The Birching

DAVID F BURROWS

PLATEN PUBLISHING

978-1-9164050-6-6
Illustrations by Steve Royce Griffin
www.steveroycegriffin.co.uk

David F Burrows
www.dfburrows.co.uk

Published by Platen Publishing an imprint of David F Burrows, 2022

Dedicated to all those poor children throughout time who suffered so much through man's inhumanity to man.

The Dirty Duck Inn

I was a Detective Sergeant when I first met Detective Constable Richard Head at the Dirty Duck Inn.

Having been out investigating the murder of a prostitute, I went back to the Yard where I was informed that Detective Superintendent 'Shifty' Shaver had gone off to the Dirty Duck for lunch, taking D.C. Head with him, and I was to join them there as soon as.

The Dirty Duck Inn was originally called The Dirty Dick Inn after one Dick Archer, the very first landlord back in the eighteen thirties when the inn was built. Dick was renowned for being unwashed, unkempt and smelling like a bad case of the shits. However, he was a popular landlord, he ran a pub where anything goes so long as he could make money from it. The place was frequented by criminals, chancers, prostitutes and lunatics. Dick died in his fifties from food poisoning; along with six of his customers who had been foolish enough to buy one of Dicks Sunday Roasts when his usual cook was off, leaving Dick to do the cooking. After that the place went downhill until it was eventually taken over by Tony Bright in the seventies. Tony had the place done up and set out to attract a better type of clientele, but somehow ended up attracting the police instead, but at least the majority of them were clean and not likely to steal beer glasses, ash trays and spittoons.

With a surprisingly warm October sun in my eyes, I head off for the short walk to the Inn only to spy 'Shifty' striding purposely towards me.

'Ah… Sergeant Potter,' says he screwing up his over long face and twiddling his ridiculously waxed French style moustache. 'I've done the rounds with Detective Constable Head. Told him what's what and what's expected of him. He's a bit of a rough diamond.' He pauses to flick his shifty eyes all around the street as if he's expecting someone to confront him. 'Good copper, apparently. Intelligent and brave. Big fellow like you. You can't miss him, bit scruffy with a bushy tash. I'll leave you to it. Must get on.' With that he crosses the road right in front of a horse and cart and gets the, 'Watch it you Pratt!'

On reaching the Georgian style inn I pause to contemplate what's upper most in my mind. Whatever possessed Heads parents to name him Richard, surely, they must have realised he'd be forever tormented as Dick Head? Secondly, was he as bent as the usual copper or as honest as the Chief Constable, meaning he was only half bent? Pushing open the door I go in.

The Dirty Duck has a large barroom, a long bar, a few tables and chairs, red velvet effect diamond patterned wallpaper and nicotine yellow ceiling, and always smells of beer, cigars, cigarettes and sweaty armpits. Busy as always there's several noisy plods propping up the bar alongside a few much quieter detectives. Over by a window sits a lone bruiser of a figure sipping at a pint gripped in a big hand while he stares blankly towards the bar.

'Usual Gov'?'

'Thanks Tony. How are things?'

'Good,' says he, his powerful hairy arms tensing as he pulls the pump. 'Part from this.' Curling back his swollen lip I see a broken tooth. 'Bit of a ruck last night. Pollard was in, sat at a table for a bite to eat. Maisy served him a pie and mash, but as soon as she set his plate down, he grabbed her, pulled her onto his lap and started mauling her, she tried to wrestle free, he started forcibly kissing her hard, then,' he points, 'see that fellow over there?'

'My new partner I believe.'

Tony hands me my pint. 'We didn't know that at the time. Anyway, before I could go around the bar and sort out Pollard, yon fellow was there demanding that Pollard let Maisy go.'

"Or what?" 'Pollard sneered.' "Stand up an' find out," 'said yon fellow. Pollard shoved Maisy off his lap so hard she hit the floor, then he leapt to his feet and went for yon fellow. Pollard threw a punch, yon fellow blocked it and then laid Pollard out cold with a single right hook.'

'Did he by Christ!'

Tony leans closer and drops his voice, 'Course everyone had waited years to see Pollard get a hiding, but no one *ever* expected just one man could do it. Trouble was no one knew yon fellow and assumed he was just some low life who'd wondered in. A couple of plods dragged Pollard away while three more drew their truncheons and went for yon fellow. I flew around to calm things down, by which time yon fellow had taken a couple of hits but given out a lot more. I got between them and the plods backed off on pain of getting banned. Yon fellow went back to his pie and pint as if nothing had happened. But I asked him to leave before Pollard regained his senses and all hell broke loose. He just shrugged, downed his pint and walked out chomping on his pie. Then 'Shifty' comes in an hour or so ago and introduces yon fellow, but I didn't quite catch his name.'

'D.C. Head. How did you get the fat lip and broken tooth?'

'Forgot the bleedin' cat was nappin' behind the bar, I tripped over the prat and connected me gob with the best bitter pump.'

'Well, it hasn't spoilt your good looks.'

'What bleedin' looks,' laughs he.

Slapping a penny ha'penny on the bar I take my pint and head over to meet my new partner.

'Detective Constable Richard Head, I believe,' says I.

'That's me,' says he getting to his feet.

'I am Detective Sergeant Gerald Potter.'

'Pleased ta meet ya, gov,' says he holding out his hand.

Dumping my bowler onto the table I shake his hand and then sit down opposite him. I note his frayed white shirt collar, his untidy tie and tatty fawn jacket with its leather elbow patches are all well past their best. He looks a scruff and needs a haircut, and to stand closer to his razor. But at least he doesn't smell and his teeth are clean. I take a swig of my beer and then say, 'Right, Constable. Tell me a bit about yourself.'

And he does, rabbiting on like a parrot, 'Come from the Eastend, but moved to North London when I got accepted by the force. Cause I couldn't do me copperin' round hear 'cause I was too well known. Ya knows what it's like, don't ya gov'?'

I nod and am about to speak when he goes on, 'Had a couple of commendations for bravery, solved a murder case an' got recommended for detective work and here I am. Now that…'

'Are you married,' cuts in I, otherwise I'd never get a word in.

'Yes. To Clarissa. No kids yet; we're trying to save up for our own place first. But…'

'I am also married. Betty and I would like children but nothing's happened as yet.'

'Oh. Sorry to hear that, gov'. When you say nothin's 'appened yet, do ya mean you ain't, ya know, done it yet? Ya know, dipped the wick?'

I am astounded by his rudeness. The man's as coarse as a fish wives fanny. 'Let us exit the domestic rhetoric for now, Constable and talk about how we are going to get along together.' I sip more beer as he empties his glass while gazing at me with trepidation. 'For one thing I would prefer you to address me as sergeant rather than gov' or even serg'. I am your superior and as such command respect. In time we may well adhere to a more informal approach towards each other, but until then we must maintain standards.'

'In other words, know ya bleedin' place,' says he narrowing his eyes.

'I wouldn't have put it quite like that, Constable. Allow me to explain. Now that you are a Detective Constable with Scotland Yard, you will need to up your standards and leave the plod behind. We must portray an image of superiority over lesser beings while about our duties if we are to command respect. Are you following me thus far?'

He scratches at his scruffy hair, 'Not really.'

'Not really, what?'

He appears confused and I'm wondering if 'Shifty' has dumped an idiot on me.

'Um… Not really, um…'

'You think about it while I fetch us another pint.' I down my beer and take the glasses over to Tony for a refill.

'Thanks, gov'. I mean Sergeant,' says Head as I hand him his beer and retake my seat. 'What you're sayin' is we got to seem like we're better than others.'

'Not exactly. Listen, by the proper use of the Queens English you will find you'll command more respect than someone who's more colloquial. If you sound like you're from the slums people will treat you as such.'

'But I am from the slums.'

'So was I, once.'

'Oh…' says he and takes a gulp of beer. 'I get it. You're sayin' I need ta improve me speech.'

'No. Improve *my* speech.'

'What yours as well?'

'No. Not mine as well. You can't say improve me speech, you say improve *my* speech.'

'But I can't see how I can improve ya speech, it sounds all right as it is.'

'No! What I'm trying to get through to you is this: Stop saying phrases such as: 'Ow are ya, gov'? And, you ain't done it, 'ave ya? Replace them with: How are you, Sergeant? You haven't done it, have you?'

'Right, I'm gettin' it now. But I ain't bein' funny, Sergeant, I can't just change the way I talk right off.'

'Of course, you can't. Fear not, Constable, I don't expect you too. I will help you to improve your demeaner so you command more respect from all you come into contact with. Whether they are lower, middle or even upper class.

Light finally shines in his eyes. 'So that I'll be listened to and taken seriously by all and sundry.'

'Exactly. Now, improving your aura isn't just about the way you speak; it is also about how you present yourself.'

'How I present myself?'

We are interrupted by Maisy leaning across the table to taunt us with her wonderful wobblers, her bright smile and long silky dark hair.

'I wanted to thank you personally for what you did last night, Detective Constable,' says she before planting a kiss on Heads hairy mouth.

'Think nothing of it,' says he.

'I best get back to my baking. Perhaps we could have a drink together sometime?'

'I'll look forwards to it,' says he watching her hips swaying as she goes off. 'Ya can't beat the heady aroma of a woman who smells of bakin', can ya Sergeant? Keep ya smelly perfumes, give me a girl who smells of meat pies and fried bacon. That Maisy's the perfect woman with the attributes to go with it.'

'I hadn't noticed,' lies I. 'Now, where were we?'

'How I present myself.'

'Indeed. Which means improving your outward appearance. Hair and moustache neatly trimmed with other parts cleanly shaven of Bristol's…'

'Bristol's?'

'I meant bristles. Shirt collars that aren't frayed. Your ties neatly tied. Jackets presentable and unpatched.'

His face drops, 'Trouble is, Sergeant I can't afford new clothes at the moment, we had to pay a deposit on our new rental. It may only be a terrace…'

'I understand, but I can't have you walking alongside me looking like a tramp. I shall fund you for now for some new clothes, and you can pay me back later when your finances are more stable.'

'That's err kind of ya,' frowns he.

'No catch, Constable. Trust me, I am not out to trick you. Above all else it is imperative that we quickly learn to trust each other if we are to do our job well and survive. Do you have a hat?'

'I do,' smiles he and promptly produces a well-worn flat cap from the seat beside him and slaps it on his head. 'This is me cap.'

'No. My cap.'

'No! It's definitely mine 'cause I came in it.'

'I know it's *your* hat! I was merely correcting your speech. This is *my* hat not *me* hat.'

'Yeah, course. I get it.' His eyes open wide and he stares behind me. 'Oh… Here comes trouble.'

Craning my neck around I see Constable Pollard storming towards us in full uniform with his helmet tucked under one arm. Six feet of solid muscle, shaven head and face like it's been ironed with a sledge hammer.

'Detective,' says he giving me a nod as I note the massive bruises across the bridge of his boxer's nose where no doubt Head's fist connected. 'Sorry to interrupt.' He glares down at Head. 'You caught me a lucky punch last night, old son, when I was a bit pissed and not ready. Now then, are you man enough to stand up to me when I'm sober an' ready for it? Or do you just want to apologise by kissing me bum-hole?'

'That way inclined, are ya?'

Pollards hammer fists clench, the vein in his bull neck vibrates like mad while his face contorts in fury, 'Meet me at the station's gymnasium. You an' me are going to settle this today to Queens Berry rules an' all that.'

'Suits me. What time?'

'After I finish me shift.'

'My shift.'

'What!'

'Ya should have said: my shift not me shift.'

'I don't give a fuck about your shift. Six o'clock in the gym. If you don't turn up, I'll take it you'll be kissing my hole the next time we meet.'

'I'll be there,' says Head as if he's meeting someone for a nice cup of tea instead of a blood bath. He meets my, don't do it look. 'That's if it's alright with me new governor.'

I shrug, what can I say?

'Good,' growls Pollard. 'Bring plenty of bandages D. C. Dick Head. You're gonna need 'em. And I'd lay off the beer if I was you, I don't want you spewing up all-over the ring when I punch a hole in your guts.'

'I'll make this my last,' grins Head.

Pollard grunts like a boar before sauntering off to the bar where he's greeted by a couple of his mates.

'I do not wish to belittle you, Constable, but take my advice, you'd be best served kissing his bottom then getting in the ring with him.'

'Why so when I dropped him with a single punch last night?'

'Because he is currently the forces heavy weight champion of all of London. Previous to that he was bare knuckled champion of all of Essex.'

'So, ya thinkin', like him, I just threw a lucky punch?'

I shrug.

'I still dropped him,' says Head pulling a smug face.

'You did indeed,' relents I. 'Very well, if you wish to commit suicide who am I to try and talk you out of it? Anyway, let us finish our beers and get out of here.'

Back outside thick clouds have appeared and the temperature has dropped, but it is still mild for the time of year. The streets are as busy, noisy and as smelly as ever, endless traffic and all manner of people going about their business, most of whom know we're coppers and give us a wide birth.

'Might rain,' says Head skipping over an urchin scraping up dog mess for his bucket of 'pure'.

'Indeed.' I clap my hands together. 'Right, let us go and get you smartened up before we go too far. We can't have you looking like one of the locals.'

'I don't look that bad, do I?'

'Not really. Some will perceive you as being quite well off.' I hold up a hand to flag a hackney down. 'Barkers the tailors,' says I to the cabby as we climb aboard.

Ten minutes later we are inside the tailors to find it quiet with just one bent up old man pawing through the various clothes rails that half fill the shop. Behind the long wooden counter stands Mr Barker himself, short and round with a hairy chubby face and bald head he is a pleasant man but a shrewd operator. Behind him, floor to ceiling, boxed shelves are filled with everything the discerning male could wish for, shirts, jumpers, socks and hats to name a few.

'Good afternoon, Sergeant Potter,' says Barker above the rattling din of sewing machines sounding from out back.

'And to you, Mr Barker.' I place a hand on Heads shoulder. 'This is my new colleague, D.C. Head. As you can see, he requires some new clothes.'

'Full works?'

'Full works.'

'Suit or jacket and trousers?'

'I've got me best suit at home,' says Head.

'Jacket and trousers, it will be then. White shirt, black trousers, bowler and plain tie.'

'Two of everything if you please, Mr Barker,' says I. 'Plus, one pair of black shoes.'

'Very good, Sergeant,' says he rubbing his hands together. 'Would you like tea while you wait?'

'No thank you, Mr Barker.' Taking a chair by the window I pick up the local rag and settle down for a read.

Barker comes around from the counter and sets to measuring up Head, 'What side do you dress, Constable?'

'I'm not with you.'

'What side does it hang,' whispers Barker.

'What side does what hang?'

'Your cock!' shouts the old man who's straightened up to eyeball Head.

'What's that gotta do with anything?' says Head looking horrified.

'He needs to measure you up,' says the old man.

Head backs away from Barker, 'Why do ya want ta measure up me manhood…?'

'I don't,' says Barker. 'It's your inner leg I need to measure up to ascertain what size trouser leg you require.'

'Oh…,' says Head.' Can't say I've ever had that done before.'

'It doesn't hurt,' says the old man. 'Just a quick poke around your groan area and it's all over. Can be quite pleasant sometimes.'

'You are not helping, Mr Jones,' grates Barker. 'So kindly mind your own business.'

'Perhaps I should go to Man's Outfitters instead,' snaps the old man. 'As you obviously don't want my custom.'

'Perhaps you should, Mr Jones. Then he too can enjoy your daily visits to just mill around his shop while messing up his clothes rails and never buying much more than the occasional pair of socks.'

'No need to get shirty you old women's blouse!' snaps he before heading for the door.

'Perhaps, Constable,' sighs Barker, 'we should start with upper body measurements before we tackle the lower regions.'

An hour later, Head is at last dressed in more suitable attire for his position in life, even if his face is still as red as a pimple. Barker bags up Head's old stuff and his spare set of new stuff. I go and settle the bill.

'Can you deliver the bags to the Yard, Mr Barker?' says I.

'Of course, Sergeant. Addressed to you?'

'The constable please.'

Back outside we find the clouds have thinned and rain now seems unlikely. We set off on foot towards the slums, but I intend calling in at a brothel before we hit the poorest areas.

'Long time since I've been around this way,' says Head. 'Don't suppose anyone will recognise me in me new clothes. Talking of which, when will ya want paying back for them?'

I shrug, 'Whenever, Constable. Don't stretch yourself. Pay a bit here, a bit there, it doesn't matter.'

'That's very generous of ya, Sergeant.'

Not really, thinks I. I want Head on side, not only to feel he's obliged to me but also to ensure he'll be up for making a few quid on the side. I'll gradually lead him into my world but initially I'll need to tread carefully, just in case he turns out to be a man of honest principals.

***

Twenty minutes later we come to a halt outside Sadie's Place, a three-story terrace with red curtains in every one of its nine front windows.

Head states the obvious as we face each other, 'A brothel.'

'Indeed, Constable. But not just any brothel. This one is run by probably the most formidable madam in all of London. Sadie Place is her name and you'll find her hard work. She's as hard as concrete, as slippery as snot and more devious than your average politician. I am investigating the murder of one of her top girls, one Mable Calver. Mable's body was found two days ago in an alleyway just off Pickle Lane, her neck had been broken. Estimated time of death between one and four am on the Tuesday. On Monday she'd set off around noon to go and see her mother. She had a bite to eat with her mother and a good chat. After giving her mother a few shillings, she left just after one pm.'

'She'd be no doubt well known in the area,' says Head. 'Easy to find out where she went after leaving her mums.'

'At first it was. Mable was indeed well known and various people saw her throughout the day. She went into several shops to spend her earnings, buying clothes, sweets, tobacco and alcohol. Just after four pm she was seen talking to a notorious ponce known as 'Razor' Williams. Nasty bit of work who runs half a dozen street girls. Rough, bottom of the ladder penny prostitutes. Thus far, I haven't been able to trace where Mable went after that.'

'So, it could be the last time anyone saw her alive,' says Head. 'Was this Mable a step up from 'Razor's' girls?"

'Mable was young and pretty and very popular with her clients, those who could afford her. She was in a different class to 'Razors' girls that's for sure. Now, Razor was later seen in the Dogs Head between seven and nine pm downing gins by the pint. He'd staggered in on his own and staggered out on his own. He hasn't been seen since. I paid a visit to the hovel he shares with one of his girls just off Fish Bone Alley this very morning, nothing.'

'Not being funny, Serg' why did ya leave it so late to look his place up?'

'Simple. The plods were handling the investigations at first. They covered the rest of Tuesday into Wednesday when it was suddenly and unexpectedly handed over to Superintendent Shaver, who handed it to me.'

'Because?'

'You tell me, Constable,' says I to test his levels of detective intuitions.

'A common prostitute's murder would be handled by the

local coppers. They'd likely know the victim well and as such are better placed to find out where she went and who she talked to. And in most cases, except for Jack the Ripper style murders they'd solve the case pretty damn quick without bothering the detectives. Which makes this case sound like there may be a lot more to it than just another murdered prostitute who no one much gives a shit about.'

'Dead today forgotten about by tomorrow and arrest any low life you want to get rid of for the crime. So, you see, Constable, I haven't had much time on this since taking it over. Most of what I know comes from the plod's reports, which aren't that detailed and are open to scrutiny, or better still to ignore and start again from scratch. And yes, I agree with you, something already smells fishy about this case.'

'Where was this Razor fellow after he spoke to Mable and before he entered the Dogs Head?'

'No idea. According to the plod who investigated, no one remembered seeing Razor during those times.'

'So, he could have been with Mable. Maybe he even imprisoned her somewhere and went back later to kill her.'

'Perhaps. Here's a snippet to set your brain ticking, it was Constable Pollard who was put on the task of tracking down Razor, and Pollard is heavily in league with Shaver.'

Head frowns, 'In what way?'

'Let's just say they get on *too* well together. Right, let's see what Sadie and her girls have to say before we go any further with the suppositions and guess work.'

I pull the bell cord, within a minute the door is opened by Sadie's doorman, all six feet of him, built like a bull with a face moulded from a gorilla.

'Yus?' demands he fixing me with bloodshot evil eyes.

'I am D. S. Potter. I request an audience with Miss Place.'

'I'll see if she's in. Wait there.' He slams the door in our faces.

'Moronic moron,' says I. 'Do you know, Constable? I get this every time I come here.'

'You come here a lot then?' says he with an admonishing glance.

'Only for my investigations. The moron's name is Bruno, by the way.'

'That's an unusual name: Bruno by the way.'

I catch the twinkle in Heads eyes and realise I have a bit of a wit on my hands. The door opens again.

'Miss Price will see ya now,' says Bruno stepping aside.

We go in and Bruno slams the door behind us so hard it shakes the walls.

'Ever thought of just gently shutting the door?' says Head.

'What fur?'

'So, the walls don't collapse.'

'What wus that? Speak up.'

We follow Bruno down a long narrow hallway decorated with photographs of naked girls on its purple papered walls and then into Sadie's gaudy parlour. A wide room with a pair of long red velvet sofas where the girls usually sit while waiting for clients. It being too early for opening legs time the sofas are empty. The indomitable Sadie is sat by a round table playing patience, she looks up, her round ruddy face with its sagging jowls complementing her baggy watery eyes and bleached starchy blond hair.

'Well, well. About time you visited me, Sergeant. Ain't seen you since God made Adam. Heard you'd taken over the case. Who's the dick head wiv ya?'

'This is my new colleague, Sadie; Constable Richard Head.'

'You taking the piss! No one's called Dick Head.'

'Well, I am,' says Head.

'Really?' says she putting down her cards. 'Who the hell gave you such a rotten name?'

'Me ol' man did. He said: "Son, life out there is fucking hard and the sooner ya get used to it the better you'll be. That's why I named ya Richard so's you'd get tormented and learn ta fight early on in life so you'd survive better later in life."

'Well, I never. Apologies, Constable for calling you Dick. Bruno, go tell that drip of a girl to make a pot of coffee for me an' the detectives.'

'Yus, Miss,' says he sloping off.

'So, Sergeant, what can you tell me?'

'Not a lot at present, I haven't been on the case long enough and am still following up on the plod's reports. Most frustrating of which is where Razor Williams has got to, he being the last person known to have been seen talking to Mable before she disappeared…'

'I can help you there,' smirks she. 'Me spies told me one of Razors girls let slip that Razor bumped into Mable around four pm and offered her a pound in advance to become one of his girls. She told him to clear off, but instead he nigh on frogmarched her into the Skinners Arms where he bought her a couple of gins and a meat pie. They chatted amiably for a bit before things got heated and Mable stormed out with Razor following her. I rest my case. Razor done for her and now he's on the run.'

'I know he was in the Dog's Head between seven and nine pm, drunk as a skunk,' says I. 'After that, nothing. Maybe he did have Mable locked up somewhere and went back to kill her, but that is only supposition.'

'He done for her alright, you mark my words. Turns nasty

after he's had too many does our Razor; especially when he don't get what he wants.

'We've got half the force looking out for him, he'll turn up sooner or later. I'd like to talk to your girls, Sadie. They may know something that could further our investigations.

She shrugs, just as a young maid comes and sets down a tray with coffee for three on it.

'Anything else, Miss Sadie?'

'Yes. Go tell the girls to get down here right this minute and make sure they're decent. I don't want the policemen embarrassed by having to question girls with their tits hanging out.'

'I don't mind,' says Head.

'Well, I do,' lies I.

'Well get going,' snaps Sadie to the maid. 'Help yourself, gentlemen. I don't do the mother bit. I like mine with plenty of sugar and no milk, it upsets me guts.'

Head pours the coffee. Sadie settles back in her chair while her face tells me nothing, but her eyes appear furtive and apprehensive.

A few minutes later eight girls traipse in and sit facing us on the sofas. Two are in dressing gowns, the rest are dressed in colourful dresses.

'The detectives want to ask you a few questions,' says Sadie giving them the evil eye. 'Give honest answers and don't rabbit on.'

'Yes, Miss Price,' says they in unison as if they're talking to a school mistress. I run my eyes over them, all are a few classes above the street girls and range from very young to about the thirties.

'Good after noon, ladies,' says I.

'Good afternoon, sir,' they chorus.

'I know that in your profession you will come into contact with all types of men. Some will be kind; many will be lonely and some downright nasty. A girl can make friends or even enemies of their customers while a client can become obsessed with a girl; the latter is often the most dangerous. So, what I want to know is do any of you know if Mable had a client who was obsessed with her to the point where she was frightened of them?'

They all give me the blank look.

'Well one of you say something,' says Sadie. 'Bridgett, you're the mouth, get talking.'

Bridgett meets my eyes, 'Mable had a *lot* of Toms who were obsessed with her, she bein' the prettiest of us all.'

'An' she had a way with men,' puts in a *very* young looking blond with an elfin face.

'But I don't think she was worried about any of her regulars getting *too* obsessed,' says Bridgett.

'Apart from that really posh one,' says the blond.

'Mable had several posh clients,' says Sadie with a hint of menace. 'Which one are you talking about, Sally?'

Sally blushes, 'The old one who looked *really* posh. Him with the fancy cane.'

Drumming her fingers on the table, Sadie looks suddenly very uncomfortable. I take a sip of coffee and say, 'Enlighten me, Sally.'

'I don't know what you mean, sir.'

Sadie says, 'About two weeks back, Mable had a visit from a new client. Tall thin fellow in a top hat and tails. Sported a full set and wore glasses, but I thought the beard and glasses were false, a disguise so he wouldn't be recognised. He carried a fancy cane with a gold top. Kept his eyes downcast and his hat on, most remove them when they come in. He asked for

Mable in a mumbled tone, even so he sounded very posh, upper class, maybe even aristocracy.'

'Did he give a name?' says Head.

Sadie shakes her head. 'Didn't say much, just that Mable had been recommended to him and he didn't want any other girl if she wasn't available. Mable was busy. I told him he was welcome to wait in the other room where we have a bar and comfortable seats. He nodded. I shew him the way and poured him a generous scotch. He went and sat in a corner while ignoring another gentleman who bade him good evening. As soon as Mable was free, I took him up to her room. He spent a half hour or so with her and came back down where he paid me and left.'

'Obviously this man returned,' says I.

'The next night, same time around eight and requested Mable. She was busy again. He waited, but once he'd seen Mable, he booked her in for three more visits for that week alone, while insisting she must be ready for him. Paid a good deposit and left.'

'Did Mable say how she had got on with this man?'

'Fine. He never asked for nothing weird, just quick and normal. Liked to chat a bit and tipped her well.'

I turn my attention back to Sally. 'What makes you think this man was obsessed with Mable? Did Mable confide in you and tell you things about her clients?'

'I have a strict rule,' cuts in Sadie. 'None of my girls are allowed to discuss their clients with each other or anyone outside this establishment. I'd have their *guts* for garters if they did.'

'But I'll bet they discuss them with you, don't they, Sadie?'

'I keep track of my girls, Sergeant by making sure they're not being treated badly. So, yes, they confide in me. But Mable never said much about this man above what I've just said. Now can we wind this up? The girls need to freshen up and put on their war paint. We'll be getting the early birds in before long.'

Sally, I notice is now squirming in her seat while her small fingers fiddle nervously with the cord on her dressing gown. 'Once I've had a quick word in private with Sally, we'll leave you in peace.'

Sadie shakes her head and glares into my eyes. 'I don't do freebies for no one, Sergeant, not even for coppers.'

'And I don't play with anyone other than my wife. I would prefer to talk with Sally now, if not she'll be coming back to the station with us for questioning.'

'Sally, stay sat. The rest of you bugger off and get ready for work.' She turns on me once the others have left. 'Don't piss me off too much, Sergeant. I've got friends in the force…'

'So, I've heard.'

'Good, so we understand each other. Take her through there,' she points. 'But I'll tell you now, the girl hasn't got much between her ears and is prone to exaggeration.'

Downing my coffee, I get to my feet as does Head.

'I don't know where you're going with this,' says Sadie staring up at me. 'Some toff visits Mable a few times more than the normal and you're thinking what? He waited around in a rough area so he could kill her? I don't think so.'

'Nor I. Sally, come with us please.'

'Am I under arrest?' says she getting to her feet.

'No. We just want to ask you a few more questions. Nothing to worry about.'

We escort Sally into the room and close the door behind us. An up market small barroom with leather bucket seats and lit by gas lamps. No windows in here. Sally sits down and we turn chairs to face her. Head goes to the bar and pours three very large brandy's, 'I'll settle up later,' says he handing the drinks around.

'Miss Sadie wouldn't like me drinking her booze,' says Sally.

'Fear not,' says I. 'We shall make sure Sadie knows we bought you a drink just to calm your nerves. Cheers.'

After a sip of what tastes like the good stuff, Sally starts to relax.

'Tell us about Mable's posh client,' says I.

'Will I get into trouble?'

'Not if you're honest with us.'

'Alright. Mable said I was to keep it a secret that the posh man was a very important person. Despite his false beard, she recognised him by his eyes the second he was shown into her room that first time. And… she recognised his knob.'

Head gives a little cough. 'She had doings with him before then?'

'We both had, cause when she told me what his knob looked like I remembered it as well.'

'Um…' ums I. 'Was it a… unusual one?'

'It was. Big and round and solid gold, so Mable reckoned.'

'The knob on his cane you mean?'

She gives a little titter, 'You thought I meant his other knob, didn't you?' She drinks some more. 'This was how it was. Mable said some time back that Sadie was robbing us blind. We get more Toms being younger and prettier and less smelly than the others. She said we could earn a lot more if we went and worked where the posh men go. So, we went and tried flauntin' our wares outside one of them gentlemen's clubs. Only we got arrested and chucked in the slammer. Next day we was up before the beak. He came in with his cane and handed it to a minion, that's when me an' Mable first saw his knob because it glinted. Then everyone sat down except us. The beak glared at us for a long time, he was stripping us with his scary dark eyes the old hypocrite. After asking us a few things he ripped us to bits and threatened to lock us up if we came around again, then he just let us go. And that was the first time we met the old bugger.'

'He's a judge by the name off?' says Head.

'Can't remember, sir something or other, but he could be the next Mayor of London.'

'And his name is Sir Arnold Falconer,' says I.

'Christ,' says Head. 'He's risking everything frequenting a whore house. Which tells me he was seriously smitten with Mable.'

'He was an' all,' says Sally. She chucks back her brandy and holds out the glass. 'Wouldn't mind another one of them, it might jog me memory.'

Head takes all three glasses over to the bar.

'Keep a tab, Constable,' says I. 'We don't want to be accused of stealing.'

'Will do, Serg'. That's six single brandies' thus far.'

Marvellous, thinks I, Head will definitely be up for making a few quid.

Head hands the drinks around, Sally takes a long swig, chokes a bit and then says, 'Anyway, on his second visit the old man told Mable he wanted to set her up as his mistress. She'd have a posh apartment with her own maid, lots of new clothes and views over Richmond Park. One of them new-fangled gramophones and she'd get electric lessons in how to talk proper…'

'Elocution lessons,' says I.

'Them as well. And he wanted her to have babies with him. He gave her a week to think it over before sayin' if she wanted to do it. She thought it over, but the trouble was the old man wasn't much good in bed and she couldn't imagine being a bird in a gilded cage just waiting around to be fed with his smelly seeds.'

'What smelly seeds?' says Head.

'His smelly man seeds. Not only that she reckoned she could get a lot more from him just for keeping quiet about his visits.'

'Oh dear,' says I. 'Mable intended to blackmail him?'

'She did an all. She said she'd earn a packet and then use the money to open her own place, somewhere even posher than here and far away from the slums.'

'Taking you with her,' says I.

'Of course.' She pauses to down her brandy; her eyes are sparkling as she begins swaying in her chair. 'She, said us being the youngest and prettiest we should be earning a lot more than the others who were gettin' to be old hags anyway. That's it really. Next thing she's gone off and got her neck broke, leaving me here with that old witch on my back to do more tricks now Mable's gone.'

'Did Sadie know what Mable intended doing?' asks I.

Sally shakes her head and then shrugs. 'She ain't said nothin' to me, but I know she had words with Mable before she went off to see her mum. That was the last time I saw her. She was my best friend.'

The inevitable happens, Sally breaks into tears. We allow her a few minutes, then Head hands her a handkerchief. Sally wipes her eyes, blows her nose, pokes a finger up, screws a bogey onto the hanky and then hands it back to Head.

'Is there anything else you want to tell us before we leave?' asks I.

She shakes her head.

'Ever thought of doing something else to make a living, Sally?' asks Head.

'No. I don't mind the job, it's better than bein' on the streets or working in a match factory.'

I down my brandy and get to my feet. 'If you recall anything else, Sally don't be afraid to contact us. If Sadie asks you what we talked about just tell her we asked about the posh man and you couldn't help much. Definitely do not tell her the part about you and Mable planning to run off and open up your own place.'

'I ain't that stupid,' says she with a hiccup. 'The less the old witch knows the easier it is for all of us.'

'Good. Thank you, Sally.'

'You've been really nice for coppers,' says she gazing up at me. 'If you want to come back and see me, I promise to pretend to enjoy it.'

'Sally,' says Head. 'Have you already told Sadie what you just told us about the judge?'

'Nah. Thought it best not to. Cause she knew we got nabbed and spent the night in clink. She got really mad about it, but then let it drop after warning us we better not try earning outside her place again or we'd get a good hidin' and then get thrown out.'

'And you've no idea whether Mable spilled the beans or not?'

She shakes her head then wobbles up onto her feet. 'Cor… I feel a bit inebriated.'

'Best go and have a lay down before you start work,' says I.

'Nah, I get enough laying on me back as it is. I'll have a bath and get ready.'

We step back into the 'waiting' room with Sadie's eagle eyes not missing a thing. Certainly, she couldn't miss Sally staggering as she heads out the room.

'We owe you for six single brandies,' says I.

'Ya bleedin' liar,' spits she. 'More like half a bottle. Anyway, forget it, it's on me just this one time. Now, did you get anywhere with Sally?'

'Nowhere special.'

Scrutinizing me and Head she lets out an indignant grunt. 'Have it your way, I'll get it out of Sally anyway. Time you cleared off. And take my word for it, Razor done for Mable, no ifs nor buts. Like I said, he'll turn up eventually.'

'Dead or alive,' puts in Head.

'Bruno,' shouts she. Bruno appears in a loping flash. 'Show the gentlemen out.'

'Yus, Miss Sadie.'

***

'What do you think, Constable,' says I as we walk away from Sadie's Place and join the throng.

'I'm thinking the last thing Sadie needs is one of her girls bringing the establishment down on her by trying to blackmail one of their own.'

'My thoughts exactly. Mable had become a liability. And what do you do with liabilities who threaten to bring you down.'

'Break their necks. Trouble is we ain't got a thing to go on. An' I don't know about you, but it wouldn't be a good idea to go and see if this Falconer toff knows anything worth knowing.'

'Not yet anyway. Not until we have something worth questioning him about. In truth he might not know anything about anything anyway. He visited Mable and had his oats, but that's not to say he asked Mable to become his mistress. Mable could well have just fantasized about it all, and, after visiting her a few times, it's probable that Falconer then moved on to someone else, somewhere else.'

'Agreed. What we need is to find this Razor bloke.'

'And to try and find out where Mable went during those times we haven't accounted for.'

As we swerve out towards the kerb, to avoid a row of costermongers selling everything from homemade food poisoning dishes to second hand anything's you could wish for, we are accosted by a matching pair of skinny, rat faced urchins with long greasy dark hair and sharp slitty eyes. Twins?

'Oy!' says one. 'Don't pass by without lookin' at what we got.'

I take a look into a large wooden fruit box that appears to contain a lot of hair. 'I have looked and cannot see anything I want,' says I.

'Maybe not now, but ya will later on when ya 'air starts fallin' out.'

'We got it all,' says the other who appears to be a few inches taller as he takes out a dark haired, very badly made wig and holds it up. 'Real 'air this is gov' an' cut from an aristocrat who wanted ta become bald for a bit.'

'Why did he want to be bald for a bit?' asks Head.

'Ta get rid of his nits I reckon. Now, how about a nice hairy chest wig?' he holds it up for our perusal. 'Women love a hairy chest. Stick this on ya an' they'll be fallin' over 'em selves ta run their claws through it.'

I am about to walk off when something comes to mind. 'What have you got for the ladies in a man's life?'

Chucking the wig back in the box he knowingly taps the end of his long thin nose. 'Show 'im, Bob.'

Bob bends down under their table and brings up a smaller box. 'Here they are Bill,' says he.

'Now then,' says Bill holding up a small triangular shaped blonde wig. 'Gentlemen like the natural look. Nuthin' worse than a bird with blond hair who's got a black thatch down below. Stick this bugger over her thatch and she'll look natural. We got all colours, brown, black, ginger…'

'Marvellous,' says I taking hold of the wig and holding it out to Head, who gives me the: Are you mad, look? 'Where on earth did you obtain all this lovely hair?'

That's it for Bill and Bob, they make to flee but I just manage to grab Bill by his greasy hair only for it to slip through my fingers. Head throws himself over the table and just misses grabbing Bob by a split second. They are off, winding and tearing through the crowds and across the road while narrowly avoiding a coal waggon going one way and a beer waggon going the other.

'Shall I chase 'em?' asks Head.

'No point, Constable. Only a greyhound would catch those little bastards.'

'So, what's it all about, Serg'?' asks Head as we walk on.

'About three weeks ago a mortuary over Hackney way was broken into. Rings and things were stolen from the six bodies in there and all six had been given a shave. That's a shave all over, well where the hair was thickest.'

'Bloody Nora! The evil little shits even shaved off the pubic bits.'

'They did, even from two ladies who were well into old age.'

'I didn't see any grey wigs in their box.'

'They probably dyed them.'

'What now?'

'We haven't got time to waste on those two right now, but the first plod we see I'll order him to go confiscate their wigs and take them to the Yard. If we get time later on, we'll see if we can't run the little buggers down.'

Walking on I spy a plod I know coming towards.

'Afternoon, Sergeant Potter,' says he.

'Constable Fuller,' says I. 'How are things?'

He nods and gives Head the once over. 'You must be the fellow who dropped Pollard.'

'I am,' says Head. 'Sorry if he's a mate of yours.'

'No mate of mine. And I'd like to shake your hand.'

They shake hands then Fuller says, 'Heard you've taken over the Mable Calver murder, Sergeant. Did you read my report on it?'

'I did. Not much to go on though.'

'We didn't find out much that's why. But not everything that should have been said has probably been said.'

'Enlighten me.'

He leans close to me, hitting me with beery breath. 'Pollard had a confrontation with Mable in the High Street just about six o'clock on the Monday evening. I know because I saw them just as I came out of Swanson's sweet shop, having been in there to see if they'd had any trouble from a pair of greasy urchins who'd been stealing from other shops. I darted back so Pollard didn't see me. Now I didn't hear anything, too far away, but it was obvious whatever Pollard said to her she didn't like it because she wrenched her hand from his grip and flounced furiously off and turned down Carters Lane, but Pollard didn't follow her, he just stomped off up the High Street. And I'm betting there was no mention of this in Pollards report.'

'Indeed, there wasn't. Interesting. Thank you, Constable Fuller, I owe you a pint.'

He shrugs, 'It mightn't be anything more than Pollard trying to get a free one. You know what he's like.'

'Even so, it should have been in his report. These greasy urchins you are after, are they an identical looking pair of rat-faced, long haired, evil looking skinny little shits?'

'They are. And they're twins. Robert and William Boyle, more commonly known as Bill and Bob. Nasty little sods who'd sell their own mother if they could get a few pence for her. The trouble is, catching the bastards. What do you know about them?'

I tell him about our confrontation with the twins and ask if he'd gather up the wigs and take them to the Yard.

'Not at all,' says he. 'But I better hurry before someone else runs off with them.' He smiles at Head. 'It's been spread around you're up for a match with Pollard at the gym tonight. Is it still on?'

'Not unless Pollard has chickened out.'

'No chance of that. They'll be a big audience for it. Shaver's already taking bets.'

'What are the odds?' asks Head.

'Last I heard, Pollards on evens, while your twenty to one against.'

'Make sure ya bet on me then if ya want ta cash in.'

'I will. Best get on.'

'Wasn't expecting that one,' says I as we walk on. 'We shall be questioning Constable Pollard before the days out to see what he has to say for himself, Constable. But for now, keep it under your nice new hat and don't tell a soul where the information came from. If Pollard found out Fuller had snitched on him, he'll beat him to a pulp. Right, let's try the Skinners Arms and see what we can turn up. Sadie said her spies informed her that Razor was in there with Mable around four pm. Assuming Sadie is telling the truth why then didn't Pollard have that information also in his report, especially as he was the one who reported on the confrontation between Mable and Razor in the first place.'

'As ya say, Sadie could have lied. If not, then Pollard didn't investigate the incident properly or he deliberately withheld the information.'

'Because?'

'No idea, Serg'. Sorry, Sergeant.'

'Nor I. Let's see what the landlord of the Skinners has to say.'

After talking to the landlord of the Skinners who confirmed what Sadie told us we head back to the Yard for a bite to eat in the canteen. It is now four thirty, leaving just an hour and a half until the blood bath between Head and Pollard.

Despite my advice to have something light, Head orders a pie and mash which is gobbled up so fast he barely takes a breath.

'That's better,' burps he rubbing his belly. 'That'll put some fire in me punches.'

'Or sick all over the ring if he gives you a good one in the guts.'

'He won't be around long enough to give me a good one anywhere. Trust me, it will all be over in seconds.'

I am astounded by the man's arrogance. He has no idea what he's up against. Pollard is a brutal, dirty fighter who knows every trick in the book. He has never been knocked down for a count above five while most of his opponents end up being carried out in round one. Heads one off lucky punch was just that, a one off. He's going to get slaughtered!

'What's for pudding?' asks Head as the canteen lady comes over to pick up his plate.

'What do you fancy, handsome? Apple pie and cream, chocolate sponge or something saucy?'

'Surprise me,' grins he giving her a wink.

She giggles before shooting me a can't be bothered glance, 'Do you want anything else?'

'No thank you, as you can see, I've still got half a plate full to finish.'

'Why's that! Is there something wrong with the pie?'

'The mash is a bit lumpy and the gravy's a bit weak, but the pie is fine.'

'There's always one. Good job your mate appreciates good grub or I'd be in despair.'

With that she flounces off while I'm thinking that Head has a way with women that defies explanation. I suppose he is a handsome chap in a rugged kind of way, but once Pollard's finished with him, he'll probably be unrecognisable.

The Fight

There are over thirty plods still in uniform, a dozen or so detectives and a few senior officers all sat on benches surrounding the ring and making more noise than a bunch of school kids.

D. S. Shaver is hosting the event while his minion, Detective Sergeant Bartley is taking bets. Officially no betting is allowed, but everyone ignores the fact. I've placed five shillings on Pollard to knock Head out in round two, and a shilling on Head to knock Pollard out, also in round two, well you never know, with luck they'll drop each other at the same time and I shall clean up.

Head stands beside me kitted out in borrowed gear from the gym. He's wearing black boxing boots, knee length black shorts, a white vest and a black robe. Around his neck is a red towel, which is good as it won't show the blood so much. He'd bandaged his own hands and I must say did so rather professionally. I put on his gloves and have volunteered to be his assistant second. Pollard is over the other side of the ring glaring at Head. He's dressed in a blue robe beneath which he'll no doubt be wearing his trade mark black vest and calf length blue and white stripped tight thingies that clearly show off his oversized genitals, the dirty sod.

Shaver, standing mid ring, claps his hands together, 'Quiet please gentlemen. Quiet! I call the contestants to enter the ring.'

Cheers all-round as Head and Pollard climb into the ring and stand facing each other while Shaver gives them the usual talking to. I go over to the red corner and say hello to Sergeant Billy 'The Bruiser' Baker who runs the gym and teaches boxing.

''Ow are ya, Gerald?' asks he smiling the smile of the toothless, oft broken-nosed ex-boxer.

'Alright, Bill. How are you?'

'Good. Now then, apart from your boy dropping Pollard with a lucky punch what form has he got?'

'No idea.'

'Well, I ain't never heard of him, so, I reckon he ain't got any above street brawlin'. Which is good cause I need to get away quick. I'm on a promise with someone's wife.'

'Lovely, so long as it's not with my wife.'

He grins. 'Placed ya bet yet?'

'Five shillings on Pollard and one shilling on Head, just in case. Well, you never know.'

'You don't.'

Shaver bellows out, 'Gentlemen of the audience. The contestants know the rules. No biting, no punches below the belt, no eye gouging, no spitting, no head butts and no kneeing in the nuts. Six three-minute rounds with a knockout or the judge's decision to decide the winner. Judges are: D. C. I. Wheeler, C. I. Duffield and myself, D. S. Shaver. Our referee is Sergeant Scofield. In the blue corner weighing seventeen stones four pounds of solid iron, the undefeated heavy weight forces champion of all of London; Constable Robert 'Poleaxe' Pollard.'

Cheers and whistles from most of the audience as Pollard dances around, shuffles his feet and raises his arms.

'In the red corner weighing sixteen stone six pounds the unrated challenger; Detective Constable Richard 'Suicide' Head.'

Boos and jeers from most of the audience as Head raises one arm while looking a bit sick.

Shaver hands over to the referee who gives the fighters the usual I want a clean fight, feels their gloves and gets them to shake hands, he then says, 'Fighters go to your corners and disrobe. Then, on the bell come out fighting.'

Head comes over as Billy swings into the ring to help him off with his robe. Head is well toned but doesn't look half as hard as Pollard. Billy gives Head a pep talk, and then leaves the ring. Head sits on the corner stool while Pollard has the ring to himself. Playing to the cheering audience, shadow boxing then flexing his powerful biceps while dancing around with fancy footwork.

'Bloody great tart,' growls Head. 'He'll be dancing off my fist in a minute.'

The bell goes, Head jumps up, rolls off a long rotten fart and dances off to meet Pollards charge. They clash, Pollard gives Head a good one on his chin, Head stumbles back several feet, the crowd cheer. Pollard charges back in and straight onto Heads fist, Pollards legs wobble but he's quick to come back with a swinging left hook, only to miss his target. Head catches him unguarded with a flurry of punches which forces Pollard to cover up and stumble back onto the ropes. The crowd boo and cheer as Head keeps up the pressure by pounding at Pollards arms trying to break through his defence. Pollard's head drops, he looks about to hit the floor, Head goes in and makes a big mistake, his chin is over Pollards head, Pollard brings it up hard, there's a sickening crunch as it connects to Heads chin, Head falls on Pollard, Pollard shoves him backwards then drives in with a flurry of brutal short punches, body shots and head shots. Heads defence is down, the crowd go mad, an upper cut from Pollard threatens to knock Heads block right off, he grabs hold of Pollard and they start dancing around, the referee breaks them up. Head staggers back, he looks done for. Pollard smirks and then charges in to finish the job only again he runs straight onto Heads fist; causing him to stagger back out of reach. Both boxers appear stunned as they trade punches at arm's length, punches that are not having any real effect on either of them, then they're in a clinch, then back to trading weak punches. At last, the bell sounds and both boxers stagger back to their corners.

'Fuck this,' gasps Head as he flops down on his stool.

Billy swings into the ring where he wipes him down with a towel and starts giving him more pep talk. 'Listen to me son. I ain't never seen Pollard so breathless. He's out of condition and he ain't used to someone standing up to him and givin' as good as he gets. Next round go for his body, guts an' heart, guts an' heart. Forget his head, guts an' heart.'

I pass Billy a bottle of water while gazing over to Pollards corner. He is indeed breathing hard and there's something wrong with his right hand. His second has his glove off and is massaging his fingers. Pollard nods, his second slips the glove back and it is so normal an act you'd have had to be very sharp eyed to see that something else went into that glove as it was slipped on.

Head takes a swig of water then spits it out on me just us I stick my head into the ring, ignoring it I get right in and go up to the referee.

'Get out of the ring, Potter you prat,' yells someone.

I demand that Scofield check the boxer's gloves before

they continue. He agrees and I nip back to the corner.

Holding up the bell for round two, Scofield orders the boxers to the centre of the ring. He feels Heads gloves then moves towards Pollard, who suddenly slaps his gloves onto his chest and collapses onto the floor, 'I think me hearts gone,' cries he.

His second immediately throws in the towel. The crowd goes quiet. Scofield holds up Heads hand. Everyone cheers, no doubt like me they placed a small side bet on Head, well at twenty to one it was worth a try.

Pollard is helped out of the ring by his seconds and staggers off towards the changing rooms.

Elated, Head bounds across the ring where Billy helps him into his gown.

'Well,' says Billy. 'There's no way Pollard took a dive to cash in, Shaver's going ta lose a fortune through this.' He looks into my eyes. 'What was it, somethin' slipped into his glove?'

'That is how it looked to me,' says I.

'Probably a knuckle duster.'

'No wonder the dirty bastard wins so many fights,' says Head. 'I'm gonna demand a rematch and then I'm gonna turn him into minced shit.'

'Let us forget that for now, Constable. We have a murder case to solve.' And, thinks I, just consider yourself lucky you've come out of this relatively unscathed.

***

'How's the chin?' asks I as we head towards the changing rooms to a chorus of well-done Dick Head and hands reaching out to pat him on the back.

'Painful. He jarred me teeth and I near bit off me tongue, the dirty bastard. But I've had worse, it'll take more than that tosser ta bring Richard Head down.'

The changing rooms smell of bad cheese, mouldy sweat and rotten fish that floats up from the drains. Pollard is sat on a bench with a towel around his waist while taking out clothes from a carpet bag. Shaver is standing there with his back to us while whispering to Pollard, he suddenly spins around to give me his shifty look.

'Ah… Sergeant Potter. Do you wish to speak with me?'

'No, sir. I wish to ask Constable Pollard a few questions regarding his report on the Mable Calver murder.

'Oh… Yes… Um, fine. Well, I'll leave you to it. And… err… congratulations on your win, Constable Head.'

'Thank you, sir.'

Shifty goes off and we take a step nearer to Pollard.

Glaring up at us he snarls, 'If you've come to gloat, don't, unless you both want a good smacking.'

'Ya hearts alright now, is it?' says Head.

'False alarm. Just a bad attack of trapped wind.'

'Spect ya got a lot of that to go with all the bullshit inside ya.'

'Enough,' says I. 'We're not here to gloat, Constable Pollard; we just need to ask you a few questions about your report on Mable's murder.'

'Can't it wait until tomorrow?' says he getting to his feet.

'No.'

'Alright, well you'll have to talk while I get ready. I'm off duty and I'm in a hurry.'

With that he whips off his towel and starts drying himself.

It is somewhat disconcerting to try and ask someone questions while they're drying their balls and their oversized member is swinging about. 'Do you mind wrapping that towel back around your waist or at least pull on your trousers?'

'What for? You shy or something?'

'What do you mean, or something?'

'You know, likes what you see does ya?'

'Just shut ya fat gob an' put ya towel on,' says Head clenching his fists.

Pollard stops rubbing his balls to glare into Head's eyes, 'Or what!'

'Or my boots will double the size of your nuts.'

'Try it Nancy an' I'll break your fuckin' legs.'

I draw out my revolver and point it at Pollards member, 'Do that and I'll shoot your big ugly spotty cock off. You're a hard bastard, Pollard but you are nowhere near as hard as the bullets in this revolver. Put your damn trousers on, *right now*.'

'Alright! Alright! The pair of you are just jealous? Got little boys ones 'ave ya?'

He pulls on a pair of trousers and then faces me with his arms folded.

'Thank you,' sighs I holstering my weapon. 'You were seen having a confrontation at around six o'clock on Monday evening with Mable Calver. What do you say to this allegation?'

'Load of shit. I don't know who told you that, but it ain't true.'

'I believe it was true. What were the two of you talking about?'

'I just said, it's a load of shit.'

'Start telling me the truth, Constable or I'll be talking to your chief about what I've found out about you.'

His eyes go dark with fury. Pollard hates a snitch. 'Alright. But not with that prat listening in. Tell him to fuck off and I'll talk.'

'Constable Head. Kindly go and get yourself dressed while I talk to Constable Pollard.'

'Do I have to?'

'It's an order.'

Pollard slips on a shirt as Head goes off; then he sits down to pull his socks on.

'Mable,' says I. 'What were you talking to her about?'

He sits up straight and shrugs. 'Nothing much really, just tryin' to be a good neighbourhood copper. I told her a pretty girl like her could do better for herself. She should give up whoring and maybe find a good man who'll look after her and cherish her. Someone like me for instance.'

'Rubbish. I'll ask again. What were you talking to her about?'

He starts pulling on his shoes, 'Like I said; just bein' friendly.'

'Last chance. Either you tell me the truth or I'll put in a report to your chief, suggesting that your report was unprofessional and probably dishonest.'

'Alright. Truth is I told her I'd ensure she'd get protection providing she agreed to the usual like the other girls I keep an eye out for.'

'I shall also spread it around that you threw the fight rather than be exposed as a cheat. Oh, and that you've got a nasty suspicious spot on your knob.'

His thing is out in a second, yanking back his foreskin he peruses it and then tucks it away.

'You had me goin' then Potter, but then I never took you for a lying shithouse. Alright, this is how it was. Razor Williams collared me about five on the Monday afternoon. He said Mable had tried to get him involved with blackmailing one of her wealthy clients. Course you know Razors been done for blackmailing clients before. But when she told him who it was, he backed off and tried talking her out of it…'

'Am I right in saying she intended to blackmail, Sir Arnold Falconer?'

'How did you find that out so quickly?'

'Never you mind. Please continue.'

'Anyway, Mable would have none of it and was determined to go ahead with her plan. Razor asked me to go and warn her off. You know as well as me you don't mess with the top toffs. I caught up with her in the High Street, but she wouldn't listen, instead the stupid cow asked *me* if I'd like to help her bleed Falconer dry.' He stabs a finger in his chest. '*Me*, a bleedin' copper. I got nasty with her and she stomped off. And that was the last time I saw her alive.'

'Did you see Razor after that?'

Shaking his head, he says, 'I decided to keep out of this one.' He leans closer. 'Look, we all know the score. We make a few quid, we bend the rules a bit, what we don't do is shit on the establishment. Do we now?'

'We don't. Do you know where Razor is?'

'No idea and I haven't heard a whisper. All I'll say is anyone could have done for Mable. It could have been a random attack by a complete stranger. Who knows and who cares? Just another dead tart.'

'That is how most will see it. Me, well a life is a life and everyone deserves justice.'

He shrugs, 'Is that all? I need to get on.'

'For now. But if you hear anything you let me know.'

***

By eight the next morning Head and I are in my office going over what we learnt the day before, concluding that we don't know much and have only intuition to go on.

'I am of the belief, Constable that Sadie is more likely to be behind Mable's murder than anyone. It could even be that Mable told Sadie her plan to blackmail Falconer while naively believing Sadie might just jump at the chance to get involved.

Only, as we have pondered before, Sadie would not want the establishment falling down on her.'

'Then there's this Razor fellow. But I'm thinking, just like big knob…'

'Big knob?'

'Pollard with his; look at this boys, ain't ya jealous?'

'Are you jealous?'

He gives me the: piss off look, 'No, what's to be jealous of just because he's got an inch more than me?'

'Some men would kill their own granny for an extra inch, Constable, but I was merely correcting your speech and not implying you were jealous.'

'Oh, I see.'

'Now, where were we?'

'Um… Oh yes. I'm thinking neither Razor nor Pollard would have killed Mable just to stop her from carrying out her plan. Why would they risk it when they'd nothin' to gain?'

'Exactly. I'm also thinking that Falconer knew nothing of Mable's intention to blackmail him. We should go and see Sadie and put her under pressure just to see how she reacts. We should also grill Bruno because if Sadie *is* behind Mable's murder, she would have had Bruno do the dirty deed for her. One thing Bruno's good at is killing people, so I've heard.'

The door swings open and in comes Shifty.

'Good morning gentlemen,' says he pulling up a chair. 'Good news, Razor Williams has turned up…'

'Dead or alive, sir?'

'Very much dead. He was found in the sewer having fell in because he failed to spot that the manhole cover had been removed. Been down there for about six hours, apparently.'

'How could anyone give an estimate on how long he'd been down there,' asks I.

He looks around the room as if expecting someone to be listening in. 'A sewer maintenance fellow told the officers at the scene that he could fairly accurately put a time on how long he'd been there by the amount of flesh that had been eaten by the rats.'

'Any witnesses?' asks Head.

Shifty shakes his head, 'Razor was found around six a.m. That being the case he went down the drain at about midnight which is also about the time he died. Now the question is this; how far have you got with the Calver case?'

'Nowhere at present, sir,' says I.

'And with Razor dead you'll like as not get any further. Therefore, the case is closed. Razor killed Mable for whatever reason we want to put down, let's say he did it because she refused to join his band of unhappy hags.'

'But what if he didn't kill her?'

'Who cares, Sergeant? She may have been a class or two above the usual trollop but she was still nothing more than a cheap prostitute.'

'She was still a human being, sir and as such deserved justice.'

A flash of anger flashes from his eyes, 'The case is closed, Sergeant and I wish to hear no more about it! Complete the usual, then file it and forget about it. Moving on to more important issues. Have you heard of the Boyle brothers?'

We nod.

'Good. Apparently, that pair of delinquents have been running riot with impunity for weeks and have upset a good many gentle folks. They've been picking pockets and shop lifting and it is almost certain they were the ones who broke into a morgue and shaved off all the hair from one, Lady Anabel Shrimpton Holmes?'

'Any relation to Sherlock?' asks Head.

'Are you being jovial, Constable?'

'No, sir just curious.'

Oh… right… well. No relation. It wasn't only Lady Anabel who lost her hair, five more bodies were also left hairless, but no one much cares about them. It is Lady Anabel's family who are of concern to us. Important people of class and status, gentlemen. They are up in arms and I have been ordered to put my best detectives on the case. But, as my best detectives are busy, I thought I'd hand it over to you two.'

'Thank you for your confidence in us, sir,' says I trying not to sound too sarcastic.

'Good man,' says he getting to his feet. 'No idea where you should begin but then you are detectives, aren't you?'

'We are indeed, sir,' says I.

'Good. Of course, uniform is keeping a look out for the Boyles, but, the little bastards are as elusive as a pink elephant.' He chuckles a bit and then is gone.

I get up and close the door, 'So, no justice then for poor Mable Calver, Constable.'

'Seems not, Serg'. But it don't mean we have to give up on her. We could still poke around while we hunt down the Boyle brothers.'

'Um… Why not, so long as we keep it low key? Maybe Razor did do for her. Maybe she died at the hands of a, spur of the moment killer, or maybe Sadie had her killed. Either way I can't bear to give up on a case.'

'Nor I, Sergeant. So, we're agreed.'

'We are indeed, Constable.'

Gains and Losses

When hunting a holed-up fox, you first have to find its lair. The Boyle's lair will undoubtably be in the slum areas and that is where we head for. For a few pennies you can buy almost anything in the slums, from unwanted urchins to the shirt on a man's back. Information will only be given by the most desperate, or if whoever you're looking for isn't welcome around the area. The twins aren't welcome having brought in too many coppers to nose around. Within the hour we have an address where the twins are thought to be staying and it only cost me sixpence. We head for Meadow View Gardens

***

'Cor, its bloody rough around here,' says Head running his eyes over a narrow lane more rutted than smooth and littered with rubbish. 'An' it stinks of shit.'

Three story dilapidated tenements with rag curtained windows, rotting doors and sunken rooves with so many missing slates they must leak like sieves. Lave and plaster has rotted and crumbled to fall in heaps, but there is life, rats, cats and mangy dogs. Kids in rags, adults in rags, unkempt and at the bottom of the human pile they stand still and stare at us through weary eyes.

'I grew up in a dump,' says Head. 'But it weren't a quarter as bad as this place. Meadow View bleedin' Gardens, Sewage View Gardens would be more apt.'

'I don't ever recall coming down here before,' says I sucking in the foul air. 'It's worse than the Gut. Dear God, how can anyone allow such squalor to go on?'

'Out of sight and out of mind,' says Head. 'Besides, lookin' at this lot I'd say they're mostly all foreigners who came here for a better life and then wished they hadn't.'

'My thoughts exactly, Constable. Number fifteen,' I point, coming to a halt.

A dark skinned, or perhaps merely filthy, old hag with a walking stick suddenly confronts us, 'You look for two boy who look alike. Black hair and black eyes?'

'We do. Have you seen them?'

'No, because I am blind. But of them I know.' She cups a grubby gnarled hand to one ear. 'I hear them. They rustle around like rats inside that house.' She points to number fifteen. 'Be warned, they have a bum.'

'So, do we,' says I. 'One each in fact.'

'But they have, *big bloody bum* behind door. You knock on door. They blow you pieces.'

'What sort of bum is it?' asks Head.

'It called explosive bum. I hear fuse being lit.'

'Oh…,' grins Head. 'You mean they have a bomb.'

'Down!' yells I.

Head and I dive away from each other and hit the squelching turd mac ground. The old hag doesn't move, 'Get down!'

There follows one hell of a deafening boom, number fifteens door flies out in splinters, the windows are blown out, the old hag suddenly disappears, my bowler flies off and I cover my head as all manner of rubbish falls down on me.

'Fuckin' hell,' splutters Head as he struggles to his feet. Wobbling he shakes his head while slapping his ears.

I get to my feet very slowly, my hands are filthy, my face feels filthy and I spit out filth while I feel I've been given a kidney punch by a gorilla. But at least I'm alive. Picking up my bowler I slap it back on.

'Where did the old woman go, Serg'?'

'I glance behind me; the old woman is laid out on her back several feet from where she'd been standing. We go over to gaze down at her wrinkly face.

'Dead as a kipper,' says Head. 'What's that imbedded in her forehead?'

'I think it's a brass doorknob.'

'Well, I never,' sighs he. 'Fancy being killed by a flying doorknob.'

'She saved our lives Constable.'

'She did indeed,' says he. 'Bless her.'

'Right,' says I drawing my revolver then fanning it around to find the avenue has emptied of life except for me and Head.

Head draws his revolver and does a sweep along the houses,

'I've never fired a revolver,' says he. 'Had rifle training, so, I suppose it's the same thing.'

'More or less. Let us go see what's what in what's left of number fifteen. Be careful, we could be walking straight into hell. There had to be more than just the twins in that house.'

Now the dust has cleared a bit and with its door gone we can see right into the house. Gingerly we creep forwards at a crouch. Head starts farting to show he's nervous but he doesn't falter. Stepping straight into the parlour, no halls in these houses, we are confronted by one hell of a mess, dust and smoke billowing around, bits of furniture and junk everywhere, with half the ceiling on top of it all. Obviously, they were making bombs for criminal activities but cocked up and blew themselves up instead of blowing up whatever they had meant to blow up. It looks like there could be up to four dead bodies, but it's hard to tell as they're splattered all over the place, lumps of gore stuck on the walls, severed and shattered limbs everywhere and of course; lots of blood. Strange all the power went outwards to the front of the house.

'Christ, what a bleedin' mess!' says Head.

'They weren't expecting that one, Constable. Serves the bastards right. No sign of the twins, even bits of them. Either they weren't here or they got out. Let's look out back.'

There follows a plopping sound as something drops from the ceiling and lands on Head's bowler.

'What's that? Something just hit me on the head.'

Perusing the gory lump, I quickly ascertain what it is. 'Fear not, Constable it's just a piece of someone.'

He gives me the horror look, 'What piece?'

'An ear plus about half a pound of skull'. Removing his bowler, he shakes the ear off, says the f and c word then replaces his bowler.

'My lovely new hat,' says he looking miserable. 'All covered in blood an' gooey stuff,'

'Never mind, at least it's undamaged.'

We go through a tiny kitchen and out back to find a small junked up yard and an open gate that takes you into a narrow alleyway. 'They could have gone either way,' says I looking up and down. 'We could split up and search both ways but I'm thinking it will be a waste of time. Let's try upstairs if it's safe to do so.'

Upstairs we find two bedrooms, four filthy straw mattresses and a small table with a tin of animal glue, sacking and a box of hair.

'The twin's wig makin' factory,' says Head picking up a wig and perusing it.

'So, they *were* here. Here with whom?'

'Maybe family, or perhaps they'd just teamed up with other low life's like themselves.'

'Who knows? We best go see if anyone else has been killed then we'll get out of here, I could do with a pint after a scare like that.'

Back outside several of the locals are out surveying the scene, while a huge mangy hound is dragging away a human leg that must of shot out of the house. It is gruesome.

'Has anyone else been killed,' asks I to a tall skinny man with a dark hairy face.

'No. Many have shit themselves, but they are alright.'

Thankfully I didn't shit myself but I came close. 'Do you know the names of any of the men who were in the house?'

He nods. I wait. He says nothing. 'What were their names?'

'There was a Mr Harry. Mr Jim. Mr Ronald. Miss Fanny. Mr Scratch and two greasy boys. All bad people, killers and robbers wanted by police.'

'Thank you, Mr…?'

'Oppenheim.'

'Were they all in the house when the bomb exploded?'

'No. Greasy boys go off with Miss Fanny an hour ago. I do not know where to.'

I hand him a shilling; we dust ourselves down and then head off.

'Where to now?' asks Head.

'Let's try the nearest pub, someone there might be able to tell us where the twins are.'

***

Ten minutes later we are outside a crumbling ruin called The Pigs Trotter. Looking at the place I doubt any decent pig would even consider going into such a place. Stepping over a pile of filthy rags wrapped around a snoring vagrant we step inside.

'Cor, what a dump,' says Head. 'Smells like fermented sick in here.'

There's, half a dozen dirty old men standing at the bar drinking pints of God knows what. Three penny prostitutes at a table, and, low and behold, talking to *them*, with their backs to us, are the twins themselves.

'They haven't seen us, Constable' whispers I. 'Let's sneak up on them.'

We do so, but half way across the shit and sawdust floor someone at the bar yells out, 'Coppers! Run for it!'

Two prostitutes stagger to their feet while the third falls off her stool onto the floor, the twins though are up and running straight at us. No grabbing at greasy hair this time, I stick a foot out to trip one up, but he leaps over my leg, I try to grab him but miss, while the other twin flits around Head. They go for the door with us inches behind them, they're out the door, supremely confident that they'll get away, only they hadn't reckoned on the vagrant and trip right over him. We grab one each, give them a ringer around their lugs to stun them enough to wrench their scrawny arms around their backs and then cuff them. We haul them up by the scruffs of their tatty, moth eaten, covered in filth jackets.

'You better let us go, Copper,' snarls Bill glaring up at me and baring his sharp little yellow teeth.

'Or what?'

'You'll get dead, that's bleedin' what.'

'Yeah,' says Bob trying to twist away from Head. 'We'll cut ya balls off an' feed 'em ta the rats. We will, won't we Bill?'

'We will that, Bob. Then we'll scalp 'em like them red skins do and sell the scalps for wigs.'

'Then we'll chop off anything that sticks out, that includes ya nozzles.'

'An' ya lugs.'

We give them another ringer, which shuts them up. Dragging them along we set off to find a cab. An hour later, having been duly charged, the still screaming, threatening and cursing twins are safely locked away in the cells. Job done, time for a pint, or two, or even three.

***

A week later we attend the twin's trial to give evidence. No one could prove they were involved in the morgue incident. In the end they were convicted of shop lifting, receiving stolen hair and being disrespectful to diseased persons, or should that be deceased persons? Spared jail because of their age they were sentenced to the birch and ordered out of the area, after their punishment, never to return.

'We'll get ya back, one day,' threatened Bill as he and Bob where being taken down to await their fate the following day.

'Do ya really think a good birching will sort the little bleeders out?' Head says as we head away from the court room intent on a celebratory pint in the Dirty Duck.

'No,' I say in all honesty. 'Not where that pair are concerned. Trust me, Constable when I say; if they can, they'll be back one day to get their revenge.'

'For ten-year olds they're the evillest little bastards I've ever met. The looks of hatred they gave us could curdle milk. They even snarled at the judge like a pair of wild demons. I agree with you, Serg'. They'll be back.'

***

Two days later and with the Boyles birched and gone we are ordered back onto the Mable Calver case by Detective Chief Inspector Wheeler, no less. Shaver wasn't happy and insisted the case was a waste of police time, but as Wheeler's related to the Chief Constable, Shaver had no choice but to back down. However, I'm of the opinion that Shaver kicked up *too* much fuss about the case being reopened. Why should he care unless he has something to hide? Deciding to restart the investigation by sounding Shaver out we head to his office.

'May I have a word, sir?' asks I, sticking my head in his door.

Spinning around from his desk he gives me the sulky look. 'About what, Sergeant?'

'The Mable Calver case.'

Slapping down the pen he was holding he gets to his feet and faces me as I move inside with Head following. 'You are wasting your time on this, Sergeant. It was as I said, Razor killed her and no one cares.'

'The chief does and so does the chief constable, apparently.'

'Utter piffle! Wheeler couldn't care less about the death of that tart; he's just trying to damn well annoy me.'

'Because?'

'Because I refused to pay back the five pounds, he put on Pollard to win. According to Wheeler, the fight was rigged just so I could make a tidy sum. More piffle. Pollard lost the fight due to an unexpected heart murmur. It was all fair and above board. Look, Potter, take my advice, just mill around for a few days and take life easy, then report back to Wheeler and just tell him you have gotten nowhere with the case. Trust me, by then he would have forgotten *all* about it anyway, and that will be that.'

Meeting his shifty eyes, I know he's hiding something, but how the hell do you go about grilling a senior officer?

To my horror, Head sticks his oar in. 'Where were you, sir on the night Mable Calver was murdered?'

Shaver throws his arms up into the air, 'What! How dare you ask me such an impertinent question? Are you a foolish oaf, Constable with a brain the size of a pea?' He stabs out a finger. 'Get out of my office before I have you reprimanded and sent back to the beat. Idiot!'

I turn to leave while grabbing Head by the sleeve of his jacket. He shrugs it off.

'I'm sorry, sir,' says he. 'We are investigating a brutal murder and believe ya may be able to assist us in that investigation. So please answer my question so we can eliminate you from our inquiries.'

Shaver takes a threatening step towards Head, but then thinks better of it and steps back again. 'Just get out, Constable while you still can. One more word and you are finished in the force.'

'Out now, Constable,' says I pushing him towards the door.

***

'What on earth got into you, Constable?' says I as we head down the corridor. 'You cannot go around talking to senior officers like that if you want to get on in the force.'

We stop and face each other, 'That man knows something, Serg', but he ain't sayin', which tells me he's as guilty as sin.'

'Of what though? Do we have a single thread of evidence that he's somehow embroiled in all of this? You have more or less accused him of being involved, when for all you know he simply believes it *is* a waste of police time pursuing the case any further.'

'Yeah, and pigs might fly. You saw his eyes, shifty as fuck but also worried as fuck.'

'No need to swear so, Constable. Let us remain professional. Yes, I do believe he is hiding something, but then the man's so bloody shifty he is forever hiding something.'

'But that don't mean we can't rock his boat a bit and try an' tip 'im out.'

Scratching at my chin a thought comes to mind. 'Someone, told me ages ago, Constable that he believed Shaver receives regular pay-outs from Sadie Price to ensure she never gets raided. Whether or not that is true is open to debate. But, let us assume that it is true, that being the case then I have no doubt that should Sadie require other favours from Shaver he would have no option other than to carry them out.'

'Such as tracking down Mable Calver and tellin' Sadie before he told anyone else, like us for instance.'

'Exactly. I'm now thinking that Pollard also knows more than he's said. He's in Shaver's pockets and would do whatever Shaver tells him to do.'

'Even to kill?'

'Possibly.'

We are interrupted by a plod coming our way and Shaver coming out of his office, slamming the door and marching off in the opposite direction.

'Come on, Constable. Let's see where our shifty superintendent is off too.'

***

Outside, Shaver commandeers a police waggon and sets off. Unable to commandeer a wagon we help ourselves, only to get chased up the road by its driver while he's shaking his fists and shouting out profanities.

Head holds on for dear life as I give the horse its head, the waggon sways and bumps along until we're close enough to Shaver's waggon for me to pull back on the reins and slow the horse down.

'Thank Christ for that,' says Head. 'I don't like to be rude, Serg' but you drive like a nutter, I thought we was going to turn over back there.'

'Fear not, Constable. I have never ridden a horse and this is only the second time I have driven a waggon, but I am quite confident that I shall not get us killed. So, settle back, relax and enjoy the ride.'

The traffic is so heavy we end up going so slow it would have been quicker to walk backwards. At last Shaver's waggon comes to a halt, Shaver alights and then sends the waggon away. I rein in the horse and we alight.

'What's he up to?' asks Head as we follow Shaver at a safe distance.

'I'll gamble he's heading for Sadie's Place to report to her that we're back on the case.'

And he does. Bruno opens the door, looks all around and then ushers Shaver in, the door is then slammed shut.

'I wish that prat wouldn't slam the door so,' grates Head. 'It does my nut in.'

'We need to somehow listen in to what's being said in there, Constable. Any ideas on how to do this?'

'No.'

'Nor I.'

'Hang on. I heard somewhere you can sometimes hear what's goin' on by sticking a glass on a wall and putting your ear to it.'

'The wall or the glass?'

He gives me the: are you taking the piss look? 'The glass of course.'

'Do you have a glass on you?'

'No. Do you?'

'No. Therefore I think we should forget the glass idea and try something far more straight forward. Come on, Constable.'

Going up to the door I give it a ring. Seconds later Bruno opens it and glares at me.

'Yus.'

'We wish to speak to Miss Place.'

'She's busy, bugger off an' come back later.'

He goes to slam the door but I jam my foot in, which really hurt.

'Get ya foot out or I'll break it,' says Bruno matter or fact.

I draw my revolver, 'Let us in or I'll shoot a hole in your head.'

'Miss Sadie won't like it. Just clear off will ya.'

'I'll count to three…'

He opens the door and hurries away while I limp in with Head following.

'What next, Serg'?'

'Let's see how it pans out,' says I heading down the hallway.

'Sergeant, how nice to see you again,' says Sadie as we enter her lair. 'To what do I owe the pleasure?'

No sign of Shaver, he's probably slipped out the back. 'Just following up on Mable's murder, Sadie.'

'Why? I'd been told the case was closed. Razor did her in and that was that.'

'Told by whom?'

She smirks at me, 'Common knowledge. Now, I'm really busy, so tell me what you want and then leave me to get on.'

'What is your relationship with Detective Superintendent Shaver?'

'What's it to do with you?'

'I am asking the questions. I repeat…'

'I don't have the kind of relationship with Shaver that you're implying.'

'Do you give him handouts to ensure your business is left alone by the police?'

'You accusing me of bribing a police man?'

'Yes, I am. I repeat…'

'Repeat all you want, Sergeant but you'll get nothing out of me.'

She goes back to her cards just as Bruno comes in, only this time he's holding a sawn-off shot gun.

'Show the policemen out if you please, Bruno.'

'Yus, madam.' says he waving the gun barrels in our direction.

'You're pushing your luck, Sadie,' says I.

'And you're pissing me off.' She points a finger at me as her mouth tightens into a grimace. 'You best go before this gets really messy, Sergeant. Did you really think you could force your way into my little home by the point of a gun and get away with it?' Violently scrapping back her chair she gets to her feet. 'Now, *get out* the pair of you before Bruno does something you'll bitterly regret.'

'We could arrest the pair of ya for threating us with a weapon and for being ugly,' says Head, swiftly drawing his revolver and pointing it at Sadie's chest. 'Failing that we could shoot the pair of ya dead and then arrest ya.'

'Are you fucking mad?' demands Sadie.

'Yes,' says Head in all honesty. 'But not as mad as your dopey doorman who hasn't even cocked his hammers. The second he goes ta cock 'em, he's dead and then you're dead. They don't call me Dead Eyed Dick for nuthin' ya know.'

'Lower your weapon, Bruno,' says I, 'or your mistress gets one right between her oversized water bags.'

Bruno lowers his weapon, 'Sorry Miss Sadie, they've got the drop on me.'

Head takes charge of the shotgun, breaks it and removes the cartridges.

'I ask again, Sadie, do you or do you not give Superintendent Shaver handouts to ensure your whore house doesn't get raided?'

A big fat grin cracks her face as she sits down. 'No, I don't. But I do share my bed with him whenever he wants.'

'So, in place of money you give him sexual favours,' says I in amazement.

'No. He takes what money he wants and I give him the other for free. That's what a good wife should do, wouldn't you agree?'

'You're married to Shaver? I don't believe it.'

'I could show you the marriage certificate if you want. Ten years man and wife, that's me and my Sydney. Didn't that just take the wind out of ya arse?'

***

'That was a waste of time,' grumbles Head as we trudge to the Dirty Duck for a pint or two.

'Not really, Constable. I'm thinking that Shaver has even more motive than I thought to want the investigation into Mable's murder to be dropped. He's not only protecting his wife he's also protecting their lucrative business. One sniff of his or Sadie's involvement in Mable's murder and he and his mouthy misses will be finished. Ordinary plods may get away with being married to prostitutes and madams, but a senior officer? No chance.'

'Which beggars' belief, why the *hell* did she let it slip?'

'She couldn't help herself and no doubt thought we'd back off once we knew.'

'Are we goin' to back off?'

I shake my head.

'Going against Shaver could be very dangerous ya know.'

'It could indeed, Constable. But as I have Dead Eyed Dick alongside me, I fear nothing.'

Head lets out a chuckle, 'Fooled them though didn't it. If they'd known I've never fired a revolver in my life they'd probably have laughed themselves stupid.'

'Most certainly,' smiles I. 'Now, the plan is this. We go into the pub and if Shaver's in there we shall confront him about what we know and see what reaction we get. If he's not there we shall spread it around what we've just learnt to everyone who is present and see what turns up.'

After happily walking along for a mile or so something comes to mind. 'Um… We'll have to back track, Constable; we have forgotten the bloody wagon we came in.'

'Christ! How the hell did we forget that? What if it's been stolen?'

We face each other. 'Who on earth would dare to steal a police waggon?'

'It didn't stop us.'

Turning around we quicken our pace and after a while arrive back where we left the waggon only to find it isn't there.

'It's bleedin' gone alright,' says Head giving me the oh fuck look.

'We're for it now, Constable.'

'I ain't, but you are, Sergeant.'

'Why just me?'

'Because you're in charge and I was only following orders.'

I have to reason that he is correct with his statement and decide to be magnanimous about it. 'Alright, so we know where we stand over this issue. I get the blame and you play the innocent.'

'Correct. I mean I've only been with the Yard a few hours so I wouldn't know whether or not it's acceptable to help yourself to police vehicles.'

As I don't have an argument, I flag down a cab, we climb in and set off for the inn. But one thing's for certain, I'll have to be careful with Head from now on if he's going to be the sort who only looks out for number one.

Arriving at the inn I am relieved to see the waggon we 'borrowed' is parked outside.

'Bet that bloody Shaver pinched it the thieving bastard,' says Head.

'No doubt,' grates I. 'Let us go and confirm the fact.'

After paying the driver and getting him to sign a receipt for twice as much, me and Head stroll into the Dirty Duck. Shaver is at the bar talking to Pollard and D. S. Bartley. There's half a dozen more plods at the bar and a couple of detectives eating at a table. Me and Head get in-between the plods and Shaver. Tony comes over.

'Two pints of best bitter please, Tony,' says I.

'You made it then?' laughs Shaver.

I meet his mocking eyes, 'Obviously, sir.'

'Did you walk or catch a cab?'

Pollard and Bartley start sniggering.

'A cab, sir.'

He straightens up, 'Just make certain when you put your expenses in for the cab it reflects the true cost, Sergeant or I shall have you reprimanded. Is that clear?'

'Yeah,' sneers Pollard. 'We can't 'ave coppers falsifying their expenses now, can we?'

'Or nicking police waggons,' adds Bartley.

'What's it got to do with you?' says Head glaring at Pollard.

Pollard stabs a finger into his own chest, 'I'll tell you what it's got to do with me, Dick Head. Crooked coppers give us all a bad name, an' being an honest copper I don't like being tarnished with the same brush.'

Tony bangs down our pints, 'Something up gentlemen?' says he sweeping warning eyes over us.

'No...' says Shaver. 'We were just having a mild disagreement.'

'Nothing to worry about, Tony,' says I.

'I hope not, Sergeant. Perhaps, Superintendent, you, your sergeant and the constable might like to go sit at a table, your meals will be out in a few minutes.'

'I like it here,' says Pollard locking eyes with Head.

'I don't want no trouble so I'd rather you went and sat down,' says Tony.

Shaver steps away from the bar and spreads out his arms, 'No one's out to cause trouble, Tony. But perhaps it would be better if, Sergeant Potter and his constable took their pints out into the garden. The sun's shining and it's quite warm out there.'

'Perhaps it would,' says I. 'May I request you come out with us, sir I would like to speak to you in private.'

'Make it quick then,' he shrugs. 'I've got a pie and mash coming up.'

Grabbing our pints, me and Head make our way out back with Shaver following. The tiny garden is laid to slabs with a few benches, a couple of long tables and a lot of creeper climbing the seven-foot walls that ring the place. There's a couple of plods drinking and smoking pipes in one corner.

'Constable Head and you two,' says Shaver pointing to the plods. 'Give us a few minutes, will you?'

They nod, get to their feet and head back inside. After a slight challenging pause Head also goes back inside.

Setting my pint down on the table I swing my legs over the bench and sit. Shaver sits down opposite, leaning forward he says, 'You shouldn't keep pestering Sadie Place, Sergeant. She's got nothing to do with that stupid little tart's murder, you take my word for it. Get that in your skull before you say whatever it is you want to say.'

'Shouldn't that be Mrs Sadie Shaver who has nothing to do with Mable Calver's murder?'

Sitting right back his eyes turn very dark, 'So she opened her mouth, did she? Well, no loss there, half the force knows me and Sadie are married. What's your point?'

I take a swig of beer while contemplating what to say next.

'Cat got your tongue, Sergeant?'

'More like a rat, sir. See I cannot understand why you're still in the position you are in if it's common knowledge that you are married to a madam. And not only that, you obviously benefit from the business. Which counts as living off immoral earnings.'

He taps a finger to his nose, 'Not who you know, Sergeant, or even what you know; it's what you know about who you know. If that's it, I think it's time I ate.'

'Not quite, sir. You see me and my constable have reasoned that you and your wife would have seen your business fall apart if Mable had carried out her plan to blackmail Sir Arnold Falconer, giving you a prime reason to want to see her dead and to ensure the investigation following her death got nowhere.'

A broad grin sweeps across his mouth while his eyes

sparkle with menace, 'Now then, Sergeant. I'll say this once only. Back off, you have no idea what you're dealing with. Mable thought she was clever, but she wasn't, she was just a stupid greedy little tart with a pretty face and a good body who stepped *way* out of line. She paid the price for trying to mess with the establishment, just make sure you don't do the same.'

With that he reaches across the table, taps the side of my face a few times, then, getting to his feet saunters away.

Head comes back out carrying his half-drunk pint and sits where Shaver had sat.

'How did it go, Serg'?'

'It didn't, the bastard warned me off. I think, Constable we are up against one hell of a conspiracy that may well close so many doors on us that we will struggle to open again.'

'Um… Can you put that in English?'

'We're fucked.'

Five Years On

We are in, Clumps office, the whiskeys not out so it's likely we won't be here long.

'I received a letter to pass on to you, Inspector,' says Clump passing over a brown envelope. 'Apparently it is from a former uniformed constable named Pollard.'

'Pollard! I thought he was dead,' says I perusing the envelope.

'Not yet, but dying of a sexually transmitted disease according to the desk sergeant who brought the letter to me.'

'Which disease is that?' asks Head.

'The sergeant didn't say and I didn't ask. How many are there?'

Head shrugs, 'No idea, Chief. Lot's I shouldn't wonder.'

'Having had relationships with half the prostitutes on his patch apparently, this Pollard fellow is probably dying from all of them. Anyway, there are more important issues on the agenda right now. I need you to get over to Hampstead High Street and go see one Franklin Frobisher at his photography shop. Yesterday this Frobisher was kidnapped, assaulted and robbed by a pair of thugs. Frobisher reported the crime to his local constabulary who have passed it on to us. Why pass it on to us, you ask?' He pauses, no doubt waiting for Head to annoy him by asking why did they pass it on, but when Head says nothing, Clump continues. 'This Frobisher is a highly regarded society photographer considered so well healed that the local constabulary felt a lot out of their depth, especially as Frobisher actually demanded that you two should be put on the case. What do you think of that revelation, Inspector?'

'Perhaps, sir our reputations precede us.'

'Perhaps,' frowns Clump. 'Now, before you rush off, not that I am being nosey, what is the letter about, may I ask?'

'I shall open it and see,' says I and do so. Reading it to myself I'm astounded by what it says. 'It is a request from Pollard to go and visit him immediately, before he dies, because he wants to confess something to me.'

'Confess what?' asks Clump.

'It doesn't say, sir. But I wouldn't be surprised if he wants to admit to a murder committed five years ago on a young prostitute named Mable Calver.'

Clumps bushy brows go up, 'Really! Odd that, a policeman, even a former policeman admitting to anything at all let alone a murder, especially five years on.'

'Just wants to get it off his chest before he pegs it,' scoffs Head. 'And to have the last laugh because we never solved the case.'

'I see,' ponders Clump scratching at his beard. 'Before my time at the Yard I believe. However, I shall dig out the case and take a gander at it. Unsolved cases always interest me. Right bugger off and get cracking.'

'Can I go see Pollard before we travel to Hampstead, sir?' asks I. 'If I leave it until we get back it might be too late.'

'Permission granted, Inspector. Just don't be too long about it.'

***

Outside we take a cab to Tannery Street of all places and finally arrive at number twelve; the address given in Pollards letter. After asking the driver to wait, Head and I go up to the front door of the half decent looking two-story little terrace. I am just about to knock on the door when it is opened by a pretty young blond who looks familiar.

'You came,' says Sally, 'I knew you would.'

'The last time we met you were working for Sadie Place,' says I.

She steps back and bades us in, closing the door she faces us, 'Finished wiv all that when Johnny Pollard asked me to marry 'im two years back.'

'That was good of him,' says Head. 'Was that before or after he got knob rot?'

'After. And he ain't got what you said, he's got the clap.'

'Which means you have also got it,' says I.

She shakes her head, 'No I ain't got it. I'm clean.'

'How the hell could you be clean?' grates Head. 'If he's got it, you've got it unless you don't do it together.'

'We don't an' never have. Johnny proposed to me knowin' he had the clap. He didn't want to end up dyin' alone and offered me a way out of the game an' I took it. I look after him an' he's looked after me up until a couple of months back when he slid downhill. An' his will says I'll get everything once he's gone. He's a good man is Johnny an' I love him.'

'Well, if it suits you both then who are we to judge,' says I. 'Now, we haven't got long, Sally, so if you'll show us to Pollard, please.'

'Do you want tea and cake? I baked it myself, it's a Victoria Sponge.'

'Sounds lovely, Sally,' says I softened by her beaming smile and blushing cheeks.

'A nice big chunk for me,' says Head.

'Alright. Follow me up an' then I'll make the tea an' that.'

We follow her up the narrow stairs to one of only two doors at the top. She taps on one, 'The police men are here, Johnny. Shall I show 'em in?'

'Show them in girl.'

'In ya go,' says she gently pushing open the door and closing it behind us.

Pollard is propped up by starched white pillows in a double bed complete with brass knobs. He looks very old, the skin on his face has shrunk to the skull and covered in the hideous mask of venereal disease. But his eyes are surprisingly bright and there's a smile on his face.

'Thank you both for coming,' says he. 'Please, pull up a chair.'

There are two ordinary chairs in the room along with a wardrobe and a dressing table and not much else, but everywhere looks clean and polished.

'Sally appears to be looking after you well, Pollard,' says I.

'She's a diamond that girl. And that's why I married her. Not for anything else she could offer you understand. I needed a companion who I could trust, someone to stand by me as the disease gradually ate me up. I knew Sally was a good one, heart of gold and believe it or not she loves me.'

'Good,' says I, though in truth I doubt if she loves him for himself or more because he rescued her from the very fate he is now facing. 'All things aside in the past, I am sorry to see you ending up this way.'

'Thank you, Detective Inspector it means a lot to me.'

'Can I ask you?' says Head deadpan. 'Is it true your knob drops off before you get covered in scabs or is it the other way around?'

'Ignore that question, Pollard,' says I shooting Head a back off glare. 'We are pushed for time. You wish to confess something to me. Something I have no doubt is in regards to the murder of Mable Calver.'

Taking a deep breath followed by an unmistakable groan of pain, he says, 'On the dressing table there's a copy of the original detailed report I made back then that was squashed by Shaver. I was then made to write out another stating what he wanted me to say. He then burnt the original but I rewrote it. Take it, but don't read it know it'll take too long.' He starts wheezing, struggling to get his breath as his body jerks forwards.

'Pat his back, Sergeant,' orders I.

'Piss off, I might catch the clap! You pat his back.'

'Are you refusing to carry out an order, Sergeant?'

'Yes, sir I am.'

'Stop,' gasps Pollard struggling to hold up a stop it hand. 'I don't want anyone except Sally patting my back, I'm so weak heavy hands could finish me off before I right several more wrongs I have to do so God will forgive me and take me into his fold.'

'You have found God?' says I.

'No, he found me.'

'Where did he find you?' grins Head. 'While you were cracking someone's head with your truncheon or forcing some poor bitch to spread her legs?'

'Enough, Sergeant,' warns I. 'If you don't start acting with more propriety, I will send you to wait outside and you will forfeit your slice of sponge. Please continue, Pollard.'

'Thank you, Inspector. Ask me anything and I swear upon Almighty God that I will answer those questions in all honesty.'

'Did you cheat by shoving a knuckle duster in your glove when we had our fight?' asks Head before I can say a word.

'I did. And I am sorry for it.'

'Did you…'

'Kill Mable Calver,' cuts in I before Head starts asking all kinds of crap.

'No, sir I did not.'

'Then who did?'

'I'm not sure, so I'll refuse to answer that one. But hopefully my report will lead you to the killer. I know the answers in there somewhere but I've never been…' He breaks off and begins coughing and shaking like a man with a serious illness.

Sally comes in, 'Johnny,' she gasps.

'I'm alright, love,' gasps he back. 'Water, please…'

Brushing past me she picks up a glass of water from a small table by his bed, slips a hand around his neck then holds the glass to his mouth. He drinks slowly, she withdraws the glass and with a sigh he lays his head back.

'Do you want anything, Johnny?'

'No. Only to sleep and dream of sheep in meadows and gambolling lambs. Take them downstairs, I have no more to say.'

'Well good luck,' says Head getting to his feet.

I throw Head an admonishing stare before thanking Pollard and picking up the envelope. We follow Sally downstairs and into a neat and very clean little kitchen. Sally washes her hands in the butler sink and then bades us sit at the table where she's laid out tea and cake for three.

'Johnny looked alright a few months back,' says she pouring the tea into china cups. 'Now he looks terrible an' he's like that all over his body.'

'At least his eyes appear bright.'

'They do, but he's blind now.'

'Really?' says I. 'I suppose he's incompetent now as well.'

'Um… Well, he can't do much for 'imself, that's for sure and I have ta change him because he's become incontinent as well as incompetent.'

'How long's he got left?' says Head grabbing the biggest slice of cake as usual.

'The doctor said he'll be gone before the end of the month. The vicar come's regular and hears Johnny's confessions and he said the same yesterday.' She passes over the teas and sits down. 'Would you both come to his funeral else there won't be many there 'cause he weren't that well liked. Don't know why 'cause he's always been good to me. He never was as bad as people thought ya know.'

It strikes me that it may well be worth going depending on who turns up, we may learn something about Mable's murder. 'Send a note to the Yard addressed to me, Sally and we'll make all effort to come. I promise.'

'Thank you, you are sweet.'

'This cake's bloody lovely,' says Head licking his jam smudged lips. 'Got any more?'

'I like a man who likes his food,' smiles she getting to her feet. 'I'll be looking for a new man once Johnny's gone if you're interested.'

Head shows her his wedding ring, 'Sorry, already taken.'

After cutting more cake and setting it down she sits and looks me in the eye, 'You know that judge who was smitten with Mable?'

I nod.

'Well, he started coming to see me for the usual about a month or so after Mable got done in. Then he asked me if I wanted to be his mistress after about the third visit just as he did to Mable. I said alright I'd give it a go, but then I never saw him again. How odd is that?'

'Very odd,' puzzles I. 'We were ordered off the case at the time, then ordered back on it and finally ordered off it for good. Falconer never got the mayor's job and as a consequence, apparently, retired from judging and public life to spend his time playing golf and tending to his orchids.'

'But did he give up rogering young prostitutes,' puts in Head before ramming another wedge of cake into his mouth.

'Probably not,' says I. 'Anything else you can recall, Sally before we leave?'

'Don't know. If I do, shall I let ya know?'

'Please do. Right, sup up Sergeant it's time we were off.'

***

The cab takes us to the train station for a short journey to Hampstead, once settled on the train I flick through Pollards original report.

'Anything new?' asks Head.

'I can't go into it now; I will study it in depth tonight at home over a scotch.'

'Bet it'll be a waste of time, Pollard's full of crap. He just wanted to ease his conscience and make sure he gets into Heaven.'

'What if there is no Heaven?'

'Then he's knackered, he'll have to go to the other place instead, that's if they've got any room left.'

'What if there's no Hell either, Richard?'

'God knows,' grins he.

Once off the train we take a cab to Hampstead High Street where we are dropped off outside Franklin Frobisher's Photographic Shop.

'Posh stuff,' says Head as we view the framed photographs on display in the window.

'Indeed, Richard.' I point to one on particular, 'The

wedding of the century, as decadent as a royal wedding. I'll bet her dress cost way over a hundred pounds and the men's top hats and tails came to hundreds more.'

'Her tiara must have cost an arm and leg. All that money spent didn't make her look any more lovely than my Chloe on our big day. Or, I've no doubt your Betty,'

'True, but this bride and groom must be at least in their late sixties.'

'Not likely to have been much of a honeymoon there then, Gerald. By the time she got all that lot off and laid on the bed ready for it he'd probably given up and dropped off. Mind you too much shagging at their age could kill them off. I reckon…'

'Let us get on, Sergeant. It will be time for lunch and a few beers soon and the quicker we see to this Frobisher chap the longer we'll have in the pub.'

'I'll go for that.'

We enter the shop to a tinkling bell and go up to the mahogany counter.

'There's some money's worth in here,' says Head gazing around at the cameras on tripods, hand held and all manner of things the budding photographer would need if they wanted to take really good photographs. The walls festooned with, I have to admit, exceptional, almost magical photographs of panoramic views of the heath, the wildlife and the people who work the land alongside the more well healed, squires and gentry.

'Wonder if he's got any nudes,' sighs Head. 'If I took up photography that's what I'd like to specialise in. Can you image getting paid to take…'

Thankfully a tall skinny man with a thin moustache beneath a nose pointing up to the sky comes in from out back. In his black suit with gold waste coat and yellow bow tie he looks seriously posh, if somewhat of a drip.

'Gentlemen,' says he looking us up and down through assessing eyes that say he's already decided we are not worthy enough to be customers. 'You are the detectives from Scotland Yard, I presume.'

'We are,' says Head. 'I am Detective Sergeant Sir Richard Head and this is my superior: Detective Inspector Lord Gerald Potter.'

'Oh! Really? Goodness me I do apologise; I had no idea Scotland Yard contained such important gentry within its lower ranks.'

'It doesn't, sir. My sergeant will have his little joke. You are Mr Franklin Frobisher I presume?'

'I am Inspector. And welcome. I will close the shop and we can retire to the parlour for refreshments while I relate my story to you.'

'Thank you, sir.'

We follow him out back, through a studio complete with a stage and a back drop of a tiger hunt and some toff stood on a dead tiger while holding his rifle and looking very proud of himself.

'Just one of the many scenarios I create for my customers,' says Frobisher with a sweep of his arm. 'Whatever background my customers require I will ensure they receive it. From the Garden of Eden to Heaven itself if they so desire.'

We walk on and into an upmarket parlour where he bades us sit at a round table.

'I am in need of a brandy, gentlemen,' says he. 'Will you join me or shall I call my wife to make tea or coffee?'

'A brandy would be most welcome, sir,' says I.

Brandies poured, Frobisher sits and raises his crystal tumbler, 'Your good health gentlemen.'

'Cheers,' says Head before chucking the lot down in one go.

'A fine brandy, sir,' says I taking a more genteel sip.

'Thank you, Inspector. Where shall I begin?'

'Right from the start.'

'Very well. I had just opened the shop at ten o'clock yesterday morning. My wife, thankfully, was not here having gone to her dressmakers to be fitted for an evening gown…'

'Sorry to interrupt, sir,' says I. 'Please stick to whatever is relevant to the crime or you will lose momentum.'

He takes a swig of brandy before letting out a long sigh. 'I was about to go to my developing room when the bell rang and in sauntered a pair of long greasy haired, tall scruffy youths, with narrow eyes and hard pinched faces while exuding that sickly stench of unwashed flesh.'

'Was one a little taller than the other?' asks Head.

'One was indeed taller, Sergeant. Do you know who they are?'

'I believe we do. But please continue.'

'I recall demanding what did they want. You could see they were up to no good.' "We want ya ta shut ya gob and listen," said the tall one as he came right up to the counter and produced a sawn-off shotgun then banged it down hard on the counter. "You're goin' ta take pictures of me an' my brother while we race a couple of sheep over on the heath." "But we ain't goin' ta pay ya for it," said the other. "So, get ya gear an' come with us." 'Of course, I refused and demanded that they leave immediately or I would summon the local constabulary. To which the tall one then aimed his shotgun and blew off Sir Trevor Parker's head.'

'Good God!' gasps I. 'You didn't say you had other customers in the shop!'

'Because I did not have any. He blew off the photographic head of Sir Trevor. And if that wasn't enough of an abomination the other took out his unmentionable and urinated all over Lady Anabel Parkers satin dress. They then threatened to destroy everything in the shop and give me a 'good kicking' unless I followed their instructions to the letter. Which culminated in my fly being loaded to capacity with my photographic equipment along with the louts and I having to whip my poor horse into a cruel fast trot, for their entertainment, as we sped off towards the heath.'

At this he drops his eyes and stares into his brandy.

'Recollecting events is always traumatic, sir,' says I. 'But you must remain focused and calm or you will allow your emotions to overtake you and we shall get nowhere.'

'In other words, get some balls,' grates Head holding out his glass for a refill.

Frobisher sits up straight as a look of determination flashes in his eyes, 'By God, Sergeant you are right. Balls it shall be and to hell with convention! I went through hell on earth yesterday and now I want revenge. Grab the decanter of brandy, Sergeant and top us up.'

After a toast to the Queen and determining that Robert and William Boyle, the infamous Bill and Bob, were back on the scene, Frobisher continues.

'It was the drive from hell, gentlemen, those monsters dropped their lower garments to bare their posteriors to nearly everyone we passed by. They screamed out abuse of the foulest nature while including the F and C words. They spat at people, but thankfully we were going so fast they only succeeded in spitting against the wind and showering themselves, which they found riotously hilarious. But without doubt it was Bill who achieved the most notorious of vile acts I have ever witnessed nor less could have even imagined. The disgusting creature wrenched off my hat which he had previously rammed on and proceeded to fart into it before ramming it back on my head. At this point I wanted to die and couldn't imagine it could get any worse, but much worse was to come. Dear God, however shall I live with the shame of it all?'

'Fear not, sir,' says I. 'We will catch the swine's and you shall have your day in court to turn the tables on *them*. Now let us take a small respite while you gather your self-esteem. Plus, I could do with a visit to the lavatory if you don't mind.'

'Of course not, Inspector. Through that door into the hallway and then second on your right.'

So, the twins from hell have returned ponders I as I urinate into a porcelain bowl decorated with blue chrysanthemums. And I have no doubt they have come back for their revenge on me and Head. Five years on they would now be probably as tall as myself and an awful lot harder than before while obviously having become far more dangerous. After a flush and a quick hand wash, I head back towards the parlour where I meet, I assume, the lady of the house, a short nicely rounded red cheeked woman with a pretty face and a nervous smile.

'Oh. Please excuse me, sir,' says she in a quiet tone. 'I was intending to keep out of the way during your visit but I must check if my bread has risen. I am Mrs Priscilla Frobisher.'

'How do you do, madam,' smiles I. 'I am Detective Inspector Potter. Should you wish to join us, madam please feel free. After all this concerns you as well.'

'Thank you, Inspector but my husband does not wish me to hear some of the more lurid accounts from his ordeal. Me being a lady of course.'

'Of course,' says I knowing she is hiding something. 'However, I will want to speak to you, madam once I have finished with your husband.'

'Oh! I can't think why, Inspector. I was out and by the

time I returned those vile creatures had gone. Apart from untying my husband I had no involvement in this dreadful incident and fear I have nothing of worth to assist you with in your enquiries.'

There was a nervous tic in her eyes just then that tells me she's definitely hiding something. 'Perhaps, but we shall see, madam. And fear not I doubt if I will keep you for more than a minute or so.' With a short bow I leave her and go back into the parlour to find Head is still taking notes having continued the interview without me, which doesn't matter as I trust him and it is getting ever closer to lunch.

'I was just saying to Franklin,' says Head with that crafty eyed look of his. 'That we will have to break off for lunch soon, as we've been up since dawn with barely a small piece of cake inside us since breakfast.'

'Lunch is on me,' cuts in Frobisher. 'They do a great Porterhouse steak at Jack Straws and it is not far away at all. If you want, we could go right now and continue the interview there.'

'Very well, sir we shall take you up on your kind offer. And then after lunch we will want to see where the twins forced you to take them. I met your good wife, sir on my way back in the hallway. Would Mrs Frobisher care to join us as she might not want to be left alone?'

'I would prefer her to remain here, Inspector. I do not wish her to hear what I shall be relating to you; it would horrify her.'

'As you wish. Before we go for lunch, I assume you have copies of the photographs you took of the incident.'

He shakes his head, 'Unfortunately I do not. They took everything, the plates, negatives and photographs, all bar one, which they ordered me to present to you personally.' Taking out a small envelope from his pocket he hands over a single photograph.

I peruse it and pass it to Head who says, 'It's a photo of someone's bare arse!'

'With what appears to be exceptionally brutal scars, probably from being birched,' adds I.

Frobisher grimaces, 'The photograph is of Bob's posterior. It was the last to be taken and was taken here once we had returned from the meadow. Bill suddenly said to Bob: "Bob, drop ya trousers and bend over so Frank can take a picture of ya arse." "What for?" demanded Bob. "So, he can give it to the coppers. Then them bastards can see what was done to us when we was just kids." "Why don't ya drop ya own trousers and let 'im photo *your* arse?" "Cause mine ain't as scarred as yours. I want them bastards ta know why we're comin' for 'em. I want them ta sweat blood. I want them to know that we, an' especially you was birched way beyond what we should 'ave been. Scarred for bleedin life ain't ya Bob?" "I is that, Bill. But I did sink me teeth into the birching coppers leg, didn't I?" "Ya did. Now, get 'em down and bend over." 'Bob did so, and reluctant as I was to photograph Bob's nakedness, I of course did so from fear of my life.'

'You did right, sir,' says I. 'What happened next?'

'They thanked me for all I had done then tied me up to a chair and gagged me. Then I could hear them going through the house obviously searching for items of value. A short while later they returned, said goodbye and left, taking my fly with them and abandoning it at the station.'

'Have you a list of what they stole from you?' asks I. 'Stolen jewellery in-particular will often turn up in pawn shops and then may be traced back to whoever pawned it.'

'Yes, Inspector. I have a copy of the list and photographs of the most valuable items of jewellery for you.' He takes out another envelope from his pocket and hands it over before stressing: '*They only took cash and jewels.*'

He stated this with such firm conviction it leads me to believe he is lying. 'Nothing else was taken?'

He shakes his head.

'Are you sure?'

'I am, Inspector.'

'Very well,' says I pocketing the envelopes. 'Let us go for lunch?'

***

After a fine lunch of steak and accompaniments washed down with a few beers we set off for the heath, until finally we find ourselves gazing over meadows, trees and hedges that afford fine views of distant church spires and rustic villages. There are sheep in our sloping meadow and a small timber shed. Frobisher parks the buggy beside it and we alight.

'Hard to believe we're so close to the fumes and chaos of London,' says Head.

'It is indeed,' says I. 'Right, Mr Frobisher. Tell us what happened and please try not to leave anything out no matter how foul it was.'

His eyes say it all. The man is still in a state of profound shock.

'What I have to tell you, Inspector is so vile I doubt you have ever personally encountered anything worse.'

'Just say it how it was,' says Head scratching his crotch. 'Spare not our feelings, sir because we don't have any when it comes to victims. You will not shock us, trust me.'

'Very well,' says he dropping his eyes. 'The twins jumped down and went to the shed and opened it. Inside there was a pair of horned sheep tethered to rings with halters. They brought them out and ordered me to start photographing while they posed with the sheep. I had taken my field camera which

I use for wildlife and scenery, it is portable, easy to use and I can change plates quickly and had taken several with me. After a few poses, Bob held onto the sheep while Bill went back into the shed, returning with a large sack. I noticed when he opened the neck there appeared to be clothes and blankets in there…'

'Obviously they had been sleeping rough out here.'

He nods. 'Dear God, gentlemen! What happened next came straight from hell. Out of the bag appeared what looked like two large sticks of dynamite and a ball of string. Working together they inserted a stick of dynamite half way into each of the poor creatures' rectums and them tied the protruding end to the sheep's docked tails while I took more photographs. "Did ya get all that, Frank?" said Bill grinning at me. 'I just nodded for I couldn't speak.' "Now then, Frank," he continued. "This is what's gonna 'appen. We light the fuses. Then we let go of the sheep and scare 'em off." He then casually pointed down the hill. "They'll run like fuck while the fuses fizz and we shout out encouragement to our own sheep. See, we got bets on this. We've bet on our rams, mine's called Randy and Bob's is called Bandy. Now, the one whose ram gets the furthest away before they're blown up will be the winner. What do ya thing of that bugger for a great bit of sport then Frank?" 'Of course, I felt sick to my stomach and couldn't speak, then Bob said to me:' "Do ya want ta bet, Frank. Ya can join in if ya like. Perhaps ya like to get kitted up and race against the rams." 'Then who would take the photographs?' I asked. "Good thinking," said he. "Let's get racing."

'They lit the fuses, whipped off the halters and then Bill extracted that vile little shotgun and shot it into the air. All the other sheep in the meadow panicked and fled down towards the far end, Randy and Bandy fled down the hill while Bill and Bob screamed out encouragement like demented banshees.

The dynamite turned out to be fireworks as blue flares shot out, sparks flew and they crackled and banged, one flare shot past my face. Bandy's firework popped out from his rectum and fell to the ground, Bob shouted out, "Foul play, let's start again." 'But it was too late, both fireworks erupted with a final huge bang and a flash of white, Bandy was bowled over but got up and carried on running while poor Randy was blown apart as lumps of him went up into the air and spread across the meadow. It was terrible!'

'Not so much a ball of flame as a ball of wool, then,' says Head dead pan.

'Woolly bits everywhere, Sergeant, floating down like bloodied snow.'

'And you photographed it all?' asks I.

He nods. 'Dear God I don't know how I did it, but then I was terrified I would be next if I did not comply with their demands. Of course, I knew most of the photographs would come out all fuzzy…'

I place a reassuring hand on his shoulder, 'You did right, Mr Frobisher. What happened next?'

'Bob refused to honour the wager, quoting a default in the terms and conditions that they'd agreed on. Bill called him a welshing F word followed by the C word. They then set too fighting, kicking, punching and even biting before wrestling to the ground where they rolled all over the sheep droppings until at last, Bob yielded. They stood up, Bob handed over a shilling, they shook hands and then embraced. Following that we loaded the fly and went back to the shop where upon they watched in fascination as I developed the photographs. The rest you know.'

'Right, Sergeant,' says I. 'Take a look around inside the shed and see if you can find anything that might be relevant and then we'll look around the field to see if we can find the burnt-out firework cases.' Facing Frobisher, I ask, 'Did the local force investigate the incident before we took over?'

He shakes his head, 'Not that I am aware of, Inspector. They took my statement and left it at that and appeared somewhat relieved that Scotland Yard would be taking over, as was I. The twins had demanded that detectives,' he pauses and turns bright red, 'um…'

'Out with it, sir,' demands I. 'Whatever it is and no matter how disparaging towards us it might be.'

'Very well, Inspector.' He coughs a bit and then says, 'They demanded that detectives Piss Pot and Dick Face investigate or they would return, whereupon I would get it up the 'ring piece' with the barrels of his shotgun.'

'That would make your eyes water,' grins Head coming out of the hut carrying an evidence bag.

'Anything?' says I.

'Nothing much; a few dog ends from rollups, wrappers from sweets and this empty gin bottle.' He holds it up for my perusal. 'And finally, this.' From the bag he takes out a used shotgun cartridge and hands it to me.'

'Could well be from their shotgun, Sergeant. When we catch the bastards, with luck ballistics will be able to match this cartridge to their shotgun giving us even more evidence to easily convict them.'

'I say,' says Frobisher. 'You fellows are so clever. I wish I were as clever.'

'Your rich and we ain't,' says Head. 'So, who really is the clever one?'

'I was fortunate enough to have been born with the proverbial silver spoon, Sergeant, I must admit. Even so…'

'Let's search the meadow,' grates I before Head go's off on one of his them and us lectures.

After a fruitless search we headed back to the shop. I asked Frobisher again if he knew of anything else that was missing along with the cash and jewels. He brusquely answered, "*No!*"

Back in Frobisher's parlour we go over everything again in case he'd missed anything while we wait for Mrs Frobisher to make coffee and join us. Ten minutes later she's sat beside her husband at the table opposite me and Head having set down coffee along with a plate of delicate little fancy iced cakes, which Head seems to think can only be eaten two at a time while ramming them down his gob, chomping on them a few times and then washing them down with coffee by the cup full.

'Lovely buns, Mrs Frobisher,' smiles he gazing at her bust.

'Thank you, Sergeant,' coos she totally missing Heads double entendre. 'I do love to see a man enjoy his food.'

'Excellent,' says I having managed to grab two before Head scoffs the lot. 'Before we leave you in peace, Mr and Mrs Frobisher, I must thank you both for your hospitality along with your strength of resolve in answering most of our questions with honesty and clarity. However, you really must tell us what else was stolen from you.'

Frobisher sits bolt upright while I note his wife squeezes his hand with such force her knuckles turn white, 'I have said there was nothing else, Inspector and I take affront of your continuing to press the matter. In fact, your underlying insinuation is one of an accusation that I and my wife are hiding something and therefore are also lying to you. Am I correct in my assumption?'

'You are, sir,' says I with more than a touch of venom in my tone.

'Look!' snaps Head. 'Just admit what else has been stolen from you or we'll tell *you* what we believe has been stolen.'

'You couldn't possibly… know,' says Frobisher as it dawns

on him that he's just stuck his size elevens straight into the shit. He and his wife suddenly turn into beetroots, still he holds out. 'There is nothing else I or my wife wish to tell you, gentlemen. I am sorry, but this interview is over with and if you press the matter any further then I fear I shall have to report your harassment of ...'

'I wouldn't even think of it if I was you,' warns Head giving Frobisher his narrowed eye look.

'Photography!' snaps I. 'An art in its own right. Why if I had your knowledge and talent Mr Frobisher, I would use that talent not only for business purposes but also for personal pleasure. In short, I would love to take private photographs of my beautiful wife and she would love to take private photographs of me...'

'Even though he isn't beautiful,' grins Head.

I shoot him my, watch it glare. 'You, sir, and you, madam have done nothing wrong. Even the church gives its blessing to married couples enjoying each other's bodies in wholesome activities within the privacy of their own home.' Having fully grabbed their attention by the way they're staring at me I go for it. 'The twins have also run off with your private photographs, have they not?'

Frobisher's mouth gapes open while his wife covers her face with her hands.

'Dear God, Inspector,' says he. 'What on earth can we do? If the photographs, or at least the knowledge of their existence becomes public knowledge then we are ruined. People will believe we are perverted and no one will want to have anything to do with us. My business will fail, I and Priscilla would find ourselves ostracised and caste out of polite society. We would even be thrown out of the bridge club.'

Priscilla, tears swamping her eyes, says, 'And can you

image how this will damage our two sons. They are in boarding school. Oh! They will be tormented and ridiculed. You know how cruel children can be?'

'Fear not madam,' says I. 'My Sergeant and I will do our utmost to secure the return of your photographs before too much damage has been done. Now, I suggest you both have a good tot of brandy to calm your nerves while I reason where we go from here.'

'A good idea, Inspector,' sighs he getting to his feet. 'Will you gentlemen both join us.'

'Of course, we will,' says I.

Frobisher goes over to the sideboard to pour the brandies while Priscilla produces a handkerchief to dab at her eyes. Both are mortified and I feel for them, but I can also see a fat wad of money coming my way.

'Now then,' says I once Frobisher has re-joined us. 'Drink up, gather yourselves together because I do not intend being gentle with you. Cheers.'

We toast the Queen again. Frobisher and I sip our brandies, Head chucks his down, Priscilla follows suit, chokes and splutters a bit before fixing me with determination in her brown eyes.

'The twins will hold onto the photographs for their own amusement while deciding what to do with them,' says I. 'Undoubtably they will then approach you, Mr Frobisher and demand a ransom for their return.'

'Thank God for that!' says Priscilla.

I hold up my hand, 'It will not be that easy, madam when it comes to blackmail. It is vital that you inform us immediately when the twins contact you. They will demand and threaten you that if you go to the police the deal will be off and the photographs will then become public knowledge. All rubbish, before they are done with you, they will have bled you dry, and then they will still sell the original photographs to the highest bidder while no doubt ensuring they retain copies. The best way to deal with this is for you to completely trust us and follow our instructions to the letter. I believe the photographs will turn out to be the twin's nemesis, they will become increasingly greedy and thus will start to make errors of judgement that will assist us in not only returning your property, but also aid in our capturing the evil rats. Now, listen very carefully while I inform you what you must do.'

***

An hour later Head and I are on the train heading back.

'Do you think the Frobisher's will remain calm enough to follow the plan, Gerald?' says Head. 'Or do you think they'll do exactly what the twins demand of them?'

'Not sure, Richard. Perhaps a bit of both. It hasn't helped finding out the photographs they took are so… um…'

'Filthy?'

'It depends on your view. Highly erotic would be how many collectors of pornography would describe them.'

'While the strait-laced would demand that the models who posed for such ungodly filth should be excommunicated and then thrown into the fires of hell.'

'They would, the pious hypochondriacs. No one else was involved in the Frobisher's sexual adventures. They kept it strictly private between themselves and I for one can see nothing wrong in what they have been doing. However, collectors will go mad to get their hands on the original photographs while being prepared to pay out a fortune.'

'Meaning our reward for securing the photos for the Frobisher's will be a lot higher than anticipated.'

'Exactly, Richard. But we should not be greedy over this.

I did feel for them you know. Nice people, but very naive.'

'Very nice. Mind you when it comes to getting adventurous that Priscilla doesn't hold back, does she? I couldn't believe you talked him into allowing us to see a 'sample' of his work along with 'lending' you a set of copies.'

'A few brandies, play to an artist's ego and before you know it, they can't wait to show off their work. Besides we needed to know just how naughty the photographs the twin's stole, are.'

'We did indeed,' says Head with a smile while his eyes go all lustful. 'And my weren't they good the few he showed us. Priscilla as a near naked Cleopatra was my favourite. Christ! I'd never have dreamed you could make a snake disappear like that. How long was it do you reckon?'

'It wasn't a real snake, Richard. I don't know, three or four feet.'

'Bloody amazing. Who'd have thought such a sweet, prim little woman like her could be so… um… how should I put it.'

'Horny. Now, can we drop the subject for now as we can't go forwards on this until the twins contact Frobisher.

'All, saying they will. They may just try and sell the photos.'

'I don't think so, Richard. They'll be out for all they can get. Let's see what Clump thinks of it all, we can trust him to keep this to himself. I also want to ask him if he'll ask the Chief Constable to help, in the strictest of confidence of course.'

'Of course. We can't have the entire force knowing that Sir Robert Briers, our illustrious church going Chief Constable is an obsessed collector of filth, now, can we?'

'And plays golf with Clump. If the Frobisher's photographs should come up for sale in the underground market, Briers, having seen the copies and informed his agents in advance what exactly he is looking for may help us to track down the sellers.

***

Back at the yard we go up to the hairy faced desk sergeant to see if there are any messages for us.

'Clump wants you in his office by eight sharp tomorrow morning,' says he pulling a face. 'And there is a parcel for you, Inspector,' adds he presenting a shoe box onto the counter.

'What is it?' asks I.

He shrugs, 'No idea, I don't open other people's parcels even when they smell like this one does.'

Leaning forwards, I take a sniff, 'Smells a bit rank, Sergeant. A kind of meat going off smell. Very odd.'

'It could be a bomb,' says Head. 'I'd open it with caution if I was you.'

'Good thinking,' says the desk sergeant. 'It wouldn't be the first we've had sent in.'

After untying the string, I take out my truncheon and say, 'Right, I shall bob down, reach up and push the lid off the box, so take cover.'

The desk sergeant disappears while Head bobs down beside me, reaching up I attempt to push the lid off the box with my truncheon only to shove the entire box behind the counter, cue a stream of foul words from the desk sergeant before his face appears glaring at us over the counter. He doesn't look happy; his forehead is now embellished with what appears to be congealed blackened blood and there's a snotty looking streak of something slowly sliding down one cheek.

'Bollocks!' says he thumping down the parcel's contents.

'Indeed,' agrees I on standing up. On the counter there now sits a pair of very large testicles wrapped in a white furry scrotum.

'Sheep's nuts,' says Head matter of fact as if receiving a

pair of balls in a shoe box is a quite normal event.

'Who brought this in, Sergeant?' asks I to the desk sergeant.

'The postman.'

'Was there a message with it?'

Bobbing down he brings up the box and peers inside, 'There's something in here. Yes, it's a note. Bit mucky. Here take, the bloody thing.'

Taking out the folded up note I open it up and read it out loud, 'Be yours next before we finish wiv ya. Luv Bill an' Bob.'

'What the hell's that all about?' says the desk sergeant.

'It's about twin brothers who are out for revenge, Sergeant. Well, we shall see whose balls get cut off first.'

'They don't scare you then, Inspector. If it was me being threatened with castration, I reckon I'd be fillin' me draws.'

'Me and all,' says Head.

'There's a PS: An' we'll 'ave Dick Face's as well.'

Head sidles right up to me, 'Let's see that note.'

I show it to him and he sighs with relief, 'There's no mention of me on that note, thank Christ.'

'No need to sound so happy about it,' grates I. 'Right, I need a drink, let's go to our office, Sergeant and review the day's events.'

'Well take your shoe box an' contents with you,' demands the desk sergeant.

'You can have them,' says I. 'Take them home for your tea. All I want is the note.'

'I don't eat balls and I don't see why I should be left to clear up this mess,' says he sweeping his arm over the counter.

'What if I order you to clear up the mess?'

'I'll make sure the balls are in Clump's office ready for his inspection the second you leave. As he's not in until the morning they'll be stinking to high heaven by then.'

'If that's how you want it.' I say to Head, 'Sergeant, pack the balls back in the box and let's get on.'

'They're your balls, you pack them up.'

We face each other, 'Are you refusing to obey your superior's order, Sergeant?'

'Yes.'

'So be it, I'll remember this act of defiance from the both of you.' Gingerly I pick up the balls between finger and thumb, drop them into the box and put the lid back on.

'What do you intend doing with them?' asks Head as we tramp off to our office.

'I shall hand them to the first urchin I see on my way home. I'm sure they'll appreciate them far more than we do.'

'They probably will. In fact, they'll think it's Christmas come early.'

Twins from Hell

Eventually arriving home at seven, by which time it is dark, I go around back and into the kitchen to find Betty setting out the table for what smells like a beef stew.

'Home at last,' sighs I dumping Pollards envelope on the table.

'Have you had a good day, Detective Inspector?' says she giving me a peck on the cheek.

'It has been an unusual day, my love. And I shall tell you all about it once I've poured myself a nice glass of scotch.'

'You do that while I put the dumplings on.'

I start taking my jacket off, Betty goes behind me to help and then says, 'The back of your jacket smells funny, Detective Inspector and there's a gooey stain right in the centre of it. Whatever is it?'

'An imprint from a pair of sheep testicles.'

'Sheep testicles?'

'Yes. Some rotten little urchin threw them at me.'

'Whatever for?' says she holding my jacket at arm's length while screwing up her face and perusing the stain.

'Let me get that drink first.'

'I'll have to put your jacket in the soak before I wash it.'

'You know best.'

'I do. Go and relax, Detective Inspector, you look tired out.'

Taking Pollards envelope, I head for the parlour, pour myself a good measure of scotch, sit down in my favourite armchair and turn up the lamp ready to read. Bliss, all is well with the world now that I am home. I have a no doubt delicious dinner to look forwards too, served by my darling wife who really appreciates me as much as I do her, followed by me relating all that's occurred during the day, including the Frobisher's antics and then… Oh fuck…'

Betty come's into the parlour and stands there with a look of 'you're dead' in her blazing eyes, in one hand she is holding a small envelope. 'Are you comfortable, Gerald?'

I was, thinks I. 'Um… It is not what you think, Betty. Those photographs are not mine they belong to someone else.'

'They all say that, Detective Inspector. Am I no longer enough for you? It was only a few months ago you were lusting after that Bullington girl. Now, I find you are in possession of several really filthy photographs that no doubt you have been luridly perusing to help satisfy your insatiable lust…'

'I have *not* been luridly perusing those photos, Betty! They are evidence in a new case that has only just been handed to me and Richard…'

'If they are evidence, why then did you not leave them at the station?'

Taking a long swallow of my scotch I fix her with the stern look. 'Because I didn't want every Tom, Dick and Hairy at the station seeing them. They belong to a couple who are mortified that the originals are now in the hands of a pair of thieves who intend to blackmail them for their return. No one, except for me, Richard, Clump and the Chief Constable will see them.'

'Is this the same Chief Constable you oft go on about who's a dirty old git who collects such filth?'

'It is, my little inquisitor.'

'Before I rest my case, I have one more question and you had better answer me honestly or you and I shall have a serious fight. Do you understand?'

'I do. What is your question?'

'Did you, or did you not, achieve sexual satisfaction from leering at these photographs?'

I need to turn this around before it gets silly. 'Did you?'

'Did I what?'

'Become aroused on seeing the photos.'

'What on earth has that got to do with anything?'

'Yes, or no?'

'I've taken the stew off the stove.'

'I'll need a wash first.'

'Hurry up then.'

***

By eight the next morning we are in Clumps office. Thankfully the scotch isn't out, one sip and I'd probably drop off.

'You appear tired, Inspector,' says Clump with a twinkle in his eyes. 'Up all night, were you?'

'Bit of a restless night, Chief.'

'Um…' ums he scratching at his scruffy beard. 'Right, first things first. I went through the files on the Mable Calver murder and unless you discovered something new in Pollards original statement I cannot possibly sanction or justify reopening the case. What did you find out?'

'I have to admit, sir I haven't actually read the report as yet.'

'Because?'

'I had a headache.'

'Did Betty have one as well?' grins Head.

I give him the shut it glare. 'No.'

'We shall forget about the Calver case for now,' says Clump. 'It has been hanging around for five years, a bit longer won't hurt. Right, fill me in on what happened with this photographer fellow.'

I do so, he listens intently, tuts a bit, growls a bit and lights up a cigar, but doesn't say a word until I have finished and handed over the photographs.

Setting down his cigar in the ashtray so it smokes all over me and Head, he says, 'Very graphic. Pretty lady. Doesn't look the type really. Rather up market. But then you never can tell. Is that a real snake?'

'I believe not, Chief.'

'Right,' says he handing me back the photographs. 'Keep these safe, Inspector. Do not log them as evidence just yet or they'll be passed around the yard and end up fingered to bits and covered in sticky stuff. Can I assume that the Boyles have returned to seek vengeance on you two for your part in having them punished for their villainous deeds?'

'Most definitely, Chief.'

'Well one thing's for certain; you are up against a pair of seriously twisted nutcases. What's your next step?'

'We shall put the word out,' says I. 'Offer, say a pound reward…'

'Make it three pounds. Continue.'

'Then hopefully someone will come forward with information as to where the twins are holed up. We also have a plan that might help track them down via another route.' I tell him of our plan to engage Sir Robert Briers the Chief Constable.

'That is one hell of an ask, Inspector,' says Clump blowing smoke in my face. 'No one is supposed to know that Sir Robert has a dirty habit, though I suspect as you know everyone knows. Even so, I doubt Sir Robert would welcome me asking him to become involved, thus admitting, more or less, that I know he's a collector of illegal naughty stuff while being a hypocrite of the highest order. In short, he'd have me carpeted and reduced in rank to a beat officer, if, I was lucky. Sir Robert is not to be approached in any way about this. But.' He holds up a hand to stop me from protesting. 'I do know someone else who would be willing to help with your plan.'

'Who is it, Chief?' asks Head.

'Never you mind,' comes the firm retort. 'His name shall remain a secret.'

'Can't you give us a clue?'

'No! I bloody well cannot,' growls Clump as he learns forward and glares into Head's eyes. 'Now, Sergeant unless you have something sensible to say I suggest you shut up.'

Head sits bolt upright. 'Well, I do have something sensible to say.'

'What is it?'

'If this anonymous person does manage to get hold of the original dirty photos while ascertaining where the seller got them and we subsequently arrest the twins, your anonymous person would have to give evidence in court thus revealing who he is, or the case will collapse.'

'Sometimes your cleverness amazes me, Sergeant. But not this time. I will ensure my anonymous person will remain so by swearing on oath that as an under-cover agent of the highest regard we cannot put his life in danger by exposing him. So, drop the subject. Anything else, Inspector?'

'Not that I can think of at the moment, sir.'

'Hand me back the photographs and I shall engage my secret friend who may well lead us to the twins. Meanwhile, I suggest you think seriously about sending your wives, and of course little Thomas to somewhere safe until the twins are caught. My gut feeling is this pair of nutters are so twisted they may well set out to target your loved ones. Who knows? They may already know where you live and have already completed a reconnaissance of your homes and families. Send them away and then I also suggest you both find somewhere else to stay until this is over.'

Clump knows something that has him very worried for our safety...

'What am I not telling you?' says he before I can challenge him.

'Who your secret person is,' says Head.

Ignoring him Clump takes out the scotch and three tumblers from his draw, and it's the good stuff but the bottles nearly empty. He peruses it before filling his glass and then barely half filling ours. 'I was recently contacted by an acquaintance of mine, no names mentioned...'

'As usual,' quips Head.

'Shut up is your final warning, Sergeant! Listen in, your lives and that of your families could well depend on it. My acquaintance was burgled two weeks ago, he lives alone apart from his servants of course, who saw and heard nothing. His safe was expertly broken into and certain letters of correspondence were stolen, but nothing else was.'

'A targeted theft then, Chief,' says I.

'Exactly. These letters were written from a lady in the highest echelons of society. They contained explicit references to her affair with my secret acquaintance who is being blackmailed over them.' Pausing he downs half his scotch. 'It gets worse; the lady in question also received a blackmail note shortly after my friend was burgled, but, being somewhat, shall we say not quite in this world she handed it to her butler to deal with. He then contacted my acquaintance over the matter whereupon I then took over and went to the lady's house to investigate. All I discovered was the fact that both blackmail letters were not written by the same hand. The one to my acquaintance was well crafted. The other, to the lady, was poorly written, obviously by someone of limited education. Until now I had no idea who wrote either of them until I saw the note you have, Inspector that we assume was written by the twins. The hand writing matches the note sent to the lady.'

'Good grief,' says I. 'You're saying the twins are behind the blackmailing attempt on the lady.'

'It appears so.'

'How on earth did they become involved?'

'It transpires they had been working as labourers for the builders who were adding a large extension to the lady's house when they were caught by the housemaid inside the house where they shouldn't have been. Namely the master bedroom where they were busy going through drawers while obviously searching for valuables. The housemaid challenged them whereupon they stuck their fingers up at her. The tallest one then produced a knife and threatened to cut out her tongue if she so much as farted too loud. She was then tied up, gagged, assaulted over her dress and shoved into a cupboard where she believes she fainted away. The twins made off with a few pieces of jewellery of no real value and the latest letter of correspondence from my secret acquaintance, the lady having forgotten to lock it away in her safe. That was three weeks ago. A week after that incident while my acquaintance was at the opera, his supposedly unbreakable safe was broken into, and as I've said, the lady's letters were taken.'

'I don't really know, Chief,' says I. 'But I doubt very much that the twins would have the skills to break open a rubbish safe, let alone a good one.'

'Agreed,' says Clump. 'The job was carried out by none other than the best of the best…'

'Larry the Lizard,' cuts in Head. 'The man who can crawl up walls and slip into bedrooms and open practically any safe without the use of dynamite.'

'He is also a gentleman thief,' adds I. 'He has never been known to hurt anyone and on the rare occasion he has been confronted, while in the act, he makes his escape even if he had to leave the goods behind.'

Clump stubs out his cigar, leans forward and raises his bushy eyebrows. 'Larry was found dead two days after my acquaintance was robbed having been shot in the face at close range by a sawn-off shotgun.'

'The twins,' says I. 'Because…?'

With a shrug Clump exhales. 'I think the twins engaged Larry to 'rescue' the letters for the sake of the lady's honour. But, when it became apparent to Larry the twins had no intention of handing them back to the lady, but were intent on blackmail instead, he refused to play ball.'

'And got done in for it,' says Head.

'Of course, this is all conjecture, gentlemen. But my coppers intuition tells me that I am not far off from the truth. Be warned, those twins are from hell!'

'What demands did they make in the blackmail notes?'

'The better written one warned about going to the police and they would be in touch. The crux of the contents from the poorly written one was to inform that they would be in touch. Do not go to the coppers unless you want the letters made public. And a postscript: Your maids got lovely tits.'

'The evil little bastards!' snarls Head.

'Not so little, Sergeant,' says Clump. 'The housemaid told me the twins were pushing five feet eight inches tall, with one being an inch or so taller than the other. Greasy long hair, pinched faces and noses…'

'Noses?' says Head looking askew at Clump.

'Yes, one each,' grates Clump. 'Anyway, it's them alright.'

'Sounds like they haven't changed a bit other than growing taller,' says I. 'Archives will have photographs of them when they were first arrested. We'll have them print off copies and hand them out to uniform who can stick them up all over the place. We'll also get copies of the jewels stolen from Frobisher and hand them out…'

'We should also get copies of Bob's arse and hand them out,' says Head.

Clump shoots him the, your dead stare. 'Do you honestly think I will sanction dozens of some urchin's bare arse being plastered all over London, Sergeant so other urchins can throw darts and dung balls at them? Can you imagine the complaints we would receive?

'I was just thinking that if anyone recognises Bob's arse, what with all its scars and stuff, they might just dob him in.'

'Brilliant! Question, Sergeant. Have you not known me for four years?'

'I have…'

'Do not interrupt when I am about to make you appear utterly stupid, Sergeant. I ask you; how many times have you gazed upon my facial features?'

'Um… Hundreds, probably.'

'And how many times have you gazed upon my bare backside?'

'Um…'

'Exactly. Now, shut up and go to sleep or something.'

'I'm wondering, sir,' says I. 'If the twins intended to cause us or our families serious harm, I think they would have acted by now.'

'Not if they intend stringing it out for the hell of it, Inspector. Just be very, very careful how you go. Take no chances and watch each other's backs at all times. Now then, I shall go and see my secret acquaintance again and the lady in question and find out if anything else has materialized. I suggest you get cracking with urgency; time is of the essence. Remember, a good copper knows when something isn't right, Inspector. You do not want your scotch, do you?'

I shake my head. 'One swig and I might just drop off, sir.'

Reaching across he grabs my glass and tips the contents into his glass, raises it to his mouth and downs it.

'I could have had that,' grates Head.

'The Lord giveth and taketh away, Sergeant,' says Clump grabbing Heads glass and downing the contents before Head can so much as blink. 'It was wasted on you anyway, especially since you pissed me off. Now bugger off the pair of you.'

Fat Fred s Funeral

'Sometimes the Chief really pisses me off,' grates Head as we head for archives.

'You shouldn't keep winding him up, Richard.'

'I'm just trying to lighten things up a bit.'

We reach archives and inform them of our requirements. Then we head to our office to discuss where we go from here.

'We shall go and find Andy, Richard and tell him to put the word out that we're looking for the twins. The plods can do the rounds of the pawn shops and dodgy jewellers to see if the Frobisher's stuff has turned up. Then once we have received the posters of the twins the plods can paste them all-over the place and then, perhaps something will turn up. Now, do you think we should move our loved ones to a safe house or not?'

'We should put them in the picture first and let them decide.'

We are interrupted by the desk sergeant coming in.

'A note for you, Inspector,' says he handing it over.

'From whom?'

'I don't know. I'm in a position of trust and don't read other people's notes.'

'Who dropped it off then?' demands Head.

'Just your usual urchin.'

'Thank you,' says I and open the note as the desk sergeant leaves.

'Who's it from, Gerald?'

My eyebrows shoot up in amazement. 'The twins. It says, more or less: Be at St Mary's church for Fat Fred's funeral service at three o'clock this afternoon if you want to have a chat.'

'Have a bleedin' chat. Are they fuckin' mad or what? What else does it say?'

I scratch my head while hoping I haven't got nits. 'Nothing else. They don't say which St Marys or who Fat Fred is.' Glancing at my fob watch I say, 'It's nine thirty, Richard which gives us plenty of time to check out the nearest St Marys Churches and find out who's being buried today.'

'It could be a trap, Gerald. We turn up all innocent, the twins pop up from behind a grave stone and blast us to bits. Game over and we lose.'

'I don't think so,' says I shaking my head. 'Whatever game the twins are playing they intend for it to go on.'

'Because?'

'Because… I think they are loving the power this is giving them. They want to torment us, to make us look stupid and to destroy our reputations. Their cockiness will be their undoing, Richard, you mark my words. Right, let's get going.'

'I could do with a nice fry up first, Gerald. Otherwise, we might not find time to eat later and you know I can't function properly without a full stomach.'

'We'll grab a couple of bacon sandwiches, Richard to eat on the way.'

Thirty minutes later we are heading away from the Yard

in a hackney. I have two rounds of white bread with three rashes of bacon in it. Head has two, two-inch-thick rounds of bread with six rashes of bacon, four sausages and an egg crammed into them. A mug of coffee and a pocket full of biscuits, plus a wedge of jam sponge wrapped in muslin for later, in case he feels peckish.'

'Did you not have breakfast before you left home this morning?' asks I.

He says something undecipherable as his cheeks are bulging with food and I wait until he's chomped and swallowed for my answer.

'Chloe made me a bowl of porridge for breakfast.'

'Really. I didn't know you liked porridge, Richard.'

He shoots me the pained expression 'I don't. Can't stand the shit, it's like eating pig's swill.'

'What does pig swill taste like then?'

'Porridge of course.'

'Why eat it if you don't like it?'

'Because Chloe made it for me one day last week and I stupidly said it was nice because I didn't want to upset her. You know what a rotten cook she still is despite Betty giving her lessons. So, when she does cook something that at least looks alright, isn't burnt or undercooked then I'll give it a try. Trouble is she keeps cooking the bloody stuff now while telling me how good it is for me. I don't want food that's good for me if I don't like it. I want real food, like pies, steaks and chops...'

'I think you're being a bit unfair, Richard. When we had dinner at yours a few Sundays back, Chloe did well and we all enjoyed it except for the batter puddings, which were a bit...'

'Like doughy pancakes. If Betty hadn't been there to assist Chloe, Gerald, we'd have had undercooked roast potatoes, raw beef, hard veg' and a gravy thinner than gnat's piss! And don't forget the only thing Chloe actually cooked totally by herself was the puddings. God, I love her bits, I mean to bits, and if she could even half cook a decent meal, she'd be the perfect wife.'

'Well, we can't have it all, Richard. Why don't you cook your own meals? That way you will always get what you love best.'

He gives me the astonished look. 'Don't think I couldn't, Gerald. But I'm a married man, and married men expect their wives to do the cooking and wait on their man when he comes home all knackered from a day's work. I start cooking and before long I'll be doing the laundry, ironing me own shirts and cleaning out the toilet.'

'Point taken. Anyway, we best eat up, we'll be at the church in a short while.'

A slight chilly breeze has picked up and the sky has clouded over as we drive down a street of terraces on both sides before turning down Church Lane. Flanked by trees with leaves turning golden brown you could believe you were heading for a village church. St Marys, is small, of grey stone and slate tiles. I ask the driver to wait, we alight and go up to a notice board beside a wooden gate.

'The Reverend Albert Shields is in residence,' says I. 'No notification on who's up for a funeral service today.'

'The doors open, Gerald. Perhaps the vicar's inside.'

'Then let us go inside, Richard. It looks like we may have some rain any minute.'

We go down a shingle path and into the church where we see an old woman tending to the flower arrangements while an aged man of the cloth is setting down hymn books on the pews. He is tall and thin with long grey hair. Straightening right up he turns to gaze at us before coming over.

'Welcome, gentlemen,' says he taking off his glasses and

wiping bony hands across his sagging eyes. 'I am the Reverend Shields. What can I do for you?'

I introduce us then ask if he is holding a service for a Fat Fred this afternoon.

'I am indeed, Inspector. Fredrick Albert Blowers, more usually known as Fat Fred. Service is at three followed by internment at the city burial ground. Will you be attending?'

'We will, Reverend.'

'You're a bit early,' says he with a rueful smile.

'We do not intend staying, Reverend and will return in time for the service. But we would like to speak to you for a few minutes if you don't mind.'

'Not at all. I shall make us a pot of coffee.'

We follow him into a small study with lots of books around the walls, a rocking chair, a pair of ladder backs, a bureau and a table in a corner for making tea on.

'Take a seat, gentlemen,' says he lighting a small paraffin stove and placing a blackened kettle onto it. Turning to face us he says, 'I am all yours,' and falls back into the rocking chair.

'We are trying to track down a pair of twins, Reverend and have sound information that they will also be attending Fat Fred's big day.'

'I see,' says he with another wry smile. 'Do you have names for these twins?'

'We do, sir. William and Robert Boyle,' says I.

'And the names of the other twins are…?'

'What other twins?'

'You said you were looking for a pair of twins. You have given me the names of two of them; what names do you have for the other two?'

'There is no other two, only this pair of twins,' says I while wondering what he's on about.

'So, you are not searching for a pair of twins but a singular set of twins.'

I give him the puzzled look. 'I have given you the names of a pair of twins and am somewhat confused as to why you keep asking me about other twins. There is definitely only one pair of twins. Is there not, Sergeant?'

'As far as we know,' says Head appearing more confused than I am.

'I am now seeing the picture, Inspector,' says Shields. 'I shall enlighten you. A pair of twins equals four people, not two people. So, therefore you are looking for two people who happen to be twins and not four people who also happen to be twins, thus making two *sets* of twins, or a pair of twins.'

The light of comprehension enters my brain. 'I am with you, sir. As, no doubt is my sergeant.'

'No, I'm not,' says Head. 'If I put two pears in a basket, I will have a pair, correct.'

We stare at him in utter confusion.

He goes on, 'If I then add two more pears, I will then have two pairs of pears and so on and so forth. Therefore, if I ask you for a pair of pears you will hand me two pears and not four pears. Am I not correct, Vicar?'

Shields puts his hands together and gazes up at the cobwebbed ceiling for divine intervention and low and behold the whistle goes off on the kettle. Mumbling incoherently to himself he shovel's coffee into a pot and pours the water in. A few minutes later we have our hands wrapped around steaming mugs of coffee.

'I am sorry, gentlemen but I cannot offer you any cake or biscuits,' says Shields while gazing forlornly at Head and sighing as if the world had just ended.

'Not a problem, Vicar,' says Head. Setting down his mug

on the floor, he takes out a bag from one jacket pocket and the muslin from another pocket. 'Have you a plate, Vicar?'

Shields reaches behind him, picks up a white plate and passes it to Head, whereupon Head tips out half a dozen biscuits from the bag, unwraps the muzzling and places the jam sponge beside the biscuits. Shields then passes Head a cake knife.

'Why don't you cut the cake, Reverend?' says I. 'I'm sure your cuts will be far more equal in measure then my sergeants.'

Head glares at me. Knowing him as I do, I know he has no intention of sharing and was intent on scoffing the biscuits and cake all to his little self. But he is now trapped and reluctantly hands the plate to Shields who cuts the cake into three equal portions, digs out three tea plates and shares out the goods.

'My,' says Shields. 'It is so much better to give then to receive. Thank you, Sergeant.'

'Think nothing of it, Vicar,' grates Head as he grabs his plate.

After a munch and a gulp of coffee I ask, 'The Boyles, Reverend. Do you know of them?'

'I do, Inspector,' says he wiping crumbs from his mouth. 'They work as walkers for Barns and Death the funeral directors.'

'Did you say walkers?' says Head. 'Or wan…'

'Definitely *walkers*,' cuts in I. Head's sulking over having to share his goodies, but there is no need for such rudeness.

'Tall slim walkers are a preference amongst the directors, Inspector. Twins such as the Boyles are much in demand and look absolutely splendid walking in front of the funeral cortege. I have observed them on several occasions doing their walks, they are magnificent.' Placing his empty mug and plate onto the table he says after dusting crumbs off his hands. 'I shall say no more, Inspector. You wait until you see them for yourselves this afternoon.'

***

'Could you Adam and bloody Eve it,' grates Head once we're back in the Hackney and heading off for the slums in search of my snouts. 'Those bastards working for funeral directors. I don't know how they've got the nerve. Christ! What next? Before you know it, you'll have mass murderers taking up Holy Orders and prostitutes becoming nuns…'

'There's a reason for the twins to be working as funeral walkers, Sergeant. And perhaps we shall find out what that reason is once we have spoken to them.'

'Well, personally I wouldn't bother turning up at the funeral. I reason we should go find where this Barns and Death directors place is and arrest the twins there. They're bound to be there sometime today to load up their customers.'

'No doubt they will be. But I'm thinking if we do arrest them there, they will clamp their jaws so tight shut we'll learn nothing of exactly what they are about or where the photos and letters are. Therefore, we shall stick with the plan and have our little chat with them.'

'And then arrest them.'

'Only if we can be confident that we shall be able to retrieve the Frobisher's photographs and Clumps secret acquaintances letters.'

'More important than that, Gerald is where are we going to have lunch?'

***

By the time we tracked down a few of our snouts to put the word out, had lunch and a couple of beers it was time to head back to the church. Arriving at two-thirty we find the lane is

111

lined near side with over fifty mourners of all ages. Furthest from the church gate are, obviously, the close family as they are huddled together while appearing much more sombre than the rest of the mourners. Head and I wheedle ourselves behind the family and up against the trunk of an oak tree where we have a clear view over their heads.

We wait quietly while listening in to the mourner's conversations where we learn that Fat Fred was only forty and died of a heart attack because he was so overweight, never took exercise and lived on fat meat, dripping and beer by the barrel. Despite this he managed to father ten kids while running a successful butcher's shop for many years, even if he didn't actually do much physically. One thing for certain Fred was very much loved and his family have nothing whatsoever to do with the Boyles.

Just as it starts to spit with rain the funeral entourage turns into Church Lane. Out front is a tall middle-aged man, splendid in his black top hat, black tails and trousers, white shirt and black tie while his shoes gleam like black mirrors. Perfectly upright he walks slowly while in tune with his cane held in a black gloved hand. In arrow formation the twins are some ten feet behind him. Dressed the same as the man in front but without canes they walk with their arms rigidly down by their sides. Their shining black hair is tied back into a tail, eyes unwavering and rigid in their movement they appear unreal, magnificent and yet poignant. Behind them comes the funeral coach pulled by a pair of beautiful black stallions, their shoes tapping rhythmically on the tarmacadam. Behind the coach walk six pall bearers. As Fred apparently weighed over thirty stone I'm wondering if six will be enough.

The second the family begin the usual sobbing and wailing, Head seizes the chance to hiss in my ear. 'It the twins alright. Just look at the pair of twats. I say shoot the bastards now before they shoot us. How dare they turn up at Fat Fred's funeral while looking like butter won't melt.'

'It is not considered good form to start shooting people at a funeral, Richard. Kindly refrain from this necrolatry and remain calm.'

'Necro what?'

'Look it up and shut up. That is an order.'

The walkers go past us as my eyes fleetingly meet Bill Boyles who momentarily glanced to his left without twisting his head. He knows we are here. As the carriage goes past the family fall in behind the pall bearers, we fall in behind them and the remaining mourners fall in behind us. The lead walker comes to a halt at the gate where the Reverend Shields now stands. Everything else comes to a stop. The pall bearers move to lift out the coffin, and I am wondering if something untoward is about to happen. Have the twins set us up? Will the handles fall of the coffin? Will it crash to ground and fall apart exposing poor Fred to the elements? Will Fred even be in the coffin? What if the twins swapped his body with someone else's? What if there is no body it having been replaced with bricks or something?

Shields and the walkers lead the way with the coffin and pall bearers now immediately behind them, then comes the family and all others behind them. The carriage remains outside being too wide to go through the gate. As the pall bearers struggle over the shingle with all that weight, I wonder why they didn't leave Fred on the carriage. After all, after the service they've only got to lug him back again and then unload him again once they get to the city cemetery.

The twins break off to stand either side of the porch's entrance. Head and I break away and step back onto the grass flanking the shingle. With the procession now all inside it is just us left facing the twins.

'Long time no see,' sneers Bill as we take a few steps closer.

'Not long enough,' says Head.

'Shall we sit in the porch out of the drizzle?' says Bill.

I nod and we follow them inside. There is embedded wooden seating either side of the porch, the twins close the heavy oak door leading into the church to shut out the sound of Shields voice before they sit down and place their top hats down beside them. Head and I sit opposite but we don't take our bowlers off.

The twins haven't changed much apart from being taller and not so weedy. Certainly, they look fit, clean and probably smell better than they used too. But the hard-little slit eyes and pinched faces are the same and they still exude an aura of menace.

'What did ya think of Bob's arse?' says Bill.

'Unjustifiable and brutal,' says I. 'And I am sorry for it.'

They nod in unison, sending out a message that they liked my answer.

'An' you?' says Bill to Head.

Head is glaring into his eyes, but Bill appears not the least bit intimidated by it.

'I agree with the inspector,' says Head without much conviction.

Bill smiles the smile of someone who can easily pick up on whether or not someone really means what they've just said. He glances at his brother and says, 'What do ya think, Bob? Think they mean it, or are they just sayin' it?'

Bob points at me, 'He means it. But,' he points at Head, 'he don't.'

'That's what I was thinkin'. Right, coppers, so here we are. Let's talk. But where ta begin.'

'Why you wanted to meet us here would be a good start,' says I acutely aware that we are just six feet away from them and should we stretch out our legs we'd touch feet.

'Alright,' says Bill. 'We want ta make a deal. Don't we Bob?'

'We do, Bill. Yeah, a deal's what we want.'

'I am all ears,' says I.

'We'll give ya back the dirty photos of Frank and his misses along with the letter we took from the old posh bird. In exchange we want ya ta find out where that bastard, Sergeant King, who birched Bob, is. See we know 'is name but we ain't been able to track him down.'

'Sergeant King left the force about three years back. Where he is now, I have no idea.'

'But if anyone can find him, I'll bet you can.'

'Perhaps I could, Bill. But then I'd be handing him to you on a plate. As no doubt you want to do him in, I can't say you're offering enough of a trade for us to be accessories to murder.'

Bill sits bolt upright; his mouth tightens and his eyes blaze. 'We wouldn't kill him. Oh no, *sir*... We'd give him a taste of what he gave Bob. Wouldn't we Bob?'

'We would that, Bill. We'd strip the skin off his fucking arse until it pisses blood. Then we'd rub salt into it until he screams for mercy, just like I had to until I passed out. Only there weren't no mercy was there, Bill? Not for me there weren't.'

'Ten years old we was, copper. When they'd done wiv us we were dumped out a back door into the gutter. Cause, King had ta carry Bob out 'cause he couldn't even stand, while the other copper, Constable Fucking French, dragged me out by me hair like I was a dead dog. We was naked from the belly down an' they just threw our ragged trousers at us and went back inside an' slammed the door. I couldn't put Bob's trousers on him, so I carried him with his trousers laid over his bits the two miles back to the hovel we shared wiv other homeless urchins. Bob bled all the way; he whimpered a lot an' he often drifted away so I had to keep talkin' to 'im so he didn't die on me. 'Ow he survived I don't know. He got infections, he got fever an' I had to stay up all night ta keep the bleedin' rats off him for weeks, and the flies off durin' the day. But there we are. Now what say you to that?'

'They should have had a senior officer there to prevent French and King from going beyond the remit, along with a doctor should there be any problems. They didn't follow procedures and were no doubt reprimanded for it at the time, when in truth they should have been charged…'

'No chance of that,' scoffs Bill. 'So, you goin' to trade or not?'

'Not. But I will help you to pursue a charge of unwarranted brutality against the officers involved…'

'Don't make me laugh, copper. Waste of time that'd be an' ya know it.'

The Lords my Shepherd being sung with feeling echoes around the church and fills the porch with its melodious tempo. Bob's eyes turn watery but Bill's just turn that bit harder. Head has stopped glaring at Bill. He gets to his feet and says, 'Just going out back for a pee.'

Silence reigns until Head returns and sits down, he appears somewhat subdued, perhaps he's feeling sorry for Bob? We wait until the singing stops and someone is reciting a eulogy before we continue.

'The other thing is this, Bill,' says I. 'Larry the Lizard had his face blown off and we…'

'Think we done it,' cuts in Bill. 'Well, we didn't, did we Bob?'

'Nah. It weren't us, copper. But we know *who* did it. Don't we Bill?'

'Same bloke who did Razor Williams in all them years back.'

'Are you stringing us along?' says I, amazed at this revelation.

He shakes his head; the end of his pony tail flicking each side of his thin cheeks. 'Now, here's the rub. I tell ya all I know. Add that to what I've already said and then we'll make that deal.'

'We'll see. You talk and we'll listen.'

'Alright. The night Razor got done in, me and Bob 'ad been out waitin' for the drunks ta stumble out of the pubs so we could steal from 'em. Easy pickin' a drunk's pocket ain't it Bob?'

'Piss easy.'

Bill continues, 'About midnight we go off home, by then it's turned misty and the gas lamps 'ad been turned low, everywhere is shadowed an' gloomy. There ain't many people about an' it's so quiet you could hear a rat fart. We're goin' along the high street; we pass a couple of ol' tarts trying ta hold each other up an' some ol' tramp havin' a crap in a shop doorway, when we spot Razor staggerin' towards us. He was well gone...'

'Drunk as a lord,' cuts in Bob.

'Now, walkin' a few yards behind Razor loomed this figure. Big bastard in a dark frock coat, swaggering like a boxer, shoulders like a bull. Hat pulled down over his eyes, neck thick as ya thigh an' 'ands like lump hammers. I knew he was followin' Razor but Razor didn't 'ave a clue. Razor's eyes were swimmin' with booze, but he still knew us 'cause he spoke when he came close to us. He said, "'Ows it goin' lads?" We said, "Good," an' he staggered off. I wanted ta warn him he was being followed but that big bloke was more menacing than a rabid dog with a bone. We passed the big bastard, he didn't even glance at us. After a bit I dared ta glance behind and that's when it 'appened. The big bastard brushed Razors battered ol' hat off his head an' then cracked him wiv a cudgel or somethin'. Razor's legs go and he drops, the big bastard then hauls Razor up by his coat to his knees an' keeps crackin' Razor's head. We could hear it; it was a sick makin' sound. Then the big bastard lifts off an iron drain cover like it was made of wood. Then he pulls Razor along the pavement like he was a rag dolly an' just shoves him head first down the drain and puts the cover back on an' strolls away. He didn't even look around to see if anyone 'ad seen 'im.

'And his name is?' says I.

Bill shrugs. 'Didn't know it back then. But I might know it now, if we strike up a deal.'

'So,' says I. 'You both witnessed a murder but neither of you came forwards. Alright I can understand that but surely you told someone what you'd seen?'

'Nah,' scoffs Bill. 'See we didn't know who ta tell in case they was somethin' ta do with whatever it was about…'

'Mable Calvers murder most likely,' says Head.

'That's what me an' Bob thought but we never found out. Anyway, we went an' took the manhole cover off so Razor could be found, otherwise it could 'ave been days before he was found and more chance of his killer getting' away wiv it.'

Applause sounds from inside of the church. Eulogy over and no doubt someone else's rendition will follow.

I ask Bill, 'How long will the service go on?'

'Good hour. So, plenty of time. Now let's talk about Larry the Lizard. Larry ain't dead.'

'Well, someone is,' grates I. 'We have a body in the morgue that came in with a fob watch engraved with Larry's name on it.'

'Means nuthin',' says Bill. 'Anyone could 'ave slipped that in your bodies pocket. Does ya body 'ave a tattoo of a lizard on its back?'

I shrug and admit we haven't seen the body.

'Well, it ain't got one 'cause the body you got in the morgue ain't Larry's. Trust me, Larry's alive an' well. Besides 'ave ya got any idea what Larry looks like?'

'No is the short answer. But we do know how he operates. We do know that he has principals, one of which is there is no way he would blackmail someone over their love affair. So, I am now wondering who *did* break into someone's safe and steal personal letters of a very intimate nature in order to not only blackmail the recipient, but also to blackmail the sender. Enlighten me, Bill.'

He's giving me the confused look. 'Ya don't know who got burgled do ya?'

'Not as yet. Our Chief Inspector is dealing with it and he hasn't said.'

Bill spreads his legs wide and shuffles himself about. It's becoming uncomfortable on these hard seats to the point it's burning your posterior. Bob stands up. By the look in his eyes, it is obvious he is in pain.

'There ya go,' smirks Bill. 'Ya boss is keeping stump 'cause of who is shaggin' who.'

'Who *is* shagging who?' asks Head, sounding enthralled by it all.

'You'll soon find out so I'll tell ya. The old bird is Lady Elizabeth Fraser. The bloke is someone called James Palmer.'

Never heard of either of them thinks I. 'Do you know who Bill is talking about?' asks I of Head.

He shakes his head and pulls a frustrated face.

Hymn number something or other is now being played on

the organ, the mourners break out into song: Jesus is my saviour. The light that leads me on. Over troubled waters to teach me right from wrong…

'The thing is, Bill, I'm not sure where you are coming from. Unless you can convince me that Larry wanted to get involved in blackmailing these lovers, I am reluctant to believe what you are telling me.'

'This is 'ow it went. We got the letter and we took it ta someone we know. She said…'

'She said! Who is she?'

'Too dangerous ta say, copper. Not yet anyway. She said let me have the letter and I'll go see someone who might be interested in it. She come back to me an' said Larry the Lizard wanted in 'cause he 'ad a score ta settle with this Palmer bloke who's shagging the old bird…'

'How old is this, Lady Fraser?' asks Head.

Bill shrugs, ''Ow the hell should I know.'

'We saw her a few times,' says Bob. 'I think she's about a hundred.'

'A fuckin' 'undred! Don't be a prat, Bob. Ain't no one on earth goes on shaggin' past fifty let alone a fuckin' 'undred.

'They might do,' sulks Bob as he sits down again.

'Nah, I reckon, she's about seventy…'

'How old is her lover?' asks Head appearing even more intrigued.

'I don't know! Never met the prat. 'Ang on though. I think he's ain't very old. About thirty so Larry reckoned.'

'So, Larry sent Palmer a note informing him that he was now being blackmailed. Meanwhile, according to my governor, Larry gets his face shot off. But you're saying Larry is alive and well and whoever's in the morgue it isn't Larry. Now, who killed this mystery body and how do you know it was the same man who killed Razor?'

''Cause we saw 'im,' says Bill. 'Me an' Bob went ta see Larry to find out 'ow he got on with Palmer. As we were about ta knock on his door, we hear a bang and instantly darted behind a hedge. Next thing that big bastard comes out of Larry's tuckin' a sawn off under his coat.'

'And it was definitely the same man you saw five years ago who killed Razor?'

'It was. We thought about following him but decided we best go see if Larry was alright. We broke in an' found this bloke laid out wiv 'is face gone, blood everywhere. Knew right off it weren't Larry despite no face. We wait, an' sure enough Larry came in half an hour later an' said: "Fuck me what have you done?" 'Well, I didn't fuck 'im but I put him straight an' he believed me. Then guess what?'

'Larry's safe had been broken into and the letters from Lady Fraser were gone,' says I.

'Cor!' says Bill wide eyed. 'Told ya he was a clever one, didn't I, Bob?'

'Ya did, Bill.'

'Seems like,' says Head. 'This big bastard took a safe breaker with him intent on recovering the letters. Once done he executed the safe breaker, the less people who know the better, then just skipped off with the letters.'

'He didn't skip,' says Bill. 'He walked off.'

'Did Larry enlighten you about what on earth was going on?' asks I.

Bill shakes his head. 'Nah. He just said:' "Lads, help yourself to anything you want. I'm off and the deals off. Don't try and find me and tell no one what you saw." 'He stuffed a bag with money an' jewels, which were hid all over the 'ouse, an' fucked off. We ain't seen or heard of 'im since.'

'Do you still intend to blackmail Lady Fraser?'

'No way. Too bleedin' dangerous I reckon. I'll give ya the letter soon as you agree to the deal.'

Shields can now be clearly heard preaching to the mourners.

My mind is going around and around as I struggle to come up with a way of tricking Bill into opening up further. He knows much more than he is saying, but either he is scared to open his mouth, doubtful, or he sees a way to profit from it all, much more likely.

'Right, Bill. I want the Frobisher's dirty photographs and the letter, plus the names of; the woman you went to see about the letters, the big bastards and whoever is laying in the morgue. Do that for me and the deal is on.'

'I could, but I won't give ya the name of the woman, 'cause I'll never be able to use her again should I need to. She's nuthin' to you anyway. I'll soon find out who the safe breaker was 'cause he ain't gonna go 'ome now, is he? The big bastard will be known by someone, trust me.'

'I think you already know the name of the big bastard,' says Head clashing eyes with Bill. 'And I'm also thinking you're not saying because your too *scared* or you've seen a way to profit from it.'

'Think what ya like, Dick Face. I ain't scared of no one, especially coppers.'

Head is on his feet and his fists are clenched.

'Sit down please, Sergeant,' says I tugging at his jacket sleeve. 'We shall get nowhere if we start squabbling.'

'Drop the insults, Bill,' says Head as he sits down. 'Then we'll get on just fine.'

'Alright,' says Bill, 'so long as ya stop starin' at me.'

'It's a deal,' says I. 'Let us move on. You two put Mr Frobisher through hell with your bizarre antics. Worse still, how could you do such a thing to those poor sheep?'

'Didn't expect them fireworks to explode like that, did we Bob?' says Bill.

Bob shakes his head and appears sorry. 'Nah. Rum bugger that was. Poor old Randy's balls got blown right off.'

'And then sent to me in a shoe box with a threat,' says I.

'Just a bit of fun,' grins Bill. 'Anyway, it got ya attention, didn't it?'

'What other *fun* have you got planned, Bill?'

'Depends how bored we get. Don't it Bob?'

'It do Bill. We've been thinkin' about goin' straight though. Ain't we Bill?'

'We 'ave, copper. See, we've been learnin' to be funeral directors. We plan to open up our own shop once we've got enough money ta buy a decent place. Bob loves shoving embalming oils an' spices into holes, don't ya Bob?'

A huge smile crosses Bob's face as his eyes twinkle. 'I love it. An' Bill wants ta learn how ta do hair an' makeup so people look nice when their family comes round ta look at 'em.'

God help us thinks I as Head shoots me the: They're fucking mental, look.

'Good luck with that,' says I as more singing comes from inside. 'Now, the thing is lads, your mugs will soon be plastered all over the place. There'll be so many people looking out for you to earn the reward for ratting on you, you'll have nowhere to hide. There's nothing I can do about that. But, as this is our case, we will be able to hold back on acting on information received until you get what we want and we get what you want.'

'Fair enough,' says Bill. 'We'll get what ya want and do a trade once you've got where King is. Then we'll fuck off an' ya won't see us again.'

'Sergeant?'

'I'm with you, Inspector,' says Head.

'Good. Does anyone have anything else to say before we call this meeting to a halt?'

'I do,' says Head. 'Now, we know we can't trust you, and you know you can't trust us. But I will trust you'll leave our families right out of this...'

'So long as ya don't double cross us,' says Bill stoically meeting Heads eyes,' ya can trust us. See, we ain't never forgotten that day years back when we was out beggin' an' shiverin' in the snow when this lady comes up an' gives us both a thick pullover to keep us warm. Known as Betty the Diamond she was an' still is. Nah, ya families are safe. Like I say, get us Kings address an' that's it.'

I get to my feet. 'Just remember we cannot be held responsible should the plods catch up with you before we've done the deal.'

Bill smiles. 'Don't ya worry, copper. They won't catch us. Will they Bob?'

'No chance.'

Who's Who

With no sign of the cab, we walk to the end of Church Lane and wait. At least it's not raining and the sun's filtering through a sky painted a light grey.

Ten minutes later the cab arrives, we board and head back to the yard.

'What now?' says Head as we settle down.

'We shall go to records and find out where King has moved to. He may have left the force, but he will have to keep the force updated as to where he resides should he be required to give evidence for any unsolved cases he worked on that may have now come to court. Then we shall go and view the body in the morgue that's believed to be Larry the Lizard and see if it has a lizard tattoo on its back.'

'It might not have a tattoo, Gerald. We've only got the twins say so that Larry had a tattoo. They could be lying or just making it up.'

'For what reason?'

'To muddy the waters and have a laugh. Let's face it, they're as mad as monks, utterly deranged and more untrustworthy than we are.'

'Agreed. Also, don't you think it strange that they did not ask where Constable French is? Surely, they'd want to get even with him almost as much as they want to get even with King.'

'Something else to find out then, Gerald. Maybe they've already gotten even with French.'

'Quite likely. What else, let me think. We shall speak to Clump, if he's at the Yard, and see how he got on before we tell him what we've found out. But…'

'But we can't say where we got our information from. So, what are we going to say?'

'We'll just tell him our snouts found it out.'

'Alright. I'm going to enjoy letting him know we know the name of his secret acquaintance along with the name of the woman he's been knocking off. That's the woman Palmer's knocking off and not the name of whoever Clump is currently knocking off…'

'Well, if he confirms Palmer and Fraser are the shaggers then we shall need to know why he wanted to keep their names a secret. Now, what's your opinion on what the twins told us about the Big Bastard?'

'The same as you, Gerald I shouldn't wonder. What are the chances that those pair of nutters not only happened to be present when Razor was killed, but also managed to turn up at Larry's house just as he, or whoever it was, was topped by the Big Bastard?'

'I would say; no chance, especially with a five-year gap between the killings.'

'So, what the hell are they playing at?'

'Perhaps you've answered your own question, Richard. The twins are playing. Playing with us. Playing with the Frobisher's along with anyone else who crosses their paths.'

'I'm all for turning this cab around, going back and

arresting them, Gerald. They're unarmed and won't be able to run very fast in those posh shoes they're wearing. Arrest them and charge them with kidnapping, assault, armed robbery, theft and blackmail. Oh yes, stealing and torturing sheep and sending disgusting parcels via the Royal Mail. Oh yes, and attempting to bribe officers of the law. Christ, they'd get forty years I shouldn't wonder.'

'There may also be murder charges to add to their crimes, Richard. The trouble is we have no evidence of their involvement in any murder. I am thinking that we should go along with what the twins want for now and see how it goes. Just in case they do give us the Big Bastards name which could solve two murders.'

'If he even exists,' says Head giving me the: you hadn't thought of that one, have you?

***

On entering the morgue, we find the pathologist has gone home and left his assistant, who took over from 'Limping' Lesly, Harold Scratcher in sole charge. Harold has modelled himself on his hero the Hunchback of Notre-dame, without the hunch. He drags a leg around the place while bent over, swinging one arm close to the ground and calling out: "The bells. The bells." He also looks uncannily like the Hunchback; moon faced, short and round.

'Afternoon, Harold,' says I.

'Afternoon, Inspector Potter,' says he while dribble runs down his fat chin. 'Who'd you like to see?'

'Larry the Lizard.'

'I shall get him out for you.'

We watch him drag himself over to chiller number one. He opens the door and goes in, cries out: 'The bells. The bells,' before pushing out, one handed, a trolley with a body on it beneath a white sheet and parking it close to us. He pulls the sheet off and we are confronted with our faceless victim.

'Bloody gruesome,' says Head.

Harold stretches himself up to his full five feet and says, 'Seen worse, Sergeant. Had one in two halves once. Split right down the middle he was, including his privates. Left him half the man he was,' he chuckles.

The body before us is long and wiry, black hairy chest flecked with grey, yellowed toe nails, an average size penis but very large testicles, which might help someone who knew him intimately to identify him. But there doesn't appear to be anything else that could help identify him such as birthmarks, scars or moles.

'Can you turn him over, please?' says I to Harold. 'I wish to see his back.'

With a grunt and a pant, Harold wrestles the stiff over onto its stomach.

'Nothing,' says Head. 'Not so much as a tattooed flea.'

Harold gives Head the goggle-eyed look. 'Why would he 'ave a flea tattooed on his back? Come to that why would *anyone* 'ave a flea tattooed on their back?'

'Why would anyone have anything tattooed anywhere on them anyway?' grates Head.

'How should I know?' grates Harold.

'Bet you'd have Esmeralda tattooed on you if you could,' smirks Head.

Harold shrugs, 'Suppose I could. But she's too sacred. No one could do her justice.'

'He hasn't been opened up,' says I. 'Why is that, Harold?'

'As he's got no face, we're leaving him as long as we can in case someone can identify the rest of him. Besides we've got a back log because people keep getting done in.'

'Thank you, Harold,' says I. 'That will be all for now.'

'Where to now?' says Head as we leave the morgue.

'Let's find out what was found at the crime scene. If there's an empty cartridge shell, we may be able to match it up with the one we found in the meadow. Then we'll find out where King and French are before we go and see, Clump.'

***

Twenty minutes later we are in Clumps office where we note that his beard and moustache have been neatly trimmed and there's a powerful scent coming off him and attacking our nostrils. He is also looking rather dapper in a clean pressed dark jacket, white shirt and blue tie with a military style motif on it.

'Going somewhere important, sir?' says Head as we sit down.

'Nothing to do with you, Sergeant. Now then, I haven't got long so let us get cracking. I went to see my secret acquaintance and am pleased to say that his letters have been returned to him and he has had no further blackmail threats. The lady in question has not had *her* letter returned, but then neither has she had any further blackmail threats. So, I think we can lay that one to rest and concentrate on who murdered Larry the Lizard, catching the twins and finding the Frobisher's photographs. How did you get on?'

'We found an empty cartridge case in the meadow at Hampstead Heath and have handed it over to ballistics. They're going to see if it matches the one found in Larry's place.'

'And if it does then it proves the twins murdered Larry,' says Clump.

'Or more likely they'll be no match, thus proving their innocence,' says I. 'You see, Chief, I cannot see any reason why the twins would kill Larry and then return the letters. Surely, they would keep them and carry on with their blackmail plans…'

'You have a point, Inspector,' says he sitting back, rubbing his hands together and frowning.

'Also, our snouts informed us that Larry the Lizard isn't dead. So, whoever is laying in the morgue it isn't Larry.'

'Who is it then?'

'The snouts didn't know, but they're pretty sure they will be able to find out, along with, possibly, who really did kill whoever is in the morgue.'

'Did they tell you where the twins are hiding out?'

I shake my head. 'No. But it won't be long before they do.'

'Right, let us leave it there for now. I must get on; I have an important meeting with my… um… bank manager.'

He gets to his feet.

'James Palmer and Lady Elizabeth Fraser,' smirks Head.

Clump sits down again as a dark cloud crosses his eyes. 'How the *hell* did you find out?'

'The twins were overhead by one of our snouts in the Skinners Arms bragging about blackmailing some toffs,' lies Head. I let him carry on as he's really good at lying. 'He also heard the twins say *who* they were going to blackmail.'

'Well, as I have said, lads, we shall forget all about this blackmailing business. It is over and done with. Put it out of your minds and plod on with the rest of the stuff.'

'The trouble is, Chief,' says Head, obviously going in for the kill. 'The, inspector and I believe that whoever was killed at Larry's place was killed by a professional hitman. Why a professional hitman I hear you ask?'

'You tell me…, Sergeant.'

Head is on the point of tipping Clump over the edge if he doesn't stop smirking, so I cut in.

'We do not know of this Palmer chap or this Lady Fraser, sir. But it is obvious they are very much a part of, or connected to the establishment, the aristocracy and no doubt to some very important people…'

'Obviously they're not very important themselves or we'd have heard of them,' says Head.

'Exactly,' says Clump. 'Therefore, as they are people of no real consequence, we shall leave it there.' He gets to his feet again and noisily scrapes his chair back.

'Except that it is obvious someone protecting Palmer and Fraser engaged a hitman, who engaged a safe cracker who he then murdered once he had hold of the letters. Of course, we could soon find out who Palmer and Fraser are and who they are related to…'

Clump sits down again. 'Have I not just told you to leave it?'

'You did, sir,' says I. 'But we have a brutal killer out there and quite honestly, I don't think they should be allowed to get away with it regardless of who they are working for. It is obvious to me and the sergeant that Palmer and Fraser are minor players in a conspiracy that is controlled by far higher up the scalers.'

'The scalers!' says he scratching his head.

'Look, Chief,' says Head adopting a sweeter nature. 'Can't you tell us who's behind it and what it's all about. Once we know how important it is that Palmer and Fraser's shagging habits don't appear in the press, we'll happily back off and keep stomp about it.'

Clump lets out a long-drawn-out sigh while gazing up at the clock on the wall. 'Right. I am only telling you what I believe to be the truth, not only because of what you have told me, but also because I have found it hard to except that the letters were returned so readily to James Palmer. You are right, Inspector. The person in the morgue was executed and, regardless of who was behind it, they are not above the law and must be caught and punished. However, this is a very sorry tale and should it get out, it will cause one God Almighty scandal. I need a drink.' Pausing he drags out the scotch and three glasses. Fills them up and shares them out. He then lights a cigar, gazes at the clock again and sighs. 'Five thirty already, lads. Shall we continue this tomorrow?'

'I would rather hear it now, sir,' says I.

'And me,' says Head.

We all take a drink, Clump blows a cloud of smoke over us and Head lets one off, no doubt hoping the smell of the cigar will mask it.

'The Honourable James Palmer is illegitimate,' says Clump as my eyebrows go up.

'How on earth did you find out that piece of juicy information, Chief?' says I.

'I have known James's parents, Lord and Lady Palmer for years. They told me ages ago, in confidence, that James wasn't their true son. Anyway, James told me that when he first received the blackmail note he went, not to us, but to his biological father, who promptly went into a rage and nearly had a seizure. He ordered James not to go to the police, saying he would deal with it. But James wasn't happy about this and contacted me as he was worried his real father might do something drastic.'

'Like have the blackmailer tracked down and murdered,' says I.

'Exactly. You see, James, personally, wasn't too worried about the blackmail attempt. He's in love with Lady Fraser and has no problems with the considerable age gap. James is thirty while Lady Fraser is fifty-two.'

'Less than a hundred years old then?' says Head. 'Or even seventy years old.'

I give Head a kick in the shins, if he doesn't watch his mouth, Clump will smell a rat and before you know it, he'll drag it out of us that we've been talking to the twins.

'Sometimes, Sergeant,' grates Clump. 'I really do not know where you are coming from. Do want to hear the rest or not?'

'We do, sir,' says I.

'Right, here comes the punch line. Elizabeth Fraser married the aging Lord Archibald Fraser when she was just seventeen. Three years later she was still a virgin. At a society ball she became enthralled with a womanising reprobate in his forties and subsequently began an affair with him. The eventual result was Elizabeth had a son. Lord Fraser was so incensed he had the boy whisked away never to be seen again, or so he thought. But Elizabeth had informed her lover their son had been taken away and her lover, I don't know how, got the boy back and passed him on to a childless, respectable couple, of poor as church mice aristocrats, to raise as their own. Now, oddly enough, Elizabeth's lover never married and by all accounts produced several more bastards, but had nothing to do with them because they came from prostitutes. But he continued to dote on and fund the illegitimate son he had with Elizabeth. Lord Fraser passed away many years ago. Elizabeth then married a foreign Count without the o which lasted several years before he was stabbed to death by his current boyfriend in a jealous rage over some other man, but at least he left Elizabeth stinking rich.'

I am now getting where this is leading to, and no doubt so is Head judging by the horrified look in his eyes.

'James's father is none other than Sir Arnold Falconer. James's mother is almost certainly Lady Elizabeth Fraser,' says Clump.

'Christ!' gasps Head. 'James has been giving his own mother one. No wonder Falconer wants to keep it quiet.'

I am struck dumb. The tale is too awful to even contemplate. On top of that, Falconer is not only back on the scene, he is now the prime suspect in hiring the killer of the body in the morgue.

'Does this James lad know he's rogering his own mother?' says Head to an increasingly uncomfortable Clump. The man is even blushing, sort of.

Clump chucks down his scotch and then refills the glass. 'He has no idea and neither has Elizabeth. So, gentlemen, you now understand why this whole sorry business is so sensitive.'

'We do, Chief,' says I. 'How on earth did you find out that Lady Elizabeth is almost certainly James's mother?'

'Her butler told me. He was a footman for Lord Fraser and witnessed Falconer flirting with Elizabeth at the ball. Over the coming months he knew full well that they were having a heated affair. Falconer was even daring enough to sneak into Elizabeth's bed even when Lord Fraser was at home; knowing full well that Fraser never entered his wife's bedroom. When Elisabeth handed over the blackmail letter to the butler, he was unsure what to do and arranged a meeting with James Palmer to seek guidance as to the best course of action. James told him he would contact his mentor, Sir Arnold Falconer for advice, and then, being in a panic, let slip that Sir Arnold Falconer was also his real father. That is when the butler put two and two together…'

'But will he keep his gob shut?' says Head. 'I mean he could make a tidy sum if he went to the press.'

'He'll keep quiet,' says Clump as his narrowing eyes zoom into Heads. 'As will you two. Not a word to a living soul, do you hear me?'

We nod.

He sits back, drops his cigar butt into Heads glass, downs his scotch and stands up.

'Right lads, I do not know where we go from here. I shall leave it with you. I must go.'

'Can I just ask, Chief,' says I. 'How did this unlikely couple meet?'

'James is an architect and secured the contract to plan the extension at Frasers Hall. He and Elisabeth hit it off the second they met, according to James. He told me that it was as if he had known her all his life. They are besotted with each other. As I have said, keep this to yourselves. Do not even tell your wives, or trust me, I shall *castrate* the pair of you.'

We nod while looking suitably miserable and subdued.

'Christ!' says Head the second Clump has gone. 'I've never heard such a tale before.'

'Nor I, Richard. And can you believe that Falconer, of all people, is involved. What a turn up for the books. I will bet he engaged the hitman to knock off the body in the morgue and if what the twins told us is true, then Falconer also had Mable *and* Razor knocked off.'

'And should Falconer find out the twins have hold of Elizabeth's letter he'll have them done in as well by the Big Bastard.'

'Not to mention yours truly and even Clump should Falconer know, or even think we know the truth behind his son's affair with Lady Elisabeth.'

'We best keep our gobs shut then,' says he, downing his scotch and then gagging on Clumps cigar butt. 'I'll do for that prat one day,' growls he spitting ash from his mouth. 'What a dirty trick, dumping his bleeding butt in my drink.'

'Never mind, Richard,' says I reaching across the desk and

grabbing the bottle. 'Let's have another. And then I think it is time we called it a day.'

'What about King and French, are we going to tell the twins where they are or not?'

'No rush, Richard. Let's wait until the twins contact us before we decide.'

Death on the Allotment

I finally make it home just after seven to find Betty in the kitchen sipping a sherry, while the waft of roasting chicken sends my taste buds mad.

'Roast chicken,' says I. 'A rare treat my little chef.'

Betty puts down her glass and wraps her arms around me.

'Your later home then I thought you'd be, Detective Inspector,' slurs she as her eyes twinkle with mischievous intent. 'I've had one too many while I waited.'

I run my hands down her back and over her buttocks. 'Are you naked beneath this thin blue dress?'

'I am. But that doesn't mean you can squeeze my bum without asking first.'

Holding her at arm's length, I ask, 'Can I please fondle your body?'

'People who ask don't get,' smiles she.

'Ah, but people who don't ask don't get anyway so you might as well ask.'

'True. But people who don't ask in the right tone of voice run the risk of getting slapped, or worse, kneed in the unmentionables.'

'True, but if people think that they may well get rebuffed should they not ask in the right way, then they'll never ask anybody anything and nothing will progress, thus leaving the world in limbo.'

'I get your point, Detective Inspector. Have you been smoking cigars again?'

'No. I don't smoke as you well know. Clump blew half a bloody chimney over me and Head while we were in a meeting…'

'What was the meeting about?'

'A man and his dog. Stop changing the subject, do you want it or not?'

'Did you bring any more of those naughty photos home?'

'No. Sorry.'

She gives a little hiccup, extradites herself and picks up her glass. Leaning back against the table she says, 'Dinner first or afters first?'

I must admit I am famished but dinner comes second when Betty's hungry for something else. And who am I to argue? 'Shall we go upstairs?'

'What! And risk the chicken getting burnt? Clear the table, Detective Inspector, I can keep an eye on the oven that way.'

We are now sat in the parlour nursing mugs of cocoa while gazing into the blue and yellow flames of the fire with only a single oil lamp to add extra light. Dinner was delicious, the love making was crippling but wonderful, except when Betty broke off to get the chicken out, stab a fork into it to see if it was done and baste it before shoving it back into the oven, saying it needed another fifteen minutes. Which was good as I didn't know if my nuts could take anymore slamming against the hard edge of the table without a break.

'Porridge,' says Betty giving me the: this is serious look.

'Should I make you porridge for your breakfast, would you eat it without complaint or would you tell me if you didn't like it?'

'The question is irrelevant, Betty,' confuses I. 'You know full well I don't much care for rabbit's food for breakfast.'

'Speaking hypothetically.'

'Ah… Is this about Richard and Chloe?'

'It is, Detective Inspector. Chloe came around today in a bit of a state. She and Richard had a ridiculous row this morning about porridge. Did he mention it to you?'

I shake my head, best to feign ignorance.

'Probably because he was too ashamed. I mean, what kind of a bully of a husband berates his wife for trying to do her best for his health. Richard scoffs far too much meat and pastry. Rarely eats fruit and is not over fussed about vegetables other than mushy peas and chips.'

'I agree that his diet could be better, Betty. But we do get a lot of physical and mental exercise along with tons of stress, danger, and Clump to deal with. The man simply can't function unless his belly is constantly being stoked up with his favourite foods.'

'And there lays another problem. Chloe struggles with her cooking, she would love to serve her man really tasty nourishing food, but despite the lessons I have given her she just can't seem to manage it. Do you know that Richard often nips into the pub on his way home, scoffs a dinner there and then when he arrives home, he makes out he's not hungry if he doesn't like what Chloe dishes up? Chloe ends up putting his on a plate and into the larder in case he should fancy it later or for his breakfast, which he never does. She then ends up eating as much as she can before throwing the rest away. Which is a disgusting waste of good food.'

'More truly, Betty, sorry to say it, not very well-cooked food.'

Betty gives me the: trust you to stick up for your mate, look. 'The thing is, Detective Inspector, no one is perfect. Chloe is a brilliant mother, housewife, lover and partner. Richard couldn't ask for a better wife even if she can't cook beans without burning them.'

'Agreed, the girl is lovely in so many ways and trust me, Richard absolutely adores her. But…'

'I knew they'd be a but! There's always a bloody but!'

'Not always, Betty. The trouble is, this but is a huge but, Richard is as addicted to the kind of foods he loves as an opium smoker is to his pipe.'

'I don't think that's a very good analogy, Gerald.'

Things can sometimes turn nasty once Betty calls me by my name. I need to think fast and be careful what I say. 'I'll have a word with him tomorrow. I will also have a think as to how we might help them sort out this problem. How was little Thomas.'

The sour face vanishes, 'Oh, he was lovely. Chloe let me change and feed him…'

'Really? I didn't know you were milked up?'

'Silly sod. Chloe's teats are sore, Thomas sucks too hard…'

'Greedy like his old man, then,' grins I.

'He's not greedy, he's a baby. Anyway, where was I?'

'On Chloe's teats.'

'Yes. She's been gently squeezing her milk into a bottle and then feeding Thomas that way.'

'And he's happy to take the bottle?'

'Not at first, but he's got used to it now. Anyway, Detective Inspector I fancy an early night before I drop off here and then wake up in the middle of the night all stiff and uncomfortable.'

I let out a big yawn, in truth I am knackered, 'Sounds good to me, my little Rip Van Winkle.'

'Good. Just don't forget to have words with Richard tomorrow.'

'I'll have to be very tactful about it.'

'Do so, but if he won't listen give him a thumping until he does.'

***

I am up earlier than usual the next morning and take the time to go through Pollards report on Mable Calver's murder while sat at the kitchen table. Betty is busying herself preparing breakfast, which isn't porridge, thank goodness.

All is much as I remember until I reach a paragraph that wasn't in the report that I read five years back. Pollard mentions that he 'ran into' one Joe Straw on the very day Mable was murdered and asked him what he was doing around the area. To which he got told, very impolitely, to mind his own business. This Joe Straw then went off. Pollard recommended in his report that Straw be brought in for questioning as the man was well known to settle scores for anyone who requested his 'services' providing the price was right. In short, Pollard obviously believed Straw could well have had something to do with Mable's murder.

There's no description of Straw, but if he's done time, I may well be able to read up all about him from his records, plus peruse any photos there may be of him. Failing that, I shall pay Pollard another visit, assuming of course he's still alive.

After a breakfast of bacon sandwiches, I head off for work at seven thirty just as Richard is about to open the front gate.

'Morning, Gerald,' says he miserably as we head towards the tram stop.

'Morning, Richard. And what a lovely sunny one it promises to be,' says I gazing up into a cloudless sky.

'Bit cold. Winter's just around the corner. I know it's still a good two months away, but can I come to yours again for Christmas Day dinner?'

'Of course. I'm sure Betty will love having you all over.'

He appears to cheer up a bit. 'Marvellous. Thanks, Gerald.'

'Just make sure that Chloe will be happy about it. After all, it's your first Christmas with little Tom and she may want to spend it with just the three of you.'

He gives me the extra miserable look. 'It would be lovely except for the dinner. I can't bear thinking about it, Gerald. God it's worse than torture. I hate myself, but the very thought of under cooked or over cooked meat and veg' all covered with a watery gravy, followed by Christmas Pudding that'll probably be like eating rabbit droppings mixed up with stodgy dumplings fills me with horror. I mean, it is the most important meal of the year, don't you think?'

We stop and face each other. 'No, I don't. Every meal's important, Richard. And any woman who loves her man wants to serve him up something special at every meal time. But...'

'If she can't cook it causes trouble in the marriage.' He spreads his arms wide. 'Why can't Chloe cook, Gerald? She's had all those lessons from Betty and still she can't fry a good old full English without ruining some of it.'

'Some of it you say. Does this mean some of the breakfast is cooked alright?'

'Yes. But, one day I'll get a nice runny yolk in my eggs but the bacon will be cremated. The next the yolks will be hard and the bottom of the egg will be burnt crisp while the bacon will be just right. One day the sausages could be burnt on the outside but raw in the middle, and the next they'll be just right...'

'There's your answer, Richard. She *is* getting there. At one time, Chloe ruined everything when she cooked, but now she's only ruining some of it. Give her a few more months and she'll be ruining even less and who knows may end up as good a cook as Betty. So, I suggest you draw your neck in and be patient and stop going on at her. I will bet you are making the poor girl so nervous she is for ever on tenterhooks and can't concentrate because you are probably looking over her shoulder the second she so much as gets the butter out of the pantry. Put it this way, how would you like to have had someone like Clump constantly breathing down your neck when you first joined the force and didn't have much of a clue about policing?'

'Um… That's not a very good comparison, Gerald if you don't mind me saying. I mean, frying an egg doesn't come anywhere near to hunting for, say, Jack the Ripper.'

'True, but the analogy is the same. You need to learn your trade; you need the opportunity to gain experience of that trade until you can be trusted to do your job to the very best of your abilities. Only then will you be relatively left alone to get on with it and it is by that time you will begin to become a seasoned professional; whether it's as an egg frier or a catcher of killers. I rest my case. Now, let's get on, we have criminals to chase and a case to solve.'

'Alright. I'll think about what you said and try to look at things from a different perspective, as I can, sort of, see your point. But if it doesn't work, can we still come to yours for Christmas?'

'Absolutely! Now, let me tell you what I found out in Pollards original report.'

***

On arrival at the Yard, the desk sergeant informs us that Clump is with two other detectives investigating the suspicious death of no other than Constable Alfred French, whose body was found in a shed on an allotment over Hackney way.

That was all the desk sergeant could tell us. We head off to records where we find out a good deal on Joe Straw which we take back to our office, picking up coffees on the way along with a huge slab of Victoria sponge for Head.

'It's obvious the twins have done French in,' says Head once we'd sat down.

'Possibly,' says I. 'But let us wait to see what Clump finds out before we get too side-tracked.'

Opening Joe Straw's file, full name: Joseph John Strawbridge, I take out a photograph taken of him eight years ago and peruse it. Six foot of solid muscle stares back at me through evil piggy eyes. A bull-necked, broad shouldered brick shithouse who looks ready to kill anything that moves. I pass the photo over to Head.

'This is the face that launched a thousand ships loaded with people all eager to get as far away from it as possible,' says Head before ramming half the sponge into his mouth. 'Christ, what an ugly, brutal looking bastard.'

'He's ugly alright, Richard. But he may not be a bastard.'

'Sorry, Gerald, he definitely is a bastard. I mean what mother or father in their right mind would admit being involved in his conception, let alone his birth.'

'True. Anyway, he's done time for GBH, ABH and endless threats with menace. He's been arrested and implicated in three murders but never stood trial for a one.'

'Too protected,' ponders Head.

'Undoubtably. You do the dirty work for the rich, well healed and important you can be assured a cover up will always be on the cards.'

'One law for them and one for the rest of us miserable beings,' says Head, before ramming the remainder of the sponge down his gullet like a demented gannet, then licking his fingers and downing his coffee in two gulps. 'Where to now, Gerald?'

'Where to indeed, Richard. We need to think carefully here. We have no evidence that Straw was involved in the murders of Mable Calver, Razor Williams or the body in the morgue, unless we believe what the twins told us.'

'*We* might believe them, Gerald. But put them on the stand and you can guarantee their unsubstantiated evidence will be ripped apart by a decent barrister and no one will believe them. End of trial.'

'Questioning Straw would be a waste of time. He'll just laugh in our faces knowing full well we have nothing on him…'

'Plus, if he gets upset, we may find our heads facing backwards and our knackers crushed into pulp.'

'So, we'll leave Straw alone for now until we have something more concrete on him. I am thinking we should pay ex Superintendent Shaver a visit and ask him why he ordered Pollard to change his report to leave Straw out of it.'

'Um… Trouble is, Clump won't like us reopening the Calver case without his say so.'

'He might if we can convince him that the Calver case is linked to the murder of the body in the morgue case because both cases are directly linked to Sir Arnold Falconer, who may well have paid Straw to sort out the mess.'

'If we go and question Shaver, we'll have to keep it quiet or Clump will go mad.'

'I think, Richard we'd be making a big mistake if we go behind Clump's back on this one. We will need his backup if we're to get involved with the likes of Straw and Falconer. If we question Shaver then what's the betting, he'll inform Falconer?'

'And then Falconer will pull strings and we're done for, having acted without our chiefs blessing. You're right, Gerald. We can't go forward with any of this without Clumps say so.'

I sit back and sigh, then run my fingers through my hair for good measure.

'You appear somewhat worried, Gerald.'

'I was thinking that this case could well turn out to be the most dangerous case we have ever been on.'

Head grins. 'You, say that about most of the cases we've been on. We'll be fine, you'll see.'

'I hope so. Right, let's see how Clump got on with French's killing before we say anything about Straw and Falconer. If it was the twins who killed French then we've got to bring them in before they kill again.'

'Which will put us in their bad books. No return of the Frobisher's naughty photographs or Lady Fraser's letter and the risk of the twins avoiding capture and then turning on us and our loved ones.'

'Which they promised not to do.'

He shrugs, 'They're wild cards, Gerald and I for one don't trust them. They're out for revenge and hell bent on becoming notorious. Even God probably hasn't a clue what they'll get up to next. Anyone who can blow up sheep for the fun of it has to be seriously warped.'

'Meaning that if French *has* been bizarrely murdered then it's bound to have been the work of the twins.'

'Any suggestions as to where we go from here, Richard?'

'Um… We could go and have lunch at the Dirty Duck while we think things over.'

'It's not even ten o'clock, Richard. The Dirty Duck doesn't open until twelve.'

'As it's us they might open up early.'

'The answer is no. What we shall do is go and see our snouts and find out if they've got anything for us. Then after lunch we'll get back here, by which time Clump may be back.'

***

We arrive back at the Yard at one thirty with mixed news. No one has a clue where the twins are hiding out. But, thanks to Andy, we now know who the body in the morgue is most likely to be. The desk sergeant informs us that Clump is back in his office so we head there right away and knock on the door.

'Come in, lads,' bellows Clump.

'He knows our knock,' whispers Head. 'How creepy is that?'

On entering we find Detective Constables Barnsley and Thompson are sat opposite Clump while all three are nursing glasses of scotch while smoking fat cigars. The room is like a bad attack of smog in a whiskey distillery.

After exchanging greetings, Clump sends Thompson off to fetch two more chairs and another glass. A few minutes later Head and I are sat either side of the constables. Clump pours me and Head a glass of scotch before keeping us waiting while he jots down a few notes.

I know the ageing Barnsley and Thompson, pretty straight coppers who have not gotten far in the force. They are good at finding clues and gathering information but hopeless at following them up unless under constant supervision by a senior officer.

Barnsley is thick set and sports a bushy greying moustache. Thompson is tall and thin with a nice shiny bald head and a full set of ginger whiskers.

At last Clump puts down his pen, and, after gazing somewhat sombrely at us each in turn, goes back to his writing for a bit longer. Then he tops up our glasses before saying, 'Any questions before we begin?'

'Yes, Chief,' says Head. 'Can we open a window and let some of the smoke out before we all suffocate through lack of air?'

'No. Anything else? Right, Detectives Potter and Head, allow me to update you. Former Constable Alfred French was found dead in his shed at first light this morning by the local beat officer, who promptly sent a local civilian to fetch further assistance from nearby Hackney Police Station, who then contacted Scotland Yard because of the brutal nature of French's murder. French's body is currently residing in the morgue while the pathologist chops him up to find out what actually killed him. My bet is after being tortured, he died from a heart attack. But we shall see. On entering the shed, we were confronted with the naked bottom half of French, face down, with his hands nailed to the wooden floor and his ankles tied together with rope. Most of his hair had been pulled out with a pair of pliers, found close to the body with chunks of hairy scalp still in it. His buttocks had been beaten raw, a bloodied cane with bits of skin on it was also close by. Easy to tell by the amount of blood that these acts were carried out while French was still alive. To complete his humiliation the killers had left a police truncheon inserted in his rectum right up to its handle. Takeover, Constable Thompson.'

'Thank you, Chief. Several residents from the row of terraces that back onto the allotment heard screams at around three o'clock this morning, along with banging and shouting. But no one dared to venture out in case Jack the Ripper was at work. No uniformed offices were in the area, they patrol up to midnight, as it's considered a safe area, and then back on the beat at first light. A Mrs Turnbull, at number six, saw two shadowy figures leave the allotment at around four o'clock, before they faded into the darkness. A Mr Flint, from number eight, saw light coming from one of the sheds between about three and four o'clock. There were no gas lamps on as they are turned off at midnight. Whoever committed this horrendous crime obviously chose the time and place well.'

'What strikes me,' puts in Barnsley, 'was their blatant indifference to the fact that anyone could have heard them, anyone could have run to try and fetch a policeman, anyone could have disturbed them. They must be the most callous and seriously disturbed killers I have ever come across. They are worse than animals…'

'You are being unfair to animals, Constable,' cuts in Clump. 'This pair of demented lunatics are monsters. And their names are, Inspector?'

'William and Robert Boyle. More commonly known as Bill and Bob.'

'The twins on the posters that have just gone up all over the city?' says Thompson.

'That's them,' says I. 'A deadly duo of cycle paths.'

'He means psychopaths,' grins Head.

'Now,' says Clump. 'French lived at number thirteen, unlucky for him, just he and his wife, his two grown up sons having left home a year or so ago. Uniform found Mrs French bound, gagged and tied to her rocking chair in the parlour, but physically unharmed. Naturally the poor woman was in a bit of a state but was lucid enough to relate what had happened. There was a knock on the door at ten o'clock last night and her husband answered the door to be confronted by the twins pointing a sawn-off shotgun at his chest. Once inside the house the twins handcuffed and gagged French then sat him down on the sofa, while Mrs French was ordered to go and make tea and provide something to 'snack on'. Mr and Mrs French were held prisoner until two thirty whereupon Mrs French was bound, gagged and tied to the chair. The twins then slipped a wire noose over French's head, pulled it tight around his neck and took him outside and then obviously over to his shed on the allotment where they began to torture him. No doubt French would have put up a fight, he being an ex-copper and still a big strong man, but with a wire around his neck the man had no hope. Uniform and forensics are still carrying out house to house, searching for clues and so and so forth. Questions thus far.'

'You told us, Chief,' says Thompson, 'that the twins were out for revenge from French and King over the birching they gave them five years ago. Now, I understand their brutal caning of French, but not the hair pulling out or the truncheon left up French's um… um…'

'Arse,' grates Clump. 'Say it as it is, Constable. Do not tiptoe around just because you are in the presence of your chief. Inspector, answer the constable's question.'

'I think. No, I believe that after his birching, Bill Boyle had a handful of his hair ripped out of his scalp by French.'

'Brutal!' says Barnsley. 'Why did French rip Boyle's hair out?'

I am about to choose my words carefully when Head cuts in.

'French did it out of sheer malice. He dragged Bill by the hair across the punishment cell floor and hurled him out into the street via a back door, whereupon a chunk of Bill's hair was ripped out.'

Clump's eyes narrow, he glares into Heads eyes.

Head gives him the innocent; butter wouldn't melt look. Only Clump is smelling a rat which is telling him that Head knows a bit too much about what happened at the twins birching.

Clump gives me the condescending look before saying, 'And the truncheon, Inspector. For what symbolic reason did the Boyles have for shoving it up French's backside?'

'I don't know, sir. Perhaps one or both of the twins suffered similar from French or King.'

'You're saying that French or King possibly shoved their truncheons up the backsides of a pair of urchins?'

'Merely an educated guess,' shrugs I.

'Makes sense,' says Clump with a smile that says it all. He suspects that Head and I could only have gotten such information directly from the twins. 'Right, Detective Constables Barnsley and Thompson, get yourselves a bite to eat first and then get down to records. I want you to go and do what you are best at, gathering information. Go through French and Kings files while concentrating specifically on their carrying out punishments. I want to know about any reprimands they'd received, no matter how far back, any complaints about them from fellow officers and from the public. I want to know how many birching's they carried out, how many times they did so without following the correct procedures and any reports by doctors or others present of *excessive* birching. Right, off you go.'

Once they'd gone, Clump tops up our glasses before fixing us with his: You're for it glare.

'Right, lads,' says he with a nice friendly smile laced with menace. 'You are both hiding something from me. Actually, I thought similar the other day. I did not fully believe your ridiculous story about your snouts having overheard about the relationship between James Palmer and Lady Elizabeth Fraser. I am now of the opinion that it was a load of old tripe dressed up as a fairy tale. Neither French or King would have written in their reports that they ripped hair out of an urchin's head, beat them cruelly and shoved their truncheons up their unmentionables. No, you could only have got that information directly from the twins…'

'It was our coppers intuition,' says Head, which is the red rag to Clump's bull.

'By God!' roars Clump shaking his fist in Head's face. 'You two have somehow been communicating with the twins, haven't you?'

We shake our heads.

'Liars! Last chance, open up now or by God, I'll have you both back pounding the fucking beat before tea time.'

'There's no fooling you, is there Chief?' says Head matter of fact.

'Not for long there isn't,' snarls Clump as his face turns purple with rage.

Time to come clean. 'We had a meeting to discuss the twins demands to see if we could come to some arrangement beneficial to all.'

Clump's eye balls swell out of their sockets. 'A fucking arrangement beneficial to all! Are you both fucking mad? Don't answer that, I already know the answer. Right, tell me everything, and believe me it better be good because if it isn't, I'll bypass your reduction in rank and have you shipped off to Australia, in chains, for good.

****

We tell, Clump everything, he isn't amused or forgiving, but he's far more understanding than we thought he'd be. That's after he'd ripped us to shreds of course.

'You, say the twins have no idea where, King is. Well, I will bet they do now, having tortured French into telling them. Assuming of course he knew where King lives. That being the case is it not reasonable to also assume that the twins have already gotten to King and we will shortly be presented with another mutilated corpse?'

'Agreed, Chief,' says I.

'Go and commandeer a police waggon and a driver. Get yourselves over to King's place as fast as you can while praying that you get there before the twins. Because, gentlemen, if you don't then it is the end of both your careers in the force. Do you understand me?'

Looking suitably miserable, with gross overenthusiasm, we nod.

'Right, I want you to arrest King and put him in the cells for his own protection. Bring back anyone who's living with him. I will find them a safe house until this is all over. The second the twins find out we have King in custody they will no doubt contact you to find out what's going on.'

'How will they find out we've got King in custody?'

'You'll think of something. Once the twins contact you, you will arrange another meeting to renegotiate. Only this time we shall have laid a trap and we will arrest the bastards just as you should have done in the first place.'

'We do that, Chief and I'll bet the twins will have arranged for someone to immediately release the naughty photographs of the Frobisher's along with Lady Elizabeth's letter.'

'Perhaps. It is a gamble we will just have to take, Inspector. Look, lads, the twins are psychopaths of the highest order. We cannot have them running amok for even another day. No, the sooner they're swinging from a rope the happier I shall be.'

'They might be too young to hang, Chief. Failing that they will no doubt claim they're mad to escape the noose…'

'They can claim all they like, Inspector, but trust me; they will be old enough to hang, and they will not be found insane enough to end up in the nut house. As to this Straw thug being responsible for the murders of Mable Calver, Razor Williams and the safe breaker with no face, what's his name?'

'Don Picket, Chief.'

'Picket, an apt name for a safe picker.' He chuckles, which is a massive release of our stress modes. 'The theory that Sir Arnold Falconer hired this Straw to assist him in covering up his own shenanigans and that of his sons is a reasonable one to consider. But as the information came from the *slightly* questionable source of a pair of deranged killers it is just as likely to not have an ounce of truth in any of it. In short it is probably a pile of bullshit to over burden you with work while they manipulate you into doing what they want.'

'So, we do nothing about what the twins told us even if there might be some truth in it?'

'I am not saying discount it, Inspector. I am saying, no ordering you, to leave it for now and prioritise the orders I have just given you. Right piss off and don't come back without King, preferably alive and not butchered to bits.'

The Kings

Outside the front of the building, we find half a dozen various carriages parked up, but only two drivers who are fussing over their horses while obviously waiting for something to do.

'Alright for some,' says Head as we make for the driver whose black painted Paddy Wagon would be our best choice as you can cram ten people into it.

'We need a driver to ferry us to Shoreditch to pick up some people,' says I.

Turning away from the pair of heavy black geldings he fixes me with confrontational watery eyes. Stretches himself up to a lanky six foot, plus his peaked black hat and says,' Do what?'

'Can you take us to Shoreditch?'

'Not without permission from my governor.'

'We have never met,' says I. 'But as I am a Detective Inspector and thus out rank you, a mere constable, I am as much your governor as your governor is. Allow me to rephrase my request. Mount up, Constable and take us where we want to go. That is an order.'

'No need to get blousy, Inspector. The thing is I can't take anyone anywhere without direct orders from *my* governor. Besides, you could be anyone. You could be a member of the public who's trying to con me into taking him home having just been let out after spending a night in the cells for being drunk and disorderly.'

'Do I look like a drunk and disorderly?'

'Yes. Plus, you appear to be a bit shifty and stink of cigars and booze.'

The other driver comes over, 'Having trouble, Ted?'

'Yeah, I have, Jim. This fellow reckons he's a detective and is demanding I take him and his pal to Shoreditch.'

'But you ain't had your afternoon tea yet.'

'Identification,' says I fanning open my jacket to reveal my holstered revolver. 'Warrant card,' adds I fishing it out and shoving it in his face. 'Last chance before I fetch *my* governor, will you mount up or not?'

'Who's your governor?'

'Detective Chief Inspector Clump.'

'You best get cracking, Ted,' says Jim. 'You don't want that Clump on your back.'

'Or his size twelves up your arse,' grates Head.

'Alright,' says Ted. 'Do you want to ride in the back or up front with me?'

'As it's a pleasant day, Constable, we shall ride up with you and enjoy the scenery.'

'Alright for you then. Me I've got to drive…'

'Just shut up and mount up!' growls Head clenching his fists. 'Christ I've never known such a miserable git as you, Constable Grumpy.'

'His wife left him,' says Jim.

'I am not surprised,' says I. 'Let's go, Ted. Time is of the essence; lives may depend on it. Dwell on this, your actions this day could save innocent lives. What more could a serving policeman want?'

'His tea and cake first would be nice.'

'I'll go along with that,' says Head.

'Let us get going before I bloody explode.'

Jim starts to say, 'You…'

'Can shut up and piss off, Constable Jim before I arrest you for construct… I mean obstruction.'

'It's bloody hard being without a wife,' moans Ted as we trot along as fast as the traffic will allow us. 'You get home and there's no one there. There's no smell of a nice roast wafting around the place. No housework's been done and you're running out of clean underwear.'

'Why don't you wash your own underwear?' says Head who's sat next to Ted while I'm on the outside and now wishing I was riding inside the waggon just for the peace and quiet.

Ted shoots Head the blank look, 'Washing my underwear's a woman's job. I never asked her to drive my horses, so why on earth should I wash my own underwear. Christ, Sergeant, whatever next? Come home and find the woman sat in your favourite armchair closest to the fire, smoking your pipe and drinking your beer. Dear oh dear. Perish the thought.'

'You should spend a day with my wife,' says I. 'She loves men like you.'

'I should never have married a girl from the countryside,' moans Ted. 'I always knew she'd bugger off back there one day. Rather smell cow pats and pigs than live the city life. Wouldn't have been so bad if she'd have left, Rose, the eldest daughter behind so she could do the woman's work. Every time the wife was having another kid, Rose would take over.'

'How old is Rose?' asks Head.

'Twelve. I think. Only girl. Got six boys but you can't expect them to do a woman's work.'

After sighing miserably, he glances behind him over the roof of the waggon, 'Don't look now but there's a pair of Chinese looking men driving a hackney right behind us.'

Head and I take a look. Behind us are sat two Chinese men, both sporting long black droopy moustaches and wearing the umbrella type hats favoured by the Easterners. One hat is bright yellow the other is bright red. They're wearing brightly coloured tops and trousers heavily embroidered with colourful patterns of flowers and exotic birds, their clothes appear very expensive. Head gives them a wave and they wave back.

'Don't bloody encourage them,' grates Ted. 'The next thing you know they'll pull alongside you and offer you those stupid fortune cookies. Accept a bloody cooky they'll then try and sell you a duck or something. Before you know it, they'll have moved into your house and taken over.'

'But at least you'd get your laundry done,' grins Head.

'Can't abide foreigners,' grates Ted. 'Eating all that weird stuff. Stir fried cat and dog mixed with toad stools and worms, so I've heard. Don't know why they let them in.'

'You've never been to China town for a meal, then?' says Head.

Ted shoots him the horrified look. 'No, I bloody well haven't. The only time I've been that way was for cab pickups or help round up triads and convey them back to the station. Eat foreign muck, no chance.'

'You should try it,' says Head. 'You might be pleasantly surprised.'

'I doubt it. Now then, where exactly do you want to be in Shoreditch.'

'Hoxton Street. Do you know it?'

'I used to be a cabby before I joined the force, so I've got the knowledge. Cause I would have stayed a cabby if I'd got more tips. Without tips a cabby doesn't earn a lot, but you do get lots of offers from the tarts who're looking for a ride for a ride.' He guffaws a bit then says, 'Which can help cheer you up when you're on nights and getting bored.'

'Bit risky, Ted,' says Head. 'Some of them girls are dangerous. Once your drawers are around your ankles, they'll punch you in the nuts, take your money and run for it.'

'That never happened to me,' he says smugly. 'The only bad thing I got…'

'Was?' says I on reasoning he wasn't about to finish his sentence.

'Nothing much. Sometimes they'd, um… *short change you.*'

'Or give you the clap,' says I.

'I never said that, Inspector,' says he giving me the get stuffed look.

'So, Constable. Can I assume you caught the clap and then passed it on to your long-suffering wife who then left you, taking the children with her?'

'Have you got any evidence for that accusation?' demands he.

'No,' says I. 'Just a coppers intuition.'

He mumbles something under his breath and at last goes quiet and falls into a sulk.

The sky has clouded over and there's a sharp drop in temperature, but the traffic hasn't thinned out and we are making slower progress than I would have anticipated. I am about to ask Ted if he could speed things up when he turns off into a very narrow alleyway.

'Bit of a rat run,' says he. 'Could come unstuck if we meet something wide coming the other way. But it'll cut the journey down considerably.'

With that he slaps the reigns down on the horse rumps and they break into a canter. A narrow lane with very narrow, crowded pavements is not conducive to a swaying and bouncing about waggon. People jump out of our way, others shake fists, stick up two fingers and shout out obscenities that are very insulting towards police personnel. But it is the small group of urchins up ahead who appear to be armed to the teeth with balls of dung that are the real worry.

'Watch out!' yells Head. 'Shit bombardment up ahead.'

Holding our bowler's, we duck our heads as the front wheel of the waggon bangs up the curb and threatens to career into the urchins and squash them against the shop front of a butchers. Urchins scream out profanities as they dive out of the way, but still, they manage to throw several dung balls our way.

I get hit on the bowler with one ball while another thuds into my ribs before another smacks the side of my neck, thus no doubt, leaving horse shit all-over my lovely white starched shirt collar.

'Ease up boys,' cries Ted as he pulls back on the reins. 'Relax, gentlemen we are through the worst part. Anyone hurt?'

Just my pride ponders I giving the idiot a cold hard stare. The man did that detour on purpose knowing full well we'd likely get pelted.

'A strange, shitty form of revenge, Constable Ted,' says I as I take out my handkerchief to try and clean myself up.

'I don't know what you mean, sir,' says he, oh so smugly.

'Can't believe I didn't get hit,' says Head, oh so joyfully.

'Probably because I shielded you and got your share,' grates I. 'Pull another one like that Constable and I'll make sure you don't see day light for a while until someone pulls your head out of your horse's arse.'

'I'm still not with you, sir,' smirks he.

'Wipe that smirk off your face and just concentrate on your driving, Constable. Any more from you and you'll find yourself up in front of the Chief Constable and facing the firing squad. In short you career will be over with.'

'Who cares,' says he. 'I'm not that happy being in the force anyway. Six months of misery it's been, what with the wife buggering off. I might go back to being a cabby.'

'Good choice,' says I while wiping the mess from my jacket with an already heavily shitted up handkerchief. 'Richard, have you a spare handkerchief I can borrow?'

'I don't have a spare, Gerald. I could lend you my only handkerchief but then I won't have a clean one if I needed it.'

'That's not very kind of you, Richard.'

'I know, sorry, but that's the fact of the matter.'

'Why don't you tear off your shirt tail,' suggests Ted with a chuckle, as the waggon moves back onto the main road.

Enough is enough. 'Change places please, Richard.'

'What, while we're moving?'

'Yes, while we are bloody moving!'

'Be careful,' grins Ted.

'If you swing this waggon about while we're standing up, trust me, Ted the wooden head, I will smack you around the head with my revolver so fucking hard you ear drums will be playing the fifth concerto for weeks. *Do you hear me?*'

'I do,' sulks he.

Head and I stand up, sort of hold hands and start to shuffle around each other, just then I notice that the Chinese men are still directly behind us. Smiling happily, they wave at me and I stupidly wave back.

'Watch out!' yells Head. 'What the hell are you doing letting go like that?'

'Sorry, I didn't think.'

Somehow, we manage to change places without falling off the waggon. Once comfortable I whisper to Head that I require the use of his flic knife.

'What for?' whispers he back.

'To wipe the shit from my shirt and jacket.'

'Will you return it to me in the spotless condition you received it?'

'You have my word of honour.'

He hands me the knife.

Ted, I can tell isn't too happy to have me sat beside him. He is about to be even less happy.

'Right, Ted,' smiles I waving the knife in front of his widening eyes and flicking the four-inch razor sharp blade out. 'Do as I bid, or you'll get this in the side of your arse. Now, shuffle forwards a bit, there's a good lad.'

He shifts himself forwards and I pull up the back of his tunic to get at his shirt.

'What's going on?' demands he.

'I need your shirt tail for wiping the shit off me. Keep very still or you might get your back sliced.'

Tugging out his shirt tail reveals a disgusting skid mark that I refuse to have anything to do with, so, as the traffic is at a standstill, I demand he stands up and takes off his tunic.

'This is a violation of a serving officer's uniform,' says he, even so he does as he's told.

'That's better,' says I as deftly I cut a nice big square of white shirt right out of the middle. 'All done, Constable. Kindly put your tunic back on.'

'You've cut a big hole in my shirt,' moans he, feeling around his back. 'I can't carry on with my duties while being unsuitably attired.'

'Oh, just shut up and get on with it,' grates Head. 'If you

hadn't set us up to get splattered in the first place, you'd still have all the shirt on your back.'

Ted fixes Head with a scathing glare. 'I'm going to report you pair of delinquents the moment we get back to the station. Then you'll be for it.'

'Hurry up, Constable,' says I. 'The traffic's on the move.'

Ted tucks his skiddy shirt tail back in his trousers, puts on his tunic, buttons it up, sits down and picks up the reins. I hand back Head's knife. Ted slaps the reins and the horses move forwards. Glancing behind us I note the hackney is still behind us but with no one in it.

'The Chinese men have deserted their carriage,' says I to Head.

He glances behind him. 'So, they have. Perhaps they decided to walk, it's quicker. In fact, Gerald at this rate we'll be lucky to make it to Kings before dark. We'll have to pull into a pub and have dinner…'

'That is a no, Richard. Don't forget you promised to make more effort to enjoy whatever Chloe has cooked for you, and your blatant attempt to stuff yourself to the gills before you get home is pitiful.' Our eyes meet and he doesn't appear happy. 'Once home you can then say that your superior officer, yours truly, ordered you to join him for a meal because we were out late and I was worried you were so hungry that you couldn't function properly. Hence the reason you are too full to eat any of the delicious dinner set out on the table.'

'What a load of rubbish, Gerald.'

'The inspector has a point though,' chips in Ted.

'Keep out of it, Constable,' says I.

'Yeah, shut your face, Ted,' says Head. 'Speak when you're spoken to from now on or you'll get a slap.'

'No need for that,' grates Ted.

At last, we arrive at ex-Sergeant Kevin Kings home. A nice semi of red brick and tiled roof with a nice mahogany front door complete with monkey head doorknocker. It even has a small frontage that still has a few flowers displaying bright colours, a nice short privet hedge surrounds the garden and a nice little black painted metal gate dead centre sets the whole thing off. There shines a welcoming orange glow from an oil lamp through the sash window. It is getting dark, partly because night is falling, but mostly because above us thick rolling very dark clouds are threatening to dump a flood onto us.

'Looks nice,' says Head as he stands up and stretches. 'I need a drink, Gerald. My throats drier than a camel's armpit.'

'I'm sure Mrs King will make us a coffee…'

'What about me?' says Ted.

'What about you?'

'Do I get to go inside for a coffee?'

'No. You can stay out here and tend to your horses while making sure no one steals the waggon. I'll bring you a cuppa out.'

Mumbling incoherently, he gets down from the wagon and has a good stretch. 'Cor, my back's stiff as a board. I'm a martyr to my back. Cor…'

'I take it you have provisions for the horses in the back of the waggon, Constable,' says I.

'Of course, I do.'

'Good. Well, relax and we shall be as quick as we can be.'

The curtains are open and, having met her a few years back, I spy Mrs King sat by the fire knitting as Head follows me down the path. Mrs King's a comely woman with a pleasant nature who is much maligned by her bullying husband. Having had dealings with King in the past, when he was a serving officer, I must admit I never liked him. Too in your face, confrontational and undisciplined. But, handy in a barroom brawl. I doubt he has changed.

I rap the monkey head knocker.

'Nice place,' says Head as he looks around. 'Very neat and tidy.'

'King's one of those who likes everything kept neat and tidy. But, be warned he can be a right arsehole.' I give the knocker another rap.

'All right! All right!' growls a voice from inside. 'Hold your bleedin' horses I'm on my way.'

The door opens and we are confronted with a craggy, late middle-aged, clean-shaven face and cold, cold dark eyes. It seems the only thing that has changed is King's hair has receded and turned grey and he's wearing a thick grey pullover when he used to be forever in uniform, even when off duty.

'Good grief,' says King, looking me up and down. 'Potter and Head of all people. What the fuck do you pair of twats want?'

'I'll thank you, Mr King to be a bit more civil. And it's Inspector to you. May we come in as I do not wish to talk on the step?'

With a shrug he pulls an indifferent face, waves us in and slams the door.

'Who is it, Kevin?' calls his wife.

'Visitors, Glenda. Best put the kettle on. Go on then,' says he waving us down the narrow hall and into a nicely furnished parlour.

'Oh,' says Mrs King as she gets to her feet. 'Sergeant Potter and…?'

'Sergeant Head,' says Head.

'Potter's an inspector now,' grates King.

'Oh, how lovely,' says Mrs King. 'How nice to have visitors. Would you care for refreshments?'

'Thank you, Mrs King,' says I. 'Coffee would be nice and would you mind making one for our driver who's outside seeing to his horses.'

She goes and peeps out the window. 'Oh, my there's a big black waggon out there, Kevin. What's that about?'

'I don't know because I can't read bloody minds, woman. Just go and make the bloody coffee, will you?'

Once she'd gone King goes over to the mantlepiece where he picks up a pipe and puffs it into life. 'Good tobacco this is,' says he pointing his pipe at me. 'You can set it down and pick it up five minutes or more later and it will still smoke.'

'Marvellous,' says I.

'Marvellous, says Head.

'Still, you didn't come here to talk about pipes, did you? Sit down and tell me what this about. No, don't, I'll tell you. You need my help, don't you? Got yourself a case that you can't solve without old Kevin King's expertise.'

'We'd rather stand if you don't mind, Mr King. It's taken us a staggering two hours to get here and we're a bit stiff. The reason we are here is to take you into protective custody on the orders of Detective Chief Inspector Clump.'

Moving away from the fire he takes a seat on the arm chair where his wife had been.

'Protective custody? You having a laugh?'

I shake my head while trying to look solemn. 'Have you not heard about your former college, ex-Constable Alfred French?'

Taking out his pipe he says, 'Heard what? No, I ain't heard nothing.'

'French was butchered to death at around three o'clock this morning.'

This gets his attention as he stands up and moves closer to me. 'Was he by fuck? Butchered by whom?'

'The main suspects are a pair of twins known as Bill and Bob Boyle.'

He narrows his eyes but he doesn't say anything.

'You may have seen their wanted posters stuck up all-over the place.'

'Nah. Can't say I have. Who are the other set of twins?'

'There isn't another set of twins. Just the Boyles.'

'You said the main suspects are a pair of twins.'

'I meant one set of twins. Two young males who happen to be twins.'

'Got it. What's this got to do with me?'

'Don't you remember the Boyle twins?' puts in Head.

'Should I?'

'You ought to,' says I. 'You and French birched them five years ago.'

Shaking his head, he goes back to his chair. 'Pair of skinny little bastards,' says he after a minute of thought. 'One bit me in the thigh, just an inch from my dick. He wished to Christ he hadn't done that by the time I'd finished with him.'

'So, we have heard,' says I. 'In fact, Mr King, you and French were so brutal in delivering the punishment to those boys back then they bear the scars to this day, along with a burning hatred to get even with anyone who did them wrong.'

'They got what they deserved the shitty arsed little bastards.'

'I would appreciate you toning down your language, Mr King,' says I.

'I speak how I find in my own home, Potter. Obviously, you haven't apprehended the little bastards yet and you're reasoning that they'll be coming for me.' He laughs, a sinical deep throated laugh. 'I'd like to see the little shits try.'

'They're not that little any more,' says Head. 'And you better take this seriously, or trust me you could also end up like French with a truncheon shoved right up your rear end.'

'I don't care if they shoved a cricket bat up his arse, there is no way I'll be leaving my wife and kids here while I hide in a bloody cell.'

'Your family are to come with us as well, by order of Clump,' says I. 'He will find them a safe house until we've, killed or apprehended the twins.'

Just them Mrs King comes in carrying a tray with biscuits, coffee pot, milk and sugar jugs along with five china mugs.'

'You shouldn't honour this pair with the best china,' says King. 'They're more used to chipped and stained tin ones.'

'It's nice to use the best mugs, Kevin,' says she setting the tray down on the small dining table tucked up against the wall.

Then it hits me. China. china mugs. A pair of Chinese men driving a hackney. No wonder none of my snouts have heard a thing as to where the twins are hiding out if they can disguise themselves that well. Damn it, why the hell didn't I question myself earlier? I knew something wasn't right with those China men. My inner ear said so.

'Milk and sugar, Inspector?' asks Mrs King.

'What? Oh, yes please. One sugar and a splash of milk.'

'Sergeant?'

'Three sugars, nice and milky. Thank you.'

Now I think I'm being paranoid. We left the Chinese behind over an hour ago. They had abandoned their vehicle. Perhaps they had to run to attend something rather than be held up. *If* they were the twins, did they follow us on foot? Easily done until the traffic cleared and we were able to speed up for over half a mile.

'Does the officer outside take milk and sugar?' asks Mrs King to no one in particular.

'One sugar and no milk,' says Head. 'Oh, and no biscuits either he's watching his weight.'

Leaving all the more for you, thinks I.

She is about to take Ted's coffee out when King snarls out, 'You're forgetting someone Glenda. Someone you should have served before anyone else.'

'Sorry, Kevin. I…I wasn't thinking.'

'I do the thinking, Glenda. All you have to do is smile and remember the rules.'

'Yes dear.'

She puts down the mug intended for Ted, pours King's coffee, hands it to him with a shortbread and then picks up the mug again.

'May I open the door for you Mrs King?' says Head.

'She can manage without you fussing over her,' says King. 'Take yourself into the kitchen, Glenda when you come back, we've got things to discuss.'

'I would rather Mrs King was here to join in the discussion, Mr King.'

'She's got to finish getting the meal ready for the family. My boys and the girl will be home within the hour from work, and they will be hungry.'

'They'll be no time for meals, Mr King. The sooner we get you all safely back to the Yard the happier I shall be.'

'What is this about, Kevin?' says Mrs King. 'What does he mean he's going to take us to the Yard?'

'Never you mind. We're not going any bloody where. Get that coffee to the officer outside before it gets cold.'

Once Glenda has gone, I say, 'If you refuse to come voluntarily, Mr King, we have orders to arrest you.'

'On what charge,' laughs he.

'Needlessly endangering the lives of yourself and your family. You need to take this very seriously, Mr King. Allow me to enlighten you on exactly how Alfred French died.'

He listens, nods a bit, pulls a few faces and scratches his nuts. I am definitely getting through to him.

'Where's that stupid woman got too,' says he going over to the window. 'I can't see her or your driver. If she's gone into the back of that waggon with him, I'll bleedin' kill the sods.'

Standing beside King I take a look outside while Head seizes the opportunity to grab the rest of the biscuits. There doesn't appear to be a soul about; which is somewhat eerie. My inner ear tells me to make a move.

Drawing out my revolver I say, 'Sergeant, draw your weapon and follow me.'

'What's this, Potter?' demands King.

'Something and nothing, I hope. But you can't be too careful when you're dealing with the likes of the Boyles.'

'You think they may be out there?' says he. 'Well, if they are, then it's your fault you pair of twats, they must have followed you. I'll get my revolver; I'm coming with you.'

'I would rather you remained here,' says I.

'No chance. She's, *my* wife. And it's *my* duty to protect her.' Going over to a sideboard he takes out a small revolver and checks it's loaded. 'I'm ready.'

'Alright, have it your way but you follow my orders. Keep your eyes peeled, don't go off half cock and start a shootout at the OK Corral. I warn you Mr King, if the twins are out there, they'll be armed and won't hesitate to use their weapons.'

'Fuck the twats,' snarls he waving his weapon in my face. 'I'm a crack shot with this little beauty. I don't miss even when under fire. Bet you can't say the same, Potter.'

I shake my head. 'The twins may be rotten shots for all I know, Mr King, but a sawn-off shotgun at close range, even in the hands of a toddler, is deadly.'

'Ah… But could a toddler even lift a sawn off, let alone…'

'I don' know!' says I. 'Keep behind me and the sergeant when we're out there. That is an order.'

Just then a door slams somewhere outback and I jump out of my skin.

'That'll be the girl home,' says King. 'She always slams the door just to bloody well annoy me.'

'Only me,' cries a female voice followed by the entering of a dark haired, pretty plain young girl. 'Oh! Whatever's going on, Father?'

'Nothing for you to worry about, Fanny. You go on, Potter. I'll stay here with the girl.'

'Lock your back door.' Says I.

Fanny's eyes open wide. 'Father, what's happening?'

I lead the way up the hall with Head just behind me. At the door I pause and we face each other. 'When I go out, you stay in the doorway ready to dive back in and shut the door should something happen. I'd rather just the one of us goes out to check all is clear.'

'That's very brave of you, Gerald.'

'You have a child as well as a wife to support, Richard.'

'Be careful, Gerald.'

I nod and slowly open the door, jerk it open and you might scare whoever may be out there into opening fire. All seems quiet. The street lamps are now on, so someone came by to light them. I step up to the gate and look up and down the street. Nothing other than a few drops of rain gently pattering onto my bowler. No sign of Ted or Glenda. Walking over to the horses I find them happily munching away with their heads buried in oat bags. Turning around I can just make out Heads shadowy figure in the doorway. He holds up a hand. I shrug and point to the rear of the waggon. Stepping up to the rear door, I peep through the grille but can't see anything it's so dark inside. There are only one of the three bolts locking the door. With a squeal I pull it back, open the door and point my revolver into the darkness while keeping my body as much as possible out of direct fire, should anyone be inside. Nothing.

'Is there anyone in there?' says I, licking dry lips.

'Is that you Inspector?' says a voice squeakier than the bolt.

'Mrs King?' says I while wondering if she's on the floor with Ted on top of her.

'Yes. I'm tied up and the driver's unconscious on the floor.'

'Richard!' yells I. 'Get back inside and shut the door behind you.'

'What's up?'

'Just *go*.'

'I am coming in, Mrs King,' says I taking the two steps up into the back of the waggon. I can just make out a figure sat in the corner. But as I go towards it, I trip over Ted's body, his black uniform is perfect camouflage. Feeling around I feel for his pulse and call out his name, he's alive but not responding.

'Are you hurt, Mrs King?' says I as I reach her and fumble around to place a reassuring hand on her shoulder but manage to place it on a sizable breast instead.

'Oh…' says she.

'Sorry, Mrs King.

'It's alright, Inspector. The touch of a friendly hand made me feel safer.'

Her hands are tied to one of the iron rings used to subdue prisoners. Still thumbling around I untie the rope. She's breathing hard and trembling like the proverbial jelly.

'They hit the policeman on the head, Inspector. Then they tied me up and told me to count to one hundred and then it was alright for me to scream.'

I reason that while she was screaming, and me and Head were running over towards the waggon the twins intended to slip into the house.

'Why didn't you scream once you'd counted to a hundred?' says I.

'Because I kept losing count and had to start again.'

'I want you to remain here, do not try to get back inside the house...'

'But. But. I need Kevin. I want my husband.'

'Do as I tell you, Mrs King, or I shall tie you up again.'

'Alright.'

'Good. Were there two men or more who attacked you?'

'Two men. They were Chinese, I think. Dear God, do you know they had the cheek to drink the policeman's coffee.'

'Don't say anymore, Mrs King. I want you to get down on the floor with the policeman and maintain a low profile. Keep quiet and try to keep the policeman quiet if he comes around. I shall close the door behind me, but not lock it. Should you hear gunfire, do not stand up and try to remain calm.'

'I think I need the toilet.'

'Either hold on to it or go in the corner. Do *not* go outside.'

Revolver out in front of me, I gingerly make my way outside and shut the door behind me, just as Ted starts groaning, and no doubt moaning once he's gathered his limited senses.

Despite telling Head to shut it, I see that the front door is on the jar. Worse than that the curtains have been drawn? Perhaps Kevin drew the curtains to keep out prying eyes, or to prevent anyone from taking a pot shot at him through the window? However, it's more likely that the twins are inside because King never went and shut the back door like I told him to.

'Inspector Potter coming down the hallway,' calls out I.

'Don't come in, Gerald,' calls out Head.

'Do come in, copper,' calls Bill. 'But chuck your pistol in first.'

'I don't think so, Bill.'

'Do as I say, copper and no one except for King will get hurt.'

'It's a hard call you're making, Bill.'

'It's up to you. Should ya refuse to chuck your weapon in, ya better choose who ya want to die first. Ya mate or the girl?'

'Don't bargain with them,' calls Head.

'Shut up, copper or you'll get it in the fuckin' legs,' snarls Bill.

In the legs, thinks I. Messy, but may not be fatal. Bill doesn't intend killing me or Head and it's unlikely he'll hurt Fanny. If he was on a real killing spree, Ted and Glenda would already be dead. All Bill wants is King. I reason that's a good trade.

'You win, Bill,' calls I. 'I'll step up to the parlour door and throw my revolver in.'

'No tricks, copper.'

'No tricks.'

'Told ya he was sensible, didn't I, Bob?'

'Ya did, Bill. Ya did.'

I throw the revolver into the parlour.

'Come in, copper,' says Bill.

So, in I go. The twins are indeed dressed in Chinese costumes. Bill is standing by the sideboard. King is kneeling on the floor while his eyes stare wildly up at the ceiling. His hands are around his back and no doubt tied or cuffed. He has a thin wire noose pulled tight around his neck. Bill has hold of the other end of the wire in a leather gloved hand, telling me the wire is razor thin. In Bill's other hand he holds a sawn-off shotgun with both hammers cocked while pointing it at the back of Kings head. Head is sat cross-legged on the floor with his hands behind his head. Fanny is sat on a chair by the table, her hands are tied in front of her. She looks absolutely terrified. Bob is stood close to Fanny and is pointing Kings revolver at Fanny's chest which is pumping up and down like a pair of pistons.

'Kick the pistol over to Bob,' says Bill.

I do so, it stops close to Bob's feet.

Bob bobs down, picks it up and puts it in a bag sat on the table. No doubt, Heads revolver is also in there.

'Go kneel beside your sergeant,' says Bill.

I do so and put my hands behind my head.

Apart from my short truncheon and knuckle dusters, I am unarmed. Head, probably, still has his flic knife, short truncheon, knuckle dusters and pot of pepper. None of which are a match against a sawn off and a revolver. Resistance is futile. Besides, King got himself into this mess and I for one do not want to be a hero and chance losing my life for such as he.

'This is how it's goin' ta be,' says Bill. 'Bob will lead the way outside, he'll 'ave the girl with him. Then you two coppers will follow six feet behind. I'll bring up the rear with King. Now then, you, coppers try anything, anything at all, and Bob will shoot the girl and I'll yank the noose on Kings neck so it cuts into his flesh. He'll be like a rabbit in a snare, the more he struggles the deeper the cut until it severs his artery while strangling him; he'll be dead in minutes. At the same time as I yank the noose I'll let loose with the shotgun. At close range It'll cut you coppers in half.

'Once you, coppers and the girl are in the back of the waggon, me an' Bob will take King around the corner where we've parked the hackney. Then we'll be gone. This is for you, ex Sergeant fuckin' King! You try to kill yourself by jerkin' forwards to tighten the noose to try and escape ya punishment we'll kill the girl and your wife. Then we'll come back and kill your boys. Now, we ain't goin' ta kill ya, but by the time we've finished with your backside you won't be able to sit on it for months. And just like, Bob, you'll never, ever, sit comfortable for more than a few minutes for the rest of your life.

'That's it, let's go. Bob, slip the handles of the bag over ya arm. Take the girl by the arm, keep that pistol pointed at her head and make for the front door. Remember, all of ya, do as I've told ya and ya get ta go 'ome to ya loved ones. Cross me and the blood bath that follows will be a one-sided slaughter.'

Bob crosses the room with, Fanny, then disappears into the hall.

'Coppers, you follow on, and keep those hands behind ya heads,' says Bill.

I do so. Head is close behind, in fact he's so close I can feel his breath on my neck. But at least he hasn't started farting.

Keeping our distance, we follow Bob over to the waggon. It is now raining quite steadily, large icy droplets. Flicking my eyes all around I note the street is devoid of people.

'Open the door, Bob,' calls Bill. 'Send the girl in.'

Bob opens the door,' Go in,' he tells Fanny.

She steps up just as Glenda cries out, 'What's happening?'

'It's me, Mother,' says Fanny.

'Go back,' says Glenda. 'I'll come out.'

Bob points the revolver into the waggon. 'Come out, Mrs an' you're a dead woman.'

'Right, coppers,' says Bill. 'Get in the waggon.'

I am about to move when an elderly couple, arm in arm beneath an umbrella and with a small dog on a lead, materialise on the path before us.

'Oy,' shouts the old man while shaking his walking stick in the air. 'What's going on here, then?'

'Turn around an' piss off!' yells Bill.

The dog starts yapping and pulling on its lead. It's so loud it's in danger of attracting too much attention from the neighbours. This could turn very nasty.

The old man appears astounded. 'I don't take orders from no China man. Do I Flo'?'

'I'd say not, Bert. Bloody foreigners.'

'Shut that mutt up,' snarls Bill. 'Or I'll blow it's fuckin, head off.'

'You touch my little Willy and I'll give you a damn good bashing,' says Bert as he takes a step closer while violently shaking his stick around.

Glancing behind me I see Bill's eyes are blazing, he is on the point of losing it.

'Permission to shut the dog up, Bill?' says I.

'Yeah. Boot the bastard,' says Bill.

Hands now in the air I step towards the dog which is three feet or so closer than the couple. It is now going crazy, leaping up and down, yapping and snarling and in danger of strangling itself to death.

'Don't come any nearer,' warns Bert. 'There's a pair of policemen around the corner. They'll soon give you what for.'

'Calm down, sir,' says I stepping closer.

'Help police!' shouts Bert. '*Police. Help. Help.*'

Striding forwards, I punch Bert in the gob just as Willy sinks his vicious little teeth into my calf. Flo' starts screaming like a demented banshee. Screams are then heard coming from the waggon. Drawing my truncheon, I give the mutt a rap on its bonce as Bert hits me hard on the side of my arm with his stick. Willy has backed off whimpering, but Bert and Flo' go for it, Flo tries to claw my face with one hand as Bert swings his stick right back behind his head, nothing else for it, I headbutt Bert, my bowler flies off, Flo' claws my face so I give her the slap from hell on her cheek, she lets go of the umbrella and staggers back a few feet. Bert is now wobbling on his feet; I give him a push and he goes down, letting go of the lead. The dog runs off yelping and Flo' collapses onto Bert. It is a mess, but at least virtual silence is restored.

Just then a pair of plods appear a good sixty feet away. For a moment they appear mesmerised, then it is out with the truncheons, whistles in mouths and peeping like crazy as they charge straight at *me.*

'Bollocks to this!' cries Head.

'Stop! Stop!' cries Bob, pointing the revolver at the plods.

The plods are ten feet from me when I hold up my truncheon and shout: 'I am a detective Inspector. I order you to stop.'

Four feet from me they stop whistling and come to a skidding halt. They are confused, disorientated and in a state of panic as they scan all around the area. They look uncannily like King. His boys are home.

'What the devils going on?' demands one.

'That's our nan and grandad down there,' says the other.

'We have a situation, lads,' says I holding up a restraining hand. 'Now, if you want to avoid a bloodbath, I suggest you lower your truncheons and listen to what I tell you.'

'Is that my father over there with that Chinese fellow?' says one while pointing his truncheon.

'It is,' says I. 'Only he's not Chinese. His name is William

Boyle and he has a wire noose around your father's neck, plus, in case you hadn't noticed, he also has a sawn-off shotgun pointing at the back of your father's head.' I raise my eyebrows for dramatic effect. 'Over there by the waggon is William's twin brother, Robert. Inside the waggon is your mother, sister and a comatose police officer. Robert you may notice, has a revolver in his hand.'

'Oh God,' says one. 'They don't look nothing like their pictures on the posters, but you're saying they're the mad twins everyone's looking for.'

'Well, you've found us,' says Bill, oh so cold and threatening. 'Now, I ain't mad, I'm a fucking lunatic and so is my brother. Now, either you drop the truncheons and do as you're told or the killing will start.'

'Do it,' orders I.

The brother's eyes meet. 'I don't know if we can do that…' says one.

'And I don't know if I want to die because you pair of wooden heads haven't got the sense you were born with,' grates Head. 'Do as you're bleedin' told, or me and the Inspector will hammer the shit out of you.'

'What do you think, Ben?' says one.

'I think we best do as we're told, Jack,' says Ben.

They drop their truncheons. I glance at Bill. His eyes are stone cold, his face is contorted, but somehow and for whatever reason I am thankful he held back. Bob is still pointing the revolver towards the plods; he looks out of it, and so far, away he could be anywhere. I know that should Bill have told Bob to shoot, Bob would have done so, firing indiscriminately until the gun was empty. Hopefully, the panic is over and the bloodbath has been avoided.

'Bob,' says Bill. 'Step back from the waggon, but keep ya

pistol aimed at them uniformed coppers. Detectives, get into the waggon.'

We do as we are told.

'You two,' says Bill to the plods. 'Pick up the old couple and help them into the waggon. Don't try anything unless you want ta see ya old man's head fly through the air.'

We help the brothers to bundle the old couple into the waggon then climb in ourselves.

Bill steps over with King, who's eyes are now full of trepidation. I've no doubt the man has never been so terrified or felt so hopeless. He can't do anything except go along with whatever Bill demands. Bill points the sawn-off into the waggon while his eyes tell me he'd happily shoot King's sons. Then he steps back.

'Bob, pull the door shut and then bolt it,' says Bill.

'What, run off?'

'Nah, ya pratt. Bolt the door, not bolt off.'

'Right, Bill,' says Bob. He shuts the door, thus plunging us into darkness, then slides all three bolts in place.

I hear Bill say,' Right, Bob, let's go.'

***

There's an awful smell inside the waggon, the air is suffocating and everyone is squashed up. But at the moment all is quiet as no doubt everyone is trying to come to terms with what has just happened.

'Does anyone have a light?' asks I.

'I don't think you should smoke in here,' says Ben. At least I think it was Ben.

'I do not intend to smoke,' snaps I. 'We need light.'

'I have a box of matches,' says someone. 'Somewhere. Um… Yes.'

A match is struck, highlighting worried shadowy faces that

appear somewhat creepy. Glenda is embracing her daughter at the front of the waggon. Ted is sat on a side bench nursing his head in his hands. The confused looking old couple are sat across from Ted, while the brothers are literally stood to attention with Jack holding up the burning match.

'Right,' says I. 'Open up the port-holes. There are six on each side covered over with wooden circles, just swing them open and let some light and air in.'

'What's that awful smell?' says Ben.

'Sorry my darling,' says Glenda. 'I was so scared it set my trouble off. Try not and stand in that corner,' she points.

'What's going on?' demands Bert, having come to his senses.

'We are temporarily imprisoned inside a police waggon, Mr King' says I.

'What's going to happen to my son?'

'Yes,' cries Glenda, breaking away from her Fanny. 'Where are those vile Chinese men taking him?'

I ignore the question for now and say, 'We must get out of here. But trust me there is no way we would be able to bust out. That would take a battering ram or a kick from an elephant. Our best hope is that someone passes by, we attract their attention and ask them to let us out. Meanwhile I suggest you all try and stay calm. Now, I am Detective Inspector Potter and this is my colleague: Detective Sergeant Head. We are in charge and you will *all* do as we tell you.'

'What about my head?' pipes up Ted. 'I need medical attention. I've got a lump on the back of my skull the size of a very large testicle.'

'Keep rubbing it,' says Head.

'Once we are out of here, I will have you up on an assault charge, Inspector,' says Bert. 'You punched and head butted me, slapped my wife and hit my Willy with your truncheon.'

'Do be quiet, Grandad,' says Ben. 'You are *not* helping the situation.'

Bert is up on his feet, 'Don't you dare talk to me like that, Ben my boy.'

'Someone's coming,' says Head.

I put an eye to the porthole next to where Head is stood. A short skinny tramp in a battered felt hat and ragged coat, while smoking a pipe, is swaying about while sauntering along on the path.

'Excuse me, sir,' yells I. 'Would you mind coming over here?'

He comes to a halt, stares at the waggon for a moment, sways a bit, then says, 'What for?'

'We are locked inside this waggon; would you be so kind as to unbolt the door at the rear and let us out.'

'Bugger off. Do I look like a moron?'

'Regardless of what you look like, sir,' says I. 'Please open the door.'

'What! And let a load of criminals run off into the night? Piss off with ya.'

'I am a policeman. We have been locked in here by criminals who are getting away. Now if you do not let us out this very second, I shall arrest you.'

'No need for that,' says he. 'Look, if you can prove to me, you're a copper, I might let you out if the price is right.'

Ben calls out through another porthole, 'Mr Hind. It is I, Constable Benjamin King. I am trapped in here with my brother, Jack, my sister Fanny, my mother, my grandfather and my grandmother. Will you please let us out and I promise to forget about your little peccadillos?'

'Nothing wrong with havin' a little peccadillo,' says he.

'Oh, what's this then?' Turning his attention to the discarded items we had to jettison he bends over and picks up the umbrella, opens it up and holds it up to keep the rain off. Mumbling away to himself he picks up and pockets the whistles. He then spies my bowler hat. Throwing away his hat he puts my bowler on and looks over. 'Fits like a sheath,' slurs he.

'You may keep the hat,' says I. 'If you let us out.'

Ignoring me he picks up my short truncheon and shoves it in a coat pocket, leaving the end sticking out. He then decides to take the other truncheons which disappear inside his coat. Lastly, he picks up the walking stick.

'Listen here, my good man,' says I. 'If you do not let us out right now, you will be in serious trouble.'

'So, you say,' says he.

With that he saunters off while whistling a happy tune and swinging the stick up and down.

'I'll have him for that,' grates Jack. 'How dare he walk off with other people's possessions, not to mention government property?'

Five minutes later we hear singing. Peering through the porthole, I spy a pair of hatless, thickset labourers with their arms over each other's shoulders while swaying along in the road.

'Gentlemen,' calls I. 'Can you come over here.'

They stop singing, turn to the side and stare over.

'Could you kindly help us,' says I. 'We are locked in this waggon.'

Unlocking arms, they come over.

'Locked in, is it?' says the dark haired one. 'How did ya manage that, me ol' darlin'?'

'It is a long story,' says I. 'Would you be so kind as to go to the rear of the waggon and unbolt the door?'

'What do ya think, Patrick?' says the ginger haired one.

'For sure it'll do no harm to take a look, Shaun.'

'I'm with ya there, Patrick. So, I am.'

They disappear from view; we hear the bolts rattling a bit and then they return.

'To be sure, you're locked in,' smiles Patrick. 'And with no way out unless someone unbolts the door. But then I'm thinkin', so I am, that you're probably criminals and it'd be a bad thing to let you out, so it would, the police wouldn't like it.'

'We *are* policemen,' grates I.

'I don't believe it,' says Shaun.

'Well, it is true. In fact, there are five policemen inside this waggon along with an elderly couple, a mother and her daughter.'

'What do you think, Shaun?' says Patrick.

'I'm thinkin', Patrick, havin' been locked inside one of these myself, so I was, there's no way they'll be able to bust out unless someone lets them out.'

'I'm thinkin' the same. So, I am.'

'There will be a reward if you let us out,' says I.

'We'll have to discuss it,' says Shaun.

Stepping back out of ear wigging range, they face each other and have a whispered discussion. After swaying about and nodding to each other they disappear towards the front of the waggon.

'What's going on?' says Jack.

'Not sure,' says I. 'But I could hazard a guess.'

The rattling of harnesses being uncoupled tells me my guess is correct.

'I believe they are stealing the horses,' says I.

'Stealing my horses?' groans Ted. 'Please tell me it isn't so.'

Only it is, confirmed by the clip clopping of hooves on the road with Patrick and Shaun's voices singing merrily while fading away into the night along with the horses.

'The bastards,' says Ted. 'I'm bloody well for it now.' He's up on his feet and pointing a rigid finger at me, while his face is twisted up with temper. 'It's all your fault. Call yourself a detective. You couldn't detect a gas leak without lighting a match.'

'Please…' cries Fanny. 'I must get out of here. It's smelly and I can't breathe properly.'

'Fear not, madam,' says I. 'Someone will come along shortly and let us out.'

'Well, I'm not waiting any longer,' says Ben. 'Come on, Jack, let's bust our way out.'

'You'll be wasting your time,' says Head. 'And the only thing you'll achieve is to give yourselves… um… what are they called, Inspector?'

'Hernia's.'

'Not Hyena's then?' grins he.

'Not of late,' says I. Typical of Head to take the piss just because I occasionally mix up my words. But then, doesn't everyone at times?

'Hernias and Hyenas aside, sir' says Ben, 'we have to at least try. If everyone will squash up and give us more room, we shall charge the door.'

What can I say, I did warn them? 'Alright everyone, squash up, please.'

'Move along the tram,' says Head.

We squash up to the front of the waggon.

'Bloody hell!' moans Bert. 'I've just put a foot into that mess in the corner.'

Ben and Jack remove their helmets and jackets and place

them on the bench. Stepping back a few paces they brace themselves. Ben counts to three and they charge, slamming their shoulders into the door with a loud thud, but to no avail. The door doesn't even groan.

'Let's try again,' says Jack.

They do so, again and again, until after six attempts they abandon their human battering ram act and have a go at trying to kick the door down. Apart from creating an unbelievable amount of noise which would scare the pigeons off Nelsons Column two miles away, again they fail miserably. But we did warn them.

'It's no use,' says Jack, breathing heavily while rubbing his shoulder.

'What now?' gasps Ben as he wipes the sweat from his brow.

His heart is beating that loudly I can hear it. On top of realising their efforts were utterly wasted they will have some serious bruises to contend with for a few days.

'We keep looking out and hope someone else comes by before too long,' says I. 'As no doubt the neighbours heard the noise, perhaps one of them will venture out to see what's amiss.'

'I'm thirsty,' says Fanny.

'Plenty of water in the horse's barrel,' says Ted.

'Which is attached to the waggon on the outside,' grates I.

Suddenly we hear the unmistakable sound of a dog yapping.

'That's my little Willy,' cries Flo' as she pushes her way through and sticks her face to the grille. 'Willy! Willy! You're back. Oh, you clever boy. Mummy's little angel. Now listen, Willy, mummy is trapped in here, be a good boy and undo the bolts and then you can come in and join me.'

'She's lost the plot,' whispers Head. 'Stark starring bonkers.'

Willy is now yapping like crazy, but I don't think he's quite understood what he's supposed to be doing as I cannot hear the bolts being shifted. Just then a voice from outside speaks.

'What's up little chap?'

Willy cuts the yapping and replaces it with whimpering.

'Dear Mr Crisp,' says Flo' through the grille. 'Poor willy wants to come in and join the family but he can't undo the bolts.'

'Ah… So, you want to go inside do you, little chap? That's it, you sit and Uncle Morris will undo the nasty bolts for you.'

The sound of the bolts being pulled back floods my senses. Never in the history of mankind has such a joyous sound been heard. Within a moment the door is opened and everyone cheers. Willy leaps into the waggon and jumps up into Flo's crushing embrace. In an orderly manner we all push, shove and pile our way out.

Outside, with a face like an acorn, stands an elderly gentleman in a dark dressing gown and indoor slippers.

'Thank you, sir, for letting us out,' says I.

He gives me the once over through baggy bloodshot eyes and says, 'I didn't let you out, I let the little chap *in*. There is a difference.'

'There is indeed,' confuses I.

After very reluctantly finding himself having to shake hands with everyone while receiving pats on his back and shoulders, Mr Crisp mumbles his excuses and slopes off.

Glenda invites us all into the house for a stiff one, drink that is and not the other kind of stiff one. Everyone is now relieved and subsequently relaxed. As no one has mentioned him, I fear Kevin King has been temporarily forgotten while they all celebrate their release. So, once coffee and brandies have been handed round and the hero of the day, Willy of course, has been toasted, I feel it is my duty to inform the Kings of the possible consequences of Kevin's kidnap. It is a sobering moment as the reality of Kevin Kings terrible predicament fully sinks in. Glenda falls into Flo's arms as they both start wailing, while Bert rants and raves about what he's going to do to those twins when he catches them, and the brothers make a vow to track the twins down and render them impotent for ever.

After promising the King family that we will do our upmost to save their loved one, and reassuring them that they are safe as the twins will not return, Head, Ted and I say our goodbyes.

It is raining steadily as we head to the end of the road to hopefully catch a hackney back to the Yard. Half way up the road the sky decides to dump an ocean on us. We are soaked to the skin by the time we eventually flag down a hackney and climb wearily in.

'Scotland Yard, please driver,' says I. 'And don't spare the horse.'

The cab takes four passengers, if you don't mind being squashed up, or knee touching whoever is opposite you. Head and I sit together with Ted opposite us. Head is unusually quiet and close to dropping off, probably because he hasn't had his dinner and isn't likely to get it until well after seven. Apart from the occasional mumble and grumble, Ted seems somewhat subdued and deep in thought.

If I've learnt nothing else this day, I am thankful for the lesson in life that Glenda King gave me. Head and I assumed the woman was somewhat of a drip when she asked Morris Crisp to open the waggon door so Willy could get in, when she should have simply asked him to let everyone inside, out. But she was right: "If I'd have asked Morris to let us out, he would have snubbed me and walked away with Willy following," she'd said. "You see, Morris has had several confrontations over the years with my Kevin. As a consequence, Morris has no time for anyone in my family except for Willy. I applied a little psychology on Morris and it worked. As for Willy, he may belong to my mother in-law, but he is a treacherous little devil who will go to anyone who'll spoil him, and Morris spoils him rotten."

Head and I haven't had a chance to discuss the consequences of today's events as I'd prefer not to discuss such matters in front of Ted. I am dreading reporting back to Clump on our miserable failure to complete what should have been a relatively easy task. Clump is going to have us keel-hauled while facing a firing squad, beheaded while being burnt at the stake and for a piece de resistance, to ensure we can never return to earth, he'd fire our ashes from a cannon towards the moon. But if he's in a fair-minded mood, we might just find ourselves paraded before the Chief Constable for demotion and excommunication to police some distant colony that's notorious for cannibalism.

This time there is no escaping our fate. The twins have been a step ahead of us all the way. They set us up good and proper by gambling that once we'd had word that French had been butchered; we'd get the order to bring the Kings in. All the twins had to do was wait, watch and follow. No doubt the twins have ruined our careers and left us at the mercy of all those who have dreamed of seeing the day when Gerry Pot and Dick Head got knocked right off their perches and landed in the gutter. We practically delivered one of our own, rotten as King is, straight into the arms of a pair of psychopaths. We will *never* live this down.

Despite everything, I cannot hate the twins. Bill and Bob could have easily topped me and Head. Done serious damage to the King family or slaughtered them all. So why didn't they? Certainly, Bill looked on the point of losing it when the King brothers turned up, but he remained calm, in control and very much on the high ground.

What the twins did to French was like something from the Spanish Inquisition. Considering the fact that Kevin King is their main target; I dread to think what they're probably putting him through at this very moment. Much more than a severe caning across his naked rump, I fear.

Ted suddenly comes to life. 'I've been thinking, sir,' says he, while smiling at me. 'That I should receive some kind of a reward for injuries sustained while in the dereliction of my duty.'

'Or even in the dedication of your duty,' corrects I. Ted got hit on the head and locked into the waggon he was in charge of and had his horses stolen while doing nothing of any worth that showed heroism or fortitude in his policing. I can't see him receiving much more than a spit in the eye reward. However, I can't be bothered to argue and fish out my note pad and pen. 'I shall put your case to my chief. If he thinks it has merit, he will forward it on to the Chief Constable. Full name, please.'

He sits up straight. 'Constable Edward Archibald Leach,' beams he. 'Ted to my friends.'

'Edward it is then,' says I and duly jot down a few notes.

With a gloriously happy smile on his face, Ted slumps back and closes his eyes.

***

Clump is stood up behind his desk, I believe he dare not come out from behind it in case he tries to strangle us. His scruffy mop is standing on end all stiff and spiky as if it's been electrified, his eyes are on fire while flames and steam shoot out from his ears and mouth.

Head and I are sat facing him having shrunk to the size of cringing worms.

'Allow me to abbreviate all you have told me while putting it in laymen's terms,' says he like a scorpion about to strike. 'You useless moronic imbeciles not only allowed a pair of weedy urchins to kidnap your prisoner from right under your noses, you also handed them your revolvers without so much as a protest. You then allowed them to herd you, near on the entire King family and this Constable Leach into the back of a police waggon meant for criminals, like lambs to the slaughter.

'You then allowed a tramp to skip off with three truncheons, two whistles, an umbrella and a walking stick. Oh… not forgetting your bowler hat. Still, it gets worse. A pair of friendly Micks happened by and merrily walk off with two of the finest heavy horses the Yard has ever owned. On top of all this, you, Inspector, managed to punch and headbutt an elderly gentleman, give his wife a slap and give her Willy a resounding rap with your truncheon.'

I could try and protest here; Willy's teeth were imbedded in my calf at the time. Better to keep quiet and let him rant on.

'It was fortunate for the pair of you that Willy had no malice towards you or he may not have helped to secure your escape.'

Sitting down he opens the draw and pulls out a bottle and one glass. Then he gives us an odd look before taking out two more glasses. Good, Head and I are desperate for a drink.

'Still,' says Clump as he fills the glasses. 'We have all had days when nothing goes right.'

I venture to ask, 'What will happen to us, Chief?'

'Nothing for now. I need to get my head around it all. Our priority is to catch the twins before they commit ever more horrendous crimes. Unfortunately, I need you two to help with that. I hate to say it, but you two are still the best hope we have. God save us.'

He fills the glasses and pushes two over. 'Right. I shall update you on what, Detectives Barnsley and Thompson unearthed. In a nutshell, French and King sailed very close to the wind throughout their careers in the force. Both had been reprimanded on numerous occasions for insubordination, gross brutality towards the criminals they arrested, not that anyone cared in most cases. But we are still answerable to the do-goods out there and of course we should be above criticism.

'Several complaints from members of the public regarding their delivering of punishments, particularly the birching of the twins. The Reverend Albert Shields, who you met,' he raises his bushy eyebrows, 'wrote a scathing half a book on the: "Revolting excessive punishment" the twins received at the hands of French and King.

'However, French and King were also extremely brave and formidable officers when it came to tracking down and arresting some of the most dangerous criminals you could come up against. Both received numerous awards, including bravery awards, while blind eyes were turned when it came to, shall we say, French and King going beyond the call of duty. French in particular got away with, shall we say, his penchant for young boys.'

'Ah…' says I. 'Hence the truncheon up his ring piece.'

'Exactly. I fear it is already too late to rescue King before too much damage has been done. Strictly between these four walls, I do not have much sympathy for King, but I do for his family who sound pretty damn decent.'

Head and I nod our agreement.

'Drink up lads,' says Clump with a wry smile.

We drink up. he refills the glasses and then lights a cigar before glancing at the clock on the wall.

'Good grief, is that the time? Nine thirty. Let's hurry this up or we shall be here all night. We have the autopsy in on French. He died, no less, of a heart attack obviously brought on by being tortured. I sent two officers to the funeral directors to ask if they knew where the twins are holed up. They couldn't help except to say the twins told them they would not be working for them for the forceable future. With no one coming forwards with any information as to where the twins might be, we are nowhere.'

'The trouble is, Chief,' says Head. 'If we couldn't recognise them, even close up, in their Chinese costumes how the hell would anyone else recognise them? For all we know they could be in this very station right now having a look round, just for the hell of it.'

Exhaling dramatically and hitting our faces with a cloud of smoke, Clump appears, for once, somewhat defeated. He doesn't know where to go next on this.

An idea springs to mind. 'I have a friend in the theatre business,' says I. 'Amongst other things he rents out costumes to individuals and especially theatres all over London and beyond. I shall go and speak to him; you never know he might just have rented those costumes to the twins.'

'Not a bad idea, Inspector,' says Clump. 'It's better than doing nothing while hoping something will turn up. Any other ideas?'

We shake our heads just as Heads stomach gives out a rumbling groan.

'If you are on the point of delivering us gas, Sergeant,' grates Clump. 'Kindly go outside and let it off.'

'It's not gas, sir,' sulks Head. 'It is hunger. My stomach thinks my throats been cut, as nothing has been delivered to it for hours other than liquids.'

'You'll survive,' sighs Clump. 'Right, piss off the pair of you. Go home, fill your belly's, cuddle your loved ones and get a good night's sleep.'

'What if King's body should turn up?' asks I.

'Then someone on night duty will have to deal with it until we get there in the morning. Get going and straight home with no detours to the pub.'

'I'll have to nip in somewhere for something to eat,' says Head.

'Can't you wait until you get home?' grates Clump.

'What for, Chief? Burnt offerings all dried up on the plate and as appetising as a fermented turd sandwich?'

'I did not send messages to your loved ones to warn them that you will be late home. No doubt you did the same, despite it being standard practice. Your dinner may well be ruined, Sergeant Head, but I don't give a rat's arse. Get yourselves home, now! That is an order.'

Head stands up while glaring into Clumps even more furious glare. I am thinking we are on thin ground here and do not want to push it, we are in enough shit now without exasperating the situation just because, Head's guts are empty.

'Right,' say I grabbing Head's arm. 'Time to go.'

Walnut House

I finally make it home just before ten, having made certain, Head went straight home and straight indoors. We'd managed to scrounge a lift with a police waggon that was then about to depart for a ruckus in an inn not far from Heads place. Head was keen to join in the impending assault on the fighting drunks at the inn, but I knew he was really hoping to get a meal and I was having none of it. If he is ever to sort his problem out with Chloe's cooking, running away from it isn't the way.

On entering through the front door, I find Betty sat in the parlour reading a book.

'Goodness, Detective Inspector,' says she, putting aside her book and getting to her feet. 'Wherever have you been? You should have let me know you were going to be this late.'

I take her in my arms and give her a big squash and a long kiss on the lips.

'Sorry, my darling,' says I holding her at arm's length. 'It has been one hell of a day.'

'Well, you're home safe and sound and that is all that matters. Now, take the weight off your big plates of meat and sit down with a scotch while I heat up the lovely lamb casserole I made. Then you can tell me all about it. Unless of course you'd rather do something else first?'

'I best unwind first, Betty. Drink, relax, dinner and then decide what's next.'

She gives me a kiss and swings away to the kitchen. I noted no scent of sherry or anything else on her and am pleased about it. It often worries me that when I'm going to be late home, Betty sometimes hits the bottle too much. It is her way of coping with the fear, the worry and the what ifs. One day it may happen, I leave home and I don't come back except via the angels. Such is the lot of all who work in dangerous occupations. All that aside there's a thousand and one ways to find yourself dead before your time even if you never leave your house. I settle down on the sofa with a scotch, just as Betty returns.

'Dinner is in the oven,' smiles she plonking herself down beside me. 'Half an hour should do it. Now then, Detective Inspector, tell me how you got on with, Richard. Has he agreed to try an awful lot harder to eat his dinners and make Chloe happy?'

'Hopefully, yes. Unhopefully no. I shall be finding out tomorrow. However, I am assured that he is at least going to try a lot harder.'

'Good, I hope so. Because if he doesn't, he's going to find that when he comes home there will be no wafting aromas of delicious meats roasting in the oven. No beer poured and should he want a bath he'll have to fill it himself…'

I shoot her the 'oh hell' look. 'Chloe's going to leave him?'

She shakes her head. 'She loves him too much to leave him. She's just not going to be treated like a servant any more. Or come to that, a sex Goddess.'

'Ah…' says I while thinking that an awful lot of women would like nothing more than to be treated like any kind of Goddess. 'So, Chloe will be shutting up shop in more ways than one. Obviously, she has been around today for the woman-to-woman chat, more commonly known as a war counsel, or a how to psychologically castrate a male by downing tools, kind of counsel.'

'That, Detective Inspector is a vile analogy and is unworthy of you. Chloe did pop round, just for a few hours. She's still so upset over not being able to please Richard at meal times. But in every other way she knows she more than meets the criteria of a wonderful wife…'

'So, your plan of action is for Chloe to stop doing all those things he loves her for, while sort of appeasing him by not cooking for him.'

'Exactly. But if she doesn't cook for him, he also doesn't get to drink in those wonderful aromas as he comes trotting into the kitchen after a long hard day, or even a short easy day…'

'Oh… I get it now.' I take a swallow of my scotch and have to admit it doesn't taste as good as Clump's. Perhaps I can 'borrow' a bottle from him.

Betty gives me a jab with her finger. 'You're drifting off, Detective Inspector.'

After a long yawn, I say, 'I am tired, Betty. In truth I am so tired I have not only lost my appetite, I'm not even that interested, at this particular moment in time, in Richard's domestic problems. Can we talk about it later?'

She takes the glass from me and sets it down on the floor. I wasn't really enjoying it anyway.

'You really have had a bad day, haven't you?' She cups my face and gazes into my eyes. 'Something has upset you beyond the usual, hasn't it?'

I nod, but how to explain it to her. For now, I would rather just leave it.

She reads my mind. 'Forget everything for now, Detective Inspector. You shall eat as much of your dinner as you fancy. Then I shall get you stripped off, freshened up and ready for bed.'

'Not sure if I can even raise the enthusiasm for love maker…'

She puts a finger to my lips. 'Say, nothing more, my love. Close your eyes for a bit, while I boil up a few gallons of water enough to give you a strip wash. We can leave everything else until the morning. But should you come out on parade during the night I will be ready. In fact, I shall check whether or not you are stood to attention or merely at ease before I cuddle right up to you.'

***

By morning, after a decent night's sleep, I am feeling better in my mind. Although I still cannot get the twins out of my head, they are not taking over my every thought, but they are certainly invading it. What is it when it comes to them? They seem to have a hold on me, almost as if I have to continually question myself over whether or not I want to see them succeed in their quest for revenge, or, I want to see them caught and punished. In this job it doesn't pay to have any kind of empathy with criminals of the twin's calibre. They are brutal, clever, well Bill certainly is, unforgiving and determined. Yet they are vulnerable, almost innocents, still boys.

'You look lost in thought,' says Betty as she places a plate of bacon and eggs before me on the kitchen table. 'Are you still mulling over the ethics of what you know you must do?'

'Sorry my little mind reader. I am indeed still mulling over how I feel about the twins. They are killers, torturers, thieves and ne'er-do-wells, but still, I have this guilt inside me, for it is the very institution I work in that set the twins on their pathway to hell. In short, French and King lost the right to call themselves upholders of law and liberty the day they tortured two undernourished urchins.

'No one took French and King to task. They were not tried for their crimes. The law cannot ever justify itself when it does not treat everyone the same. I know I'm no angel, but I do have standards, and although I'm happy to give an urchin a ringer around the lugs I could not beat any of them half to death.'

'And no one cares, do they, Detective Inspector?' says Betty as she sits down beside me and takes my hand. 'But actually, there are *those* who care and are forever trying to improve the lot of the poor. It is an uphill battle, but gradually things are improving…'

'But not fast enough, Betty.'

'True,' smiles she. 'However, life will go on and you must go on while remembering all the filth you have helped to clean off our streets. But if the job has become too much for you to bear, then you must get out…'

'And do what? I love my job, most of the time, and cannot image doing anything else.'

She gives me a peck on the cheek and stands up. 'Then you must do what you think best. If this case is eating you up then ask Clump if he can replace you and put you on something else. Now, eat your breakfast, Detective Inspector, Richard will be here in a bit.'

'Well, he better be in a good mood, because I am not in the mood to put up with his moaning and sulking should he not have enjoyed whatever, Chloe dished him up last night and this morning. If he goes off on one, he'll be receiving the biggest ear full he's ever had.'

***

'I couldn't believe it,' beams Head as we board a tram at the end of my street. 'I walk in to the kitchen to be greeted with hugs, kisses and tears from a woman trembling with relief that I was home safe and sound.'

Relieved that he's in a great mood, I joke, 'What woman was that, Richard?'

We sit down side by side, the tram is packed so whatever you say, be assured that someone will be earwigging.

'Chloe of course. But, Gerald, what amazed me the most was, afterwards…'

'Afterwards what exactly?'

He gives me the odd look. 'You know, the… um… comforting her part. Anyway, where was I?'

An old witch behind us leans forwards and sticks her warty nose in, 'What amazed you the most.'

'Oh… yes. Thank you, Mrs, but kindly mind your own business.'

'Or what?' snaps she.

'You will find your broomstick lacking sunshine.'

'Are you going to let that great big oaf talk to me like that, Cyril?'

I crane my neck round to see a cringing in his seat very small man who was wishing he was somewhere else. 'Yes,' says he.

'So be it,' sulks she sitting back and folding her arms.

'To continue,' says Head. 'Chloe served me up a warmed-up steak pie, mash and gravy. The pastry was well charred on the edges, the gravy had all but been boiled away to a thick gloop and the mash was a bit lumpy. But my goodness, was it lip smacking delicious.'

'Good,' says I. 'And breakfast?'

'Ham and eggs with crusty bread and butter. Marvellous.'

'The moral of this tale, Richard, is that last night you were genuinely really hungry and realised that Chloe's cooking is nowhere near as bad as you think it is. And I believe you have finally turned a corner.'

A broad smile crosses his mouth. 'By God, am I one lucky man or am I not?'

'You are indeed a lucky man, Richard. As am I.'

'There you are, Cyril,' pipes up the old witch. 'Men who appreciate their wives, unlike you!'

'But then they are not married to *you*,' drawls he.

Fortunately for us the pair get off at the next stop to be replaced by a pair of noisy giggling girls who are so wrapped up in each other they couldn't care less about anyone else's conversations.

'So,' says Head. 'What's the plan of action, today?'

'We are going to see my friend, Robert Soberly, the costume supplier I mentioned last night. If he doesn't know where the twins hired the Chinese costumes from, he will still be able to give us the addresses of all the hirers of costumes in and around London.'

'There could be loads of costume hirers and fancy-dress hirers,' says Head. 'But what if the twins didn't hire the costumes? What if they stole them? Or hired or even bought them from somewhere way out from London.'

'Then we will have wasted our time. The trouble is, Richard I am at a loss what else we can do. We have not had one snippet of information as to where the twins could be hiding out. No one's heard a thing, or they're not saying because they see the twins as heroes. French and King made a lot of enemies in the underworld. An underworld that will be celebrating their demise.'

'You think, King will turn up dead?'

'Most likely. If he turns up still alive, rest assured, he will never ride a horse again.'

***

Just under an hour later we are stood outside a neat detached Georgian house in white stone with a cast iron railing and a set of steps up to the black door. We are in a narrow muse just off from Bond Street.

'Very posh,' says Head gazing up to the third-floor windows. 'If it wasn't for the brass plate on the wall, you'd have no idea this was a costume hire shoppy thing.'

'Very much aimed at the wealthy, Richard,' says I. 'Quality costumes from all over the world. Robert Soberly and I joined the Met' together. We became good friends and he was on course to becoming a good copper. But he got the bug to get rich and turned to crime instead…'

'You're pulling my plonker,' says Head.

'No, I'm not. Robert opened a clothes stall and sold affordable, quality clothes all-over London. Only on the best market patches I might add…'

'Where was the crime in that?'

'Half the stuff was nicked. He did a couple of years in the nick, came out and then went into supplying theatres with costumes. Long story, but he has done well. Let's hope he's in.'

We go up the stairs and I ring the bell. The door opens in under a minute and we are confronted with a suitably uniformed young maid with a bright smile and shiny red hair beneath her maids cap. She curtsies.

'Good morning, gentlemen. ''Ow may I be of assistance,' coos she.

'Good morning, Miss,' says I flashing my warrant card. 'I am Detective Inspector Potter and this is my college, Detective

Sergeant Head. We wish to speak to Mr Robert Soberly.'

She curtsies again. 'Do you 'ave an appointment, sir?'

'We are policemen, Miss and do not need an appointment.'

Now she appears somewhat worried. 'I'll 'ave to ask Mr Soberly if it's all right for you to come in.'

'Whatever for?' grates Head.

'I can't say,' says she with another curtsy.

'It is an offence to refuse to answer a policeman's questions, Miss. And can carry a prison sentence for perverting the course of justice. Do you understand what I am saying?'

'No. But I ain't done nothing wrong and I ain't perverted no one. You see if I ain't,' says she as her cheeks turn as red as a cockerel's woggle.

I lean a little closer to her and whisper, 'Tell us what you can't say and I promise you will not feel the strong arm of the law.'

'I don't know what you mean. Strong arm of the law, what's that about?'

'We will not arrest you,' smiles I.

'Alright,' says she so quietly she is barely audible. 'Robert. I mean, Mr Soberly, 'as told me that if the police call, I'm not to let them in without telling him first in case he has to make a run for it.'

'Thank you, Miss. Go then and inform Mr Soberly that the police are here to arrest him and if he whips out the back and over the wall he will probably get away.'

She curtsies then gives me a wan look before shutting the door in my face.

'You were a bit cruel there, Gerald,' grins Head. 'The poor girl looked terrified. Why didn't you tell her you're a friend of this Robert Soberly?'

'Sorry, I couldn't help it, Richard. Anyway, knowing

Robert as I do, I would image the young maid's real duties stretch far beyond opening doors to callers.'

'Bit of a dirty old man, is he?'

'He's the same age as *me*,' protests I.

'Exactly. I rest my case.'

The door opens again and this time we are confronted by a tallish fair-haired man with a neat moustache and long sideboards. His peacock patterned cravat and tweed jacket give him an air of sophistication, while his soft blue eyes give out an aura of deep understanding, intelligence, breeding and class.

'Well roger a donkey,' laughs he holding out a hand. 'Gerry Pot you ol' cock sucker. And with reinforcements,' grins he giving Head the once over.

'Detective Sergeant Richard Head,' says Head.

'Come in, come in,' says Robert as he steps aside and waves us in.

After handshakes all round and the usual; how are you, how's this and that, Robert leads the way down a long corridor with pale walls covered in quality paintings. Having previously done the grand tour I know how stylish, Robert's home, stroke business, is. The drawing room is furnished in the French style, very baroque and very expensive. Robert shows us in and we sit down on a bright blue settee with deep red hard wood ends that curl up and then twist around and around at the end like a sailor's rope. It is pure luxury.

Robert falls back onto a matching settee opposite us.

'Tea, coffee or something stronger, though I must say it's a bit early?' says Robert.

'Coffee please,' says I.

'Coffee please,' says Head. 'And a few biscuits if you don't mind.'

Robert picks up a small bell that was on the coffee table that stands between the settees.

'I've yet to install bell cords in this room that connect with the servant's hall,' says Robert. 'So, if I call or tinkle a little bell, no one will hear unless they're within ten feet of the door. So, I clang this evil sod.' He holds it up to show us. 'Cover your ears.'

We do so. Robert clangs the bell and it is so loud it could not only wake the dead but make them stone deaf in the process.

The maid we have already met appears. 'You rang, Rob', I mean, sir,' says she with a curtsy.

'I did, Mary. Go and tell Margaret to rustle up coffee for three with a few cakes and biscuits.'

'Would that be the best cakes and biscuits or the cheap shit ones? Sir.'

'These gentlemen are my friends, Mary. Do you think they look cheap?'

She shrugs with obvious indifference.

'Never mind,' sighs Robert. 'Bring the posh stuff.'

'Very good, sir,' says she with a curtsy.

'She's getting there,' says Robert. 'I've only had her three times over the last month or so since she's been here, and it's taking time to coach the slum out of her and turn her into something more genteel. But then I must admit I do send out mixed messages to the girl, because I myself, still can't get the slum fully out of my system.'

'Nor I,' says I.

'And I'm the same,' says Head. 'Once in it never forgotten. No matter how well you're doing in your life you'll still have the occasion nightmare of how miserable your life was as a kid. And there's always that haunting fear of falling on hard times and ending up back there.'

Robert sweeps an arm around the huge room and says, 'I

have all this. Any one room in this house, including the toilets, contains more wealth in it then the entire wealth of the street where I grew up, times ten, maybe even times a hundred. I also have those nightmares, Sergeant, but nowhere near as real as they used to be. Obviously, you're not here to arrest me, or you would have done it by now. I assume you need a favour.'

'On the information side, Robert,' says I. 'We need to pick your brains.'

***

'You could have knocked me down with a brick,' says Head as we leave Robert's house behind and head for Marylebone in a hackney. 'Who'd have thought half his huge garden would have a posh warehouse in it that contained over a thousand costumes.'

'He has hundreds more, Richard if you count all the costumes that are out, plus two other outlets that cater for those with not so deep pockets. Robert is the biggest supplier of costumes in all of London. He is a darling to the rich and the aristocratic. Whatever they want he will supply even if he has to have it made.'

'I liked the bloke. Bloody funny sod as well.' He smiles to himself. 'I loved the tale of the naïve young couple who'd been invited to a posh naturist party and had no idea what costume to wear. "Are you sure you do not mean a naturalist party, madam, sir?" He'd asked them in his posh voice. "One is not sure what you mean, Mr Soberly," said the gentleman. "A naturist is someone who enjoys the alfresco life while dressed in the altogether, sir," said Robert… Then, before Robert could explain what a naturalist was the gentleman said: "Then, sir, that is what we require. Two altogether costumes."

'Marvellous,' chuckles I. 'It proved a point though, Richard. Not all aristocrats are decadent pleasure seekers.

When he finally got through to them that they were expected to turn up for the party stark naked, and as such did not require a costume, the lady passed out on the Persian carpet and the gentleman broke out into a sweat and started to shake like a jelly.'

'I wouldn't mind spending a boozy night with your friend, Gerald. I reckon it would be one hell of a laugh.'

'Robert was keen to have us back, so, Richard, I think you and I should have a man's night out sometime soon. Down to business. According to Robert, the most likely candidates from whom the twins may have obtained the posh Chinese costumes are; one Cedric Bolsover and one Harvey Major who live together at Walnut House, on Marylebone High Street opposite a small row of very upmarket shops and restaurants.

'If the twins did not obtain the costumes from these gentlemen, then I'm afraid, Richard, you and I will have an awful amount of foot slogging to do.'

Head lets out a groan. 'Theatres, shops that rent out or sell costumes, other individuals and not to mention all those all over London who manufacture the costumes. We'll be tramping the streets for ever, Gerald. By the time we find out where the twins got the costumes, we'd have probably died of gout through too much leg use.'

'Sometimes, Richard your cynicism appals me.'

'And rightly so, Gerald. It even appals me at times.'

We continue the journey in relevant silence, while I wonder whether or not, King's body has turned up yet and who's next on the list. Would it not be a good idea to try and find out more about the twins' past? It may lead us to others who crossed their paths and thus place us in a position where we, for once, are a step ahead. The process would be daunting, but if the line of enquiry we are on now doesn't bear fruit, I cannot think of any other way forwards.

At last, we reach Marylebone High Street and I call for the driver to take it slowly so we can keep an eye out for Walnut House. I then spy a plod heading towards us and tell the driver to pull over and stop.

'Constable,' calls I sticking my head out of the hackney. 'A word if you please.'

He stops and says, 'Certainly, sir. How may I assist you?'

After a quick introduction I ask, 'Can you tell me where, Walnut House is?'

'I can, Inspector,' he points. 'The fifth house along on this side. Would you care for me to show you?'

'Very much so, Constable Soames. Thankyou.'

I pay the driver and we alight. The path we are on is wide and relatively devoid of people. Across the road there are many more pedestrians going about their business. There's half a dozen posh shops and two very expensive looking restaurants.

Constable Soames has a full set of mostly grey hair covering his jolly round face and he marches along the pavement in a way that portrays how proud he is of his position in life.

'What can you tell us about this, Bolsover and Major, Constable?' says I.

'Nice fellows, sir. Late middle-aged eccentric academics. Very wealthy, but you wouldn't think so when you see the state of their house. That's inside and out. They've been burgled a few times but it doesn't seem to bother them much. They take life as it comes and are equally at home in the company of toffs or street urchins.'

'That is odd,' says I. 'The wealthy normally avoid the poor like the plague. What makes these two so different?'

'Experiments, Inspector. Bolsover and Major are forever into something that requires volunteers from all walks of life.

It is all academic stuff. They record information from their experiments and then write pamphlets and articles about their findings to present to scientific bodies.'

'That all sounds rather creepy to me,' says Head. 'They're not into sawing off people's skulls to poke around in their brain boxes, are they?'

'Nothing of the sort, Sergeant,' chuckles Soames. 'They are, like I say eccentrics, but they are harmless. May I ask why you wish to speak to them?'

'You may. We are on the trail of a pair of twins, that's one set not two, known as the Boyles. You may have heard of them, Constable.'

He stops dead and we face each other. 'I *certainly* have heard of them, sir. Their wanted posters are all over the place, except around here, too posh to have to suffer the ugly face of the criminal class. I also heard about that Constable French's murder before it appeared in this morning's papers. Not only that I knew of the twins a few years ago. I even saw them alight a carriage and then enter Walnut House…'

This revelation smacks me in the face.

'Tell me more, Constable.'

He shrugs, 'Not much to tell, sir. The twins were escorted into the house by a very shifty looking character, who I found out later was one: Razor Williams…'

'We are familiar with the name, Constable. Please continue.'

'Well, that was more or less it, really. By chance I saw this Williams character and the twins come out of the house roughly two hours later at about ten pm, climb into a carriage and head off.'

'And the twins looked none the worse for wear?'

'No. Perfectly fine.'

'Can you recall how they were dressed?'

'Quite smart. Dark trousers and jackets with white shirts and decent shoes. I'd never have believed they were anything other than fairly posh kids if it wasn't for who they were with.'

'Do you know what went on inside the house while Razor and the twins were there?'

'No idea other than to say it would have almost certainly been something experimental.'

The mind boggles, thinks I, but I won't speculate at this moment. Head has other ideas.

'Razor Williams was a pimp,' says he. 'And pimps sell flesh. If he dressed up two ragged urchins in fine clothes, he would have known he was going to get his money back plus a profit. The twins would be a gift to those with perversions, male or female.'

'I'm not following, Sergeant,' says Soames.

Head gives him his don't be a twat look. 'The poor little sods probably got rogered, Constable along with God knows what else.'

'Oh…' says he with an inflection of guilt. 'I never thought.'

'Something we are all guilty of at times, Constable,' says I. 'Did you report what you've just told us to your superiors at the time, or have you done so recently?'

'Neither.'

'Why not?'

'Um… I didn't think it was worth reporting at any time.'

I shake my head in frustration. 'If you'd have reported it at the time, something may have been done about it, Constable and five years on we might not be where we are now. And if you'd at least mentioned what you witnessed back then, the second you saw the wanted posters, we may have been where we are now two days ago and thus caught the twins before they tortured, Constable French or kidnapped Sergeant King. Assuming of course the twins have been hiding out in Walnut House.'

'Sorry, sir,' says he looking suitably glum. 'I've been keeping an eye out but I haven't seen the twins around this area. I suppose I reasoned they'd be hiding out in the slums.'

'In truth, Constable we all thought the same. Now, have you seen anyone odd looking going in or out of Walnut House recently.'

'Yes, I have, sir,' says he excitedly. 'There were two females who went in there at about five pm the other night. They looked odd to me because they were both dressed in exactly the same theatrical red dresses with big hats decorated with Ostridge feathers…'

'Were they about the same height?' says I. 'Roughly five feet seven?'

He nods. 'I didn't see *them* come out, but then I can't stand around watching one place all night, but I *did* see two Chinese men come out at about seven. Pleasant chaps, they spoke to me in Chinese…'

'Do you speak Chinese?' says Head.

'No, Sergeant I don't.'

'So, you didn't understand what they said to you?'

He shakes his head. 'But they sounded pleasant and they smiled at me, so I thought they'd probably just wished me a pleasant evening. Which is exactly what I wished them in return.'

'Brilliant,' smiles I. 'Constable, your powers of observation transcend universal expectations for a humble policeman.'

'Thank you, sir,' says he. 'Just doing my duty.'

'The, Inspector is being sarcastic, Constable,' says Head. 'Translated, he has just told you; you may as well be policing on the bloody moon for all the good you are.'

'Enough of this, Sergeant. Walnut House, here we come,' snaps I.

Now miserably, miserable, two minutes later, Soames presents Walnut House to us and we all pause at the rusting iron railings with its rusting, hanging off its hinges gate, to peruse the veritable jungle before us. Two gigantic Walnut Trees stand either side of the expansive frontage which is packed with straggling bushes and shrubs that haven't seen a pair of sheers for years. A narrow weed strewn path leads down to a massive three-story house with two bow fronted windows first floor and several sash windows on the other two floors. The sun is out and the day is pleasant for the time of year, but in this garden, it is dull and depressing.

'Do you know if there's anyone inside the house, Constable?' says I. 'As I note that all of the tatty grey curtains are drawn in every window.'

'Their curtains are always drawn, sir. But usually, they are in at this time of day. They take breakfast across the road in the Café Paris, for an hour or so. Then dinner there again, at about six pm, for a couple of hours. Then…'

'Thank you, Constable Soames,' says I. 'My, Sergeant and I shall seek entrance into the house. While we are doing that, I want you to get back to your station and inform your superior that we, that's me and my sergeant, believe the Boyle twins might be hiding out in this house.'

I point at the house to ensure he knows we mean *this* house and not one on the moon.

'Right, sir,' says he. 'Do you want me to come back here after I've reported to the station?'

'Yes please, Constable, if it's not too much trouble. And hopefully you will also return with at least half a dozen well-armed, colleagues.'

This lifts his equilibrium as he says with stirring enthusiasm, 'Will do, sir. When it comes to armed conflict, I am your man.'

'Marvellous,' says I. 'Off you go, Constable.

With him gone, Head and I draw out the revolvers we were reissued with last night, and walk slowly down the path towards huge porticoed, paint peeled blackish double doors. We step up three stone steps and I take hold of the bell ring and give it a tug. It doesn't move and feels as if it's cemented in.

'I'm thinking, Richard,' whispers I. 'Perhaps we should go around the back first.'

'Agreed,' says he. 'We might then take the occupants by surprise.'

Leading the way, I push a way through the bushes to get to the corner of the house. On doing so we are confronted with a mass of evil brambles ten feet high and no doubt stretching to the very rear of the house. After trying the other side of the house, we find it much the same and return to the front door.

'If I bang on the door, Richard we shall lose the element of surprise. Have you got your lock picks on you?'

'I have. But try the door first it might not be locked.'

'Good thinking,' says I, as reaching for the green tarnished brass knob I try turning it. 'It's stuck fast, Richard.'

'The bastard,' hisses he. 'Stand aside and let me have a go. It's stuck fast alright, Gerald, we'll just have to knock on the door.'

With that he gives the door a thump with the side of a clenched fist and to our amazement the door opens a tiny bit.

'It's open,' says he, and pushes it right open on squealing hinges.

We are now confronted with a long hallway. A wooden floor covered in dust and grime. Dark brown wall wallpaper that is tatty and hanging off in places, with the only bright spots being where paintings once hung. A huge oak sideboard blocks half the hall. Hanging on by a thread there's a hideous elk horned hat stand screwed onto the wall, and a gigantic cracked terracotta olive jar beneath being used as an umbrella, stroke, walking stick stand. You can tell this because there are lots of sticks and umbrellas rammed into it.

'It stinks in here,' whispers Head, fanning his revolver all around the place. 'Like dog shit mixed with mouldy cheese and rotten sperm.'

I gaze up at a ceiling covered with dust laden cobwebs and a gas-powered chandelier that looks as if it might crash to the ground at any second. The worst of it is, is the darkness, it feels more like dusk in here then early afternoon.

Still keeping our revolvers pointing forwards we cautiously advance. If the twins are here, they could be anywhere and we could be jumped on at any second.

The sound of voices echoes down the hall, 'Well,' whispers I, 'there's life up ahead, Richard. Take it slow and quiet.'

We pass closed doors either side of us. Light shines out from an open door a few yards further on. The voices become louder, male voices, but not the twins. Head holds up a hand.

'It's probably Bolsover and Major talking,' says he. 'I don't think the twins are here. So, what do we say when we come face to face with the occupiers?'

'I'll think of something, Richard. Shall we go for it?'

He nods.

Quickening our pace, we stride with purpose through the open door and confront two men sitting opposite each other on a very long junked up kitchen table while nursing chipped mugs of what smells like hot chocolate, but could just as easily be fermented sick.

'Armed police,' barks I, pointing my revolver. 'Do not move, keep your hands on your mugs where we can see them.'

'Oh! How exciting,' says the one facing me. 'Is this a raid?'

He may be sat down, but it easy to see he is a tall very skinny object with an elongated thin face, wide open bright eyes surrounded by hand bags that stare at me over thick rimmed glasses resting on a pointed nose. He sports a patchy, tobacco-stained grey beard and fuzzy sticking up straw textured hair. He has a holey tartan scarf around his scrawny neck and a white shirt, with scuffed dirty collar, beneath a grey cardigan that has leather patched elbows.

The other fellow twists his head around to stare at me like a mad man. He is also tall and skinny, with sunken, dark ringed eyes. His face is covered with a virtual bush of wild black hair streaked with grey and a mop of hair to match. A thick knit round neck jumper in bright, grubby green hangs on him as if he were a coat hanger.

'How jolly is this, Cedric?' says he, with a hint of an American accent. 'Big strong policemen have turned up to entertain us.'

'Is there anyone else in the house?' demands I.

'Only Fabio,' smiles Cedric.

'And where might he be?' says I, still keeping my weapon pointed at him.

'Where is, Fabio, Harvey?'

'Probably out in the back garden hunting rats for his tea,' says he.

'Is Fabio a cat?' grimaces I, because if he isn't the mind boggles.

'No, he's a dog,' says Cedric. 'Well, officer, to what do we owe this fascinating intrusion into our home?'

I lower my weapon. 'I shall come to that, sir,' says I

scanning my eyes around a kitchen with plaster flaking white stained walls, a double butler sink, full of pots and pans, crockery and all manner of odd-looking utensils. There's a huge blackened range piled up with more pots and pans and a falling to pieces, seriously on the lean, Welsh dresser that has stacks of crockery piled upon it. But at least it is bright in here as there is nothing on the large window to prevent the sun from shining in and displaying the clouds of dust that flouts around.

Apart from the obvious back door and the one we entered there are three more doors, one beside the dresser and two more on the opposite wall.

'Do any of these doors lead to anywhere?' points I.

Cedric answers, 'No, they are for the walk-in larder and cupboards. Take a peep if you like, but be careful when you open the door by the dresser as it is rather full, and all manner of things may fall out upon you.'

'No need for that, sir,' says I. Relaxing a little I holster my revolver. 'Sergeant, keep an eye out in the hall. Gentlemen, I am Detective Inspector Potter and this is my colleague, Detective Sergeant Head. First of all, I want to apologise for this rude intrusion, but needs must. We are of the belief you may be harbouring two dangerous individuals by the names of William Boyle and his twin brother, Robert Boyle. What say you to this accusation?'

'I would say, Inspector,' says Cedric, 'that your accusation is correct except for the inference that we are *harbouring*, Billy and Bobby, when in fact they are our guests. As for them being dangerous, I would say they are of no danger to us, whatsoever.'

'Why don't you and your sergeant sit with us?' says Harvey. 'Would you care for a warming mug of cocoa?'

'We'll pass, thanks,' says Head.

'And I'll stand for now,' says I. 'Do you know where the twins are?'

'They went out yesterday, Inspector and haven't returned as yet,' says Cedric. 'I believe they were going to a fancy-dress party and were stopping over.'

'Dressed as Chinese men,' says I.

'Oh… You are correct, Inspector,' says Cedric. 'Billy and Bobby love to dress up, don't they Harvey?'

'They do, and *my* how fabulous they look. They can even dress in female attire and carry it off with great aplomb. My word, they've even been approached by naughty men looking for love before now. One brute even tried to forcibly fondle Billy up against a wall at one time while he and Bobby were parading along the Strand swirling their parasols.'

'Of course, the brute was somewhat perplexed when Billy kneed him in his delicate area,' titters Harvey. 'My, the tales those boys tell us. Such joy they are. Are they not, Cedric?'

Cedric's arms shoot up to the ceiling, 'Delightful boys. Gifts from heaven. Bless their little cotton drawers.'

'They are also wanted for torture, murder and kidnapping amongst a string of other crimes,' says I. 'Leaving you, gentlemen as their associates by aiding and abetting them by allowing them to hide out in your home.'

'Oh dear,' says Harvey, as a hand goes to cover his mouth. 'I don't believe it, Inspector. Surely you are mistaken. Billy and Bobby are gentle souls who would not harm a fly unless they deserved it, such as the brute whom Billy was forced to ward off.'

'How long have the twins been hiding out here?' says I.

Cedric shrugs, 'Oh, about three months or so. They turned up of out of the blue, we hadn't seen them for what, five years or so?'

'About that,' says Harvey. 'We were amazed by their progress; they had improved immensely academically. Billy in particular is very intelligent, don't you know.'

'I have come to realise that, sir. Can I ask how you came to know them in the first place?'

'About five years ago,' says Cedric, 'we were researching the theory and practice of eugenics…'

'You what?' says Head.

'I'll explain later, Sergeant,' says I. 'Please continue, Mr Cedric.'

'We advertised in the papers for twins of any age and sex to assist us in our studies. Subsequently that Razor Williams fellow contacted us and we engaged the twins. We paid Razor a fair rate for the twin's involvement, but how much the twins saw of the money I don't know. You will have to ask Razor.'

'Dead five years ago, I'm afraid,' says I.

'Oh. How did he die?'

'Clubbed over the back of head and then thrown down the sewer.'

Harvey chuckles. 'No doubt he was at home there.'

'Razor's murder was witnessed by the twins. How much truth was in what they told us is open to speculation.'

Head says, 'Do you not have any servants?'

Cedric shakes his head. 'We are self-sufficient, Sergeant, and prefer it that way.'

'We do indeed,' says Harvey.

'Anyway,' says Cedric. 'The twins helped us, over several weeks, with several ongoing projects we were involved in at the time. Extra sensory perception and sexual preferences to name a couple.'

'Sexual preferences?' says Head, sounding somewhat confused. 'What do you mean by sexual preferences?'

'Did they like girls or boys or both? Did they differentiate in their preferences? Just because they are twins and share the same genetics, it doesn't mean they think or act exactly the same.'

'Oh, I see,' lies Head.

'We must suspend this conversation for now, gentlemen, before we lose the plot,' says I, 'Very shortly we shall be joined by several more armed police who will be deployed around this house to hopefully catch the twins when they return…'

'What if they don't return, sir?' says Head.

'Who knows, Sergeant,' sighs I.

'Oh, they will return,' says Cedric, with confidence. 'Unless of course something dire has happened to them. I will say, Inspector, I hope there will not be any violence. We do not want to see blood shed on our doorstep or the twins harmed in any way.'

'That will be up to them, sir. Now, if one of you will show me where the twins have been sleeping, the other must remain here with my sergeant.'

'I will take you,' says Cedric, as scrapping back his chair he stands. 'Follow me.'

I follow Cedric into the hallway, up a flight of thread bare carpeted stairs and into a surprisingly tidy double bedroom with twin beds and the usual bedroom furnishings, including a dressing table, where no doubt the twins sit to put on their facial disguises and make up. The beds are made and there is very little of anything left out to peruse.

'This room used to be my mothers,' says Cedric, watching me as I open the large mahogany wardrobe and go through the few clothes that hang inside. 'The twins cleaned it up and have made it their own. They're not afraid to work, Inspector, unlike Harvey and I. By God, we're a pair of idle buggers we are.'

Turning away from the wardrobe, I say, 'If you can afford to be lazy, sir, then that is your choice.'

Going over to a bow fronted chest of draws I go through the draws and find nothing of interest amongst the drawers, socks and pullovers. But on opening the top drawer of the dressing table I find a wad of notes and beneath them a large envelope. Taking it out I peruse its contents. One diary and two smaller envelopes. Inside one envelope, there is a single photograph of the twins at about four years of age, sat on a woman's lap. She is sat on a ladder-back chair, with his hand on the top of the chair, behind the woman, stands a rather hard looking man with cold eyes. The twin's parents, no doubt and no doubt this is the only photograph of the family together.

'I am not sure of the legality in what you are doing, Inspector,' says Cedric, as he comes over to look over my shoulder.

I face him, 'Nor am I, sir,' says I, with a back off glare. Opening the other envelope reveals the naughty photographs of Frobisher and his wife along with the letter belonging to Lady Elizabeth Frazer. They are the originals.

'Oh, I say,' says Cedric. 'He's a big boy.'

'Do you mind standing back, sir,' grates I.

He steps back and folds his arms. Hoping to find our stolen revolvers, I go through the other draws, look under the bed and then, satisfied that there is no more to find, I keep hold of the envelope and its contents.

'Are you seizing that envelope, Inspector?' says Cedric.

'It is evidence, sir.'

'Do you think, Harvey and I might take a peek at those, um… How shall I put this?'

'The answer is no; you cannot look at the dirty photographs. They are not only evidence of the twins' blackmailing attempts on an innocent couple, it also illegal for anyone to show them to anyone.'

'That is a shame, Inspector. I did not wish to see them for my own sexual gratification, but for our current research into:

Pornography and its effects on the mental and physical wellbeing of the viewer. Or, to put into layman's terms; Does excessive masturbation over graphic images of a sexual nature, over a period of time, really effect the viewers eyesight while causing mental anguish and irreparable damage as to how they perceive the opposite sex, or the same sex. Especially mother and father figures.'

'The answer is still no,' smiles I. 'I have seen all I wish to see, sir. Let us go back down.'

On reaching the hallway one of the front doors starts to open very slowly. Drawing my revolver, I put a finger to my lips so Cedric keeps quiet and hand him the envelope to hold. Head is leaning halfway out of the kitchen with his revolver pointed towards the front door, we nod at each other. It is so eerily quiet you could hear a dead man breathe. The door opens a tiny bit further, whoever is behind it is being very, very cautious. Head then makes a move, silent but deadly he swiftly covers the distance from the kitchen to the front door in two seconds, then presses himself back onto the other door, revolver gripped with both hands and pointed to the side ready to point it at the head of whoever enters. Pushing Cedric back out of sight onto the stairs, I step into the spot Head just vacated.

The door opens a bit further and then someone peeps around it, but it is so bloody gloomy I can't make out who it is. With baited breath I crouch down to present a smaller target should the door suddenly fly open and Bill's sawn-off shotgun discharges up the hall.

One hell of a roar echoes up the hall followed by an ear banging thump. The part open door flies off its hinges and crashes onto the floor sending up a cloud of dust. The door Head is sheltering behind slams him back against the wall and his revolver goes off. The Elk's head, complete with cobwebs, falls off the wall as half a dozen, armed with rifles, plods cram into the hall and let off a volley.

Diving back into the kitchen I yell out, 'Armed police! Hold your fire.'

'Come out with your hands up,' yells a voice. 'We are armed police and will shoot you if you don't do as you're told.'

'This is Detective Inspector Potter,' yells I. 'Lower your weapons, you pratts, we are on the same side for God's sake.'

'So, you say. You could be anyone, and you fired the first shot.'

'Get off the fucking door,' yells Head. 'You're crushing me!'

'Christ, there's another one hiding behind the door,' says another voice.

'I'm a policeman,' growls Head. 'Get off the door before I lose it.'

'Not until we've seen some form of identification,' sounds the first voice.

I've had enough of this. 'Hold your fire,' yells I. 'I'm coming out with my hands up.'

I slip my revolver into its holster, raise my hands and step out just as the gas chandelier gives out an unmistakable cracking sound, followed by a weird squeal, before crashing to the floor along with ten ton of plaster, dust, cobwebs and a big fat rat jerking around on the floor in its death throws. Arms still raised I wait to be shot to pieces. Nothing. All is quiet. As the dust settles, I can see six covered in dust plods staring towards me while pointing their rifles.

'That's Inspector Potter alright,' says Constable Soames.

'Lower you weapons men,' orders a sergeant.

'And get off the fucking door!' yells Head.

'No need to keep swearing,' says the sergeant. 'Men, step back from the door.'

Lowering my hands, I brush dust from my face and step towards the plods as Head, one hand over his nose where blood is seeping through his fingers, comes out from behind the door.

'I am lost for words, Sergeant?' says I to the plod.

'Bright, sir.' He holds out a huge hand. 'Pleased to meet you.'

He is a big rotund man with a thick bushy moustache, thick sideburns down to his square jaw and thick hairy caterpillar eyebrows and I'm thinking the thickness continues into his brain where it has become cotton wool.

With reluctance I shake his hand. 'Sergeant Bright, this is my colleague, Sergeant Head.'

Bright holds out his hand to receive a frozen stare so cold he retracts it.

'Can you all step into the hallway,' says I.

They do so while brushing dust and cobwebs off their uniforms while avoiding Heads scathing eyes and my look of disdain. To say they are now feeling very foolish is an understatement.

'Why on earth did you charge the doors like a herd of rampaging bulls, Sergeant Bright?' says I. 'Why didn't you just knock on the door like normal people do?'

There is indignance in his eyes as he stretches himself up to his full height. 'We tried ringing the bell, sir but no one answered.'

'That's because it doesn't work,' says I.

'Then I noticed the door was actually slightly on the jar and was just cautiously trying to open it when I heard the distinctive sound of a weapon being cocked. I thought, what if those mad twins are hiding behind the other door waiting to blast us the moment, we stick our heads in? So, I gestured to my men that we back up and then, on the roar, charge the doors. We've done it before and it worked a treat. But this time… sorry, Inspector, I got it wrong.'

'I'm oof do fix my dose,' says Head.'

'Carry on, Sergeant,' says I. 'Please check Cedric and Harvey are alright. They must have at least filled their drawers over this. Now then, Sergeant Bright. Ask your men if they can try and put the door back on…'

'It's come off its 'inges,' informs a plod. 'The woods rotten. I don't reckon it can be fixed. You'd need a carpenter.'

'Just shove in place and prop it up,' snaps I. 'Hurry it up. I want those doors closed as quickly as possible.' I am suddenly aware that there is a distinct smell of gas.

'I need a smoke ta calm me nerves, Sergeant,' pleads a plod.

'In a *minute*, Constable,' says Bright. 'I'm sure we all could do with a short break.'

I am tempted to leave them to it while I make a sharp exit out the backway while taking Head, Cedric and Harvey with me just in case there's a gas explosion. However, if the twins should turn up, they are going to be wary enough as it is when they see one of the front doors propped up, and should they peer inside and see the devastation that's been caused, I've no doubt they'll be off like cats with their tails on fire. Should they turn up and find the house demolished they'll be doubly suspicious that something isn't quite right.

Cedric comes up to me. 'I've turned the gas off, Inspector,' says he, appearing somewhat bemused at all the devastation before him. 'It's rather a mess, isn't it?'

'You will be able to put in a claim for compensation, Mr Bolsover,' says I, without a shred of enthusiasm that he would receive a single penny.

'Oh, it doesn't matter, Inspector. I recently agreed to sell the house to relatives. We have to move out in a few weeks once all is finalised. Harvey and I have decided to retire to Brighton. Fresh sea air, beautiful views and lots of super healthy young men for distraction.'

'Lovely,' says I, while, at this moment, wishing I too could retire to the seaside. 'Can I ask if you have a room where I can brief everyone on why they are here, sir,' says I.

'Use the study, if you want, Inspector,' smiles he. 'You'll find there's a nice big bottle of scotch and plenty of glasses in the bureau. Help yourselves. Drink it all. Harvey and I do not care for scotch. We love cocktails.'

Without the tail in the word, thinks I. Still, live and let live, I am so pissed off at this moment I couldn't care less about Cedric and Harvey's life preferences, besides, they seem nice enough fellows who are doing no one any harm. I just hope they haven't harmed the twins in the past. The twins may only be using Cedric and Harvey while they hide out and carry out their revenge, while all the time knowing that Cedric and Harvey are the last on their list. And don't they say; save the best for last.

Stake Out

Ten minutes later, except for Head who's with Cedric and Harvey, we are in a huge study that has piles of books stacked everywhere, including hundreds in cabinets all around the walls, a long table and chairs, two bureaus and loads of dust. In one of the bureaus, I find a large, thirty-year-old, bottle of single malt and plenty of crystal tumblers that are reasonably clean. I tell everyone to grab a glass and then I pour them all a single and no more. We can't have half a dozen drunken plods armed with rifles falling all over the place, or worse, shooting at anything that moves. I could just image a blissfully happy, holding hands, little old Chinese couple walking past the house and getting mistaken for the twins. Six pie eyed plods then leaping up out of the bushes and blasting the couple to pieces.

After drumming it into their heads that I want the twins caught alive because we don't know what has happened to Sergeant King, and we may just be able to reach him in time to save his life, I instruct them on the plan of action. Having learnt from Cedric, that access into the house from the rear is impossible, due to eight-foot walls all around it topped with broken bottles, tons of bramble bushes and years of shit from Fabio's bum, I am content to concentrate on the fact that the twins will most certainly come in via the front door. But when?

The aim is to have four plods hiding amongst the shrubs and bushes out front, two inside resting and ready to relieve two plods at a time every hour, as no one could stay squatting down for too long. Head and I will take turns up at a front window where we can peep through one of the many holes in the curtains, for two reasons, one to keep an eye on the plods so they don't wonder off, and the other is to ensure, the second we spy the twins coming in the gate, we'll be down stairs to confront them before the plods leap up from their hiding places and all hell breaks loose.

'Any questions?' says I.

A plods hand goes up. 'What if I want to go to the toilet while I'm crouched beneath the bushes?'

'If you're desperate just do it there and then. But don't stand up or make a sound.'

'Trouble is, Inspector, my farts are really loud…'

Heaven help us, groans I to myself. 'To ensure quiet farts, place a hand on each bum cheek, pull the cheeks apart just as you're about to let rip, you will find that enlarging of the escape route for the gas helps to quieten it. Next question.'

Soames puts his hand up. 'My shifts over in another hour or so, can I leave on time as I have a funeral to attend?'

'Whose funeral, is it?'

'My neighbour. Nice old boy…'

'As he's not family and he is dead, he won't miss you, Constable. Send his family some flowers, duty comes first. All of you will be expected to stick with this for as long as it takes. Is that clear?'

They all nod. 'Good. Do not forget to keep low and quiet

while hiding out. No talking, not even whispering, no coughing or loud farting. And no smoking. The twins could be disguised as anything. Chinese cooks, tarts, cowboys, anything…'

'Will they be disguised as jam tarts or custard tarts?' grins a plod. Everyone laughs.

'Neither, most likely they'll be apple tarts,' smiles I. 'If anything goes wrong, and you have to fire your weapons, try to bring the twins down by aiming at their limbs. My hope is that this will end without bloodshed, but the twins are loose cannons and there's no knowing how they'll react once confronted.'

'How well armed are they, sir?' says Bright.

'They are in possession of one sawn off shotgun and three revolvers that we are aware of.'

'And they *will* use them,' says Bright, giving his men the you better believe it, look.

'Without hesitation, Sergeant. Do not underestimate the twins, men. They are reckless beyond belief and have a very low opinion of the police.'

'So, do we, sir,' laughs the joker from earlier.

'Thank you for that, Constable,' says I. 'Always good to have a giggle. Let's get to it.'

***

During my periods of inactivity while we waited, I used the time to go through Bills note book, while keeping an eye on Cedric and Harvey who'd been joined by Fabio, who, having taken an instant dislike to me, laid on the kitchen floor intermittently growling and baring his evil, surprisingly large fangs while maintaining an attitude of, if you make any sudden moves I don't like, you'll feel my teeth clamped on your balls.

Bill's writing was illegible at times but easy to follow thanks to the sketches that accompanied each passage. He'd tracked French down by simply going to the records office and looking up the 1891 census. French hadn't moved since the census, but King had, and there was no record of to where? Most disturbing were the sketches of what the twins had planned to do to their victims. Graphic sketches of French and Kings torture. King was to get exactly what Bill told me he'd get when we met at the church. Do not kill, had been written beside each sketch. The planning for their intended crimes is detailed but didn't say where or when, thus giving nothing away. Bill had named French and King, but the next intended victims weren't named. After King came: 'That fat bitch along wiv 'er 'usband.' A sketch showed a large, naked woman being tortured while hanging by her arms from a beam. Bill and Bob were portrayed as stick men, both wielding instruments of torture from hot pincers to huge carrots. The woman was being sexually violated, while, trusted up naked like a chicken, a gagged man watched in horror at the scene before him. Must be the husband, I'd assumed, but again no name. Bill had stated that: 'Once the filthy bitch had spilled all the beans, he'd finish her off.' Her old man would follow, but his death may be a bit quicker, cue question mark. Bill wanted names from the couple, names of whom and for why it didn't say, only that once he had those names and had: 'Slaughtered the fucking lot of 'em,' it would be over and done with. I found the last sketch of Bill and Bob swinging from the gallows to have been the most disturbing, whilst also being the most poignant with a pair of doves flying up to heaven. They *didn't* expect to escape justice, but *did* expect to go to heaven?

After hiding out in the bushes for a change, by which time it is getting dark, and once back in the kitchen I finally accept a coffee from, Cedric and say to hell with catching the plague from his grubby enamelled tin mugs. By now everyone has become fed up with waiting for something to happen. I also realise that no one, except for present company, know where Head and I are or when we'll be back. Do we continue waiting? Or do we abandon the operation? One thing's for certain, I can't keep six plods stuck here for much longer. They have other duties and homes to go to. But leaving now may ruin any hope we have of catching the twins before they begin their next killing spree.

Suddenly hit with a brilliant idea I jump up from the kitchen chair I'm on having forgotten all about Fabio, who goes for my crutch like a flying vampire. Sheer instinct has me swiftly move the tin mug to cover my privates, Fabio's teeth clamp onto the mug and pierce the metal. Like the proverbial snarling terrier with a rat, he refuses to let go, or he can't let go because his fangs have become stuck. Luckily Fabio's masters have just taken tea and biscuits for the plods waiting in the study and fail to witness the part where, with furious intent, I swing the mug with Fabio still attached right behind me, then up towards the ceiling and let go. There follows one smashed window and one vicious little mut flying out into the brambles.

I am just contemplating how to explain the broken window to Cedric when in they come.

'We heard a crashing sound,' says Cedric, his eyes scanning all around the kitchen.

'It was, Fabio,' says I, innocently. 'For some strange reason he leapt up onto the table, sunk his teeth into my mug and then went berserk. Growling and snarling he tore around the kitchen trying to shake off the mug, but it held fast. I tried to get hold of him to help but he would have none of it. Then the next thing I knew he dived for the window and went straight through it and disappeared.'

Both stare at me with expressions of sheer incredulity.

Cedric says, 'He did that once before. Did he not, Harvey?'

'He did indeed, Cedric. But then there was a cat pressing its nose against the window at the time. Fabio hates cats and went for it by leaping up onto the table and then going for the window. *Smash* and he was gone.'

'Dogs can be utterly reckless when it comes to cats,' says Cedric. 'It is understandable.' He shoots me the puzzled look. 'But why on earth did he sink his teeth into your mug and then leap through the window, Inspector?'

I shake my head. 'I am one of the most revered detectives in the Yard, Mr Bolsover, but even I haven't a clue as to why Fabio attacked my mug and then descended into canine madness. Perhaps he only meant to play with it but when it got stuck, he couldn't handle it?'

'Go and see if he's alright, Harvey,' sighs Cedric, as he takes a seat opposite me. 'Harvey and I usually go out for our evening meal about this time, Inspector. Will that be possible?'

'Providing you both give me your word that you will have your meals and then return immediately to the house.'

He nods. 'What will happen to the twins should you capture them, Inspector?'

'They will be tried and found guilty of murder, sir. We have too much evidence against them for any other verdict.'

'Will they be sentenced to death?'

'Not necessarily. If they plead insanity and it is accepted then they will escape the gallows, but will spend the rest of their lives in an asylum. The trouble is, Mr Bolsover, I do not believe they are insane and neither will a jury, regardless of how brilliant their defence is.'

'You have read my mind, Inspector. I will not hesitate to secure those boys the very best defence, money can buy even if it should be futile. If nothing else they deserve to be heard for all that they have suffered. Then, perhaps, some good might come from it and they would not have died in vain. For is it not time that the poor and destitute in this glorious country, especially the children, have the full protection of the law in place of being ignored by the law. Is this not a society that brutely punishes the poor, for even the smallest misdemeanour, whilst allowing the rich and powerful to commit the most heinous of crimes whilst knowing that they will rarely be held to account, unless they committed their crimes against one of their own?'

'It is as you say, sir. But slow as it is, progress is being made. No child for years under sixteen has been hanged. All children have the legal right to schooling. Laws have been passed to protect the very young from being used as nothing more than slave labour in all kinds of industries. There is still much to be done and I believe that one day the law will protect everyone; no matter their social standing and regardless of age or sex.'

'Or who they choice to love, Inspector?' says he with cold cynicism.

'Who knows?' says I. 'Time will tell. Would you kindly bring my sergeant and I something back to eat from the restaurant once you've had your meal?'

'Of course, Inspector. What would you like?'

'Steak sandwiches in thick crusty bread with tons of butter and lots of horseradish, would be nice.'

'I will ask, Pierre to prepare you the finest steak sandwiches you will probably have ever tasted. Anything else?'

'A receipt, please. Then I can claim back the cost.'

Harvey walks in carrying a, minus the tin mug, trembling, Fabio in his arms. Considering he went straight through a pain of glass; Fabio appears to have escaped any serious injury. There really is no justice, sometimes.

Cedric is up on his feet and holding out his arms. 'Poor little chap. Come to daddy and tell him all about it.'

I can only pray the vicious little bastard doesn't speak English. Trembling and whimpering though he is, his hate filled, staring right at me, devil red eyes are telling me in no uncertainty that he intends to get his revenge.

Cedric is now smothering the brute with kisses while cooing endearments. I too would like to smother him, but with a cat.

After fetching their hats and coats, Cedric and Harvey head off for dinner. Thankfully they take Fabio with them. Having decided to allow Sergeant Bright and his men to leave I head for the front door only to pause at the chandelier still laying where it fell. I can still smell gas.

Stepping into the darkened room where Head is taking his turn to spy out front through the tatty curtains, I ask, 'Can you smell gas, Richard?'

'You made me jump,' snaps he, turning his shadowy features towards me. 'I thought the bloody twins had sneaked up on me. Yes, I think I can smell gas. But as the house smells of damp, decay, dog's shit, mould…'

'A simple yes or no would have sufficed,' grates I. Head is hungry, hence his grumpy mood. 'You might like to know that Cedric will be bringing us steak sandwiches from the restaurant across the road once he and Harvey have had their dinner.'

'Marvellous,' says he. 'I'm so hungry I could eat a twenty-pound turkey. Did you tell him I want door stop bread, thick butter, loads of horseradish and at least a pound of good steak?'

'More or less. I'm going to tell the others to go, Richard. We have no idea when, or even if the twins will return tonight and I cannot justify keeping the plods here any longer.'

'Agreed, Gerald. We might be better off without them, anyway. I watched Cedric and Harvey head down the path and was then horrified to see one of the plods jump out of hiding to confront them. The prat pointed his rifle at them while no doubt demanding to know where they were going. Harvey pointed back to the house before speaking to the plod, who nodded before creeping back behind the bush…'

'They've no doubt become very bored, Richard and bored plods become careless. I'll send them off and ask Bright to contact the Yard to update them on what we're about and request relief. Then they can inform our good ladies that we have no idea when we'll be home.'

'If Clump is about, he'll soon send out help. Did you ask Cedric to bring back seconds as well?'

I shake my head. 'Hopefully we won't be here for too much longer. Right, I'll go and speak to Sergeant Bright, he's in the drawing room…'

The unmistakable sound of a gunshot has me jump so high I nearly hit the ceiling. Head yanks the curtain aside and says, 'No sign of the twins. I'll bet one of the dopey plods let a round off by mistake.'

I look out the window to see two of the plods having an assignation on the path.

'Well, if the twins were nearby, Richard, they aren't now,' says I before stepping out into the hallway where I meet, Sergeant Bright and Constable Soames heading for the front door.

'What happened, sir?' says Bright.

'One of your men fired his rifle,' grates I.

'The bloody fool. I'll sort him out.'

Bright is obviously furious, as am I as we step out front.

'Who fired that shot?' demands Bright.

'I did, Sergeant,' says the joker. 'A bloody great rat fell on me 'ead from the bush I was hidin' under. I jumped out of me skin and squeezed one off by mistake.'

Hands on hips, Bright barks out, 'Every bloody criminal from here to Buckingham Palace must have heard that shot, including the two we're after. You've just fucked up the entire operation, Constable and shall be reprimanded for it by the Chief Inspector...'

'May I have a word, Sergeant?' says I.

Taking a few steps away from his men I advise Bright to take it easy. Having become very bored and disinterested the men had no doubt slipped into lethargy, therefore they were also off guard and in truth; having a rat suddenly drop on your head in the dark is enough to make anyone fill their drawers.

'As you say, sir,' says he. 'I will keep this off the record. But I can't apologise enough. How can we possibly make this up to you? You must think we are a bunch of incompetents.'

'I do not think you are a bunch of incompetents,' lies I. 'We all make mistakes. What I propose, Sergeant is that you and your men step down and leave this to me and my sergeant...'

He appears somewhat aggrieved. 'Then you do think we are incompetent?'

I shake my head. 'I had already made up my mind to call it a day for you and your men, Sergeant, before the shot was fired. There is no point in all of us remaining here until the cows come home when we don't know when, or if, the twins will turn up.'

'Agreed,' says he, sounding relieved. 'And I do have other pressing tasks that require sorting out.'

'Good,' smiles I. 'Then gather your men together, Sergeant. I shall give them a quick pep talk and then you can get off.'

***

Two hours later, Head and I are still sat in the front room looking out for the twins to return. We are both pretty pissed off and yawning well. We haven't heard a word from the Yard and I can still smell gas. But Cedric assured me on his return that the gas pipe supplying the chandelier is definitely *off*.

'Those steak sandwiches were the best I've ever had,' says Head, smacking his lips. 'And that crème, thingy brolly, French desert was lovely, thanks to Cedric guessing I'd love one. I might ask, Chloe if she can make me one. But then perhaps not. How much bloody longer have we got to stay here, Gerald? My backside aches through sitting on this lumpy old chair for so long. A man could get piles from it, I reckon.'

Or worse, thinks I, like a thumping headache from your constant moaning. 'As long as it takes.'

'Which could be forever,' groans he. 'The twins could be anywhere. They may have gone to the theatre or something. Or jumped on a train and gone off to the seaside for the weekend. They could even be in a brothel dipping their wicks…'

'Dipping their what's?'

'Wicks! Dicks!'

'Oh, sorry I wasn't listening. It's like this, Richard. Catching the twins *here* is the best option we have at present. If we bugger off now and they turn up ten minutes later we'd be pretty damn pissed off about it, wouldn't we.'

'No, we wouldn't, because we wouldn't know they'd turned up, because we wouldn't be here. Therefore, we wouldn't give a rat's arse about it.'

'Probably not,' sighs I.

Cedric sticks his head in the room. 'Would you gentlemen like a nice mug of fortified coffee to cheer you up?'

'We would, sir,' says I. 'Thankyou.'

'Any biscuits with that?' says Head.

'We are out of biscuits, I'm afraid,' says Cedric. 'But I do have a jolly nice cream sponge that Harvey made if you would like a slice.'

'How about a nice big fat wedge instead,' smiles Head.

'A man after my own heart, Sergeant. A big fat wedge it shall be. And you, Inspector?'

'A small piece, thank you, sir.'

'Why not have a fat one like me, Gerald,' says Head. 'If you can't eat it all then I could eat it up for you.'

'A small piece will suffice,' grates I.

'Ah, but when you take a gander at my big fat wedge you will wish you had one just like it in place of your little one.'

'I am sorry, Sergeant. But I won't care a fig if yours is bigger than mine. I never have in the past and I don't see why I would care now.'

Sitting up straight in his chair, he fixes me with the; you're a liar look. 'Sorry, sir, but the size of your portion compared to my portion has always been an issue as far as you're concerned. In fact, I could go so far as to say that you are obsessed with the size of my portion compared to yours.'

'Excuse me, gentlemen,' says Cedric, sounding rather excited. 'Are you still referring to portions of cake or some other portions, such as, um…'

'There are two major reasons that spur the sergeant on, Mr Bolsover. One is food and the other is more food. He is a glutton of the highest order. If he'd have been born a pig, he'd be gloriously content to have his nose in the trough twenty fours a day.'

'I think you're over exaggerating,' grates Head, giving me the; do you want a thump look? 'I don't eat that much and I'm not a glutton; just a growing lad.'

'The only growing you're currently doing is outwards at the stomach. Now, Sergeant let us drop the subject before it turns nasty.'

'I shall fetch the coffee and cake,' says Cedric.

'Thank you,' says I. 'And please disregard our ridiculous conversation. Occasionally we have such trysts when we are tired and stressed.'

'Speak for yourself,' grates Head.

'As your senior officer, Sergeant, it is in my delegated vernacular to speak for you whenever I want.'

Head stares at me. 'Delegated vernacular. What the hell does that mean?'

'I believe the inspector meant delegated vicariousness,' ventures Cedric. 'Vernacular is relevant to language, whereas vicarious authority is relevant to the church and vicars…'

'Who cares,' says Head. 'I just want my cake so I can eat it.'

'I rest my case,' says I.

'Back in a short while,' says Cedric.

'That Cedric's a clever chap,' says Head, the second Cedric had gone. 'You'd do well to have a few lessons from him on the English Language.'

'Fuck up, Richard. Now, how's that for the kind of language you fully understand.'

'No need to get grumpy just because you said the wrong word, *again*. If you didn't try being so clever you wouldn't get in such scrapes.'

I have had enough of this silliness. 'It is obvious, Richard, that we are both tired and fed up with waiting. But we are stuck here until God knows when and must therefore make the most of it. May I suggest we just get on with it and cut out the squabbling.'

'Agreed. Sorry, Gerald, I did get a bit silly. I just want to go home. What time is it?'

'Eight o'clock.'

'I should be relaxing in my armchair by the fire, having had a lovely dinner, and enjoying a beer and a good fart. I wonder what, Chloe had cooked me for tonight. It's probably ruined by now, anyway.'

'Probably,' yawns I. 'Betty was going to make me an Irish stew tonight. One of my favourites. I'll have to have it warmed up tomorrow.'

Cedric returns carrying a tray with two huge wedges of cake, a pot of coffee, two dirty mugs and a half empty bottle of brandy.

'It is rather dark in here, gentlemen,' says he setting the tray down on a small side table. 'Can you see well enough or shall I bring you a lamp.'

'The street lights outside afford us all the light we require, sir,' says I, while reasoning that as I can still smell gas, a flaming lamp could be dangerous. 'But thank you anyway.'

'I shall leave you to it. Call if you need anything else.'

***

'Apart from the dog hairs that cake was delicious,' says Head, eyeing what's left of mine. 'Do you want the rest of yours, Gerald.'

'Feel free, Richard. I couldn't eat another crumb.'

'All the more for me,' grins he, reaching out to take it from the plate on my lap.

I grab him by the wrist. 'They're here, Richard,' hisses I.

'Who is here?'

'The twins you prat.'

'Christ! There they are coming up the path. Hang on. Are you sure it's them?'

'It's them alright.'

'What dressed as women complete with big wide fancy hats?'

'Along with scarlet dresses and suitable wigs.'

They walk side by side, one, who I assume is Bill, carries a valise which no doubt has their weapons inside.

Putting aside the plate I stand up and draw my revolver. Head draws his and we gingerly make our way into the near dark hall, where we press ourselves up against the wall behind the door where Head hid before. I hope that when the twins push the other door open, it opens without coming off its hinges again and falling onto the floor, thus panicking them into backing off and drawing weapons.

The door begins to open, a polished ankle boot steps in, the door opens wider and with a swirl of scarlet, Bill steps right in to be followed by Bob.

They fail to notice us as they head up the hallway, pausing to look down at the chandelier before continuing. Head and I step away from the wall, take two strides closer to our prey and then challenge them.

'Halt!' demands I, pointing my weapon at Bill's back. 'Armed police. One wrong move and we will fire.'

'Oh, heaven,' cries Bob, sounding incredibly feminine.

'Drop the valise,' says I. 'Then both of you turn around with your hands held up high.'

Bill drops the valise. They raise their hands and, very slowly, turn to face us.

'Go behind them, Sergeant and frisk them for weapons.'

'We haven't got any weapons,' says Bill, sounding even more feminine than Bob did.

Their faces are difficult to define in the near dark along with their dark hair curtaining their cheeks and those big hat rims shielding their eyes. Their brilliant impersonation of females would fool most men, but not me. It's them alright.

Head, still pointing his revolver, goes behind Bob and,

using his free hand, runs it up Bob's legs, over his buttocks and then across his false breasts, giving each one a good squeeze, and finally under his arm pits.

'Ooh.' Is all, Bob cries.

Head frisks, Bill. He's just over the buttocks when, Bill says, 'If you dare to run your filthy hands over my bosom, Sergeant Idiot, I will have your hide.'

'And if you don't shut up, you'll feel my weapon up your ring,' growls Head, as he gives both of her, his, breasts a quick squeeze. 'All clear, sir.'

'Gentlemen,' says I. 'Carefully lower your arms and put your hands behind your backs so my sergeant can handcuff you.'

Nothing happens. Neither of them moves.

'Don't try playing silly buggers,' snarls Head, grabbing one of Bill's arms and yanking it down. 'Hands behind your backs, *now*,'

Just then, Cedric and Harvey, followed by a fang baring, Fabio, come out from the kitchen.

'Whatever is going on?' cries Cedric, as a hand goes to his mouth. 'That's my niece you are man handling, Sergeant.'

'Is it really?' says Head, interjecting a good deal of sarcasm. 'You'll be telling me next their tits are real!'

'They are you, oaf,' snaps Bill.

I suddenly recognise that voice, and it isn't Bills or Bobs. It's that stuck-up, upper-class witch who caused us a heap of trouble a year or so back when we were on the: Jack the Flasher case. Amelia Richardson and her twin sister Rebecca. Rich, spoilt madams who have no idea about anything beyond their gilded life styles. A pair of young beauties as fickle as fleas, but so well healed you'd have half the top toffs in London on your back should you dare to cross them. Nothing for it but to do a little crawling.

'Ladies, I must apologise unreservedly for the... um... assault on your persons. We thought you were the twins: William and Robert Boyle who are wanted for murder along with a host of other violent crimes. You may have read about them in the papers...'

This could be going well. They are both staring at me open mouthed and may well be amazed that they have inadvertently been drawn into a major criminal investigation. On the other hand; they may just be shocked dumb.

'I find it very difficult, Inspector,' says Amelia, oh so snottily, 'to believe you could have possibly mistaken me and my sister for a pair of guttersnipes. I would have thought that the fact we are wearing expensive dresses might *just* have given you a small clue as to our sex. Nor less the fact that our very deportment could not possibly be imitated by *any* male.'

Rebecca buts in, 'We have been schooled in the art of being a lady by the finest of the finest, Inspector... Potty, isn't it?'

'Potter.'

'I think, Potty suits you better,' smirks she. 'In short, we do not accept your feeble apology and will take this matter further. I am of the opinion you both knew exactly what you were about, having instantly recognised us, to opportunistically cause us immense embarrassment in a pathetic attempt to gain revenge, having been yourself highly embarrassed because we out witted you and made you appear fools when we crossed swords some months ago. We will destroy you, especially as we have a witness of considerable statue. Do we not, Uncle Cedric?'

'Let us withdraw to the drawing room and discuss the matter,' says Cedric. 'I believe brandies all-round might be just what is required to sooth tempers...'

'I do not want my temper soothed!' snaps Amelia. 'I want,' she points at Head, 'that idiot up before a judge for his brutal assault on my person…'

'It wasn't brutal,' says Head. 'In fact, it was rather gentle considering I thought you were violent criminals.'

'Shut up, you, silly man,' snaps Rebecca. 'No, Uncle. I will not discuss the matter further with these imbeciles until I have spoken to my solicitor.'

'Even so, Amelia, I insist that *we* discuss the matter,' says Cedric. 'Let us retire to the drawing room.'

All four tramp off with a growling Fabio trailing behind.

'You couldn't make it up,' says Head. 'Fancy that pair of spoilt brats turning up out of blue like that.'

'It's diabolical, Richard. We're right in it now.'

He gives me the quizzical look. 'Not we, you. You ordered me to feel them up…'

'Stop right there,' demands I, holding up a, stop right there, hand. 'I didn't order you to feel them up, I ordered you to search them for weapons. Is it my fault you went beyond what would be classed as prudent just to have a quick grope?'

He scratches his scalp. 'Why on earth would I grope a man dressed up as a woman, when I knew she was a man? While under orders; I pattered around their bodies, over their dresses I might add, to search for hidden weapons. It's not as if I shoved my hand up their dresses and had a good poke around, is it?'

'But you did grab their breasts. Didn't you?'

'No, I didn't, I skimmed over them.'

'You must have realised you were groping real breasts and not false ones that were stuffed with socks or whatever.'

'Oh, fuck this, Gerald. I've had enough, I'm off.'

'Off where?' says I to his back as he makes for the front door.

'Home,' says he, glancing back.

'Wait! I'll come with you,' says I, as a brilliant idea hits me. 'I've also had more than enough for one day. Just let me speak to Cedric for a minute or two.'

'I'll wait outside for you. But I won't be hanging around, so hurry up, I'm still hungry.'

I find Harvey alone in the kitchen putting coal into the aga.

'May I have a word, Mr Major,' says I, stepping in.

He straightens up and faces me, 'Of course, Inspector.'

'My sergeant and I are going to go over the road for a beer and a break. We can of course keep watch from there should anything untoward turn up.'

'Oh. Very well, Inspector. The door will be open as always it is, should you wish to return.'

'Thank you, sir. No doubt, Mr Bolsover will want to speak to us once he's spoken to his nieces.'

'Only to inform you that the ladies will have dropped any notions of pursuing charges against you or your sergeant. They have set their hearts on buying this house and intend bringing it back to its former glory, with all the modern conveniences, of course. Electric lighting, telephone and centralised heating. It will all cost a fortune.'

'All paid for by daddy, no doubt.'

'Indeed. Anyway, do not worry, Inspector, Cedric *will* persuade the girls not to pursue charges against you to avoid a scandal.'

'Thank you, sir.'

Once settled in the very posh, very French Restaurant, and afforded a clear view of Walnut House, we order two pints of bitter, only to be informed they serve only French beers. We are then given menus that, thankfully, are in English as well as French.

'They haven't got steak sandwiches on this menu,' grates Head.

'This is not the kind of place that normally serves sandwiches, Richard. No doubt they did them as a favour for Cedric. Besides, surely even you couldn't possibly eat another one, they were huge.'

'Bloody delicious they were,' says he, smacking his lips. 'I might never get the chance to have another one if I don't get one now.'

'It's up to you, Richard. But you will have to pay for it yourself. There's no way you'd be able to claim for two sandwiches at the prices they charge.'

'How much were they, Gerald?'

I show him the receipt that Cedric gave me.

'How much?' gasps he.

'Ten shillings, Richard. Enough to feed a poor family for weeks.'

'Christ!' says he, looking very downcast. 'I suppose I'll have to go without. I mean, how can I justify spending *that* much on a sandwich?'

'You can't, Richard. In truth, I will have trouble getting my money back as it is. I doubt, Clump will authorise such an expense just for a couple of sandwiches. Thankfully, Cedric treated us to our sweets or goodness knows what the final bill would have been.'

'Let's hope this foreign beer's good, or I'll sink into depression.'

Pierre the waiter returns with two small bottles of beer and two small schooners on a silver tray. He sets them down on the lacey white table cloth and pours a few drops into each glass.

'Would, Messieurs, care to order?' says he.

'We only want the beers, thank you,' says I.

'I am afraid, Monsieur, that we cannot serve alcohol in this restaurant without a meal.'

'You what?' grates Head. 'I've never heard anything so stupid…'

I show, Pierre my warrant card to shut Head up before he starts ranting.

'Ah… You are the detectives I made the sandwiches for?'

'We are,' says I. 'And they were superb, Pierre. Thank you. The problem is we cannot afford to buy a meal, but we need a beer and a break from the house.'

'Cedric informed us of you and why you are here. Please, stay as long as you wish. It is no problem,' he waves an arm around the place. 'You can see we are quiet now.'

He is summoned by a customer and immediately goes over to him. The place is quiet, three couples and a group of four. All are well healed and expensively attired. The ambiance is one of slow, sleepy and cosy. You could drop off in no time.

'Oy,' hisses I. 'Wake up, Sergeant.'

Shaking his head, Head lets out a yawn and scratches his scalp. 'Christ, I was gone then for a moment. How long before we can pack up and piss off home, Gerald? I need me bed.'

'My bed.'

'My, me, who cares? It's nice in here, Gerald but I'd rather be in an ordinary pub where we fit in.'

'Let us give it another hour, Richard. Perhaps by then the calvary will have arrived.'

'I doubt it. Either, Bright didn't pass on the message or no one at the Yard can be bothered about us. Let's face it, if the wrong person got the message, they wouldn't even bother passing it on because they don't like us.'

Allowing him to ramble on uninterrupted I watch the pathway leading up to the house, along with the people who are about and the light traffic that passes by. All in all, between both sides of the road there's a half a dozen couples strolling arm in arm, a few lone walkers, two with dogs and three children accompanied by two nannies in standard black uniforms; one of whom is pushing a pram. I suppose you might wonder if, Bill's pushing the pram with Bob squashed up inside it. But as the children and the nannies all turn to enter the high scrolled gates before Walnut House you can suppose they all live there. Pierre returns with two more bottles of beer.

'On the house, Messieurs,' says he, setting them down.

'Thanks,' says Head. 'They're alright these beers, considering they're foreign.'

'But not as good as English beer, hey, my friend?'

Holding the glass close to the table lamp, Head says, 'True, but the colour is like golden lemons and clear as a crystal stream, unlike some of our beers that are the colour of cats piss with lots of dregs in the bottom.'

'That is awful,' ponders Pierre.

'Not really,' says Head. 'Well not to us it ain't.'

Nabbing the Twins

We are on our third beer when I spy the Richardson's leaving the house and stepping up to the road. After looking both ways they cross over.

'Those dopey trollops are coming over, Gerald,' says Head.

'So, I see, Richard.'

'I wonder what they want.'

'God knows. Perhaps they intend coming in here to verbally attack us some more.'

'Or, perhaps they're after another frisking session. That Rebecca enjoyed it.'

I shoot him a don't be a prat look.

'It's true, Gerald. I'm telling you, she enjoyed it.'

'And I'm telling you, you're the one who enjoyed it, Richard. Good grief man, do you honestly believe a female of her class would enjoy a lowly sergeant pawing her with his great big dirty hand.'

He looks at his hands. 'They're not dirty and not that big. Believe what you want, Gerald. I know what I know.'

'We all know what we know, Richard. But sometimes we

don't know if what we know is worth knowing. If you know what I mean.'

The sisters enter the restaurant to be greeted by Pierre. After a short exchange of words, the sisters point to the table next to ours, and over they come.

Amelia gives me the once over, then says, 'Would you object to us taking this table so close to you?'

'Feel free, Miss,' says I with a hint of sarcasm.

Pierre draws back a chair and Amelia sits. He does the same for, Rebecca, who to my amazement throws, Head a saucy smile.

'Champagne, Mademoiselle?' asks Pierre.

'What else, dear Pierre,' says Amelia, fluttering her long dark lashes.

There may be far more to these snotty creatures than I imagined. Perhaps they like more earthy men than the type they usually consort with.

Once Pierre has gone, Amelia says, 'You are off the hook, gentlemen. We shall not be pressing charges over the unfortunate incident in Cedric's hallway.'

'Thank you, Miss,' says I. 'I would offer to buy you a drink in recognition of your kindness, but I am afraid a lowly policeman's income does not run to Champagne.'

'I should hope not, Inspector. Otherwise, we might think that you are corrupt. Are you corrupt?'

'Absolutely not,' lies I.

Her eyes twinkle as she stares seductively into mine. 'Then, Inspector, perhaps you will allow me to *utterly* corrupt you before the evening is out.'

'And I you,' says Rebecca to Head, as her beautiful pink tongue flicks over her ruby lips.

Head is all but drooling, but then I catch, Amelia's quick

furtive glance at the window we have momentarily taken our eyes off. I look out just in time to see a figure step out from the pathway of Walnut House, onto the pavement and hurry away.

'With me, Sergeant!' says I, jumping to my feet.

'What about my beer?'

'Sod the beer. Come on.'

'Don't go, please,' says Amelia.

Ignoring her I head for the exit with Head on my heals.

'Unless I'm mistaken, Richard,' points I. 'That is, Cedric hurrying away over there.'

'Where's he off to?'

'To warn the twins, I shouldn't wonder. Come on.'

Crossing the road and narrowly avoiding getting flattened by a speeding hackney we make the other side. Cedric is a good fifty yards ahead of us and not so easy to see in the shadowy light from the gas lamps.

'Those bloody sisters were trying to distract us,' says Head as we break into a trot to close the distance between us and, Cedric.

'To allow, Cedric to leave the house unseen by yours truly,' says I.

'The devious little vamps. But why? What's it to them if we catch the twins.'

'Nothing,' pants I, too long sitting around and a couple of beers have left me a bit breathless. 'No doubt, Cedric persuaded them to conduct their little charade as a way to punish us and make fools of us in revenge for the hallway incident.'

'Shame on them,' sighs Head. 'I just about convinced myself, Rebecca really fancied me.'

'That's your ego shattered, then. Shit, I've got a stitch coming on.'

Slowing down I clutch at my side and fall against the iron railings beneath an overhanging tree.

'Don't drop out now, Gerald,' spits Head. 'We have to keep up or we'll lose him.'

'Give me a few seconds,' gasps I. 'Christ, it's like being stabbed.'

'Do you want a piggy back?'

'No, you'll only drop me.' Sucking in air I force myself on at a slow walk.

'Shall I go ahead, Gerald.'

'Too dangerous to… go it alone,' pants I.

'I can't see, Cedric, Gerald. He's too far ahead of us. Or maybe he's veered off or crossed over the road?'

'Keep going. With luck we may well pick him up again.'

After another hundred yards or so, by which time my stitch has abated, we come to a halt.

'We've lost him, Richard. No point in going any further. He could be anywhere.'

'One thing's for certain, Gerald, Cedric must have known all along when to expect the twins home. He's conned us.'

'And didn't he do it well?'

We are close to a small park to which the gates are still open. 'I could do with a pee, Richard.

'Me too, Gerald.'

Nipping into the park we take ourselves in hand under a mighty oak tree as our feet crackle acorns on the ground. Gazing down I ponder over little acorns growing into mighty oaks and reason that such analogies aren't always true.

'The air's getting colder,' says Head, as he squirts up the bark. 'Winter's just around the corner.'

'Careful, Richard,' snaps I. 'You're splashing me.'

'Sorry. Just trying to see if I can beat my ten foot in the air record.'

Sometimes I despair about Head. I am just tucking myself

away when through the dark and descending curling mist I spy what looks like someone heading our way.

'Get behind the tree, Richard,' whispers I. 'Someone is coming.'

We sneak behind the tree where I stick my head around the trunk enough to see what's coming. Definitely one person and perhaps two others walking slowly beside him. But they blend into the darkness making it hard to fathom out if I am peering at one large person or two smaller ones practically touching each other. As they come ever nearer, I can hear a voice softly speaking. As the mist parts so I can make out *three* figures, two are dressed in black with highlights around their faces. *Wimples*, they are dressed as nuns and are walking alongside, Cedric. Slowly I draw my revolver. Head follows suit. We nod to each other. I gesture for him to go one way while I go the other, but to stay still for a moment longer. As the figures close on us, we jump out in unison.

'Stand still!' says I, pointing my revolver at the nun in the middle who's carrying a large black valise. 'We will shoot if we have to.'

'Told ya he was clever. Didn't I, Bob?' says Bill.

'Ya did, Bill. Ya did.'

'Let go of the bag, Bill,' says I. He lets it fall to the ground.

Cedric takes a step towards us, 'Stop, Cedric,' demands I. 'Move one more inch and I will shoot you. Hands in the air. Now!'

All three raise their hands, but Cedric speaks out, 'It does not have to be this way, Inspector.'

'It does, Cedric. Now shut up and speak only when spoken too. Bob, take one pace to the side away from, Bill. Cedric, you do the same. Keep those arms up high. Sergeant, pick up the valise and put it at my feet.'

Head steps forward while keeping his eyes firmly fixed on Bill and his revolver pointed at, Bill's head, as he bobs down and picks up the valise. Taking four steps to the side he dumps the bag at my feet.

'Sergeant, frisk Cedric first.'

Head steps over to Cedric and using his free hand frisks him all over. 'All clear, sir.'

'Cedric,' says I. 'Sit down on the grass and hold your hands around the back of your neck.'

Once he is down, I tell, Head to frisk, Bob.'

'I'd rather you did it, sir,' says he.

'Why?' grates I.

'I don't want to be accused of groping a nun even if *she* is a man.'

Here we are in a park having confronted two of the most dangerous criminals we've ever come across and what does Head do? He plays silly buggers. 'Just bloody well get on with it, Sergeant.'

Keeping his eyes and his revolver pointed at, Bob's head, Head bobs down. He runs a hand up the inside and outside of, Bob's leg and then the other. On patting around, Bob's backside, Bob lets out a cry of pain.

Bill jerks forward, 'Stop, copper. Ya hurtin' 'im…'

'I hardly touched him,' says Head.

'Bob is in a lot of pain, Inspector,' implores, Cedric. 'Please, be gentle with him.'

Head is on his feet, his nose barely an inch from, Bobs as he sticks the point of his revolver onto, Bob's temple. 'Like he was gentle with, French, and no doubt just as gentle with, King.'

Now comes a threat from, Bill, 'I'm tellin' ya, copper; leave 'im be or I'll cut ya fucking black heart out!'

'Back off, Bill,' warns I. 'And you, Sergeant, change places with me and keep your weapon pointed solely at, Bill.'

We change places. Cedric remains sat on the grass. With care I finish frisking, Bob.

'All clear. Bob, go and sit down besides, Cedric, with your hands behind your head.'

'He can't sit down on this cold hard ground,' says Cedric.

'Then kneel down, Bob,' says I. 'Bill, I'm going to frisk you. Please do not try anything untoward or you and your brother will find yourselves leaking blood.'

'What, say ya, copper, if I say we don't give a fuck? May as well end it here, right *fuckin'* now.'

His eyes blaze, demonic, cruel and determined. He lowers his arms a few inches as if he might be going for a weapon hidden beneath his habit. He isn't bluffing. But the last thing I want is for this to end in what would be the twin's virtual suicides. There are too many questions I want to ask them. First and foremost, where is, Sergeant King, and is he still alive?

'Back off, Bill,' says I, moving my aim to cover, Cedric. 'You may not care if you and Bob die here, Bill, but I'll bet my soul you won't risk, Cedric gaining a nice big hole through his brain.'

Panic swamps, Bills eyes. I was right, Cedric has obviously been so kind to the twins they couldn't bear being instrumental in the man's destruction.

'Alright,' says Bill, as he shoves his hands back up high. 'I give ya me word. Leave, Cedric be an' all will be well.'

'I'll trust you, Bill.'

'Well, I fucking wouldn't,' snarls Head. 'It'd be like trusting a rabid dog just because you gave it a bone.'

Going over to, Bill, I bob down and start frisking his legs over his habit.

'Kings small revolver is tucked in me trouser belt,' says

Bill. 'Ya'll 'ave ta go under me 'abit ta get it.'

'Always dreamed of putting my hand up a pretty nun's habit,' says I, to lighten the atmosphere.'

'Ya won't find nuthin' ya want up this 'abit,' laughs Bill.

After fishing out the revolver and tucking it into my holster I back away. 'Lower your hands, Bill, and put them behind your back.'

After cuffing him, I tell him to go and sit beside his kneeling brother. Head cuffs, Bob, but with, Bob's hands in front of him so as to be more comfortable. Out of handcuffs, I ask Bill if *he* has any in his valise. He does, two pairs, I use one to cuff, Cedric's hands behind his back.

'What now, Inspector?' asks Cedric.

'It's back to yours, for now. Sergeant Head will lead the way with you, Cedric, a yard behind him. Bill and Bob will follow on, side by side, while I bring up the rear. Do not try anything stupid, any one of you, unless you want this to end in one hell of a mess. There will be others out there. Couples, mothers, fathers and children. We do not want anyone forced to give us a wide berth by stepping onto the tarmacadam to go around us and getting run over. Nor do we want any shooting in case an innocent gets shot. Do I make myself clear?'

There comes a cry of "Yes," from all. 'Once out of the park, my, Sergeant and I will hide our revolvers so as not to panic anyone we see. Should anyone try to pass us, just squash over as far as possible and let them through. Does anyone need a pee before we set off?'

'I do, please,' says Bob.

'Sergeant,' says I. 'Please assist, Bob in relieving himself.'

Head gives me the horrified look. 'How exactly do you expect me to help him take a piss? I mean I can't do it for him, can I?'

'Ya gotta get his knob out an' 'old it for 'im, ya prat!' says Bill.

'Fuck off. I ain't holding no male's private part except for my little lads.' He gives the back off glare as he points at me. 'And he can't make me, do it. So, either you uncuff him so he does it himself, or he pisses himself, or someone else helps him.' He stabs a finger in his chest. 'I will *not* be helping.'

'Very well, Sergeant,' says I. 'If you wish to be silly about a willy, that's your prerogative.'

'He's my bruva,' says Bill. 'Uncuff me an' I'll 'elp 'im.'

I shake my head. 'No way, Bill. You'll stay cuffed until you're in the slammer.'

''Urry up,' cries Bob. 'I got enough pain wivout 'addin' piss to it. It'll sting like a bastard.'

'I will do it,' says Cedric.

I uncuff him. 'I trust you will not do anything silly, Cedric?'

'You have my word, Inspector.'

Cedric helps, Bob to his feet. Lifts up his habit and holds it away while he unbuttons, Bob's flies to extract his manhood. It is then that I realise we are all watching intently, as does, Bob.

'Do ya mind?' grates he. 'It ain't right ya all watchin' like that.'

'Turn your back on us, Bob,' says I.

Bob does so. We all hear the tinkling of water falling on the grass. A minute later, with me carrying, Bill's bag, we set off and exit the park, to begin our slow walk back to Walnut House. I allow, Cedric to remain free of handcuffs.

The pavement this side is clear, there's no one heading away from us or towards us.

'Is, Sergeant King dead or alive, Bill?' says I to his back.

'Very much alive,' says Bill, without turning his head. 'But he won't be able ta sit down for weeks. And 'e'll be in pain an' discomfort for the rest of his life.'

'And where is he now?'

He shrugs. 'In hospital I reckon. I gave an urchin a penny ta deliver a note to the cop station at Brixton tellin' them where we'd left the bastard.'

'Where did you leave him?'

'In a workman's shed on a derelict site where they've been knockin' down some slums.'

'How badly hurt is he.'

Pausing he turns to face me. 'We beat the skin off his arse, till he bled like a stuck pig. Just like he did ta, Bob. Didn't we, Bob?'

'We did, Bill. Just like he did ta me.'

Turning around, Bill continues the walk.

As we near the house a pair of, swaying all over the pavement, posh prats in top hats are headed towards us.

'Good evening,' says one to Head, before hiccupping loudly. 'A splendid night for a stroll.'

'If you say so,' says Head, coming to a halt to allow the prats to pass by safely.

'I do, sir,' slurs the toff, as he passes around, Head, while his companion steps into the road to pass.

'I say, Algernon,' says the one on the road. 'Nuns. And my, are they not the most beautiful angels you have ever seen?'

'Wonderful, Bertram. I look forward to going to heaven if all the angels look like this. That's if we are eligible,' he guffaws.

'Perhaps,' slurs Bertram, staring dreamily into, Bills eyes. 'The divine sister can put in a good word for us.'

'Perhaps ya'd like a good fuck with it as well?' snarls Bill.

'I say, sister. No need for profanities,' says Bertram as he wobbles further out into the road. 'Your boss won't be too happy having heard such filth coming from one of his staff.'

'Just move along, gentlemen before someone gets hurt,' says I,

It is at this point that, Bertram gets hit by the side of a carriage and knocked back onto the pavement to career into Bill and Bob. Bob hits the iron railings with a scream of pain. The drunken toff stumbles to the ground then rolls over and on to his back as he starts laughing. Before I can stop him, Bill stamps the heal of his boot into, Bertram's face with such vicious intent that I know he has done the toff serious damage.

'Back off, Bill,' yells I, yanking him back by his wimple.

'Christ!' says Head, looking down at the toff. 'That flattened his big conk.'

Algernon challenges, Bill by taking up a boxer's stance, 'Have at you, you dirty cow,' snarls he as he starts dancing around.

Stepping in between them I hold up a hand towards, Algernon. '*Police*. Cease this stupidity right now, sir, or I shall arrest you!'

Algernon staggers back a few feet while giving me the confused look. 'Arrest me? Are you a half-wit, sir? You should arrest that evil bitch for assaulting my brother, by George. Do you know who we are?'

'No idea,' sighs I. As if we haven't enough on our plates without having to deal with a pair of drunken upper-class twits. 'Just grab your brother and piss off before I lose my temper.'

Bertram is now being helped to his feet by, Head; his hand covering a nose that is leaking blood by the cup full.

After wobbling a bit, Algernon fixes me with watery eyes and says, 'We shall not be going anywhere until you arrest that vicious trollop for assault.'

'I'm already arrested ya twat,' snarls Bill, as he turns to display his cuffed hands.

'My dose is broken,' says Bertram.

'Oh, God! What absolute bunkum this all is,' says Algernon. He points at, Bill. 'You, madam must be a prostitute pretending to be a sister of the holy order. By heaven, how dare you soil the good name of the church, you should be whipped.'

That's it for, Bill. Before I can hold him back, he leaps forward and head buts, Algernon on the nose so hard, Algernon stumbles backwards before collapsing to his knees.

'You, slag!' yells Bertram as to my horror a derringer appears in his hand. Head swiftly grabs, Bertram by the wrist and wrenches his arm into the air just as the gun goes off to discharge a shot harmlessly into the air. Head wrenches the derringer from, Bertram and puts him in an arm lock.

Algernon, complete with bleeding nose, is up on his feet while fumbling for something beneath his posh frock coat, obviously a weapon of some sort. That's it for me. Shoving, Bill aside I give, Algernon a well-aimed boot between his legs which sees him fall backwards with both hands grabbing at his crotch as he struggles to catch his breath. After finding a derringer inside a coat pocket, I haul him to his feet and ram his top hat back on his head.

'You will pay for this, you brute!' gasps he.

'Damn you,' spits Bertram.

'Surname, please,' smiles I.

'Smythe,' says Algernon miserably.

'Algernon and Bertram Smythe you are both under arrest for attempting to assault officers of the law while they were about their lawful business. Discharging a firearm in a public area in an attempt to cause serious injury, or even death, to known persons. Resisting arrest and being drunk and disorderly.' says I. 'Do you have anything to say?'

'Yes,' says Algernon. 'Fuck off, you swine.'

'Sergeant, cuff, Bertram while I cuff, Algernon.'

'Have you got any spare cuffs?' says Head.

'There's a set in the bag,' says I. Rummaging around I take out the cuffs and hand them to Head. Then I cuff, Algernon with the cuffs, Cedric had on. It is then that I notice, Cedric is nowhere to be seen. 'Cedric's buggered off, Sergeant.'

'He went into his home,' says Bob, oh so matter of fact.

'Great!' That's all we need, a prisoner wandering off willy 'bloody' nilly. 'You all, right?' says I to, Bob. 'You don't appear well.' In fact, he is looking very pale and sickly.

'I need ta lay down on my tummy,' says he.

Bob's going to faint, stepping forwards I grab him before he goes down. 'He's fainted.'

'Uncuff me so I can carry 'im,' says Bill.

'What's up with him?' demands Head.

'Probably suffering from the clap,' sneers Bertram.

'He's real sick,' snarls Bill, glaring at Bertram with murderous intent. 'So, fuck up ya stupid twat before I kill ya!'

'Enough,' says I. 'Sergeant, uncuff, Bill so he can help his brother.'

'Is that wise, sir?'

'I promise not ta run for it,' says Bill.

'I'll take your word for it, Bill,' says I.

'Bill?' says Algernon, who seems to have sobered up remarkably fast. 'Strange name for a female prostitute.'

'It's short for, William Anna,' snarls Bill.

Head uncuffs, Bill, who takes hold of Bob as I release him. Bill lifts him up as if he's weightless with one arm around his back and the other under his legs at the knees. After searching the toffs and finding no other weapons, Head forces the toffs onwards with, Bill following on and I bringing up the rear. It is barely a hundred yards to Walnut House, but far enough when you're carrying a dead weight, yet Bill seems unperturbed by the task. For his size he is obviously very strong indeed.

'Thanks for this, copper,' says Bill, without looking back. 'I won't forget it.'

Let's hope I don't regret it, says I to myself. 'What's wrong with him, Bill?'

'Come closer. I don't wanna risk, Bob hearin'.'

'I'm listening,' says I, now barely a foot behind, Bill and wondering if this could all be a trick to get the better of me.

'Bob's dying,' whispers he. 'He's got cancer in his backside an' it's speadin' fast, accordin' to the specialist.'

'What specialist?' says I.

'A mate of Cedric's from a posh hospital. A Mr Parkhurst.'

'He's not a doctor, then?'

'Yeah, he is a doctor but he don't like bein' called doctor. Ya 'ave ta call him Mr.'

'I see,' says I even though I don't. 'Did, Cedric pay for the consultation?'

'Bless his heart, he did. Cedric an' Harvey are the kindest men on earth,' says he coming to a halt and facing me. 'Ain't none better. God made men like them, an' mothers like our mother, while the devil made all the evil bastards in this world.'

'You believe in heaven and hell?'

'I do. Once this is done, Bob will be goin' ta heaven while I'll be goin' ta hell. And that, copper will be the first time we'd ever have been apart. But I don't mind burnin' so long as I know he'll be with our Ma.'

He walks on. In truth he's just punched a hole right through my armour to leave me exposed to his strength of will. There's something very special about, Bill Boyle, despite his bloody crimes. I am feeling sorry for him and his poor brother when I should remain impartial and uphold the law to the letter. They are brutal, merciless criminals who have nowhere to go except towards the gallows or being shot dead where they stand. I arrested them at the park and in the dark, which was a very dangerous, and some would say, stupid action to take when others would have just opened fire without warning. But my inner ear keeps telling me that, Bill and Bob at least deserve to be heard in a court of law for the injustices they suffered as mere children, to highlight the failings of an uncaring society and a police force that should be striving to protect *all* children, not just the rich and privileged, but also the unwashed slum kids riddled with lice and rickets.

As we walk it hits me that the Smythe's are twins. Which sets me to pondering over the fact that in the entire history of the modern police force it is extremely unlikely that anyone has ever before arrested two sets of twins, with a third set, the Richardson brats, to also be arrested once we are back inside Walnut House. Assuming of course that they haven't run off, I will charge them with attempting to pervert the course of justice by assisting one Cedric Bolsover in his attempt to assist wanted criminals in avoiding arrest.

On arriving at Walnut House, we find the front door has fallen off its hinges again and has been propped up in the hall against the wall. Head skirts around the fallen chandelier followed by the Smythe's, who have been very quiet since we set off. Bill is still carrying Bob. Bob is now sort of awake and muttering incoherently.

I call out, 'Inspector Potter and Sergeant Head have entered the building along with their prisoners. Be aware we are armed and dangerous.'

Laughter erupts from the kitchen, with one voice more distinct than the rest. Clump!

Cedric steps out from the kitchen, 'I see you have gained more prisoners, Inspector,' grins he. Then on seeing Bill carrying Bob, he says, 'Oh dear. What's wrong Bill?'

'Bob passed out Cedric. I need ta lay him down.'

'Bring him into the drawing room, we shall lay him on the chaise lounge.' He looks at me. 'Chief Inspector Clump is here, Inspector. He's in the kitchen.'

'Thank you, sir. You shouldn't have skipped off the way you did.'

He shrugs. 'I thought I'd get the kettle on. Anyway, come on Bill.'

'Go with them, Sergeant,' says I. 'Once Bob is settled, cuff Bill again.' I turn to the Smythe's, who appear none too happy. 'In you go, gentlemen.'

On entering the kitchen, I find Clump along with Constables Barnsley and Thompson sat opposite Harvey and the snooty Richardson brats. The aroma of coffee, brandy and walnut cake would have been a welcome boost to my equilibrium if it wasn't for the stink of cigars and a cloud of smoke hanging over the table like a dense smog.

'Well, Inspector,' says Clump, running curious eyes over the Smythe's. 'You do realise you have the wrong pair of twins with you. They may be disguised as villainous gentlemen hiding behind bloody faces, but they definitely are not the Boyles.'

'They've gone into the drawing room, Chief with Cedric and Sergeant Head. Bob is poorly and needs to lay down.'

Clump's eyebrows go up. 'Really. What's wrong with the poor lad? Exhaustion from torturing and beating policemen I shouldn't wonder.'

'Something like that, Chief,' says I.

'I trust, William Boyle is suitably shackled.'

'He is, Chief,' lies I.

'And who are these pair of shifty looking devils?'

'We, sir,' grates Bertram. 'Are Bertram and Algernon Smythe who have been falsely arrested on trumped up charges,' he glares at me, 'by this idiot.'

'They do a lot of that,' sneers Rebecca.

'Would you and your… um… guests, care for a fortified coffee, Inspector?' says Harvey.

'We would, sir,' says I. 'Thank you.'

'If you would all care to retire to the drawing room,' says Harvey with a wan smile. 'I shall serve in there. More space and comfort.'

'Good idea, Mr Major,' says Clump.

'We have to get off, Harvey,' says Amelia clipping her fancy valise together and standing up along with her sister.

'You are going nowhere,' snaps I. 'Amelia and Rebecca Richardson; I am arresting you both for perverting the course of justice by aiding and abetting one, Cedric Bolsover in his attempt to assist two wanted criminals to avoid capture.'

'What utter rot,' snaps Rebecca. 'I and my sister shall leave right now and if you know what's good for, Inspector Numbskull, you will *not attempt* to stop us!'

'No one is going anywhere until my officers have updated me on what exactly has been going on,' barks Clump, as he stabs his cigar at the sisters.

'I thought we had reached an understanding, Chief Inspector,' says Amelia, all doughy eyed.

'We did, Miss,' smiles Clump. 'But you have just been charged with a serious offence and until I have all the facts, so I can judge whether or not a simple formal warning will suffice to allow you to depart, I must warn you to behave or find yourselves gagged and shackled.'

'Well, I…'

''Shush,' says Clump, finger on lips. 'To the drawing room. Lead on, Inspector.'

We find Bob lying face down on a chaise lounge and sound asleep. Bill is sat at the head of the huge table with one hand cuffed to the heavy looking calver he is on. His wimple has been removed, but with his long hair and makeup, he still appears very feminine.

'That bitch assaulted me,' snarls Bertram. 'She stomped on my face and broke my dose.'

'And the swine head butted me and broke *my* nose,' growls Algernon, before giving me the evil eye, 'I was then booted between the legs by that brute. God knows I may never produce an heir now. I demand satisfaction.'

'Sit down and shut up,' barks Clump. 'Everyone will have their say once I am aware of all the facts. Until then you will do as you are told and remain quiet.'

'You will regret this,' says Bertram. 'Do you know who we are?'

'Last warning,' yawns Clump. 'Speak only when you are spoken to or I will have my officers lock you both in a cupboard. Inspector, you and Sergeant Head sit beside me. Constables, sit the other side of me. Ladies, you and the Smythe's sit the other side of the table…'

'May I sit with, Bill?' asks Cedric, as he shifts a pile of books on the table to make more room.

'No, sir. Leave him sat by himself,' says Clump flicking a glare at Bill. 'Now, everyone, sit *down*, please…'

After a scrapping of chairs, we all sit. The table is so big it could accommodate twice as many people. Everyone, except the sisters, removes their hats to place on the table before them.

'We shall wait until, Mr Major has joined us before we

begin,' says Clump. 'While doing so, I advise all who have been charged with a criminal offence, to consider the possible consequences of the situation you currently find yourselves in; so that when I hear your side of events you may do so with honesty and integrity. Is that clear to you all?'

Except for, Bill, who stares unflinchingly at Clump, they all nod.

'Good. Well, done men,' says Clump softly, smiling at me and Head. 'What you have achieved this day is nothing short of miraculous. In bringing in two of the most dangerous psychopaths ever to cross swords with the Met' you have excelled yourselves and undoubtably saved lives. There is no way those evil little bastards would have stopped their brutal killing spree until God knows how many more victims had turned up. Your bravery and devotion to duty will not go unrewarded.'

'Thank you, Chief,' says we in unison.

'Now,' continues Clump. 'I apologise for not getting here sooner. I received your message from a Constable Soanes, strange fellow, not all the ticket, but at the time I had also received information of the most sobering kind. Sergeant King had been found over Brixton way in a shed and taken to the infirmary at Brixton Prison for medical assistance, because it was close by and he looked close to death. After visiting the prison and finding, King unconscious but stable, despite having his arse skinned, we headed to the crime scene to investigate. At the time I reasoned that you might be on a fool's errand and we were more likely to come up against the twins than you were. I was wrong and again I apologise profusely to you.'

'To be honest, sir, we too were wondering if we were on a fool's errand.'

'I realise that you must both be exhausted...'

'Fucking knackered more like,' says Head.

''Yes, thank you, Sergeant,' grates Clump. 'Let us sort this out as quickly as possible and get back to the Yard. Your good ladies have been informed not to expect you home until you arrive, which, hopefully will be sooner than later. Now, what is wrong with the Boyle laying on his stomach?'

I tell him what I know and to my surprise he displays some sympathy for Bob.

'French and King could not have imagined the future trouble that would result from their brutalisation of mere boys. Obviously, they were cock sure that there would never be any recriminations for their wicket acts. They were wrong and I have little sympathy for them, but a lot for their families. But we cannot have vigilantes running amok however justified they feel their quest is. Not against us or the ordinary citizen. Where would it all end gentlemen if we did not maintain law and order?'

'A right mess,' yawns Head. 'God I'm bloody starving.'

Heads eyes have focused on the huge cake being carried in on a tray by Harvey. Setting it down along with twelve small plates of dubious origin, that are well cracked and chipped, along with a cake knife he says. 'Rebecca, will you be mother?'

'If the Chief Inspector allows,' says she in challenge. 'And the Inspector doesn't shoot me for fear I shall attack him with the knife and cut off his ugly head.'

'Just cut the cake, Miss and leave the vitriolic wit to my sergeant,' grates Clump.

Harvey goes off and returns five minutes later with a huge pot of coffee, mugs, cream and sugar bowl that has naked ancient Greek males upon it. The cream jug is very graphic with the Greeks up to all sorts, Betty would appreciate it but Head, judging by his sour face doesn't.

Once everyone has cake and coffee, Harvey goes around pouring a drop of brandy into the mugs for anyone who wants a drop. Cedric feeds Bill while, Bob, still sound, starts snoring like the proverbial pig.

'Heaven help us,' sighs Clump, his eyes gazing up at the cobwebbed ceiling. 'Let us begin.'

***

We don't leave Walnut House until eleven, by which time I've gone beyond tiredness to reach a state of unhappy resolve that I'll never sleep again. Clump had a Paddy Waggon parked around the corner to which we are all in the back while a pair of plods man the reigns. When I say all, I mean Bill and Bob, the two constables, Clump, me and Head. Clump let Cedric, The Rotten Richardson's and the Smythe twats off with a warning after talking to them in private. How much they paid him to turn the other cheek, I have idea, but it wasn't pennies.

As we trot along, Head drops off and starts farting which is worse than Bob's snoring. Bob woke up for a while in the house and had a cup of tea and a slice of cake. He and Bill also changed into more suitable attire while under close watch. All their possessions, along with any evidence, was bagged up to be taken back to the Yard. Bob managed to stay awake for an hour before dropping off again. Head carried him out to the wagon and we settled him down with thick duck down cushions provided by Cedric, who told us to take it easy and avoid any holes and bumps so Bob didn't get hurt during the journey. Cedric and Harvey were allowed to give the twins a quick hug. As tears streamed down their faces, they promised the twins they would visit them in prison if at all possible. The Richardson sisters went off arm in arm with the Smythe's, who all appeared deliriously happy with the outcome of their strange day out.

Clump, as ever, doesn't appear the least bit tired. Apart from a few words he has all but ignored Bill and Bob despite Bill constantly goading him by giving him the: Go on copper, have a go, I dare ya look. But Clump wouldn't bite. Bill is handcuffed to a bull ring which forces him to sit side on, leaving him in some discomfort thus unable to sit back and relax. He doesn't complain once. All he cares about is that Bob is as comfortable as he could possibly be.

'I'm asking you, Chief,' says I once we are barely a mile from the yard. 'To ensure that Bill, and especially Bob, are treated well in the cells.'

'You want me to keep the wolves from tearing the rabid dogs to pieces, do you?' says he coldly. 'Perhaps I should ensure they receive a nice mug of hot cocoa before they go to bed and get tucked in, then read them a nice fairy story. You know the score, Inspector, they'll be queueing up to take a swing at those monsters.'

'That's why I'm asking you to put muzzles on them, sir. The twins hold vital information regarding the Mable Calver murder. The death of Razor Williams. The murder of Don Picket the safe breaker and heavens knows what else. I also want to know who else the twins intended going for and for why. Bill will take whatever you throw at him and wouldn't talk even if you roasted his nuts over hot coals. You hurt Bob even a little and Bill will not help us. But if you show Bob even rudimentary compassion, Bill will help us.'

'And you can guarantee what he tells us will be the truth, the whole truth and nothing else?' says Clump with a puff of smoke into my face.

'I believe he will be honest, Chief. What's he got to lose?'

Clump points his cigar at my nose. 'Exactly. He knows he will hang so he has nothing to lose. But then what can he hope to gain other than keeping the wolves off his brother.' He drops his voice to a whisper. 'He could lie through his teeth just to cause trouble for anyone he has a problem with while sending us out to run around all-over the place with ever increasing egg stains on our hairy beards and moustache's. However, Inspector, I am intrigued to know who the fat bitch in Bill's diary is, along with all the others he was going to slaughter once she'd opened her mouth and dropped them in it. It could be very interesting. I'll have strong words with the lads on duty at the cells to lay off and keep everyone else at bay. I think it is imperative we get the twins into the relative safety of Pentonville as soon as possible. They will be welcomed as heroes by the inmates. But, Bill in particular, will be in dire danger should he dress up as a girl and a different pack of wolves go for him with far worse intentions then just giving him a thumping. I will do as you as ask, Inspector.'

'Will you also ensure they are not separated at any time?'

He nods. 'Now I have a request, Inspector.'

'Anything, sir.'

'You be the one who wakes the sergeant up when we get to the Yard.'

'I had a feeling you'd ask me that, Chief,' says I.

'Let us hope he doesn't wake up fighting,' grins Clump.

'Or it could be lights out for me,' says I without a smile.

Grilling the Twins

Having gone through the rigmarole of 'signing' Bill and Bob in at the Yard, and seeing them safely into their cell, Clump gathered together all the plods who were on cell duty for a talk. By the time he'd finished with his threats of severe disciplinary action against anyone who so much as spat at the twins, they'd gotten the message loud and clear.

After a quick debrief and a scotch in Clump's office, Head and I were given a lift home. I finally let myself in the front door just before two in the morning while announcing that I was home. I got no reply, Betty must be sound asleep in her bed, or on the sofa.

Taking myself into the parlour I find one table lamp still alight, but struggling as the wick was burnt right down. Betty is not on the sofa. After turning up the wick I carry the lamp into the dark and very quiet kitchen where the faint aroma of an Irish stew still wafts around. No doubt my share is in the pantry and covered over with a muslin cloth. But do I fancy eating at this time of the day? No. Time for a quick wash and bed.

Twenty minutes or so later and relying only on the moon light shining in through the window, I creep over to the bed where, Betty is sound and snoring like a lady. That's soft and gentle with no eardrum busting snorts. Slipping in beside her I give her a kiss on her forehead, pull the blankets up to my chin and close my eyes.

***

When I open my eyes, Betty is stood by the bed fully dressed with a mug of tea in her hand and gazing down at me through questioning, sparkling eyes.

'You're awake at last, Detective Inspector. Tea?'

Somewhat grouchy I sit up and let off a big yawn. 'What time is?'

'I'm fine thank you, Detective Inspector. More to the point, how are you?'

'Sorry, my little wasp. I'm fine and all the better for seeing your lovely grimace.'

Setting the tea down on the bedside table she sits down on the bed.

'Whatever time did you come home?'

'Oh… About two.'

'Goodness me, no wonder you look so grumpy. You should have woken me up.'

I take a sip of tea. 'I didn't want to disturb you. Besides, I went out as soon as my head hit the pillow. What time did you say it was?'

'I didn't. Eight thirty.'

'Which gives me thirty minutes to have breakfast, a wash and shave and get to the Yard for nine.'

'What about going to the toilet?'

'I won't have time.'

'But you always go before you leave for work.'

'I'll just have to pass on this occasion and save it up for later.'

'It' isn't a good idea to deny the course of nature, Detective Inspector, you could end up with a blockage that would require a pint of syrupier figs to shift it.'

'Clump told me he wanted me in for nine this morning, Betty…'

'Well, it's alright for him, he only needs an hour or so of sleep and he's as fresh as a kipper.'

'A kipper?' grins I.

'Sounds better than a daisy, in his case. I mean; could you image saying to Clump he's as fresh as a daisy. But then I don't suppose you'd dare say he was as fresh as a kipper anyway. Still, it brought a smile to your face. Now, as you are going to be late for work anyway, do you want a little love and attention followed by a breakfast of ham and eggs, or would you prefer no love and a round of toast to eat while hurrying up the street to work?'

'I suppose I had better go for the quick option,' sighs I.

The sudden knock on the door has Betty going over to the window.

'It's, Richard. I'll go let him in. There's a kettle of hot water ready for you in the bathroom.'

I down my tea in one, which burns my throat, then stumble out of bed and make for the bathroom to the sound of Head wishing Betty good morning. He sounded even more grumpy than me. After a reckless shave, a lick and a prayer I head down to the kitchen.

'Morning, Gerald,' yawns Head, staring gloomily into his mug of tea.

'Morning, Richard,' yawns back I, as I sit down opposite him. 'You look how I feel.'

He lifts his head to give me the baggy eyes look. 'What a bloody awful night. I got home to find no dinner on the table and Chloe asleep in the bed with Thomas beside her…'

'Would you like a ham sandwich to take with you, Richard?' cuts in Betty.

'If it's no trouble,' says he, instantly cheering up.

'No trouble. I'm making, Gerald one so I may as well do you one as well.'

'Thank you, Betty,' smiles he. 'Where was I. Oh… yes. Well, I hadn't the heart to disturb Chloe and the boy, so I went back down stairs to conduct a search for my dinner. I found it in the larder in a stew bowl. It smelt like a mutton stew, looked like a mutton stew, and although I ate it cold and it was a bit greasy, it actually tasted like a mutton stew. Lovely.'

'A triumph for Chloe then?'

'It certainly was.'

'So, not such a bad night after all, Richard?'

'After my meal it all went downhill,' sulks he. 'I thought I'd kip down on the sofa and went out as soon as I pulled a coat over me in case it turned a bit chilly. The next thing I knew I was woken up by the boy screaming his head off. Course you're instantly terrified some mad man has snuck into the house and has gone for your loved ones. I leapt off the sofa and charged into the hall, stubbed my toes on the stair, tripped up the stair and twisted my back, but still kept going by clawing my way up. Trouble was it was so bloody dark; I couldn't see bugger all. On reaching the top of the stairs I was suddenly hit on the head with something hard…'

I am thinking if this sorry tale goes on for too long, we won't make the Yard before lunch time.

'Course I fell halfway down the stairs before I regained enough control of myself to scramble back up, only to hear Chloe scream out: "So you want some more, do you?"'

'Oh… dear,' says Betty. 'Poor Chloe. She must have

thought you were a burglar. Or something even worse.'

'When she hit me the second time on the head it felt like I'd been hit with a hammer…'

'Was it a hammer?' asks Betty.

'No. It turned out to be the piss pot, I realised this when it smashed on my skull and wet stuff ran all down my face.'

'Just wet stuff?' says Betty. 'No little boys pooh or sick with it?'

'No, thank Christ.'

I am staring from one to the other unable to understand how they have become so wrapped up in this, everything else has been forgotten. Betty has stopped making the sandwiches and Head has completely forgotten that we need to get a shift on.

'As I stumbled back down the stairs,' continues Head, 'I managed to call out: "Samantha, It's me your beloved."'

'Samantha?' says Betty as a hand goes to her mouth.

Head pulls a what a prat I was, face. 'The knock on my head must have jumbled up my brain. I don't even know a Samantha. I've never known a Samantha…'

'We need to get a shift on, Richard,' cuts in I.

'He can't leave it there all up in the air,' says Betty. 'It'll drive me mad if I have to wait until later to hear the rest.'

'Nip around to Chloe's and get the rest from her,' snaps I. 'We really must go!'

'Why the rush, Gerald?' grates Head.

'Because, Clump is expecting us to be at work by nine.'

'No, he isn't.'

'He bloody well is, Richard. He quite emphatically told me to get in tomorrow by nine o'clock.'

'No, he didn't. What he actually said was: "Do *not* come into work tomorrow before nine o'clock." 'And I said: "Would about ten o'clock be alright?" He replied: "Absolutely fine."'

'Are you sure he said that?'

'Absolutely. We have plenty of time, Gerald…'

'Good,' says Betty. 'What happened next, Richard?'

'Realising it really was me, Chloe let me into the bedroom. We lit a lamp and then picked up Thomas from the floor.'

'What was the poor little mite doing on the floor?' gasps Betty.

'Trying to crawl under the bed to get away from the fracas,' says I.

'It was no joking matter, Gerald,' says Head, giving me the stern look. 'The poor little lad must have fell out of bed and hit the floor boards. Shocked and disorientated he awoke screaming, which set in motion the chain of events that followed…'

'Goodness me,' says Betty. 'Was Thomas hurt?'

Head shakes his head. 'He's like his dad, tough as old socks. Anyway, after he'd had a drop of mother's milk, he dropped off again and me and Chloe had a talk. Well, more of an ear bashing really. Chloe demanded to know who this Samantha tart was. I told her I had no idea as I'd never known a Samantha.'

'But she didn't believe you, did she?' says Betty caustically, hands on hips.

'No, she didn't,' says he appearing amazed by the fact. 'No matter how much I pleaded my case she refused to believe me and accused me of all sorts. Oh… And that's where you come into it, Gerald.'

'Me! What the devil has your row with your wife got to do with me?'

'Chloe, amongst other stuff, accused me of paying a plod to deliver a false message informing her that I would be late because of work. When, the truth was I was with this Samantha tart…'

'How did Chloe know she's a tart when she's never met her?' says I.

'A natural assumption,' grates Betty. 'Be quiet, Detective Inspector you're interrupting Richard's story.'

'Sorry,' says I. 'Where do I come into this, Richard?'

'You're my cast iron alibi. Once you confirm to Chloe that we really where out until the small hours just doing our duty, then peace, love and passion will quickly return.'

'I will go and see her, Richard,' says Betty, 'and confirm that you were telling the truth…'

'But what if I was also lying as to where I'd been?' says I.

'I know when you're telling me porky pies, Detective Inspector. I also know when you are stretching the truth and when your eyes start wondering no matter how furtive you think you are. You were one hundred percent genuine last night and I am proud of you. Of you both, even though I don't know exactly what you were up too last night, I know it was Kosha and to do with the Boyle twins.'

'We captured them, Betty,' says Head. 'Thanks mostly to Gerald's brilliance and my dogged determination to catch the sods come hell or high water…'

'Good God!' says Betty. 'Was anyone hurt?'

'No one, except for Bob Boyle when I felt up his bum.'

Betty's face is a picture, her eyes open extraordinarily wide and her jaw drops.

'It's a very long story, Betty,' says I. 'I will tell you all about it later. Now, this is an order: Sandwiches please and then we must go.'

'Just a minute, Detective Inspector,' says she, sitting down opposite Head. 'I need to explain something to Richard first.'

Going over to the work top I pick up where Betty left off.

'Leave those,' says Betty. 'I'll finish them in a minute.'

'I am quite capable of making a couple of sandwiches, Betty. Just say what you have to say so we can get off.'

'No need to get grumpy, Detective Inspector. Right, Richard. The thing is this, even if Chloe believes you were working last night and not messing around it doesn't alter the fact that you called out another woman's name and not hers. Calling your wife by another name is one of the worst things a man could do, especially during moments of conflict between you or even casually. She says: "Did you enjoy your dinner, Richard?" You answer somewhat absent minded: "Lovely thank you, Samantha." Another is to call out another woman's name during sleep. But the absolute pits, is to call your wife by the wrong name during love making just as you… you… you know?'

'You know what?' frowns Head. 'I'm not following, Betty.'

'Just as you release your little tadpoles into her pond,' says I.

'Thank you for that brilliant repartee on the miracle of conception, Gerald,' grates Betty.

'I'm with you now,' says Head as he spreads his arms wide. 'I do not know a Samantha now, or, at any other time of my life. Now I get what you're saying, Betty, but how the hell can I convince Chloe that I'm telling the truth…'

'Right!' snaps I. 'Time to go, Sergeant. We shall discuss your problem on the way to the Yard.' I hand him his sandwich suitably wrapped in wax paper. 'I will see you later, Betty.'

She gets to her feet and gives me a peck on the cheek. 'Any idea what time?'

I shake my head and shrug. This is the worst part of being a copper, the never being sure when you'll get home. Or, even *if* you'll get home.

'I will talk to Chloe, Richard,' smiles Betty. 'Don't worry, it will all turn out fine.'

Time to go.

***

Thirty minutes later we are in Clump's office where we find him polishing up a pair of derringer pistols which look just like the ones, we took from the Smythe brothers.

'Take a seat, lads,' says he. 'Do you know these little pistols came all the way from the American Wild West. Those Smythe brothers had them sent over from relatives they have living in a place called Baltimore.'

'You didn't give them back to them, Chief?' asks I.

'No. I confiscated them,' smiles he. 'For the Police Welfare Fund, of course. They must be worth a few bob.'

'Undoubtably,' says I.

'Right, to the business in hand,' says he, putting the derringers into his drawer. 'The Chief Constable came to see me an hour or so ago. He is cocker hoop over the arrest of the Boyles. And sang your praises like an Irish Linnet. Well, more like a strangled cat really. Bravery awards, exceptional devotion to duty awards.' He holds his hands up. 'You name it and he intends to shower you with it. What do you say to that, lads?'

'Marvellous,' we chorus. However, I know Clump and there is that look in his eyes that says he's not so happy about something.

'Did the Chief Constable visit the twins, Chief?' says I.

'He did,' frowns Clump. 'I went with him, to also ensure the twins were being treated well. The Chief Constable did not speak to the twins, he just glared at them. But, nowhere near as fiercely as Bill Boyle glared back at him.'

Clump goes quiet and appears deep in thought, then, snapping out of it, he says, 'What do you think of the Chief Constable, Sergeant? I am asking you because I know you will answer me without any bullshit.'

'He stole our Aphrodite statue,' says Head. 'The man's a

hypocrite and a serious pudding puller.'

'Was that the same statue you stole from lost property?' says Clump.

'It was, Chief,' says I.

Sitting right back, Clump gives us the searching look. 'What I am going to say to you now, must be kept strictly between us. Is that understood?'

'It is,' says we, even though we are agreeing to something we might not be happy to keep secret once we know what it is.

'After visiting the Boyles, the Chief Constable and I had coffee in this very room. Just the two of us, that is. He demanded that the twins be tried, convicted and hung before the weekend.'

'But that's only three days away,' says I. 'Giving us limited time to question them over the killings of Mable Calver, Don Picket…'

'Or over anything else,' cuts in Clump. 'I told him that you would require considerably more time to question the twins over the unsolved cases and other crimes that have yet to be brought to our attention. He then demanded to know what other crimes. I answered that the twins may well have committed other serious crimes that we have no knowledge of.'

'Did you mention we also want to find out who else the twins were going for and why?'

Clump shakes his head. 'Sometimes, Inspector, you get this gut feeling that something isn't right. I got that while talking to the Chief Constable. Something said to me do not mention about the twin's determination to track down, torture and kill more people who have done them wrong. Top of their list being a woman, no less.'

'A cover up,' says Head. 'That old sod can't afford us to turn up anything that might be embarrassing to the establishment. Which means he already knows there is something to find out.'

'Exactly,' frowns Clump. 'He then agreed to extend the time to the trial, conviction and execution of the twins until Tuesday next week. I pleaded with him it would give you no time to follow up on anything the twins might tell you. He got really angry and told me in no uncertain terms that it was non-negotiable and demanded that the twins must swing within a week. I then asked him, why the rush?'

'Which was as good as accusing him of being shifty,' say Head.

'It was,' says Clump. 'He didn't answer me. Instead, he then demanded that the twins be transferred immediately to Pentonville. I asked him why? And he said: "They should be in the appropriate establishment, Chief Inspector and not held in a station cell which is for temporary custody only." I agreed with him, but emphasised that as our time was limited it would be much more convenient to hold them here for questioning to avoid all the rigmarole of arranging visits, etc.'

'He was going to have them topped, I reckon,' says Head. 'Easy as hell to have someone killed in prison.'

'As we well know,' says Clump. 'Anyway, he reluctantly capitulated. The twins will remain here until their trial date. They will then be transferred to Pentonville.'

'That's if they make it to trial,' says I. 'Over the years there has been several suspicious deaths of troublesome prisoners in our cells, that we are all aware of. Especially on prisoners who have attacked and even murdered one of our own. They really would queue up to hang the twins in their cell while making it appear it was suicide.'

'Agreed,' sighs Clump. 'We are between a rock and a very hard place, lads. The twins are only marginally safer here than they would be elsewhere. But at least we can keep an eye on them twenty-four hours of the day. I intend to select uniformed officers I trust to stand guard over the twins and see to their needs. Even so, we will run the risk of the twin's murders before they're even been tried, let alone convicted. You have a week to question the twins and follow up on anything they might tell you.'

I shake my head. 'It isn't long enough, Chief.'

'I know that, Inspector. But bear with me; I intend going way above the Chief Constables pompous head. Call it the old boy network. All being well, we shall have our extension for as long as would be considered reasonable for you to conduct your investigations. Now, whatever you do, do not allow anyone to over hear you question the twins about anything you know you must keep between ourselves. Although a few red herrings wouldn't go amiss. Is that clear?'

'You can trust us, Chief,' says I.

'With your very life,' grins Head.

'I perish the thought, Sergeant. At twelve o'clock, I will be conducting a talk in the meeting room with as many detectives and uniformed officers who can attend. I will be showing them the grisly contents of the twin's bag and then go into detail about their crimes and the reasons for those crimes. I hope to impress on those officers the importance of policing within the legal guidelines that we should all be adhering to. There's nothing wrong in giving a piece of shit a damn good thumping, but a whole lot wrong with going way over the top to fester the kind of hatred that has led to the twins, brutal, even satanic revenge. You two need not attend.'

'Thank you, Chief,' says I.

'Right lads, I need to prepare for my rendition. Bugger off and get grilling the twins.'

We thank him and get to our feet.

'One more thing,' says he, just before we go out. 'I would

happily hang the twins myself given half a chance. Just bear that in mind and don't forget what the twins have done. Do not become attached to them.'

***

After leaving all our weapons at the desk, we make our way to the cells where we are informed by the guard that the twins have been no trouble whatsoever. On entering the cell, which is barely big enough for one let alone two, we find Bob sat on a thick cushion on his bed ready nursery rhymes and Bill shadow boxing against the bleak grey walls. Neither is shackled in any way. Light comes in from a small bared window set high above Bob's bed. There's nothing in the cell other than two small wooden beds with thin straw mattresses, a bucket for a toilet and a small corner table with jug and basin for washing in. There are two towels and soap in a dish beside the basin. Naturally there is nothing to shave with as the twins don't shave yet. There's a pair of enamel plates on the floor that have been wiped almost clean, no doubt by the bread that went with the meagre breakfast. Eating implements are all wooden. There are two enamel mugs, one half full with wishy washy horribly coloured tea. Or is it something far more horrible? Bill and Bob are in drab grey prison uniform complete with black arrows. Bill turns away from the wall and meets my eyes while Bob closes his book and looks up at us.

'Ya made it then,' says Bill.

'Have they been treating you well?' says I.

Bill nods. 'The foods crap, but at least it ain't rotten. The beds are as hard as bleedin' floor boards, but at least Bob's got plenty of cushions.'

'How is your pain, Bob?' says I.

He gives a hiccup and then slurs, 'Best it's bin for years.'

'He's high on laudanum,' grins Bill. 'That hairy copper,

Clump brought it in and poured it into Bob's mug. Cedric sent it.'

'That was kind of Cedric,' says I. 'Right, Bill. We're going to go to the interview cell where we can conduct our interview and questioning of you both in relative privacy. Unfortunately, you will have to be shackled.'

'Ta make sure we don't run off,' grins Bill. 'If only Bob *could* run.'

'You still wouldn't get far,' says Head, with menace.

Bill points at him, 'Does he have ta come?'

'He does, Bill,' says I. 'Sergeant Head will be taking notes along with his own input. I trust you will behave at all times.'

'Ya 'ave my word,' says he with conviction.

'Thank you. Right, the guards will ask you to step outside one at a time where you will be shackled, wrists and ankles, all linked together. Please do not struggle as that would aggravate the guards into becoming rough. And we don't want that, do we.'

'I said we'd behave,' says Bill. 'And behave we shall.'

Shackling the twins went without an ounce of conflict. Along with three guards we escort the twins to the interview cell, passing through two thick squeaking iron barred doors, each one unlocked by a pair of large iron keys. A third, much thinner, barred door opens to the interview cell. A twelve foot-by-twelve room with a heavy wooden table and two long benches each side. The benches are screwed to the floor, not in fear of someone pinching them but in fear they'd be lifted up to hit you on the head with. Two sides of the cell are barred, the other two, grey bricked. A pair of glazed and barred windows are set high in the ten-foot walls to allow light in.

One of the guards' places Bob's thick cushion onto the bench and assists Bob to sit. The guard is one of Clumps handpicked men, I know him quite well. He'll do what Clump wants, but you can tell he'd be just as obedient should Clump tell him to slit the twin's throats.

'Could we have coffee for four, please?' says I to one of the guards.

'Would you like fancy biscuits with that as well?' says he.

'Chocolate and ginger would be nice,' says Head.

The guard stomps off, slamming and locking the door behind him. One guard stays inside the room, the other remains outside. They are taking no chances with the twins and I can't say I blame them.

'Bill,' says I. 'We only have a few days before your trial to interview you and follow up on anything you tell us. So, we shall be coming back regularly. Before the trial we will discuss your plea options. You could put in a plea of insanity for instance…'

'We'll be pleading guilty ta everything,' says he, with indifference.

'That will be your choice, Bill. How old are you?'

'I'm fifteen and Bob's an hour or so younger.'

'That's good news, Bill. No one below sixteen has faced capital punishment for years.'

'Can we talk about it later on? Just you an' me.'

I nod. Bill obviously doesn't want to discuss capital punishment in front of Bob.

'I would like to talk about your lives preceding our arresting you five years ago.'

'Why?'

'Because I am interested and want to understand what led you onto the path of criminality.'

'What's he mean by that, Bill?' says Bob.

'He just wants ta get ta know us a bit better, that's all it is, Bob. Just bein' friendly.'

Bob smiles, 'That's good init?'

Bill places a hand over Bobs and gives it a squeeze.

'Let us begin,' says I. 'Please start taking notes, Sergeant. I am curious, Bill. Why did you pick on Franklin Frobisher to kidnap? Why select that particular field to hold your… um… sheep race, and why have it photographed?'

'It all goes back to when our Ma died. Do ya want to know about all that?'

'I do, Bill. But in as brief a statement as possible.'

'Understood,' says he. 'Ma died and the ol' man died a month after, when me an' Bob was about six or seven years old.'

'That's tragic, Bill. Did they succumb to the same sickness?'

'Nah. The ol' man murdered Ma, an' then he got hung for it.'

'Then they threw us in the orphan 'ouse,' says Bob. 'An' it was terrible weren't it Bill?'

'Bleedin' 'orrible it was,' says Bill. 'We weren't nothin' more than slaves. Beaten an' abused. The food was shit an' the beds full of lice. We stuck it out through the winter an' a cold spring, then ran off once the weather was warmer. But, goin' back to before the ol' man murdered Ma, I'll tell ya what happened. The ol' man had a good job down the docks and when he was sober things were alright. When he was drunk and he'd lost money gamblin' he turned into a monster. I was in bed when I heard the door slam an' the ol' man fallin' all over the place. I knew poor Ma was in for it. She'd wait up for him in case he wanted anything, an' I mean anything. I lay shiverin' with fear. But then I heard laughter. Ma was laughin' an' the ol' man was laughin', but I daren't go down to see what was goin' on.'

The rattling of keys interrupts us. The guard comes in with coffee pot, mugs, milk and hard tack biscuits on a wooden tray. Setting it down he says,' Anything else, Inspector.'

'No, thank you.'

'I hate those hard biscuits,' says Head. 'They're not fit to give a dog.'

'It's them or nothing,' grates the guard.

'I like them,' says Bob.

'You can have my share,' says Head. 'Where's the sugar?'

'There ain't any,' smirks the guard. 'We don't give it to criminals 'cause it makes them go bonkers.'

'What a load of crap,' says Head. 'You're just being mean.'

With a sneer the guard clears off and the door is locked. I pour the coffee and place the plate of biscuits between Bill and Bob. Bill tucks in but Bob just pecks at his. He doesn't appear the least bit well, his eyes are sunken, sad and distracted. Perhaps he's just out of it because of the laudanum, or more likely he is truly dying before our eyes.

After a sip of coffee, I urge Bill to continue.

'The next morning me and Bob got up and went downstairs. Ma gave us a big hug while the ol' man smiled at us. He told us he'd taken the day off to take us all out. He'd hired a small carriage with a beautiful grey horse ta pull it. We took a posh picnic and set off for Hampstead Heath. It was a lovely day, no cloud and just a gentle breeze. It was warm for mid-autumn. We had the time of our lives.'

'We was like kings, weren't we Bill?' says Bob.

'Kings for a day, we were that, Bob. We picnicked by the sheep meadow. The ol' man played football with us. Ma just lay in the grass with a happy smile on her face. Later we went to a pub and had ginger beer and crisps. Ma had sherry an' the ol' man beer. It was the best day of our lives. The sun was setting when we finally set off for home. Dark when we arrived. The ol' man dropped us off and said he'd got to take the carriage back. He said he wouldn't be long, but he might just nip into the Ship for a pint…'

He drops his eyes and I can see they are welling with tears. Head isn't taking notes, obviously as it has nothing to do with our investigations. I'll remember it all anyway. Bill takes a few gulps of his coffee while Bob looks about to drop off.

'Once the ol' man had gone,' continues Bill. 'Ma told us he'd won a pile of money. So much that we could go for buying our own little place. That was the real reason she was so happy. The ol' man wasn't back by the time we went ta bed, but we went tired and happy. I don't know what time he came 'ome, but it were late and he woke us up…'

At this point, Bob covers his ears and closes his eyes.

'The ol' bastard was drunk. He started shouting, cursin' and bangin' things about. I snuck out of bed and out on the landin'. Ma was cryin' and pleadin' with him ta calm down. But he wouldn't, he'd lost all the money he'd won that he'd got left and more besides. Then Ma said somethin', I can't remember what she said, he went mental and attacked her. I can't say what he did, except afterwards he ran out the house and I went down ta help Ma. Bob came down, he'd wet himself and was shakin' like a leaf. Ma's face was all punched in and bloody. I… I…'

'Stop, Bill,' says I. 'No need to say more if it upsets you this much.'

He looks into my eyes. I see deep into his where I see intense pain and sorrow.

'Never told no one about this,' says he. 'But then no one ever asked before. I'll go on. I ran outside and banged on next door. The man answered, I told 'im Ma was hurt bad and he came in our house ta look. Ma was dead, he said. Then his wife came in, the door was open, others came in along with a copper. Me an' Bob were taken in next door for the night. The police soon caught the ol' man, they found him hidin' down the docks. They locked him up and he went ta trial next day. No one would 'ave believed it but the judge sentenced him to be hung by the neck until dead. He appealed, dragging his fate on for a few weeks, but he still got the rope. We went to Ma's funeral a week after she'd died. The next day the neighbours handed us over to the authorities and we found ourselves in the orphanage.'

Bob takes his hands away from his ears, and says, 'Is it done, Bill?'

Bill nods.

'Let's have some more coffee,' says Head sombrely. Even he has been touched.

Head fills the mugs up. Bill chomps on another biscuit. Bob is very quiet, just staring at the mug in his hands. Five minutes later, Bill continues.

'Once we'd run away from the orphanage, we decided we'd get right away in case we got caught an' 'ad ta go back. We went ta Hampstead, because we'd been so happy there and we could dream of Ma. It was a long walk. We only had what clothes we 'ad on. We drank out of streams and begged food on the way when we passed through a village. But no one would give us anything. They'd just shoo us away. But we eventually made it ta the meadow and hid up in the sheep shed. There were sacks in there, we used them and straw for beddin' an' settled down for the night.'

'It was nice in there,' says Bob. 'A bit smelly, but no one ta beat us an' we did what we liked. Them sheep were friendly, except for them ones with balls who kept tryin' ta ram us.'

'They were shits,' says Bill. 'We survived by stealin' from the fields and the houses nearby. We took eggs from chicken coops and vegetables from fields an' gardens. Pies and bread from a baker; we'd slip in the back when the owners were servin' customers an' help ourselves.'

'We lived like kings. Didn't we Bill?'

'We did that, Bob. We even stole clothes off linen lines. We liked ta go an' look into the shop windows, especially the photo shop owned by Frobisher. One day we promised ourselves we'd 'ave enough money ta get our photograph taken again. See, when we were there with Ma an' the ol' man we went into the shop and had our photograph taken.' He looks at me. 'Do you think we could have it back?'

'I will see to it,' says I. 'Once our governor has finished with your things, I'll let you have anything you want providing it's allowed.'

'No weapons then?' grins Bill.

'No weapons. Now, do you want to carry on or take a break.'

'I'm enjoyin' talkin' to ya,' smiles he. 'Of course, we used ta get chased away from shops an' that. Frobisher was the worst; he'd come flyin' out waving a cane and shout out somethin' like: "Be gone you thieving little rats or you will find my cane across your backsides." Anyway, after about three weeks of livin' free, we knew it wouldn't be long before we were forced ta leave. On coming back ta the shed early one mornin' with an arm full of carrots, who should be standin' there talkin' to a copper? No other than, Frobisher. We'd been rumbled, that Frobisher must 'ave followed us an' discovered where we were hiddin' out. We'd managed to avoid the farmer even when he tended to his sheep, but now we were done for. Frobisher spotted us; he pointed an' yelled out. The copper ordered us ta stand still, but we weren't about ta go back to no orphanage, so we dropped the carrots an' ran for it.'

'We ran like the wind. Didn't we Bill?' laughs Bob.

'Like sails bein' blown by a force eight,' says Bill. 'They couldn't catch us. But we were done with at the meadow and headed for London. The weather changed, it blew up a storm and we got drenched and really cold. We found shelter beneath a big tree an' shivered away all night. We was done in when we finally got ta London. We travelled all over lookin' for somewhere ta stay. We begged, scavenged and we stole, but it weren't no good, me an' Bob began ta starve and turn rotten. Better that then going into the poor 'ouse. But then our saviour came before us. None other than Razor Williams.'

'Some saviour,' says Head. 'I'll bet he snaked his way into your minds so you'd do whatever he wanted.'

'He did that an' more,' says Bill. 'He talked us in ta goin' back ta his, for food and drink. Cause we weren't about to say no. And that was the start of his controlling us. He put us up, clothed and fed us as he taught us how ta get by. He was like that Fagin in the Oliver Twist book. Cause we never thought he'd use us the way he did. Once we'd got fattened up and the scabs had disappeared, he said we was ready to start payin' 'im back for all he'd done for us. Razor had loads of tarts workin' for him, but only one was special to him. He called her Dolly. It were a Sunday, early evening in the walled little yard out back of his terrace. Dolly had a tin bath filled up. Razor told us ta strip off an' get in. Dolly gave us a scrub an' washed our long hair. Razor wouldn't let us 'ave it cut, he said it made us look pretty boys. After the bath we was dressed in nice clothes complete with top hats.'

Pausing he drinks some more of his coffee, Bob follows suit, then he coughs a bit as tears fill his eyes. He covers his ears. It is obvious where this is leading to.

'We was taken out in a hackney, but weren't allowed ta see where we were goin. About a half an hour later we was outside a house with red lights in all its windows. Cause I knew what sort of place it were. Razor hurried us inside and we were taken upstairs an' into a big bedroom with a four-poster bed in it. Gaudy colours of purple an' red with not much furniture. That's when the fat bitch came in ta look us over. "They look good, Razor," she'd said. "Let's see how good." We was ordered ta strip again. She looked us over again, even looked in our gobs and said, "Perfect. Well, done, Razor." Then she put white night gowns on us an' told us ta get in the bed. "You boys will be set up for life if you do as you're told," she'd said. "You're going to have visitors. Obey everything they order you to do and we'll get along fine. Play up and you'll find yourselves in big trouble. Ain't that right, Razor?" Razor took out his cutthroat and waved it close to our faces. "You won't be pretty boys ever again, that's for sure,' he'd snarled at us. 'You can guess the rest.'

'The dirty rotten bastard,' says Head, gritting his teeth. He's thinking about Chloe and how she was used and abused as a child.

'Do you wish to take a break, Bill?' says I.

'Nah. Cause, we were too terrified not to do what we was told. About two hours later we was taken back ta, Razors where we were fed lovely food and given beer. I prayed that we'd never have ta go through that again. But it was only the start. Razor earnt a fortune out of us over the next few weeks, but we barely saw a penny of it because we had ta pay 'im back what we owed. Then one night he took us ta Walnut House. It was a grand dump and we didn't like it. Dark an' a bit smelly. We met Cedric an' Harvey an' I dreaded what they'd do to us. We was shown into the drawing room and asked to wait. Once in there, Razor told us ta strip off. He said the men were scientists who needed twins to do studies on, and we'd better do as we were told or we'd get it. We stripped off and stood there naked and tremblin'. Razor went out the room, ta get his money in advance no doubt. Then he left. Cedric and Harvey came into the room and saw us standing there all naked and terrified. They were horrified and quickly helped us get dressed. Tea and cake at the kitchen table followed while they asked us about ourselves. We kept tight lipped about what we had been forced ta do, knowin' what we'd get if we opened our mouths. For all we knew these kind men could be workin' for Razor an' were as nasty as him and wanted ta find out if we were snitches. But they weren't an' 'ave never been anything but kind and loving.'

'What did they want from you?' asks Head, dubiously.

'They were studying identical twins for a science paper,' says Bill. 'They wanted ta know just how identical we were. Did we like the same things? Could we tell what the other was thinking? Were we intellectually the same?'

'We did games,' says Bob. 'My favourite was the ink blot game. Ya blob some ink onto a paper, fold it over and squash it. Then ya open it an' say what ya see in the picture.'

'All innocent, then?' says I.

Bill nods. 'After going back a few times, Cedric urged us ta go an' live at there's away from Razor. But that would 'ave put them in danger. Ya don't do the dirty on Razor Williams an' get away with it. He'd 'ave slaughtered 'em. But we wanted out, and that came when we met the Wild Boys.'

'The Wild Boys?' queries I.

'The ones who blew themselves up when ya came lookin' for us down at the gardens.'

'Why did they blow themselves up?' says Head.

'Just an accident. They were messin' around with explosives. They were goin' ta rob banks an' needed explosives ta blow the safes. But the twats were so stupid they just ended up killin' themselves,' He grins and Bob giggles. 'Anyway, they took us under their wing because they needed us ta squeeze through windows an' let 'em in so they could rob places. Now they were so crazy that even Razor daren't go against 'em. We was free from Razor. We didn't eat so well, or dress so well and were more likely ta get caught by the coppers. But then we didn't 'ave ta worry no more about Razor or the filth he forced us ta do. We was free an' happy until a pair of clever sods caught us.'

'Sorry,' says I. Oddly enough I meant it. 'How long were you with the Wild Boys before Joe Straw killed Razor.'

'Joe Straw didn't kill Razor. We lied,' says Bill.

'Who did kill Razor?' says I.

'We did,' smiles Bill. 'But we weren't gonna tell ya that at the time. Everything was as we told ya, except as Razor came swaying towards us, drunk as he was, he pulled out his cutthroat. He was goin' ta do us. We just lifted off the iron drain cover an' then I shouted out somethin' like, "Ya want some ya fucker? Come on then!" An' he did, he came at as like a mad bull an' went straight down the hole. But then he managed ta stand up and start ta climb out. Bob got one side of the cover an' I got the other, then we dropped it on 'is bonce an' he fell back down right into the shit. While we was lookin' down ta see if he was dead we was joined by the big bastard, Joe Straw. He looked down an' said, "Good work lads. You've saved me a job. Couldn't 'ave done better me self." Then he sauntered off.'

'So, you believe Straw was going to kill Razor anyway?' says I, glancing at Head to make sure he's taking notes.

'Cause he was. Straw killed Mable Calver an' Razor witnessed it.'

'How do you know that Razor witnessed Mable's murder?'

'We know a lot of stuff. Don't we Bob?'

We all look at Bob, his head has flopped down and he's snoozing quietly.

'He gets really tired lately,' says Bill. 'Anyway, the thing is this. I've got lots of information for ya, but I want something in return.'

'Ask away,' says I.

Bill flicks his eyes to the side, 'Not with him standin' so close behind us,' whispers he. 'He's probably listenin' in ready ta tell ya governor.'

I am just about to ask the guard to leave us for a few minutes when the third guard returns and shouts out through the bars as if we're miles away, '*The Chief Constable wants to see you and the sergeant, right now.*'

'What about?' grates I.

'*I don't know, do I? It ain't my place to ask the hierarchy what they want, is it?*'

'I suppose not,' grates I. 'We best go and see what he wants, Sergeant.'

What about them, then?' says the guard inside the room, pointing at the twins.

Having no idea how long we'll be I say, 'Best to take them back to their cells.'

'Yeah. And make sure you treat them well,' warns Head. 'Or you'll have us to deal with.'

***

'Are you going soft on the twins, Richard?' says I as we follow the guard to wherever the Chief Constable is waiting for us.

'No, I am not going soft, Gerald. But I do believe the twins weren't born evil, but have been turned evil by other evil bastards. They never stood a hope in hell of living a good life. It isn't fair and it isn't right. If we can get them off the death sentence then I'd feel better about it. But they'll still have to be locked up for good.'

'They'll hang them,' says I, soberly. 'There's no way

they're going to let them live. Whether or not Bob lives long enough to hang that is. Either way, Bill doesn't want to live once Bob has died. Bill will plead guilty and go to the noose without a blink of the eye, but I don't think Bob will be going with him.'

'I'm not following you, Gerald.

We stop and face each other while the guard carries on oblivious. 'Even if Bob lives long enough to face trial, Bill will kill him so that he doesn't have to face the hangman.'

'Oh…' says Head. 'A mercy killing.'

I nod and we walk on.

***

Chief Constable: Sir Robert Briers, having temporarily taken over the duty officer in charge of cells, office, is sat behind a desk flicking through the Times. On entering he folds the paper most neatly and waves us to sit. He is in full uniform, minus hat and looks at us through narrow, sneaky but challenging sharp blue eyes. Bushy grey moustache and hair that is cut regimentally short up the sides but thick on top. He is a tall man with ruddy fat cheeks but thin pail red lips. He is not very well liked by the rank and file, but is well received within the realms of his own kind.

'Gentlemen,' smiles he. 'Firstly, allow me to congratulate you for your sterling work in capturing those evil; Sons of Satan. I have already put in place a reception in your honours. More on that nearer the event as I am, as always, pushed for time. I understand from D. C. I. Clump that the Boyles may have important information regarding ongoing investigations to do with various unsolved serious crimes, past and present. May I ask; have you learnt anything from the Boyles as yet?'

'We have, sir,' says I. 'Bill Boyle has confessed that he and his brother, five years ago, murdered one, Razor Williams, a violent criminal who was linked to the killing of one: Mable Calver, a prostitute. They also have information regarding the murder of one: Don Picket, a safe breaker linked to robbery and blackmailing of the upper classes.'

His eyebrows go up and I notice that not only are they not bushy, I believe they are used to being plucked. 'I see,' says he, the inflection in his voice telling me he couldn't care less. 'It sounds as if, Inspector you are being forced to run around in a pointless quest to solve crimes that have as such sorted themselves out. A violent thug was killed, at the time, by a pair of delinquents who have since evolved into two of the most vicious killers we have ever come up against…'

When he says we, he meant us, thinks I, because we sure as hell hadn't noticed him anywhere about when we were out risking life and limb.

'A common prostitute was murdered, perhaps by this Razor fellow, or by some other violent pimp. Either way she chose such a life style and off course paid the ultimate price for being a lazy trollop who preferred renting out her wares in place of good honest, Godly work.'

I flick a glance at Head, his eyes are glazing over and I just pray he doesn't lose it with Briers.

Briers rabbits on, 'As for this Picket fellow, again we have a habitual criminal who destroys the lives of the good and the Godly in pursuit of easy gains no matter the suffering he causes.'

'He still had his face blown off, sir,' says Head. 'Murder is murder, is it not, sir?'

Briers' cheeks are turning crimson, a flicker of fury crosses his eyes as sitting back he says, 'It is, Sergeant. However, sometimes we must prioritise our investigations into solving crimes that affect the good people of this glorious city in preference to the gutter trash criminals that almost always sort themselves out amongst themselves anyway, if you understand what I mean?'

'We do, sir,' says I. 'But in the Boyles case we do not know what other crimes they may have carried out. For instance, you may recall the brutal rape and murder of a young socialite from a year or so back during a break in at a mansion just off Hyde Park...'

'I do, Inspector. The young lady in question was known to me. We attended the same church services. I do not recall that you were investigating the crime.'

'We weren't, sir. The case is still very much open, but hasn't gone anywhere since the murder. I believe the twins may well have information on that and other despicable crimes.'

He rubs a hand over his chin, I have cornered him and he can't get out without compromising himself. 'I see. Take my advice, Inspector, take everything they say with a large pinch of salt. They will be out to discredit the force and stir up unfounded allegations against the upper classes. Do excuse my manners, gentlemen. Allow me to offer you both a tot of the finest.'

The draw is opened, a bottle of serious single malt comes out along with glasses and a box of cigars. They weren't put in there for us, but were put in there so that we didn't see them before whoever was expected to enjoy them turned up. He pours three generous tots then passes two over. The cigar box is offered, but we politely decline.

'To you, gentlemen,' says he, raising his glass.

After a sip, I say, 'Thank you, sir. Do we have your blessing to continue with our interrogation of the twins?'

'You do, Inspector. Keep me informed on any progress. Do not forget that the twins will stand trial next Tuesday. I expect the trial will be short and that the ultimate punishment will take place the following morning…'

'The twins have informed us that they will be pleading guilty, sir.'

That brings a smile to his face. 'No plea bargains or pleas of insanity? Underage declarations?'

'None at all, sir. They have accepted their fate without complaint.'

'Excellent. Thank you, gentlemen. Needs must I am afraid. Drink up and return to your duties.'

We down the scotch, get to our feet and leave.

'That bastard is hiding something,' says Head as we make our way back to the cells.

'His haste in sending the twins to hell, can only mean he wants to shut them up as quickly as possible before they say something that he or his cronies will regret.'

'Like being linked to the madam who used the twins. We need Bill to give us her name.'

'We'll do that now,' says I.

'What times lunch?'

'Right now, if you want.'

'Lovely,' smiles he whipping out his ham sandwich from his jacket pocket and unwrapping the paper.

Pausing just before we turn the corner to the guard room, we quickly scoff our sandwiches.

'Nice ham, Gerald, but I would have liked a bit more of it along with thicker butter.'

'I shall bare it in mind next time, Richard.'

'I wonder how Betty got on with Chloe,' says he, looking somewhat worried.

'Betty will smooth things over, Richard and all will be back to normal.'

***

Back in the interview cell with a fresh pot of coffee but no more biscuits, we continue interviewing the twins.

'Right, Bill,' says I. 'First of all, I believe the Chief Constable came to eyeball you both the other day.'

'He did.'

'Have you ever met him before?'

He shakes his head. 'I stared hard at him, tryin' ta remember if he was one of the 'visitors' who used us at the whorehouse, but he weren't. But I'll bet he knows others who did visit the fat bitch's place.' His face screws up in fury. 'All toffs they were. Rich bastards. They treated us like bits of meat.'

'Like lamb chops to the slaughter, we were,' says Bob.

'We need her name, Bill,' says I.

'I thought ya would 'ave guessed by now,' says he.

'Sadie Place,' says I, her name having crossed my mind a few times.

'I knew ya was clever, Mr Potter.'

'Mr Potter, is it? What happened to copper?'

'We've got respect for ya, ain't we Bob?'

'We have, Bill. Mr Potter it is.'

'What about me?' says Head.

'Mr Dick Head it is then,' says Bill. 'So, what comes next, Mr Potter? Will ya raid the bitches place or not? If ya do, go on a Sunday night, that's when she mostly has the youngsters in, it's quiet then. No drunks or riff-raff.'

'We would have to watch the place for a period of time or have more evidence from other sources before we can raid the place. Sadie Place knows too many of the right people, Bill. We would have to have cast iron evidence to be able to try and catch her in the act of supplying children for disgusting purposes.'

'I understand that,' says Bill. 'But you and I both know that the bastards who used us will get away with it. They'll be a cover up. The fat bitch will mysteriously disappear and it will all blow over. Except, somewhere, someone will take over where she left off and nothin' will 'ave changed. That's why we intended ta sort the bitch and her 'customers' out ourselves.'

'All you say is true, Bill,' says I. 'And I'm sorry we caught you before you had a chance to get to her. What's done is done, I'm afraid.'

'Don't you know any names of those who used you?' asks Head.

Bill shakes his head and Bob follows suit. 'They were all careful not ta give away any details of themselves,' says Bill. 'No doubt the bitch put 'em straight from the start.'

'That lady told us her name,' says Bob.

'What was the ladies name, Bob?' says I.

'I can't remember, Mr Potter.'

'I do,' says Bill. 'She never came ta the whorehouse, Razor took us out ta hers a few times. She was an oldish bird, posh and good lookin'. She wanted ta paint us for a huge canvas on the Ancient Greeks. We just posed naked or in various stuff like togas. But she never touched us and she paid well, but that bastard, Razor took it all. As we knew the run of the place, we went back a few years later and robbed her ta make up for what we never got. Cause we never dreamed we'd find a letter ta blackmail her with.'

'You're talking about Lady Elizabeth Fraser,' says I 'But I thought you worked for the builders who were extending her house?'

'Nah. Don't know who told ya that, but we never worked for her except on the paintin'.'

'Then we were lied to,' says I, 'to cover up the fact that she had dealings with a notorious pimp, and to cover up her involvement with child sex slaves, even if it was in an artistic way.'

'Devious,' says Head, jotting it down in his note book.

'She was nice ta us, really,' says Bill. 'I weren't happy with blackmailin' her or her lover. So, I'm glad it all fizzled out. Now, I expect ya want ta know about everyone who was involved in the blackmail attempt, and whether or not Joe Straw really done Don Picket in, or if I just lied. And better still, who Straw works for.'

'I would, Bill,' says I.

'I'd want ta make a deal first. I tell ya everything I know in exchange for ya doin' something for us.'

'Go on.'

'They're goin' ta swing us next week, Mr Potter. Me an' Bob are resigned to it, ain't we Bob?'

'We are,' says Bob, as he gazes into my eyes and smiles, which kicks me right in the emotional stomach. 'We're goin' on the swings, me an' Bill. And then, and then we're goin' ta heaven ta be with our Ma. It's gonna be fun, ain't it, Bill?'

Bill lays a hand on Bob's shoulder and gives it a gentle squeeze. I now have a lump in my throat as big as a coconut and I feel retched. These killers before me are little more than children, Bob in particular has the mental capacity of a not very bright seven-year-old. How different would they be now if life hadn't been so cruel to them? They were doomed the day their beloved mother was murdered. Looking away from Bob I look into Bill's eyes; they are sombre and sad but somehow at peace.

'Me an' Bob wants ta go an' visit our Ma's grave one more time, Mr Potter. Do ya think ya can arrange it?'

Sitting up straight I take a deep breath. They're asking one hell of a lot. They're killers of policemen, hated beyond hate even though they had considerable justification for their heinous crimes there is little sympathy for them, from the force or the public. It is difficult enough as it is to keep the wolves from tearing the twins to pieces, let alone to grant them favours, favours that will spell sympathy and exoneration for their crimes by many. *I* do not personally hate the twins nor do I have a problem with them taking a last trip outside to visit their mother's grave, but it will not be easy to arrange.

'Where is your mother buried, Bill?' asks I.

'City Cemetery. Plot 2109.'

'You have a good memory, Bill.'

'We've been a few times since we've been back, ain't we Bob?'

'We have that, Mr Potter,' says Bob. 'We put flowers on Ma's grave. And a real fluffy kitten.'

'The cuddly toy type of kitten, was it?' says Head.

Bill shakes his head. 'Bob found it dead a few feet from Ma's grave an' he said: "I think I'll put the fluffy kitten with Ma, so she'll 'ave company in heaven." 'So, that's what we done.'

Dropping my eyes, I try counting the life grains in the table rather than show that I'm close to tears. I'm so choked up I'm finding it hard to breathe.

'Can ya do it then, Mr Potter?' says Bill.

'It will take some doing, Bill. I'll have to speak to my chief, if he can't sanction it then we're buggered. But he's got a lot of clout and the chances are reasonable. If it's a go we'll have to arrange it for tomorrow or the next day at the latest.'

'Yeah,' smiles he. 'Next week would be too late. And flowers. Could we have some flowers?'

'I'll arrange it. You know they won't allow you out without being heavily shackled. Plus, you will have a large well-armed escort in case you've set it up for accomplices to break you free.'

He shakes his head and laughs. 'No trickery, Mr Potter. I give ya me word.'

'Anything else?'

'We'd like ta see Mrs Potter. If not here then at the cemetery, if only to wave at her.'

This one throws me so far emotionally I'm in danger of landing in the Thames.

Bob says, 'If we wave at Mrs Potter, will she wave back?'

'She will, Bob. Honestly, she will. I'll er… have to ask her, but I am certain she will say yes. She'll not be allowed to come and visit you here, but as the cemetery is a public place, they cannot stop her going there.'

Bill smiles, his eyes have gone soft and he looks about to cry.

'What's up Bill?' says Bob gazing forlornly into his brother's eyes.

'Nuthin'. Just crunched me balls when I tried ta cross me legs.'

'Oh,' grins Bob.

'So, we 'ave a deal, Mr Potter,' says Bill.

'We have a deal, Bill.'

We shake on it across the table, complete with rattling chains. Bob holds out his hand and I shake that also. Then Head does something unexpected, he reaches over and offers Bill his hand. They shake hands, and then Bob shakes Head's hand, and then his brothers.

'We trust you, Mr Potter,' says Bob. 'Bill says you're a good honest copper.'

'Thank you, Bob. I am not the only one, my sergeant and many other coppers are decent human beings. Unfortunately, you've mostly had dealings with the rotten bastards.'

'Talking of bastards,' says Bill. ''Ow's king getting on?'

'He will walk again, apparently. But he'll be effectively crippled for life and his sex life is over for good.'

'Not all bad, then,' grins Bill.

'I'm really tired, Bill,' says Bob. 'Too much excitement, I reckon.'

He looks suddenly dreadful, grey and insipid as his head falls forwards and a deep sigh leaves his rasping lungs.

'I'll 'ave ta take him back,' says Bill.

Bob has passed out. I order the guard to assist the twins back to their cell. Interview over for the day.

Bill Tells All

Checking in with the desk sergeant I am handed a letter. Taking it to our office we sit down and I peruse it.

'It's from Sally Pollard,' says I. 'She's sorry for the short notice, but hopes we can attend Pollard's funeral on Friday. Details enclosed.'

'So, the old sods dead then?' says Head.

'I hope so, Richard as it isn't nice burying someone who's still breathing.'

'Sometimes, Gerald you have a very peculiar sense of humour,' grates Head. 'We're too busy to attend funerals at the moment, Gerald. But we could use it as an excuse to skip off work and go to the pub instead. We could drink a few toasts to him.'

'The wake is at the Dirty Duck, Richard.'

'We'll go somewhere else then.'

'I think it best we attend the funeral and then on to the wake. Who knows who'll turn up? I'll bet ex- Superintendent Shaver will be there and possibly Mrs Shaver also.'

'Hmmm. Tongues are loosened over a few drinks,' says Head. 'Once armed with the information we should get from

Bill tomorrow, we'll have a damn good idea how to sneakily worm stuff out of Shifty and his trollop of a wife.'

'Indeed,' smiles I. 'We may well be able to oversee the twins visit to the cemetery before Pollard's dumped in the dirt as his burial isn't until three o'clock. Thus, saving us having to wait around or having to return on another day.'

'Like killing two bodies with one stone,' grins Head. 'Anyway, isn't it about time we had some proper lunch?'

'You've only just had lunch. Was there something wrong with your ham sandwich?'

'No. I said it was lovely, but it only filled the hole a bit, I need more sustenance or I'll weaken through food fatigue and become unable to function properly.'

'Come on then, I could do with a tea and a toastie.'

'Balls to a toastie,' says he scrambling to his feet. 'Pie, mash and mushy peas for me.'

***

'I can't believe they'd ran out of bloody pies,' moans Head for the umpteenth time as we trudge back to the cells to check on the twins.

'Never mind, Richard' grates I. 'At least you managed to fill your gaping chasm with a fry up big enough to bloat an elephant.'

'But I wanted pie and mash. I'd set my heart on it. Besides elephants don't do sausage and bacon, or eggs and fried spuds.'

'Perhaps, with luck, Richard, Chloe may have a nice home cooked steak and kidney pie for your dinner tonight. That's if she's even speaking to you.'

'Do you think, Betty has soothed Chloe's furrowed brow.'

'Most certainly. I am only goading you, Richard because I am fed up with your obsession with gluttony. Let us drop the food subject and get on.'

We find all is quiet around the cells. A pair of plods are sat outside of the twin's cell around a small table and tucking into pie and mash lunches.

'Bleeding typical,' growls Head, starring at their meals with ravenous intent.

I peep into the cell to see Bob lying face down on his bed. There's an extra wooden bucket close by as no doubt the poor soul is feeling very sick indeed. Bill is laying on his back dozing on his bed.

'Has a doctor been summoned to tend to Robert Boyle?' says I quietly to the plods.

'Yes, sir,' says one, 'he said the boy should be in the infirmary, but his brother wouldn't let us take him unless he could go with him. But the super' said, no chance.'

Understandable, thinks I. 'Did the doctor give him anything?'

'Just more laudanum. He told us, out of ear shot of the twins, that he doesn't expect the boy to live much more than a week. He said he'd be sick a lot and start messing himself. I ain't being funny, sir, but we ain't cleaning up the mess when he should be in hospital.'

'How many bloody messes have you cleaned up after a murder, Constable?'

He shrugs and shoves a chunk of meat into his mouth.

'Exactly. Just do the best that you can. The twins go on trial on Tuesday and by Wednesday morning you won't be seeing them ever again.'

The other plod swallows whatever's in his mouth and says, 'The superintendent told us they've brought the trial forwards to Monday.'

I am angry and astounded by this revelation. 'For what reason?'

'The Chief Constable ordered it because he's afraid the sick one might die before they can hang him.'

'Leaving us even less time to question them,' says Head.

Careful what I say in front of the plods I pull Head a good three yards away. 'We could wake Bill up and continue the interview right here in his cell.'

'I can't see them agreeing to that, Gerald.'

'I'll order them. There doesn't appear to be anyone else about to countermand my orders. Time really is of the essence, Richard.'

'Let's get on with it then.'

Going up to the plods who are wiping bread around their plates to scoop up every drop of gravy, I say, 'We are going to interview William Boyle in his cell.'

Two pairs of challenging eyes meet mine.

'We can't allow that, sir without the super's agreement.'

'He isn't here, but I am, Constable.'

'He'll be back soon; you'll just have to wait.'

'I am your senior officer. I am ordering you to allow us access to the cell.'

'It'll be on your head, sir.'

'Then so be it. Where is your super anyway?'

'He went out for lunch with the Chief Constable and a few other high rankers. Alright, we'll open up. Who cares, we're being relieved in a couple of hours.'

The second the door opens, Bill sits up to study us through wet eyes, he's been crying.

'Are you up to continuing the interview in here, Bill?' says I.

He nods. 'Any chance of a drop of the 'ard stuff?'

'No alcoholic beverage for the prisoners allowed,' says a plod.

'Coffee it is then,' says I. 'If you don't mind, Constable.'

He shrugs. 'I'll have it sent over from the canteen. Anything else?'

'Yes. Kindly keep out of ear shot whilst we are interviewing the twins. They may relate sensitive information to us that must not become general knowledge.'

'No earwigging then?' sneers he.

***

Ten minutes later, after a coffee laced with a drop of scotch from Head's hip flask, we plod on with the interview while Bob remains almost comatose.

'Once we 'ad the letter,' says Bill. 'We went ta see Larry the Lizard while thinking that the lady must have sent letters back to that Palmer bloke. Larry robbed his safe and found a bundle of letters. Larry don't do blackmail normally, but in this case, he was right keen. Now, how the hell that Joe Straw, the big ugly bastard, became involved I don't know...'

'I'll tell you later, Bill. Just tell me what you know for certain.'

'What we told ya about Straw was the honest truth. Like I said before, we went ta see Larry, but just as we approached his 'ouse we heard a shot an' darted into some bushes. The next minute, Straw came out tucking a sawn off under his coat. Straw definitely topped Don Picket. After that I decided to drop the blackmailing of the lady and Frobisher in case Straw came after us. We had too much other stuff ta get on with. Five years earlier, Straw 'ad also broken Mable Calvers neck and Razor Williams witnessed it, but Straw saw 'im. Razor ran off an' hid up for a while until he thought he was safe. Cause he hadn't reasoned with me an' Bob. We done him in, witnessed by Straw who was obviously goin' ta do Razor in 'imself anyway.'

'How do you know all this?' ask I.

'Dolly told us. Razor told her about what he'd seen when

she was holed up somewhere with him. After Razor was found down the sewer, Dolly was lookin' for revenge and we told her the same tale we told you, that Straw done him in. She believed us an' said she was gonna pay a couple of hard cases ta do Straw in. We told her ta drop it as Straw was too dangerous, but she wouldn't listen. Two days later a pair of thugs were found floatin' in the Thames with their skulls caved in. Dolly was found the next day strangled on her bed with her own drawers around her neck. No evidence, but I'll bet Straw done 'em in.

'That Straw's like a phantom, turnin' up when least expected an' comin' out of nowhere. He always seems ta know everything about everything. Like he's got a sixth sense or somethin'.'

'More likely he's extremely well informed and has a string of narks looking and listening out for him. He's also arrogantly confident that he will get away with murder even if he was caught,' says I.

Bill gives me the quizzical look as Head says, 'Friends in high places has Straw, Bill. And you're lucky he didn't catch up with you or you wouldn't be talking to us now.'

'Maybe,' says Bill. 'Maybe not. Still, we'll never know.'

'Who do you think, Straw was working for?'

'He's free-lanced and will work for whoever pays what he demands. Sadie Place employed him ta do Mable in, I'm certain of that, because Mable had been opening her gob about all sorts that went on at the whorehouse. I don't know who paid Straw to top Picket but I'll wager it was Palmer.'

'You're not far out, Bill,' says I and go on to tell him about Sir Arnold Falconer being Palmers illegitimate father, or is that the other way around? And Lady Fraser almost certainly being Palmer's mother.

'So ya sayin' that Palmer's been 'aving it off with his own

mother?' says Bill, looking suitably horrified.

'It seems like it,' says I. 'Now, the only people who definitely know about this, apart from Falconer, is myself, my sergeant, Clump and now you… But Falconer, hopefully, doesn't know we know or we'd probably be dead by now.'

'Don't worry, Mr Potter,' says Bill, crossing his heart. 'I'll not tell a soul, and if I'd have known about it before hand, I wouldn't have tried blackmailin' Palmer or the lady.'

'But that still leaves you and Bob on Falconer and Straws hit list. And several other hit lists from those who also want you and Bob silenced before the trial over your unwilling involvement in Sadie Place's filthy doings.'

'You're not safe here, Bill,' says Head. 'Clump has done his best to keep you safe for as long as he can, but even so, every day is a bonus and the trial is still five days away.'

'But would they dare ta try an' get to us while we're in here?' says Bill.

I nod. 'As risky as it is they just might, and the trouble is, Bill, there isn't a bloody thing we can do to help other than move in with you.'

That brings a wide grin to his mouth. 'Or ya could move us out.'

'Not even Clump could get that one sanctioned.'

'I wouldn't worry about them comin' for *me*, Mr Potter if I was armed. See, there's plenty of weapons ya could use just in this cell ta defend ya-self. But if Straw turned up, you'd need somethin' special.'

'Such as?' says Head.

'A flick-knife would be good. Ya can easily hide it, it's quick ta use an' fuckin' deadly. Even Straw wouldn't last long wiv his throat cut.'

I meet Heads studious look. All of our weapons are in the

guard's office, except I'd noticed, when we emptied our pockets under the plod's watchful eyes, Head's flick-knife. The question is, dare we hand it over to Bill? There would be absolute carnage should he attempt using it to break out or just to slaughter the odd plod for the hell of it. But then he won't go anywhere without Bob while Bob's still alive. If the knife is found or turns up in someone's guts there'd be one devil of a furore to find out where it came from. And it is well known in the Yard that Head carries a flick-knife. But then several other coppers carry extra weapons that they shouldn't, but they haven't got access to the twins.

'I'm sorry, Bill neither of us carry such a weapon,' lies I.

'Just a thought,' says he. ''Ow about a small iron bar?'

I shake my head.

'Do you know the names of any of the other children, Bill who were taken to the whorehouse?' says Head, obviously to get Bill off the weapons subject.

'Nah…, we saw a couple of young girls once, but weren't allowed ta speak ta them. But I knew who brought 'em there. Curly White's his name. Do you know of him?'

'We do,' says I. 'His girls worked the slums just outside what was Razor's patch. Another nasty bit of work, is Curly. He and Razor hated each other's guts. But they kept out of each other's way out of mutual fear of each other.'

'Curly took over Razors patch an' his girls after we done Razor in. I tried gettin' Curly ta open up about the young girls he supplied ta the whorehouse, but he wouldn't say nuthin'. So, I put 'im on our list, but I'll never 'ave the chance ta go for 'im now.'

'We shall pay him a visit before the weekend,' says I. 'You never know, he may just tell us something we can use to help nail Sadie Place.'

'I doubt it,' says Bill. 'An' watch the bastard, Mr Potter, he ain't scared of no one.'

'I'll bear it in mind. Right, I think we are done for the day, Bill. We shall return tomorrow. Hopefully, Bob will be feeling better and may even tell us something important that he's remembered.'

'Not likely,' says Bill sadly. 'The poor sod can't remember what he 'ad for breakfast sometimes.'

'I will get the photograph you want from, Clump and bring it to you tomorrow. Anything else? Would you like some chocolate for instance?'

'Bob loves chocolate,' smiles he.

'Then chocolate it shall be.'

***

We head for Clump's office. By now he should have had lunch and is enjoying a cigar and a scotch.

'Come in and join me,' bellows Clump when we knock on his door.

'You must know our knock, Chief,' says I as we go in.

'It pays to remember sounds, Inspector. Like visual memory it can be invaluable. Sit down and tell me all you have learnt from the twins. Scotch?'

'Yes please, Chief,' says we in unison as we take a seat opposite.

We tell Clump all we'd found out from the twins. He listens in silence, apart from the odd fart, a few growls of anger and lots of tuts.

'We must keep the information regarding the selling of children for sex strictly to ourselves for now,' says he, as he tops up our glasses. 'It is dynamite, gentlemen and it is obvious that Briers is fishing to find out if you have any idea what has been going on for years at Place's whorehouse. We could be talking about politicians, aristocrats, business men and even high-ranking members of the force who will all close ranks to squash any investigations into the sordid secret world they frequent. To be honest, I am not the least bit sure where you should go with all this from now on…'

'On the surface we could stick with the murders of Mable Calver, Razor and Don Picket,' says I, 'while secretly poking around for information on the names of those who visited Place's place for illegal gatherings with children.'

He breathes out hard, sucks on his cigar and then downs his scotch. 'No one up high is the least bit interested in the murders of, Calver, Williams or Picket, Inspector. And once the twins have been executed, they also will soon be forgotten. The second the establishment get even a whiff of our involvement in investigating child sex slavery that may or may not name VIPs, they will swiftly ensure we drop it like the proverbial hot coal, while destroying our reputations and careers in the process.'

'We could bring the press in, Chief,' says Head. 'They'd love to be involved.'

'Wouldn't they just,' growls he. 'I would want cast iron proof on all and sundry before getting the press involved, Sergeant. Such investigations can topple governments and destroy the status quo with far reaching consequences…'

'Are you telling us to drop it, Chief?' asks I.

'No, Inspector, I am not. I am saying; be very, very careful how you go. If this Straw fellow did do for Mable, Picket, this Dolly woman and the pair of unnamed thugs found flouting in the Thames, he will certainly have no qualms about topping you two. For now, take it easy and only tell Briers enough to keep him sweet and ignorant of your true intentions. I, personally, want to see those who believe their gilded positions in life are above the law, are brought to justice and punished accordingly. Cast iron, gentlemen, so cast iron that even the most powerful maggot couldn't wriggle their way out of it.'

'There is another way, Chief,' says I.

'Go on,' says he.

'If, Bill Boyle were to escape from his cell and 'allowed' to continue his quest for revenge...'

He holds up a hand. 'I didn't hear that, Inspector. Do not forget, either of you, that the twins are a pair of seriously twisted criminals who will shortly be on trial for the most heinous of crimes. I need time to consider all you have told me. Get off home for the remainder of the day. Think about all we have said and exactly what you are getting into. Think of your families, your careers and your very lives. Sometimes, lads, we all have to put ourselves and our love ones first. Life is too short as it is without risking it being even shorter.'

'Before we go, Chief,' says I. 'Bill has asked if he could have his family photograph back.'

Opening his draw, he pulls out the photograph and handing it to me, says, 'Except for the photo, everything else in the twin's bag will be going into our black museum. Just remove the glass before you give it to the twins. I will sanction the twins visit to the cemetery, but it will have to be heavily policed. What time are you thinking of?'

'Sometime in the morning, if possible, Chief. Afterwards the sergeant and I would like to attend John Pollards funeral at three in the nearby chapel...'

'The old sods finally died then?' says Clump. 'There will not be many in attendance I shouldn't wonder. Me included. Where's the wake?'

'In the Dirty Duck.'

'Wonderful. I shall see you in there, but I could be a bit on the drag so save me a plate of sandwiches.'

'Will do, Chief. How did the lecture go?'

'Extremely well, Inspector. Only twenty could attend, but I believe they thoroughly enjoyed it. Mind you, there wasn't a one who failed to express their hatred of the twins and what they'd like to do to them.'

'No doubt,' says I.

'Right then,' smiles he. 'Bugger off and leave me to contemplate my navel.'

***

'We could ask Sally Pollard what she knows about the children who were brought to the brothel,' says Head as we head home on the tram.

'We could be putting her life in danger, Richard. Besides, she has just lost her husband and it would be somewhat insensitive at this particular time to question her about her past. We'll start with Curly White tomorrow. Who knows he may be willing to talk for a small bribe?'

'I doubt it, Gerald. Talking of money, I can't see us making anything worth talking about while we're on this case.'

'Me neither,' sighs I. 'Not even a reward for finding Frobisher's dirty photographs or Lady Fraser's letter.'

'Those photos would have looked good in the forces museum,' grins Head. 'They'd be queuing up to see them.'

'With salivating tongues and their eyes out on stalks, I shouldn't wonder.'

Tears and Revelations

'Your home early, Detective Inspector,' says Betty as I enter the kitchen to find her rolling out pastry on the table.

Stepping up behind her I wrap my hands around her waist and nuzzle my nose into her hair and drink in her sweet scent.

'You smell divine,' says I.

Twisting around she pulls me into her light blue dress and meets my eyes.

'And you just smell,' grins she.

'As in stink smell or manly sexy sweat smell?'

'Manly sweat, a bit overpowering, but it does do something for a girl. It's the kind of smell that stirs me up and makes me want to strip you naked and give you a bath.'

'That sounds lovely,'

'I'll have to finish the meat pasties for dinner first, then I am all yours.'

'All of you or just some of you?'

'That's a silly question coming from a Detective Inspector who should know by now just how well his butter is spread.'

'A strange cliché my little annalist.'

Breaking away she dusts flour from her apron off my jacket. 'There's an article in the paper about a gas explosion on Marylebone High Street. Walnut House, it said. Isn't that the house where you said the twins had been hiding out?'

'It is. Well, I was right, I told Cedric Bolsover he had a gas leak but he insisted it wasn't a problem.'

'Obviously it was,' grins she. 'The papers in the parlour. Go and relax while I finish getting dinner ready for the oven.'

'No rush. Tell me how you got on with Chloe.'

'All good. She realises that having been hit on the head with a hard wooden hairbrush followed by a chamber pot was enough to scramble the brains of an ox, let alone a man.'

'Even a man with a head as hard as Richards,' says I.

'Indeed. Anyway, to make up for not believing, Richard didn't know, or had never known a Samantha, Chloe's cooking him his favourite tonight. Steak and kidney pie with mash and mushy peas.'

'Risky…'

'Oh, thee of little faith,' grates Betty, giving me the admonishing glare. 'Chloe's cookery skills have come on in leaps and bounds of late, Detective Inspector and I am confident that her pie will be a roaring success.'

'I never said it wouldn't be, Betty. The risk comes from Richard ravishing Chloe way beyond the normal for cooking him his favourite pie when he'd been drooling over the thought of one for hours. I will bet that the second he enters his kitchen and gets a waft of the pie baking, he'll throw all pleasantries to the wind and she'll be flat on her back on the kitchen table before she's had time to dust the flour from her hands.'

'Sometimes, Detective Inspector, you can be incredibly crude and base. Just go and read your paper.'

I hang my jacket and bowler up in the hall and then pour

myself a scotch in the parlour before settling down in my favourite armchair by the fire, even though the fire hasn't been lit yet as the house is quite warm. Luckily, Cedric and Harvey were having their evening meal across the road when the blast happened. Probably caused from the fire they lit in the drawing room just before they went out. The blast wasn't big enough to demolish the house, but it did blow out the down stair's front windows, bring the ceiling down and cause a fire that swept through the hallway and into other downstairs rooms. The fire brigade turned up and quickly had the fire under control. A: 'Beware. Danger to Life' sign was placed outside the house and since then, Cedric and Harvey have been ensconced in a nearby boarding house of some repute. No mention of Fabio. No doubt he was out catching rats or he'd joined his masters for lunch across the road. Pity.

An hour later, having put the pasties in the oven, Betty joins me in the parlour, dragging the tin bath in with her.

'I've got four buckets of hot water all ready,' says she. 'Help me fill the bath and then we can get in and scrub each other's backs.'

'Lovely,' says I, putting aside the paper and my scotch. 'Then we must talk, Betty. I have a favour to ask of you.'

'What favour would that be, Detective Inspector? If it's too naughty I will probably say no…'

'It's nothing like that, Betty. It concerns the twins.'

'Oh…' says she, her smile dying on her lips. Betty has immense sympathy for the twins, she understands that what they have done can only end in death or life imprisonment. Even so, she cannot help feeling dreadfully sorry for the terrible life the twins have had to endure from such an early age. When I tell her just *how* terrible their lives have been, I have no doubt she will shed tears of utter anguish and will readily agree to the twin's request.

***

By ten o'clock the following morning, Head and I are again talking to the twins in their cell. Bob is awake and sitting up in his bed on a huge soft cushion. He is in good spirits, but still looks rough, he is also, judging by the vagueness in his eyes, still stoned on laudanum. Bill informed us that the Reverend Albert Shields was allowed to visit them in their cell that very morning and we'd only just missed him. He will now visit them every day and will accompany them to the gallows. Cedric and Harvey had also requested, several times, permission to visit the twins, but had been turned down.

I hand, Bill the photograph and two bars of chocolate.

'Thank you, Mr Potter,' says he, with a smile. 'Chocolate, Bob. We've got chocolate.'

'I like chocolate,' says Bob, his speech somewhat slurred.

Bill breaks a small chunk off one bar and feeds his brother. Bob sucks very slowly on it, he looks as if the effort is painful, even so a broad smile crosses his mouth.

'The chief has sanctioned the visit to your mother's grave tomorrow, Bill,' says I. 'Betty will be honoured to be there and promises to wave.'

'Lovely,' says he. 'Bless her angel's heart. The reverend is comin' as well. I don't suppose, Cedric an' Harvey could come?'

'No one can stop them visiting the cemetery, Bill. But they would have to stand way, way back from where we'll be. Obviously, I can vouch for Betty, but I cannot do the same for Cedric and Harvey. If they come too near the plods, who will be armed, they will get jumpy and it all could turn nasty. You and Bob will then be frog marched back into the waggon and the visit would be ruined. Sorry, Bill, that's just how it is.'

'I understand, Mr Potter. Thank you, and you, Mr Head for all you have done.'

'You are welcome. Now then, has anything else come to mind since we spoke yesterday? Any names of children who were used. Names of those who used them? Anything at all, no matter how trivial you believe it to be.'

He scratches at his head, while I ponder whether or not to tell him that Clump has ordered us not to push too hard with our investigations. I decide I can't tell him or he'll go to his grave knowing his and Bob's abusers will most certainly never be brought to justice.

'Couldn't think of nuthin',' says Bill, feeding Bob another piece of chocolate. 'I was up half the night goin' over it all, but my mind was distracted. I kept thinkin' of ma, an' the good times we 'ad when we was little. Strange I should remember so much detail, ain't it?'

'A sign of intelligence, Bill,' says Head. 'I remember a lot about my childhood as well. And, like you, it wasn't all bad.'

'No,' smiles he. 'And soon, for me an' Bob it will all be over.'

'I feel sick,' says Bob.

Bill holds a bucket up and pulls back the thick cloth that covers it just as Bob throws up. It is a wretched sight; the lad is on his last legs. I'm thinking he may not survive the journey to the cemetery, assuming he survives till then anyway. Nothing much except laudanum and chocolate comes out of Bob's mouth, obviously he hasn't eaten much, or he's constantly throwing up whatever he eats. Bill cleans his mouth up and settles him down on his side on the bed.

'I'll be alright by tomorrow,' says Bob, so quietly you can hardly hear him.

'Ya will, Bob,' says Bill, as tears swamp his eyes.

We wait while Bob drops off into a fretful sleep before continuing.

'Tell me what you did and where you went once Bob was fit enough after the birching?' asks I.

'Why?' says Bill.

'Because I am interested, Bill.'

'And me,' says Head.

'Alright,' says Bill. 'Hard as I tried, I couldn't stop Bob's wounds getting' infected. We 'ad no money so I couldn't pay for a quack. Cedric always said we could go ta him whenever we needed help. After stealin' a luggage trolley from the station, I got Bob onto it and pushed it ta Walnut 'Ouse. I had ta get a trolly 'cause Bob couldn't sit down, so he stood all the way. Cedric and Harvey were horrified at our condition when we turned up, but they was as good as their word. We moved in. Cedric got a doctor and Bob got a lot better in a few weeks. We stayed there for two years. Cedric an' Harvey taught us ta read and write along wiv a lot of other stuff, like geography and history.'

'I had wondered how you learnt to read and write,' says I. 'Especially as I assumed you had no schooling whatsoever.'

'We 'ad a bit at the orphanage,' says he with a grimace. 'But we didn't learn enough ta even sign our names. Anyway, after a while I got restless. I wanted revenge for all that we'd suffered and I needed ta learn other skills. We left Walnut 'Ouse an' got in wiv a gang of hard nuts who made their money through offerin' protection and score settlin'. I learnt ta fight, ta terrorise an' ta be clever in all I did. 'Cause Bob weren't strong enough ta learn boxin' an' dirty fightin', but he weren't afraid of no one anymore. After a year wiv the gang we left an' looked out just for us. Then I started ta plan our revenge. We went back ta Cedric's because we needed a safe haven an' somewhere ta hide out. Cedric got us work wiv the funeral directors an' we took it from there.'

'Did Cedric and Harvey know you were planning to get your revenge even if it meant killing someone?' says I.

'Maybe, but they never asked us anything about what we was about. They taught us 'ow ta dress up an' become someone else. Cause we said it was for our protection when we went out, cause too many people were after us. The rest ya know.'

'We do,' says I, while wondering just how much we do know about the twins. Perhaps, very little. Bob isn't very bright, while Bill is devilishly clever, utterly ruthless and incredibly violent. That is all by the by as their fates are sealed.

We stay with the twins until lunch time. After a canteen lunch we then spend the remainder of the day brushing up on other cases we were working on before the twins took precedence. At five we sneak off home knowing full well that Clump is nowhere to be found. Head believes Clump is probably in some posh women's bedroom and teaching her the meaning of life as he sees it. Scotch, cigars and lots of exercise beneath the covers.

***

The following morning, just before ten o'clock the entourage sets off for the city cemetery. Bill and Bob are with us, along with two armed with rifles plods, in the back of a Paddy Waggon. Bill is cuffed to a bull ring and sat on the side bench. Bob hasn't been cuffed and is also sat on the side bench with a thick cushion to lessen his discomfort. There is no doubt in everyone's mind that Bob; truly is close to dying and presents not the slightest threat. Two more armed with rifles plods sit up with the driver.

The Reverend Shields and Clump are waiting for us as the wagon pulls up as close at it can to the grave of the twin's mother. Across from the grave stands Betty, Chloe with little Thomas in her arms and standing beside her is Cedric and

Harvey. Bob, free of shackles, is lifted off the waggon first and placed in a chair with wheels, then pushed by Head towards the grave. Shackled, feet and hands, Bill is helped down from the waggon where he pauses. Throwing back his head he stares up into a sky where wisps of bright white cloud seem to herald his arrival. Breathing in deep he meets my eyes and smiles.

We are there for a full hour. The reverend gave a long moving sermon on the miracle of motherhood followed by prayers. I then stepped forwards and placed a bouquet of seasonal flowers and roses on Mrs Boyles grave and then stepped back. Betty, Chloe, Cedric and Harvey waved to the twins who in utter joy waved back. It was a magic moment that even the rattling of Bill's shackles couldn't spoil.

There then followed a ten-minute silence to allow the twins time for reflection. That then should have been that. The twins were to be helped back into the waggon to be taken back to their cell. But then Bob somehow managed to stand up. He then began to sing The Lord is my Sheppard. To everyone's amazement he sang like an Irish Linnet who had been finally set free from its small wire cage. Everyone joined in, except for Bill, whose eyes were transfixed onto Betty while tears streamed down his face. By the time the carol came to an end, near everyone's eyes were welling up, while Betty, Chloe and Harvey, like Bill, were swamped in tears.

Finally, Clump placed a hand on Bob's shoulder and said quietly, 'Time to go, young man.'

After returning with the entourage to the Yard and spending a couple of hours going over other cases with Clump, all three of us set off for Pollards big day.

On arrival we find no one there as we are too early. We wait on a bench where we share Clump's hip flask of scotch but not his cigars or his farts. At two thirty the coffin turns up, along with Sally Pollard and a few others, mostly policemen. Notably, also present is ex Superintendent Shifty Shaver and his good lady, or if you like bad lady, Sadie Place herself, who is looking rather splendid in mourning dress complete with large hat covered in long black feathers. She is also much fatter than I remember having not seen her for some time.

A simple but pleasant service followed in which no one cried except for Sally, in-between eying up a young plod that is. Well needs must when you're a widow. Best to get married again as quickly as possible in these days where a woman on her own might struggle against a system so heavily favoured towards the male of the species. Then it was off to the Dirty Duck for the wake.

Oddly enough there were two dozen more policemen already in the inn on our arrival, most of whom never cared a jot for Constable John Pollard. But then Pollard had left enough money behind the bar for half the force to drink to his memory. The spread laid on was as upmarket as you'd expect from a much more senior officer than a mere constable.

After a few drinks and something to eat, Shifty Shaver and Sadie come over to where me and Head are stood at the bar.

'How are you, Potter?' says Shifty, a bit too pleasantly.

'Fine thank you, Shaver,' says I.

Sadie takes a sip from her glass of red wine and says, 'Are the twins giving you any trouble, Inspector?'

'No. They behaved admirably at the cemetery and have done so throughout their incarceration.'

'I suppose with the rope looming they may be opening up to you and confessing other crimes they've committed.'

She is fishing to try and find out if the twins have said anything about how she sold them for sex as little kids. I am inclined to headbutt the rotten cow, thus giving me great satisfaction. But as the case against her will all most certainly be going nowhere, I have no choice but to accept that Sadie, and her Shifty husband, will probably never be taken to account. Still, no harm in tormenting her a bit.

'The twins have opened up to us, haven't they Sergeant?'

'They have indeed,' says Head, smirking at Sadie. 'You wouldn't believe what they've been coming out with.'

Her cheeks turn crimson as she downs her wine in a strangled gulp. 'Oh… What kind of tales have they been filling your heads with?'

'Can't say,' says Head. 'Privileged information.'

'I wouldn't believe a word those vicious little thugs tell you,' says Shaver pompously, as he straightens himself up and looks down his nose at us. 'They're just trying to settle scores by accusing all and sundry of crimes they never committed.'

'What kind of crimes are you referring to, Mr Shaver?' says I.

'All kinds I shouldn't wonder,' says he, with an indifferent shrug.

'What we wish to know,' says Sadie. 'Have they mentioned us at all?'

'No,' lies I. 'Should they have done?'

'Not at all. I merely mention it because I had a few run ins with the little bastards years back. Forever trying to sneak into my home and steal things while my back was turned. A few whacks around the ears sorted them out. But from what I've heard those twins' bare malice towards anyone who *they* perceive to have wronged them.'

Any doubt I had that the twins had told me the truth about how they were abused goes out the window. Shaver and his cow are as guilty as sin. But again, I can do nothing about it.

'Rest assured, Sadie,' says I. 'The twins haven't said a thing about you or your establishment.'

'Good,' smiles she, though her eyes are not smiling, she doesn't believe me.

Head decides to extricate us from the proceedings. 'Drink up, Gerald. Time to get back to work. Chloe's making me another steak and kidney for dinner and I don't want to be late home.'

'If you'll excuse us,' says I, meeting Sadie's dour face.

'Of course,' says she.

We go over to where Sally's talking to a couple of young plods.

'We have to go, Sally,' says I.

'Thank you for coming,' smiles she. 'Would you give this letter to the twins, please?'

She hands me a small envelope. 'I will have to read it first, Sally.'

'That's alright, Inspector. There's nothing untoward in there. I just wanted them to know I am thinking about them.'

'I suppose you got to know them when they were just little kids.'

She nods as her eyes fill with sadness. 'Let's just say I truly know how it felt for them.'

Leaning forwards, I give her a fatherly kiss on one cheek and we say our goodbyes.

Leaving the Dirty Duck, we head off home, sod the work, it'll wait until tomorrow.

'We could have a few pints at the Trafalgar,' says Head.

'And drink a toast to Nelson to boot.'

'That fat bitch is as guilty as sin,' grates Head. 'And no one is going to do a thing about it. It almost makes you want to let Bill out so he can do her in.'

'Only we won't, will we, Richard?'

We pause to face each other. 'No, we won't. Let's go and get a bit wobbly and drown our frustrations.'

Bill Escapes

I am rudely awakened some hours later by something crashing through my bedroom window. Somewhat disorientated I fall out of bed while fumbling for my revolver on the bedside cabinet, knocking over a half full mug of milk in the process. Stumbling over to the window I yank up the sash and stick my head out into the rain while pointing my weapon at the shadowy figure standing below.

'Don't shoot, Gerald,' cries Head of all people. 'It is I Richard.'

'What on earth do you think you are doing? You threw something through my window!'

'Sorry. I kept banging on the door but you failed to answer, so I threw a small rock at your window and it just sort of went straight through the pane.'

'Bloody marvellous,' grates I. 'What do you want, Richard?'

'Bills escaped!'

'What our Bill?'

'Yes, *our* fucking Bill!'

'How did he manage that?'

'I don't know do I? Just get down here as quick as you can. The message from the Yard was to get there fast and come as you are.'

'What, naked and unshaven?'

'Throw something on, Gerald and *hurry up*.'

Slamming the window shut and turning around I pray I don't stand on any broken glass as I fumble around for the matches to light the lamp on my bedside table. As Betty's face is lit up, I am amazed to see she has been undisturbed by the commotion and is still happily snoring away. I give her shoulder a few shakes to wake her.

'Oh, not again,' groans she, hauling herself up into a sitting position then rubbing at her eyes. 'I've had enough for one night, Detective…'

'Forget that,' says I, tersely. 'I have to get to the Yard double quick. Apparently, Bill's escaped.'

'Really! How on earth did he manage to do that?'

'I have no bloody idea as yet, Betty. Look, I must dress and get off. Be careful where you stand, there's glass on the floor.'

'Why is there glass on the floor, Detective Inspector?'

'Because, Richard threw a rock through the window in order to wake me.'

'That's a bit reckless, Detective Inspector. Why didn't he just knock on the door?'

'He did,' says I, pulling on my trousers. 'But it failed to illicit a response.'

'I see,' yawns she. 'Is it raining outside?'

Hauling my shirt on I reply, 'It is and it will come in through the broken window unless you put something over it.'

'I could shove my bare bum up against it as a temporary solution I suppose.'

'No need for sarcasm, Betty, I am not in the mood.'

'Sorry,' sulks she. 'What has happened to poor Bob...'

'I have no idea,' snaps I, grabbing my holster and revolver. I give her a peck on the cheek. 'I love you.'

She grabs hold of my hand. 'I love you too. Please be careful, Detective Inspector. Bill is unhinged and extremely dangerous.'

'Bill wouldn't hurt *me*, Betty.'

'He would if you stood between him and his quest for revenge.'

After lighting another lamp for Betty, I take mine downstairs with me. Holster on, weapon in, jacket and bowler on, shoes on, unlock the door and go out.

'I don't believe this, Richard,' says I as we hurry up the path and clamber into the back of a police cart with no cover.

'Evening, Inspector,' says the driver, who is no other than that moaning pratt, Constable Ted.

'Constable,' acknowledges I. 'What do you know about Bill Boyles escape?'

'Not much, sir,' says he, clicking the horse into a trot. 'I was enjoying a nice cuppa in the canteen when the duty inspector stormed in and shouted out: "You drivers. Who knows where Clump, Potter and Head live?" Two of us put up our hands. "You," he yelled, pointing a finger at me, 'Go and pick up Potter and Head." He then pointed at my mate Jim and yelled, "You go and pick up Clump. Tell them Bill Boyle has escaped and to get here fast and come as they are. Hurry up and don't spare the horses." We went outside where there was a hell of a panic on. Coppers everywhere. Searching the waggons, running all over the place, going mental. As I clambered up onto my waggon a mate shouted out: "Be careful Ted, that Boyle bastard left Constable Peters in the cell with his throat cut. Blood everywhere!"'

'I don't fucking believe it,' says Head.

'I don't tell lies,' grates Ted.

'The sergeant was speaking figuratively, Constable,' snaps I. 'Anything else?'

He shakes his head. 'Other than I'm bleeding soaked already.'

'You should have picked a covered vehicle.'

'This one's faster,' says he, smugly.

No doubt he chose it on purpose knowing we'd get soaked while being too much of a knuckle head to realise, he'd also get soaked. Well, I shall come up with something in which to wipe that smirk from his mouth.

Rain lashes our faces as we speed through streets that are empty apart from the odd prostitute trying to fleece drunken men who can barely stand. Tramps and urchins hunting for food or looking for somewhere to sleep for the night. And off course an unusually high number of plods in pairs. Bill has certainly put the fires of hell up everyone's backside. Houses are in darkness and if not for the gas lamps all would be in total darkness.

'What time is it?' asks I.

'Two in the morning,' says Ted. 'And what a bleeding time to have to ferry people about when I should be in the canteen enjoying the site of the night cooks lovely bouncers. Me and her are getting well. Now the wife's buggered off I might be replacing the old tart with Carol the cook before too long. She's got a lot going for her that girl. She could cook and clean for me while still going out and earning extra money. Then she can keep me warm at night while I snuggle my head down into her lovely big bouncers.'

You won't be going anywhere with Carol, thinks I, once I tell her you've got the clap.

On arrival at the Yard, we find it eerily quiet. Judging by the amount of empty carriage spaces I assume they're all out looking for Bill and loaded to the gunwales with as many plods who could be dragged in.

'You're to go down to the cells,' says the desk sergeant as we step up. 'Chief Clump is waiting for you.'

We head down to find two plods outside the cell while gawping inside we find Clump looking down at the, dressed in his undergarments, body of one Constable Gough who's gaping slash across his throat is being looked over by the pathologist, Dr Shelley.

'Been dead barely an hour or so,' says Shelley, as a blob of dark blood bubbles out from Gough's wound. 'I would say the weapon used was a cutthroat razor or a very sharp knife.'

Gough's white vest is soaked with blood. There's blood pooled on the floor and splatters all over the cell.

'Well,' says Clump. 'Bill has now had plenty of time to get as far away from here as he can.'

'Which would be pretty damn far for someone as fit as Bill,' says I, stepping a foot or so into the cell.

'Ah… You are here,' says Clump. 'Good men.'

We all exchange a quick greeting then I ponder over Bob's body. He is laid on his back on his bed with his arms folded across his chest. He appears to be at peace, his face shows no signs of trauma caused by a painful, traumatic death. For that I thank God.

'I have sent as many men as were available to search the nearest slum areas,' says Clump. 'But I am thinking Bill may be too clever to go for the obvious. What say you, Inspector?'

'If he's doing slums, he'd be better served to make for The Gut. They would welcome him with open arms. He'd be a hero for killing a copper. They would hide him so well it could take days to find him, if at all.'

'Agreed,' sighs Clump.

This situation will have severe ramifications for Clump. It was he who pressured the hierarchy to allow the twins to be detained here instead of sending them to a more secure prison.

'Do we know how Bill pulled this off, Chief?' asks Head.

'More or less,' says he, miserably. 'Constables Trent and Gough were on duty. Gough told Trent to go and get some tea and biscuits. Despite it being strictly against the rules, Trent did as he was told. He got yapping in the canteen and was gone near on fifteen minutes and when he came back, he found Gough murdered and Bill gone. Gough obviously disobeyed procedure by opening the cell door whilst having no backup and paid the ultimate price for it. When questioned, Constable Trent stated that he had no idea why Gough had committed such a foolish act.'

'Well, I do,' says I. 'Gough loved tormenting the twins through the grille. He'd mock them about their impending date with the rope and sneer how much he was looking forwards to seeing them dance the wet leg…'

'As you lose control of bodily functions,' says Shelly without looking up.

'Indeed,' says I. 'In retaliation, Bill would spit back that Gough wouldn't dare say such things to his face unless he was shackled.'

'So,' says Clump. 'Bill managed to stir Constable Gough up enough for the fool to enter the cell intending to teach Bill a lesson. Of course, he had no idea that Bill was armed and even less that Bill would cut his throat so quickly and with ease. The mark of a true psychopath. What beggar's belief is where the hell did Bill get the cutthroat razor from.'

Dr Shelley stands up and says, 'Razor. Flic knife. Even a scalpel, Chief Inspector. Small blade, but as sharp as sharp can be.'

'Someone must have smuggled it in,' says Head.

'Such as whom?' grates Clump.

'The Reverend Shields. The doctor…'

'Or even one of you two,' says Clump, giving me and, Head the evil eye. 'No gentlemen, I do not believe it for a second. Everyone who entered this cell would have been thoroughly searched for anything considered dangerous should the twins get hold of it. Unless, yet again protocol was not strictly adhered too. That being the case, I am of the opinion that Bill simply picked a pocket, helped himself and hid the weapon while waiting for Bob to pass away before he used it.'

'That's the most likely explanation, Chief,' says Head, a bit too keenly.

I am of the opinion that Head was the one who had his pocket picked because he failed to surrender his flick-knife before we entered the cell on our very first visit. I shall ask him later…

'Only Bill knows the truth of it,' says Clump. 'After killing Gough, Bill obviously stripped him of his uniform and put it on. Then he calmly walked out of the Yard with no one even noticing the blood that must have been on his shirt collar and all over his tunic, let alone the fact that he wasn't a copper. And he did all that in less than five minutes, I'll wager. So, Inspector what next? Any ideas?'

'Bill will continue hunting down all those who have done him and Bob wrong in the past. I am convinced he'll go for Sadie Place first. He'll torture her into giving him the names of those who abused him and Bob when they were small boys. I think our best bet would be to conduct an around the clock surveillance of Sadie's place. Starting as soon as is possible, and with particular enforcement on Sunday.'

'The most likely day he'll turn up,' adds Head.

'Well, it will be a start,' says Clump. 'Let us retire to the canteen for cake and coffee to discuss what else we can do, while uniform cleans up this mess. Will you join us, Dr Shelley?'

Shelley shakes his head. 'Back to bed for me, Chief Inspector. I shall continue my work in the morgue by nine o'clock.'

Once settled down in the canteen I managed to whisper into Carols ear that Constable Ted has the clap as she bent over the table close to me while laying out mugs of coffee and a plate of buns. To which she replied in a hissing whisper: "Another reason to tell the slimy toad to piss off and leave me be."

Ideas on what else we can do to track Bill down are not coming thick and fast. The usual talk to your informants, put up wanted signs and just keep searching have been cast aside by Clump. He is hoping to keep Bills escape quiet for as long as is possible while he obviously comes up with a plan to get himself off the hook. He is of course delusional, no doubt the news is already spreading like the plague.

As the meeting drags on, I am finding it increasingly hard to stay awake, as is Head, but Clump, as always, appears to be wide awake and unphased. Lovely as it was, mine and Betty's marathon love session earlier is taking its toll. Having had a few drinks and thrown our inhibitions to the wolves we had started out back on the lawn while lightning flashed and thunder roared. Then, when it began to tip it down, we retreated indoors for a short but uncomfortable session on the kitchen table followed by another on the sofa in the parlour. After that we retreated to the bedroom where we collapsed on the bed to catch our breath. After a kip we carried on in wild abandonment until; finally at close to midnight, we succumbed too slumber. Only to be awaken by Head. Glancing at the canteen clock on the wall I yawn miserably and note, that it is three thirty. My detective brilliance then informs me that so far this night I had managed to have just over one hour's sleep.

'Are we keeping you awake, Inspector?' says Clump.

'Sorry Chief, I am struggling to keep my eyes open.'

'I was about to wind this up anyway, Inspector. There's no point in us three joining the search for Bill while it's pissing down and dark as pitch. I suggest we go home, get some shut eye and meet in my office at first light. By then, hopefully one of us may well have further ideas as to where we shall go next. We need a definitive plan in which to capture Bill before he slaughters too many citizens from our glorious city. Anyway, who fancies a nice wee dram in my office before they go?'

Finally making it home an hour later I creep upstairs, so as not to awaken Betty, and slip into the darkness of our room. Only to find she is anything but asleep.

'Tell me all, Detective Inspector,' whispers she.

'Can I tell you later? My brain hurts. I need to sleep.'

'Do I smell scotch on your breath, Detective Inspector?'

'Clump insisted on a wee dram to help us sleep,' yawns I.

'Typical! You can stay up boozing but can't stay up to tell me everything that's been happening.'

'Sorry my little Nosy Parker,' says I laying my head down to find I only have one pillow. Fishing around the side of the bed I fail to find it. 'I only have one pillow Betty. Do you know where it is?'

'Yes. I stuffed it in the broken window to keep the draft and the rain out.'

'Why didn't you use one of your pillows instead of mine?'

'Because I can't sleep on one pillow.'

'Neither can I. I think it was rather mean of you to nick one of my pillows when you could have found something else to do the job.'

'I didn't think you'd be back tonight, did I.'

'Whatever,' sighs I, as my eyes close.

***

Saturday went by in a blur as I was still too tired to function properly. Head also struggled but Clump was full of beans and raring to go. Only he was going nowhere much at all. Surveillance had been set up in a three-story terrace that overlooks Sadie Places brothel across the road. Head and I are to do our stint on Sunday night. The word was put out to as many informants as we could find that we were looking for Bill, but to keep it quiet for now. Other than that, nothing much happened until the Chief Constable turned up.

Sir Robert Briers had roared into the Yard like a demented lion with toothache at ten o'clock. Whereupon he threatened to have Clump reduced in ranks to a desk clerk before going into a tirade of abuse to all and sundry who just happened to be within ear shot. In short, he was accusing the entire Metropolitan Police Force of being a bunch of incompetent useless imbeciles who were more bent than a shepherd's crook. Briers was of the opinion that someone in the force had taken a bribe sufficient enough to help and abet a brutal killer to escape from custody. And the way he kept glaring at Clump implied that Clump was his main suspect. Utter rubbish of course.

How will Briers react when he sees the evening papers I wondered? No doubt his brain box will explode at headlines that accuse he, himself, of being the incompetent behind the failure to keep such a dangerous criminal as William Boyle inside. Nor less of the accusation that he delayed the trial and subsequent executions of the twins in his quest to have the twins grilled over other past unsolved crimes that they may, or may not, have been involved in. In short, he was just trying to pin unsolved crimes on the twins merely to up his accreditation ready for the next Chief Constable's election.

How do I know all this? Simple, on our way into work, Head and I detoured to a certain reporter's home, one I trust implicitly to keep our dealings a secret, to negotiate a deal. The result was: Twenty pounds for me and ten for Head. He getting less because he refused to enter said reporters' home and hid up outside behind a hedge to supposedly keep watch in case we'd been followed. When in fact, he merely chickened out just in case it ever came out that we'd let the cat out of the bag before the official statements due the next day by the Chief Constable, along with obviously receiving payment.

By ten o'clock Head and I are talking to Andy and Nick at the end of Pickle Lane.

'Been all sorts fishing around for information, boss,' says Andy. 'Reporters after a story and bounty hunters, mostly. Prats! Most of 'em would get themselves killed should they run into Bill. Except one. Big bastard he was. Mean as hell…'

'Face like a gargoyle,' adds Nick, pulling a face.

'Sounds like, one Joe Straw,' says I.

'That's the one,' says Andy, handing me a card. 'He gave me that and said ta contact him if I hear or see anything.'

I peruse the card: Joseph Strawbridge. Private Investigator. Dept Collector. Punisher. No task too small or too dangerous. Extensive experience in tracking down missing persons. There follows an address at a Pawn Brokers in Peckham where to leave a message so that Straw can then get in touch. I hand the card to Head; he reads it and jots a few notes in his diary before handing it back to Andy.

'Any use to ya, boss?' says Andy.

'Knowing Straw is after Bill just adds to our problems, Andy. But it could also help us. We need to know where Straw lives. This Pawn Broker is just a go between. I'll bet Straw doesn't reside there and we need to know exactly where he lives. Can you keep watch on the Pawn Brokers, Straws bound to turn up regularly to see if there's any messages for him? When he does, follow him, see where he goes and who he speaks to. If he talks to any coppers make sure you get their numbers.'

'We can do that,' says Nick, always keen to earn a few shillings.

I hold up a stop hand. 'The thing is, lads, Straw is a killer every bit as dangerous as Bill, but with more experience. He won't be easy to trail or easy on you if he catches you following him. Take no chances whatsoever. Promise me.'

They cross their hearts and promise to be careful.

'Ya can trust us,' says Nick, beaming with enthusiasm.

'Do not forget, Andy that you have a family that needs you to stay alive and provide. While you, Nick, have a woman and a child to support.'

'And another one on the way, boss,' smiles he.

'Congratulations,' says Head. 'You must be the only twelve-year-old in all of London to have already fathered two kids. Christ, you could be a grandfather before your twenty-five.'

'Cor, that'd be nice,' smiles he. 'But I'm thirteen now, Sergeant Head. I'm practically a grown up. I've even got hairs on me nuts.'

Fishing out two half-crowns I press one into each of their grubby hands.

'Thanks boss,' they chorus.

'Just you remember what I've said. Be bloody careful.'

'We will, boss,' says Andy. 'Trust us.'

***

'So, Straw's looking for Bill,' says Head, as we walk the slums while asking around for possible sightings of Bill. 'I wonder who Straw's working for?'

'Sadie Place? Falconer? Who knows, Richard? There will be a few well healed gentlemen out there terrified that they may be exposed for the dirty dogs that they are. Or worse, that Bill catches up with them and administers his own punishment for their crimes against him and Bob.'

'So, what now, Gerald?'

'A couple more hours of wasting our time, then I suggest we go get some lunch and a few beers. It's going to be a long day and night.'

No mercy

Come seven o'clock we are in a small musty smelling bedroom on the third floor looking over the road at Sadie Place's brothel. The only light we have comes from the gas lights in the street below. We have two armed with rifles plods with us and it is stuffy with the sash window shut. A light fog has descended outside that slightly hampers our view of who is coming and going at the brothel. However, I am confident that we will recognise Bill should he turn up.

The rear of the brothel is being watched by Detectives Barnsley and Thompson, who also have two armed plods with them. It is unlikely that Bill will even attempt to come in from the rear. There's a six-foot-high wall, topped with broken bottles, surrounding the small courtyard. Should anyone manage to climb over that and jump down into the courtyard, they will then be met by a pair of vicious hounds who have a reputation for ripping out throats and answer to no one other than Sadie Place or 'Shifty'. The only other way into the courtyard is via a thick iron door that, apparently, is always locked and can only be opened with a huge key. If Bill comes, I have no doubt he will go straight in through the front door, and not even Bruno could stop him.

'Do you want any more coffee?' says Constable Blunt.

'May as well,' yawns I.

'I'll have another cup,' says Head.

'And me,' says Constable Grant.

'Ask the old lady if she's got any more of those little buns,' says Head.

'Alright,' says Blunt, picking up the tray with our cups on.

Light from the hallway fans in when Blunt opens the door, he nips out and closes it behind him. He'll then head to the kitchen where the dear old soul who owns the place will once again put the kettle on.

At eight-thirty, two very young-looking girls and a male step out of a scruffy hansom.

'He appears familiar,' says I.

'That's Curly White the pimp,' says Grant. 'He's on my patch. I'd recognise his gait anywhere, the cocky bastard.'

Head comes up to peer over my shoulder. 'How old do you think those girls are, sir?'

'Twelvish? But then it's hard to tell from here when you can't see their faces properly.'

'Pity we couldn't go nab that bastard,' says Grant. 'I'd love to give his bollocks a good kicking.'

'No chance of that, Constable,' says I. 'We must not stray from our task. Perhaps we can deal with Curly another day.'

'Poor little girls,' sighs Head. 'We should be going down there to rescue them from Sadie's evil clutches before they get used.'

'And mess up the entire operation, Sergeant. Hard as it is, we stay put until our shift is over, or Bill turns up.'

Fifteen minutes later we are supping coffee and tucking into coconut buns when Blunt, who's up at the window, says, 'Odd looking character crossing the road towards Sadie's, Inspector.'

I go over for a look. There's a bent over old man in a long coat hobbling across the road with the aid of a stick. He has on a flat cap and carries a small carpet bag that appears to be well stuffed and heavy.

'Look alive, gentlemen,' says I. 'This could be it.'

Head and Grant step up to peer over our shoulders.

'Just an old git,' scoffs Grant.

'I'll bet that's Bill,' says Head.

The old man pauses at the closed door. He looks up and down the street then stares at the houses on both sides before resting his eyes on our window.

'Don't move,' snaps I, grabbing Blunt by the arm to hold him in place. 'Stay still. Dart back now and you'll give yourself away.'

Satisfied he isn't being watched the old man raises his cane and raps it on the door. The door opens and Bruno appears, whereupon the old man jabs the point of his cane into Bruno's chest. Bruno's hands slap onto his chest, he staggers forwards and then collapses at the old man's feet where he receives a few fast jabs at his neck from the cane.

'That's Bill alright!' says I. 'Now, remember the drill. Your lives may depend on it.'

With me leading we tear down the narrow stairs and out onto the pavement. Grant veers off; his task is to inform those behind the brothel that Bill has arrived. They will then come around front as backup. Head, Blunt and I cross the road. Bruno is still twitching, but it is all over for him. Blood runs from his neck and chest and is pooling out over the pavement. Bill's cane obviously comes with a stiletto dagger that shoots out at the touch of a button.

Blunt, rifle at the ready, stays put while Head and I, revolvers in hand, step over Bruno and make our way silently up the hall. At the end of the hall, we pause and run eyes up the stairs. No one to see, but there's noise coming from behind closed doors. Chattering, a laugh and the sound of someone grunting like a pig. We can also hear a voice coming from behind the door that leads into Sadie's 'reception area'. That voice is definitely Bills.

Bobbing down I peer through the key hole. Sadie's sat in her usual place at the table, all I can see of her is her bulbous bum cheeks hanging out either side of the ladder-back chair. She's wearing a pale blue dress. Shifting my position, I can just see up to the nape of her neck which has a wire noose around it. Standing up I tell Head what I've just seen.

'Bill must be standing to one side of her,' whispers Head in my ear. 'We burst in and he'll yank it tight to slice through her juggler.'

I nod. Wrapping a hand around the brass door knob I turn it very slowly.

'Come in, whoever's outside,' sounds Bill's voice. 'But lower your weapons, or else.'

Lowering our weapons to our sides, I open the door and we take one step inside.

'Well, well,' says Bill. 'What a surprise, Mr Potter and Mr Head no less.'

Bill stands to the side of Sadie. She is as rigid as the four scantily dressed prostitutes sat opposite on a green velvet sofa. The two young girls, who are dressed in pink dresses with pink ribbons in their long blond hair, are also sat rigid on the sofa and appear terrified. Curly White sits alone on the other sofa. 'Shifty' Shaver is sat beside Sadie, he cranes his neck around to stare beseechingly at us. The side of his face has the brutal imprint from no doubt the double barrels of Bills sawn off shotgun which is now firmly pointed at Curly, while his other gloved hand has hold of the end of the wire of the noose.

'Now that I 'ave everyone's attention,' says Bill, as calm as you please. 'This is how it will be. You, fat woman,' he snarls at Sadie. 'If you want ta stay alive you will write down the names and titles of all those bastards who abused me an' my brother Bob all those years ago when we were just small kids.'

Bill's words are less strewn with the colloquial. Oddly enough, calm as he is, he is even more menacing than usual, topped by a piercing glare that seems to encompass everyone in the room. One false move from anyone and a blood bath will ensue.

'I don't know if I can remember names from all that time ago,' pleads Sadie.

Bill gives the noose a short tug and Sadie's body jerks as the wire tightens just that little bit more.

'Ya ol' man will help ya remember,' snarls Bill. 'How many more coppers have you got outside, Mr Potter?'

'Six,' says I. 'And more on the way.'

He grins and appears utterly unphased. 'Now, providing fatty gives me what I want they'll be no need for anyone else to get hurt. Once I have the names I will leave. It's as simple as that.'

'You'll never get out of here alive, Bill,' says Head. 'Give it up before it turns nasty.'

'It turned nasty years ago, Mr Head. I'm not ready ta die just yet. Do ya think I'd walk in here without a way out knowing you'd probably be watching the place. I knew you'd be clever enough to know I'd be after fatty an' her ol' man as top priority. Now, fatty, there's a pencil and paper before ya. Get writing.'

'Can you loosen this thing around my neck first,' says she. 'I can't drop my head to see what I'm writing.'

'Just get on with it,' snarls Bill.

'She can't do it with that…' begins 'Shifty'.

'I told ya ta keep ya mouth shut, didn't I?' says Bill. 'She'll do it or die.'

Sadie begins to write. The girls on the sofa begin to nervously fidget while Curly starts to slowly slide a hand inside his frock coat.

'At this distant you'll be fuckin' decapitated should I squeeze just one trigger, ya pimply pimp,' warns Bill. 'Keep ya hands still an' where I can see them. That's all of you except you, skinny girl,' he adds, fixing his eyes on one of the prostitutes whose small breasts have come out of her bodice. 'Shove ya tits back, it's distracting the policemen from their duty.'

I give Head a quick glance, he meets my eyes with a guilty look. This is typical of the man, here we are facing a blood bath an all he can do is ogle tits. If it isn't food, it's the other that possesses the man.

The sound of giggling and footsteps coming down the stairs fills the room. I hear Blunt's voice boom out ordering whoever's out there to get back upstairs and lock themselves in a bedroom. There follows the sound of several pairs of feet stampeding back up the stairs.

After a short while, Sadie announces that she has finished. She can't remember any other names.

'No matter,' says Bill. 'I'll get more names from those on the list. Now, fatty, stand up and stuff your list in my pocket. We are leaving. Pimp, get to ya feet, you're comin' as well.'

'I ain't goin' nowhere,' snarls Curly.

'As ya wish,' says Bill, and pulls a trigger. Curly is hit full in the face, splattering blood and gore all-over the place as he's punched back into the sofa. All the girls scream. I feel like screaming myself. I would have brought up my revolver and shot Bill, but the second his shotgun went off he swiftly turned it on me and Head.

'Don't even think about it,' says Bill, his eyes icy cold. 'I don't want ta kill you or Mr Head. But I will if I have to. You women stop screaming. You two girls can leave an' go home. Mr Potter, yell out to ya men and tell 'em to hold firm so the girls can leave without some trigger-happy copper blastin' 'em ta hell.'

I yell out his request and Barnsley yells back, 'You alright, sir?' He is right behind the door.

'Yes. We are alright. We are sending the girls out now.'

'Can we go as well?' pleads the prostitute with the small breasts which have popped out again.

'No one else leaves,' says Bill. 'Not until I've gone. You kids, get up and leave.'

They hesitate, but do as they were told. They are so traumatized they just stare as they step past Bill towards the door. Bill winks at them as his eyes fill with tears. It's enough to encourage the girls to quicken their steps and grab at the door knob, then they are out, slamming the door behind them.

'Git to ya feet,' demands Bill, glaring down at 'Shifty'.

'Shifty' stands, he is visibly shaking. All the colour has drained from his face, he looks as sick as the proverbial dog.

'We'll be leavin' now, Mr Potter,' says Bill. 'If ya follow too close, I'll kill the pair of 'em. Keep ya distance and I promise I'll let them live.'

'We shall keep our distance, Bill,' says I. 'You have our word.'

'Good. So, we understand each other. Fatty, you lead the way. 'Shifty', pick up my bag and cane and follow behind me. I'll 'ave the gun trained on ya. One false move an' you an' ya bitch will die. Understand?'

'Shifty' nods, and takes his place. Bill turns side on, he has a firm hold of the wire while pointing the gun at 'Shifty'.

'Right, fatty,' says Bill. 'Start walking nice and slowly towards the backdoor.'

I can't believe Bill thinks he's going to escape out the back. The second he makes the courtyard the dogs will pounce. Sadie's throat will be cut by the wire and 'Shifty' will have his head blown off while Bill is torn to pieces. Bill must know about the dogs? Perhaps he thinks Sadie and 'Shifty' will be able to control them? He may also think he can escape through the iron door.

Sadie opens a door in the corner of the room which leads to the kitchen. From there another door opens into the courtyard. Sadie leads the way into the kitchen and once 'Shifty' is through the door it is closed and I hear it being locked.

'Richard,' says I. 'Go tell, Barnsley to get his men around back. Then we'll pick the lock and follow through into the kitchen.'

Head hurries away and in less than a minute he returns.

'Message delivered, Gerald,' says he, looking anything but happy. 'I've got a bad feeling about this. It ain't going to end well.'

'If we have to, Richard, we must take Bill down.'

He nods, we make it to the door. I bob down to spy through the key hole, but the key is in it.

'The keys in the lock, Richard.'

Bobbing down he takes a peek, 'I can push it out and then sweep it under the door.'

He pokes one of his lock picks through the key hole, the key hits the stone floor with a tinkling sound. Head gets right down and sweeps the key under the door. We are in the kitchen in seconds where we come face to face with a pair of terrified scullery maids who are standing as stiff as boards.

'They went that way,' says one, pointing with a trembling finger at the back door.

'Something smells nice,' says Head, his greedy eyes transfixed on the pots on the stove.

'Beef stew,' squeaks the maid. 'With herb dumplings.'

'Herb dumplings,' says Head, smacking his lips. 'I may be back in a bit for a bowl full, or two.'

Glaring at the man, I say, 'Sod the stew, what can you hear?'

'Nothing except the bubbling from the stew.'

'Exactly,' says I. 'No snarling dogs, no screaming from someone being torn to pieces. No shots fired. Nothing! Are the dogs out in the yard?' asks I to the maid.

She shrugs. 'Don't know, sir. They've been really quiet the last hour or so. They didn't even rush up to meet Miss Sadie like they usually do.'

'They ain't even been scratchin' at the door,' says the other.

Nothing else for it. I open the door and point my revolver out into the near darkness of the courtyard. Head and I step outside. There's a strong stench of dog shit, cow paunch and rotting meat.

'Over there, Gerald,' points Head, towards the iron door which is wide open.

'Christ. The dogs are loose in the street.'

'With Bill, Sadie and 'Shifty'. But did they go left or right?'

'God knows,' says I, in all honesty.

Unable to see the dog turds as they squelch beneath our shoes, we stride over to the iron door and then step out onto the dirt track of a gloomy passage that runs between the rear end of several large terraces. Even so I can just make out

Barnsley and his men all pointing their weapons at us.

'It is us, Constable,' says I, as we step up to him. 'Lower your weapons. Did you see anyone come out from the courtyard?'

He shakes his head. 'Nothing, sir. We saw nothing.'

'What about dogs?' says Head. 'Did you see or hear any dogs come out?'

'No, Sergeant. But I can't half smell them,' says he, wrinkling up his nose.

'We've got dog shit on our shoes,' grates Head.

'Disgusting!' grimaces Barnsley.

'Right, Constable,' says I. 'Take your men back to the front of the house. We shall go through the kitchen and meet you there. Look sharp, Bill could be anywhere.'

'You'll trapse shit all through the place,' says Thompson.

'Good,' says I. 'Go!'

They head off as we make for the kitchen door, which ominously is now shut. I try the knob; the door is locked. 'Ladies,' yells I. 'It is I, Inspector Potter. Unlock the door if you please.'

The key is turned and the door opens. Both maids point to the other door and say, 'They went that way.'

Leaving skid marks as we go, we enter Sadie's parlour. She is sat back at the table, shocked beyond words, the noose has gone but left a ring of bright red right around her neck where in places it has cut flesh that is bleeding slightly. 'Shifty' is sat beside her, his eyes as dull as dish water.

'Where's Bill?' demands I of 'Shifty.'

He points at the door into the hall. 'He went that way.'

'Where are your dogs?'

'They're dead,' cries Sadie. 'Didn't you see them laying in the yard with their mouths all frothy. That bastard must have somehow poisoned them.'

'You must have seen us come into the yard,' says I. 'Where were you?'

'Bobbed down behind the kennels. We dare not call out, he'd have killed us,' says 'Shifty'. 'Once you'd gone past us that swine herded us back to the kitchen then left us here and then he was gone.'

'Straight out the bleeding front door,' says Head. 'The cheeky sod out manoeuvred us good and proper.'

'He did that, Richard. But at least he kept his word and spared their miserable lives.'

'And wrecked our business,' sulks Sadie. 'He, said if we didn't close the business right away, he'd be back to slaughter us. I want protection, Inspector. And I want it *now*.'

'Get stuffed you, vile cow,' snaps Head. 'You were about to sell those poor girls. You don't deserve anything other than a bullet up your rear end.'

'Enough, Sergeant!' snaps I. 'We have a killer to catch.' I cast a glance over to Curly. He is still very much dead and has left an awful mess for some poor soul to clean up. Still, that's one more piece of scum off the face of this earth. Pity someone else will quickly take his place. 'We are off now,' says I to Sadie. 'I'll send a plod in to take your statements. I also want you to write down all the names you gave Bill and hand it to the plod.'

'Get stuffed yourself,' says she, giving me the get stuffed look. 'You lot were fucking useless. Nearly got us killed. I'll be reporting you to your superiors.'

'Sadie Place I am arresting you for procuring underage girls with the intention of selling them as sex slaves…'

'Do that and I'll bet you'll be out of a job by daylight. I've got too much on too many high rankers from the Yard. You've been warned!'

'Oh! Shut up, Sadie,' barks 'Shifty'. 'Think yourself lucky

to be alive. Thank you, gentlemen. If you hadn't have turned up, I believe Bill would have topped us both. I owe you.'

'A bowl of stew would do right now,' says Head.

'We are leaving, Sergeant,' says I. 'Thank you, Mr Shaver and goodbye.'

Head touches the rim of his bowler. 'Goodbye fatty. And don't forget to rub a bit of lard on your neck to soothe it.'

'What about him?' grates she, pointing to Curly. 'You can't just leave him there.'

'Fear not, madam,' says I. 'Someone will cart him away sometime between now and Christmas once forensics have poked around and took photos. So do not move him, cover him up, or mess around with his clothes to search for valuables or you will be arrested. You will also find Bruno's body out front...'

She jumps to her feet and clasps her hands together. 'Bruno! My lovely Bruno is dead?'

'Stabbed in the heart and neck. But fear not madam, it was quick and he didn't suffer.'

'You sir, are the vilest copper I have ever known,' snarls she, shaking a fat fist at me.

'Thank you for that inspiring accolade, madam. And on that note, it's goodbye and good riddance.'

***

After wiping the dog's shit from our shoes all over Bruno, including his hairy face, I allot the constables their tasks. Barnsley and Thompson are to take statements from all and sundry in the brothel. The pair of plods with Barnsley are to inform the Yard of what's happened so they can follow up with forensics and so on. Grant and Blunt are to stand guard, one out front and one out back to protect the crime scene from anyone trying to come in or go out.

'Do you know, Gerald?' says Head, as we head for the nearest pub. 'It took Bill less than ten minutes to kill two men, save two young girls from being violated, terrorise everyone involved, make his escape and disappear.'

'And, at some point he also managed to kill two vicious curs. I will bet he tossed poison steaks over the wall an hour or so before he killed Bruno, and somehow unlocked the iron door from the outside in readiness should he need to escape that way. What troubles me is why did no one see him?'

'They should have, Gerald, but then Bill's a phantom. Now you see him and now you don't.'

'And where the hell did, he get all what he needed so quickly? Escaped on Friday night and killing by Sunday night. Someone must be helping and hiding him.'

'My bet is on Cedric and Harvey.'

'What, from their hotel room, Richard?'

'What if Bill is holed up in Walnut House? It might still be habitable out back.'

'Possibly. Let's have a beer first and then we'll go and take a look.'

After a couple of beers and a pie in the Dukes Head, we take a cab to Marylebone.

The demolition of Walnut House hasn't begun yet. Apart from the mess the blast caused the house doesn't appear too damaged. But the keep out warning signs remind us that the building is unstable and unsafe. We negotiate the rubble and broken glass from the windows and reach where the front door used to be. The smell of charred timber assaults our nostrils as we peer into the gloomy hallway to see the ceiling has collapsed, thus blocking our way in.

'It's too dark to go in,' says Head, quietly. 'And the halls impassable. Why don't we try down the sides of the house?'

We do so, but the brambles and fallen rubble prevent us getting more than a few yards.

'Let's go around back,' says I. 'Cedric told us there was no way into the house from the rear, but then he may have lied.'

After knocking on the door of the huge posh house next door, and explaining who we are, we are granted permission to go down to the bottom of their garden to see if there's a way into Walnut House from the rear. After climbing a tree to be able to see into Walnut's Garden we find it too dark to see anything much. There are no signs of life or lights filtering through the mass of brambles. Barbed wire runs along the top of the eight-foot-high wall and, as best as we can see, continues right around the rear of the house. Trying to get over the wall would be foolish, if the barbed wire doesn't get you the brambles over the other side will. However, what little we can see of the rear of the property appears relatively untouched from the explosion and the fire.

'I'll bet it's still habitable in there,' whispers Head. 'Bill could be holed up in there with everything he needs on hand. Costumes for disguise, weapons to use and lots of tinned food. Even running water most probably.'

'You could be right, Richard. If he is in there I for one am not going to risk going in there in the dark. Let's leave and return tomorrow, maybe then we can find a way in. We'll go back to Sadie's Place and see if forensics have turned up.'

'Along with Clump,' groans Head. 'He'll flip his lid when he hears we let Bill get away.'

'No doubt he'll be breathing fire hot enough to burn the hair from your ears, Richard.'

He shoots me the maligned look. 'Not just my ears, yours as well.'

'I know that,' grates I. 'We will all get roasted, Richard, but none more so than me.'

***

We are in the bar in Sadie's brothel, Clump, having persuaded 'Shifty' to allow us to use it so Clump can verbally abuse us.

'Four of my finest detectives,' says he as he stomps around with a big fat cigar in one hand and, having helped himself, a large glass of scotch in the other, but none for us lot. 'Four handpicked uniformed offices. Eight men, all armed to the teeth, but still Bill Boyle not only escapes arrest he does it with ease.' Pausing he glares only at me. 'Why didn't you at least try to shoot him? You could have tried hitting him from the bedroom window the second he stabbed Bruno. You certainly should have both shot him the second he shot Curly White. Why?'

'Everything happened far too quickly, Chief. Bill did Bruno in in seconds and then by the time we entered Sadie's, which was a minute or so later, Bill already had everyone, except for Curly, frozen in terror. Curly attempted to intimidate Bill and ended up losing his face. Bill was just too fast, too calm and too indifferent about his own safety to be caught off guard. If we had attempted to shoot him, I dread what the consequences would have been if we'd have messed it up.'

Clump lets out a long sigh. 'This list Sadie wrote out of men who abused the Boyles,' says he waving it about. 'This list is going to give us severe headaches. Everyone on it is no doubt someone of wealth and status. We are now faced with the task of trying to protect these men from Bill's wrath, while having no idea who he'll go for first. Fifteen names, fifteen different addresses that are, no doubt, spread all over London and even beyond. But first of all, we will have to find out where each one resides and who is the most important. What a bloody headache!'

'Why not just leave them to their fate, Chief?' says Head.

Stepping up close, Clump glares into Heads eyes. 'Nothing I would like more, Sergeant. Does anyone else have any bright ideas. What about you, Inspector Potter?'

'I think we should take Sadie's list with a bucket of salt, Chief. I'll bet she's put down names of those who have wronged her in the past. You may note she has put down one: Sir Raymond Fleurs, who I know is a staunch campaigner against child exploitation, especially in the sex trade.'

'As usual you are well informed, Inspector,' says he, dropping the confrontational tone. 'That being the case, we will have to go overboard in our attempts to keep everyone on this list as safe as possible. I shall head back to the Yard shortly to liaison with uniform to see how many men they can allocate for the task of protection. But first I shall be having words with Madam Place.'

Speak of the devil, in waddles Sadie. 'A Dr Shelly and several other men are here, Chief Inspector,' says she, sounding decidedly pissed off. 'I trust they'll clear up the mess once they've taken the bodies away.'

'They will, madam. You lot, clear off so I can talk to Madam Place.'

'I am busy, Chief Inspector,' says she, turning up her nose.

'It is not a request, madam. Either speak to me now or I'll have you dragged down to the station for a chat in the cells,' says he, ushering us out and closing the door.

'So that dirty cow gave Bill a list of names of innocent men,' says Head as we go outside for a breath of air. 'I'll bet it won't take Bill long to realise she's taken him for a fool…'

'And then he'll return to finish the job. I'll bet you a pound, Richard, that Sadie's dead within two days.'

'I'll take that bet, Gerald, but say that she'll be dead before daybreak.'

'No chance. Even Bill wouldn't be crazy enough to come back here tonight. I am thinking he will head home, wherever home is, and take stock. He'll want to find out where everyone who's on that list lives. Once he realises, he's on a wild goat chase, he'll be gunning for Sadie again, but this time with no clemency.'

'The trouble is, Gerald. How many on that list will suffer Bills torturing skills before he clicks, he's been had.'

I shrug my shoulders. 'Let's hope the plods keep up a good enough vigil to scare Bill away long enough for us to catch him…'

'Or kill him…'

***

Sadie Place and her husband's bodies, where discovered the next morning at eight o'clock when a maid took them up tea and buttered toast on a tray. Both had had their throats cut while laid in their huge bed. No sign that they had put up a fight, other than Sadie must have jerked bolt upright in shock as a cutthroat razor, left at the scene, sliced through her jugular vein, causing blood to spurt right to the foot of the bed.

As we peruse the gristly sight, Head says, 'So, Bill didn't make his escape last night as we believed, but instead he hid somewhere inside the house until he was ready to strike.'

'With no one the wiser until earlier this morning. Again, there were plods maintaining watch over the house all night, but no one saw or heard a thing until the maid screamed her head off…'

'Which then rolled down the stairs and then bounced out into the street,' grins Head. 'Thus, alerting the plods that something wasn't quite right.'

'Very funny, Richard. Clump's balls will do the Rumba when he hears about this one, especially as the press got here before us, having been tipped off by a: "Pretty young thing with a husky voice in a tight red dress and deep blood red painted lips." Who said, when asked for her name; "I am Lilly E Bow." Which is an anagram for William Boyle.'

'At least the plods have managed to keep the press outside. What now, Gerald?'

'I suggest we get as far away as possible before Clump turns up, Richard. Let's leave the plods to it and go check out Walnut House. By the time we return, Clump may have calmed down.'

'But *surely*, he won't be blaming us, Gerald. I mean we were in our own beds when Sadie and 'Shifty' got stuck like pigs.'

'But we did do a search of the place before Clump called us all into the bar. Clump will accuse us of not searching properly. Because?'

'We were tired out and wanted to get home because we were famished and in dire need of a little love and passion from our long-suffering wives.'

'To which, he'll then call us a pair of something very rude.'
'Such as?'

'A pair of Cs more interested in our guts and groins then our jobs. Let us get going.'

***

After following a bridleway beside a house two properties from Walnut House we find it takes us around to the rear of the properties and to the rear wall of Walnut House, where we discover a thick bramble bush with lots of dead leaves upon it. Dead or dying because it's thorny stalks had been cut off at its base to enable it to be pulled away from the brick wall, thus exposing a hole big enough for someone to clamber through. We clamber through and draw our weapons.

'I need to fart,' whispers Head, as we scan the ten-foot-high jungle before us and the worn-down pathway that cuts through it towards the kitchen.

'Well, I'm not stopping you,' hisses I.

'But it could be a very loud one, Gerald. If Bill's about it might warn him of our presence. I had beans for breakfast.'

'How many beans?'

'One tin, plus what Thomas left.'

'How much did he leave?'

'About a half a tin.'

'Isn't it risky giving a little tot so many beans in one sitting? Goodness me, Richard, the boy's little stomach could explode through all the gas that's in half a tin of beans.'

'That's an old wives' tale. Besides, he rarely eats more than half what he's given.'

'Why then do you not give him less beans if he's not going to eat them anyway?'

'Then they'll be none left for me to do my waste not want not lecture. Sorry, I need to fart.'

And he does, creating an explosion like a rumble of thunder and a crack of lightning all rolled into one. God knows what the neighbours will think, as no doubt they would have heard it, but hopefully are too far away to have smelt it, unlike myself. The question is, if Bill is about, did *he* hear it?

Keeping to the path we cautiously step into an open weed strewn area and make for the kitchen door which is open. Inside it is much as I remember, except everywhere is covered in dust, stinks of fire and the ceiling is black with smoke. After climbing over fallen charred joists we make the stairs and up into the bedroom where the twins stayed. Access to further bedrooms is perilous as floors beneath our feet groan, creak and threaten to collapse. But of Bill there is no sign. Even so I am convinced he has been here recently, where he no doubt picked up items, he required to continue his murderous quest for revenge. Somewhere amongst the mess in this house Bill had hidden what he deemed he would need.

'There's no way he's been hiding out here,' says Head. 'But I'll bet good money he's been here recently.'

'Agreed,' agrees I. 'There wasn't a single complete cobweb in the hole in the wall when we went through, Richard. Convincing me that someone had recently gone through there. And there's no foot prints anywhere on the dirty floors, because someone has brushed over them. Bill was here, but he certainly isn't here now. We may as well head back to the Yard.'

***

A week goes by, a week when nothing happened to further our investigations regarding Bill. No one on Sadie's list has been slaughtered. No one has come up with any information as to where Bill might be hiding out. In short, we have heard nothing, seen nothing and have gotten nowhere. Rumours abound that Bill has been topped. Fled the area. Joined a monastery. Signed up for the navy or the army or emigrated to Australia.

Andy and Nick continue to try and follow Joe Straw, but to no avail, the man is as allusive as the Scarlet Pimpernel. Perhaps even he has given up searching for Bill.

Two days later Andy sends me a message asking to meet up at twelve o'clock in The Skinners Arms. Going on my own I find Andy and Nick in the busy snug tucked up in a corner at a small table nursing empty half pint glasses. Nick appears to have been in a bad brawl. His face is battered and bruised, nose broken and both eyes blackened. I take a seat opposite them.

'What the hell happened to you?' asks I.

Nick opens his swollen mouth to display a broken front

tooth and a tongue that also appears swollen. Nothing comes out.

To deny anyone from overhearing, Andy answers in whispering tones for Nick. 'Straw done it, boss. Nick was trailing him late last night it bein' his turn to be upfront. The first time we'd picked up on him in days leavin' the Pawn Brokers. I kept well back, as we'd done all along so as not ta be too obvious. Straw turned a corner; Nick went after him. When I turned the corner there weren't no sign of either of 'em.'

'He grabbed me,' puts in Nick, his voice sounding as if he'd just had a tooth pulled. 'He'd hid in a doorway…' Saliva bubbles out from the corner of his mouth, he tries to suck it back, then runs his swollen tongue over his bottom lip.

Andy picks up the mantle again. 'Straw half strangled Nick as he dragged him down an alleyway. Then he punched him twice in the face with his huge fist. He demanded to know who was paying Nick ta follow him…'

'And Nick told him?' says I, the guilty looks in their eyes confirming the fact.

'Sorry boss,' gurgles Nick.

Andy continues, 'Straw told Nick he knew where he lived and if he didn't answer truthly he'd go to his home and get it out of his woman…'

'Then he grabbed me balls an' twisted 'em,' splutters Nick.

'I heard Nick scream,' says Andy. 'I'd run past the alley, now I went back and found Nick rolling around on the ground. No sign of Straw, he'd vanished.'

We are interrupted by a greasy barman with a fat stubbly face demanding to know what my poison was.

'A pint of bitter and two halves,' says I.

'Any grub?' says he.

The large meat fly crawling around his grubby stubble puts me off and I shake my head.

'Sorry boss,' says Nick.

'Worry not, Nick. I cannot see that Straw knowing that you're working for me will make any difference. Likely as not he'll give me a wide birth while he continues going about his shady business. In truth he's no more likely to find Bill then we are. Now, any joy at the cemetery?'

'Jack, one of me lads,' says Andy, 'saw a young woman turn up and put some flowers on Bill's mother's grave. Then he followed her across the cemetery where she placed more flowers on Constable Pollards memorial.'

This intrigues me. 'This woman being young, pretty and blond with a slim figure.'

'That's her. Nice little thing according to Jack. He says she didn't cry at the first grave but did sob a bit at the other. Any use to ya, boss?'

'It certainly is Andy. You've done well. Mums the word though…'

'As always, boss,' grins he, tapping his nose.

After a couple of pints, I hand Andy a pound to share out with whoever has been helping out, plus another between him and Nick. Having told the boys not to worry, I tell Nick I hope he soon heals and should he need any money for medical or dental assistance for his injuries, to just ask. I also tell them to lay low for a while to ensure that Straw loses interest in them.

As I head back to the Yard, I ponder over why Sally Pollard would go and place flowers on Bill's mother's grave. The answer is simple. Bill, dare not risk it as he knows the grave will likely be watched. As is Bob's grave, he having been laid to rest in St Marys thanks to the intervention of the Reverend Shields, who refused to allow Bob to be buried in un-consecrated ground. Bill got Sally to lay the flowers on his mother's grave, unless she did it of her own accord? Doubtful. Sally is obviously at least in touch with Bill. Perhaps even more than just in touch?

Recalling Sally's letter to Bill, which I delivered to him later that afternoon after Pollard's wake before I signed off for the day, tells me that Sally resonates deeply with the twins. They have common ground, Sally was used and abused from a very early age just like the twins. She would have known, perhaps even witnessed what they went through. Of course, she would have been a good five years older than the twins back then, but her experiences would still have been raw at the time the twins were being used. I decide to pay Sally a visit and to see what she has to say for herself.

I suppose I should have continued on to the Yard instead of heading for Sally's, so that Head could come with me just in case Bill *is* hiding out at Sally's. However, having left a moaning Head to sort out paperwork we're behind with, because he usually leaves most of it to me, I decide he deserves to suffer for a while longer.

On arriving at Sally's, I find her downstair curtains closed, which strikes me as a bit odd. It's been over a week since Pollard was buried and I see no need for Sally to shut the light out to maintain a dignified period of mourning. I have the feeling she's keeping the curtains shut to keep out prying eyes.

Taking myself around to the rear of the terraces via a passage I count along ten houses. Matching curtains in the downstairs kitchen to the front windows confirms that this is Sally's house. A feeling of dread comes over me, it's too quiet. If I go in, what will I find?

The small backyard I note is very tidy as I quietly open the gate and cover the thirty or so feet to the kitchen door. Drawing my revolver, I take hold of the doorknob and give it a turn. To my surprise I find the door isn't locked. Opening it I creep into the kitchen to the aroma of toasted cheese and freshly baked cakes. I find the table is set for two with steam coming from a matching pair of dark blue mugs filled with coffee, little iced buns on a stand and two plates with crumbs on. Whoever was, or still is, in the house has either skipped out the front door or is hiding. Either way they are obviously aware of my presence.

Now, the question is do I back out of the kitchen and go for assistance or search the house on my own? I decide to continue as I am fairly confident the house *is* empty. Desperately trying not to make a sound I take a step backwards intent on gently closing the back door only to go rigid as something hard is pressed into my spine.

'Best not move, Mr Potter,' sounds Bill's voice. 'I don't want ta kill ya, but I will if ya do something stupid. Break your weapon, then drop it on the floor.'

I do as I'm told; the revolver makes a load noise when it hits the flag stoned floor.

'Take a seat, Mr Potter,' says Bill. 'But keep ya elbows on the table.'

I sit down at the far end facing Bill and place my arms on the table.

'Ya can come out now, Sally,' calls Bill.

The larder door beside the range is pushed open and Sally steps out. She appears unafraid as she shuts and locks the back door before going over to stand beside Bill.

'How did ya know I was hidin' out here?' says Bill, as without taking his eyes off me he bobs down, picks up the revolver and sets it down on the draining board.

'Just a hunch, Bill,' says I. 'How did you know I was about?'

'I didn't. Now and again, I take a peek out front an' saw ya through a crack in the curtain crossin' the road towards the house. Then you disappeared an' I reasoned you'd gone around the back, so I told Sally ta hide while I nipped out back an' slipped into the privy, just in time to see ya creepin' up to the backdoor.

'What now?' says I.

'That's up to you, Mr Potter. I suggest we have a coffee, sit around the table and have a chat. Give me your word, that you won't do anything stupid and I'll give ya mine.'

We exchange promises. Bill sits down opposite me, but keeps the sawn off firmly pointed at my chest.

Sally leans back against the range and says, 'Would you care for a coffee, Mr Potter?'

'Yes,' says I, aware that I must look as I feel, utterly stupid having been so easily outwitted.

'Would you care for a cheese toasty as well?' smiles she.

I shake my head.

'Ya came on ya own, then?' says Bill.

I nod and then lie, 'But Sergeant Head knows I was coming here. If I don't return within the hour, he has orders to bring half the Yard here.'

Bill smiles, 'Ya came alone an' didn't tell a soul where ya were goin' didn't ya?'

'Astute as ever, Bill. I must admit to having been a truly stupid man in this instance.'

'Ya ain't stupid, Mr Potter. So, I'm thinkin' ya came alone because if ya did capture me here ya wouldn't be sure how you'd react. Should I arrest Bill or let 'im go? Or will I have ta kill him? If ya had come with back up you'd only have two options, arrest me or kill me.'

'Bang on the nose, Bill.'

Sally sets a mug of coffee down for me, careful to not come between me and Bill.

'Thank you, Sally,' says I, shooting her a wan smile. 'So, what exactly is your relationship with Bill?'

'We're in love,' beams Sally. 'We plan to get wed.'

'And then what?'

Bill says, 'Sally's gonna sell the house then we'll go ta America an' start a new life.'

'Before or after you've exacted your revenge?'

'It's over,' says Sally, injecting finality in her tone. 'Bill don't want to kill no more.'

I meet Bill's eyes, they are stoic, almost haunting.

'It's true, Mr Potter,' says he. 'It's over.'

'Then all those on Sadie's list will then escape retribution. I find that hard to believe, Bill.'

'The names on that list was all rubbish. That bitch just put down the names of those she'd got a grudge against. Knew it the second she started scribbling. Still, she's gone know, the filthy old faggot.'

So, I was right about the list, thinks I as I sip my coffee, which exonerates me a little from today's foolishness. 'You must have hidden in the house, Bill until it was quiet enough to come out and slaughter Sadie and Shaver.'

'There's a secret hide out in a broom cupboard upstairs in the brothel. When me an' Bob was there as kids, we was shown the cupboard an' shoved in it an' locked in ta get us used to it, in case the coppers came an' did a raid lookin' for kids. It's pitch black an' airless in there, and we was told not ta make a sound until we was let out, or else. Bob was terrified an' wet himself because we was shut in for over an hour.'

'So, you hid in that cupboard until it was late and had gone quiet,' says I. 'Then out you popped ready to kill?'

'I did Shaver in first. Then I shook the fat bitch's shoulder ta wake her up. I wanted her ta know what was comin'. But I reckon all she could vaguely comprehend was this dark shape looming over her. She sat up. I could just make out her wobbly cheeks from the light comin' in from the street lamps through the open curtains. I slit her throat. Ya should 'ave seen the look of pure shock in her eyes. She knew she'd been done in good an' proper as she sank back on the bed with her pudgy hands around her neck tryin' ta stop the blood gushing out. Too fuckin' late, Sadie Place, you rotten piece of shit. Too fuckin' late.'

Sally places a hand on one of his shoulders. Bill looks as if he's about to cry. But for whom? Not Sadie Place or anyone else he's murdered. No, Bill wants and needs to sob away all those terrible memories from his past while Sally holds his hand.

'After the killing, what did you do next?' says I, sipping more coffee.

Picking up his mug and slightly relaxing the hand holding the shotgun, Bill drinks his coffee without taking his eyes off me. Sally kisses him on the head and takes his mug.

'Do you want another coffee, Inspector?' says she.

'Not just yet, thank you, Sally.'

'How about wrapping your hands around my lovely little buns? They're still warm.'

'Perhaps later. What did you do after the killing, Bill?'

'I went through the bitches draws and found cash an' jewels, then I legged it. I kept ta the darkest alleys and drifts until I reached here and slipped in via the back alley.'

'Have you been hiding out here ever since you broke out?' says I.

He shakes his head. 'I made my way to Walnut House after breaking out. I had a lot of gear hidden up there which luckily had been untouched by the fire. Stayed there until the heat had died down a bit and then headed for here early on the Sunday mornin'.'

'Why here? Surely you were gambling because you couldn't have known whether or not Sally might stitch you up for the reward. After all, she is a coppers widow.'

He reaches out to take the mug from Sally and takes a sip before setting it down and saying, 'The letter you gave to me from Sally when I was in the cells told me all I needed ta know. I knew by her words that she was sympathetic to me, havin' suffered similar as a kid. She'd put her address on the letter, so I knew she wanted me ta write back. I did and told her I hoped ta see her again one day. The reverend delivered it for me,'

'I knew Bill and Bob from when they used to be dragged into the whore house by Razor Williams,' says Sally, 'Poor little sods they were. Cause I weren't much older than them, and it wasn't good, but at least I didn't have to suffer the way they did.'

'So, when Bill turned up you welcomed him in with no questions asked?' says I.

'Not quite,' grins she. 'Six in the bleedin' morning it was and someone's banging on my door. Thought it was that randy milkman, the cheeky sod. He'd been trying to get between my sheets ever since Johnny passed away. I went down in my nighty armed with the piss pot half full intent on throwing it in his bleedin' fizz hog! I threw open the door and threw a good pint of piss right into Bill's face.'

Bill laughs. 'First time in years since I had the Wind of Christ up me. Thought I'd had acid thrown in me face it stunk so much.'

'You, cheeky sod,' grins Sally, punching him in the arm. 'Anyway, I helped clean Bill's face up and then I filled up the tin bath by the fire so he could have a good soak while I washed his clothes. The rest is history.'

'Tell me about your escape, Bill,' says I, keen to get away from tales of their love life.

'Gough kept goading me. Been doin' it from the second we was thrown into the cell. He kept taking the piss out of me an' Bob. He thought it was funny, but he was about as funny as constipation. We refused ta bite, which drove him nuts. Bob was dying, fadin' fast by the Friday and I knew it was then or never ta make me move. I pleaded with Gough ta get permission for Reverend Shields ta come in so he could read Bob his last rites. Gough just laughed in my face through the grille, then he spat at me.

Gough snarled, "The little bastards going to hell and doesn't need a priest."

"Leave it, Michael," said Trent. "I'll go see the chief and…"

"You'll do no such thing," Gough barked. "Do something useful and go get us some tea and cake from the canteen."

Trent said, "Alright. But don't do anything stupid while I'm gone."

'He went off and I realised my plan ta take the reverend hostage ta aid my escape weren't goin' ta happen. So, I went to plan two and started goadin' Gough. I called him a snot nosed dog with shit for brains an' a whore's spawn. He just laughed his head off and said, "How much longer is the little shit going to last? Hey, how about I come in and finish him off? I could ram my truncheon up his arse, that'll do it."

'I stuck my face to the grille and sneered at him. "You wouldn't *dare* come in here alone, especially when I ain't cuffed. You ain't got the balls. In fact, I'll bet your balls are the size of marbles ta match ya tiny winkle." That got him going. His face turned red and steam seemed ta come out of his lugs. Then I said, "I'll bet ya ol' woman has loads of real men in while ya on nights. I reckon the poor cow needs it bein' married to a weak-kneed toe rag like you." The thing was, Mr Potter, Gough could give it but couldn't take it. He ordered me to get to the back of the cell, then he unlocked the door and came in. he went for me, spittin' an' snarlin' with his truncheon in his hand. But I did him good an' proper before he could lay a finger on me.'

'Slashing his throat with what?' says I.

'A flick-knife.'

'One you stole from Sergeant Head.'

'I saw the shape of it in his jacket pocket an' easily picked it.'

'Then you took Gough's uniform and simply walked out.'

'I said goodbye ta Bob first. He grabbed my hand and said, "Promise me you'll give it up if ya get away. Live ya life Bill, for both of us. Marry a nice girl, 'ave kids and name 'em after me an' ma. Promise me." I promised him. I hugged him, then kissed him all over his face then ran my fingers through his hair an' said, "God bless my darling little brother and look after him when he reaches heaven." Then, with a smile on his face, he was gone. 'I stripped and put Gough's uniform on and walked out of the station. I couldn't believe no one spotted all the blood on the uniform or that it was far too big for me. It was as if I was invisible.'

'That was the angels looking out for you,' says Sally.

Or the devil himself, thinks I.

'It's going to be wonderful living in America,' says Sally. 'They'll be red Indians to see, and cowboys, and fancy stores like you've *never* seen.'

'You're not there yet Sally,' says I, soberly. 'You must realise the gravity of your situation. You have been compliant in aiding and abetting a wanted criminal to evade justice by hiding him in your home. You are also an accessory in knowingly assisting him by allowing him into your home where he prepared himself to go and commit a double murder at one Sadie Place's brothel…'

'They deserved to die,' says Sally, shooting me a very dark look.

'I believe they did, Sally. Razor Williams. Constables French and King. Curly White. All deserved what they got. But, Constable Gough, though a fool and a bully did not. Apparently, he has left a widow who must now manage on her own to bring up three young children.' I stare into Bill's eyes. 'One too many, Bill. If you'd have incapacitated him instead of killing him you would still have my sympathy swinging the pendulum your way. Now I am not the least bit sure where to go from here.'

'I'm sorry, Mr Potter,' says he. 'Bob was dying and all Gough could do was vilify him. I lost control. I *just* lost control.'

'The problem now is, Bill, where do we go from here? You dare not let me go, but you do not want to kill me. Do you intend keeping me prisoner or what?'

He sweeps a weary hand through his long hair. There is a tiredness in his eyes that says he could just close them and pray that they will never open again.

'I ain't had time ta think,' says he. 'I knew if anyone could work out where I was hiding it would be you, but even then, I doubted the fact. If the roles were reversed what *now* would you do? Take me in or shoot me?'

'My wishes are irrelevant, Bill. You hold all the cards. It is your choice.' I meet Sally's eyes. 'What would you do Sally?'

'I'd wish Bill bon voyage, and part as friends.'

'Nice sentiments, Sally. Only the reality is far more difficult to resolve.'

'Sal', says Bill. 'Pass the bottle of brandy and two glasses. I think me and Mr Potter could do with a drink.'

'What about me?'

'I need ya ta stay sober for what I have in mind.'

'What do you have in mind?' sulks she.

'Just get the brandy then nip upstairs and take a peek outside. Front and back. I'll tell ya when ya come back.'

Sally does what she's asked. Bill pours two generous measures of brandy as Sally disappears upstairs.

'A toast to a peaceful solution to our problem,' says Bill, raising his glass.

'A peaceful solution,' toasts I, anything rather than have my head blown off.

'This is what I propose,' says Bill. 'You'll take ya chair over to the range and sit. Then you'll cuff yourself to the handle on the oven door and toss me the keys. One hour later, Sally will hand ya back the keys and ya free ta go. An' I trust ya won't arrest Sally thus forcing me ta try and rescue her. By then I'll be well gone to somewhere even you couldn't find me.'

'And if I refuse to comply?'

He shrugs, 'Then we've got a serious problem that won't end well,' says he, levelling the sawn off's barrels to my head.

Standing up I move the chair and sit. Cuff myself to the oven handle, then toss the keys onto the table just as Sally returns.

'I took a quick peek out front, Bill,' says she. 'Just that old couple hobbling along while holding each other up. Out back, a big man in a floppy hat passed by, he glanced into the yard but didn't stop. Oh! What's going on, Inspector?'

Bill says, 'Mr Potter's agreed to be cuffed ta the range for one hour to allow me time enough ta get away…'

'Where too?' gasps she, hands going up to her mouth.

'It's a secret, Sal',' smiles he. 'The less ya know the better. But don't worry. We'll be sailing away before ya know it. Just keep the Inspector here for one hour and then hand him the keys. Is that clear to ya?'

She nods, 'But what if he wants a wee or something?'

'Slide a potty over to him an' then look the other way. Do *not* get within reach of him for any reason. Do you understand what I'm sayin', Sally?'

She nods.

Bill gets to his feet, 'I'll get a few of me things an' then I'll be gone.'

He spreads his arms, the sawn off's barrels pointing to the ceiling. Sally falls into his arms and begins to sob as he crushes her to his body.

'You will come back, won't you?' she says, gazing up into his eyes.

'I will, as God is my witness.'

***

I spend a pleasant hour chatting to Sally about trivial matters while all the time trying to sneakily trip her up into telling me something I want to know. Such as where has Bill gone? When are you sailing to America and on what ship? Do you have a named buyer for the house? And more, but she's no fool and gives nothing of worth away except the look in her eyes when I broached the subject of where Bill might be. She probably knows, but isn't saying.

At last, the clock in her parlour chimes three o'clock and is clearly heard in the kitchen. Sally hands me the keys. I unlock the cuffs and pocket them while meeting the trepidation in her eyes.

'Listen hard, Sally,' says I. 'I'll keep my bargain with, Bill. I won't arrest you now, but I cannot promise the same should we meet again. I don't believe you're going to America. Bill knows full well that the ports are still being watched and wouldn't risk boarding a liner with you in tow. What I do believe is that the killing is over and done with. So, I don't care where your true destination is, only that you'll both be off my patch…'

'Thank you, Inspector,' says she. 'I could give you a big sloppy kiss…'

'Save it for Bill. Now, heed my warning; there's still plenty out there who want Bill captured dead or alive and will stop at nothing to get to him first. Whether for the reward or revenge, or because someone is paying them to try and stop Bill from getting to them…'

'But Bill's finished with all that.'

'The trouble is, Sally, even if they hear Bill is done with it all, they won't believe it and even if they did it will not stop them. Bill will be hunted forever until he is dead or caught. You must be vigilant. Take no risks. Lock your doors at all times. Go out only if you must. Carry a weapon with you at all times. Like a knife or a small pistol, you can hide on your person.'

She falls back into the rocking chair in the corner, 'Why would anyone come for me, Mr Potter? I'm just a girl…'

'Who happens to be William Boyles fiancé. If anyone knows where he's now hiding it's likely to be you.'

'But I don't know where he's gone. Cross my heart.'

'I don't believe you, Sally. But I have no time to try and bully it out of you. I must go. Lock up behind me.'

I leave by the back door, which she locks behind me. After walking to one end of the passage I back track to the other end, while keeping an eye out for anyone who might be lurking around. Stepping out into the street I scan both ways. It is quiet, barely a soul about, but that doesn't mean no eyes are watching me or the house. Sally saw a big man in a floppy hat walking along the passage. Could that big man be Joe Straw, or am I just being paranoid? No cabs come by until I reach the main road where I flag one down to take me back to the yard.

As I watch the world go by, I ponder on my next course of action. Should I relate all to Clump or keep quiet? Keeping quiet will make me an accessory in aiding Bill to remain at large. Telling all *may* lead to Bill's capture and eventual execution. Sally of course would easily be caught and convicted. Leading to a lengthy prison sentence, or worse, execution.

I decide to keep all to myself for now, but ask the driver to change course for where I believe Andy and Nick might be at this time of day. It takes over an hour to track them down at a butcher's where they're earning a few shillings helping out in a small abattoir at the rear of the shop.

After the usual greetings I tell the lads what I want them to do and they readily agree.

'Be done here by five, boss,' says Andy. 'Then we'll get to it.'

'Yeah,' says Nick, struggling to form his words. 'Ya can rely on us, guv'.'

'I know I can, lads. But take no chances. Just report back to me if you see anything that looks odd. Tell no one what you're about and understand that I'm treading an iffy path with all this.'

'We do, boss. Mum's the word.'

Leaving them to it I reboard the cab and continue on to the Yard.

***

Once back in the office, where I am not greeted by a very grumpy Head who was just about to sneak off home, I have to listen to his woes and grumbling before I can get a word in.

'Despite what you may think, Richard,' says I, as we sit and knock back a scotch or two. 'I have not been skiving off. And when I tell you what I've been about you will be amazed…'

'I doubt it,' grumbles he. 'Nothing you could have been up to will even come close to me having to fart around with paper work all bleeding day. Christ! I've hardly left the office since you sneaked off…'

'What, not even to eat in the canteen?'

'So, I had a breakfast and a lunch. So what? I needed it. paper work is hard work and bloody tiring. It's probably made me impotent it was so bleeding boring.'

'Well at least you can now appreciate all my efforts in that area. Now, listen in, I have one hell of a confession to make.'

Once my tale is told I sit back and ask, 'What would you have done, Richard?'

He tops up our glasses before answering. 'I wouldn't have gone there on my own for a start, Gerald. But, in truth I don't know what I'd have done if I'd have been on my own like you were. Maybe the same. The big question now is, where do we go from here?'

'We? If you become involved and it gets out you could also find yourself up on criminal charges. Do you want to take that risk?'

'Of course. Either we're partners or we ain't.'

'Thank you, Richard. I am inclined to say nothing to anyone else about what happened and let it be.'

'Meaning you are sanctioning Bill and Sally's flights to freedom.'

'Exactly. I know he deserves to be taken to task for killing Constable Gough. But then I…'

'Can't find it in your heart to send him to the gallows.

Neither can I, Gerald. Especially if Sally goes with him. So, we say nothing and do nothing while hoping they disappear as quickly as possible to wherever they truly intend to immigrate to.'

'Time to go home?'

'Just one more nip,' grins he. 'Oh, yes. Clump wants to see you in his office first thing tomorrow. For what reason you ask?'

'For what reason I ask?'

'God knows. Drink up and let's go home.'

The Shootout

It's near dark when finally, I make it home at six thirty to the aroma of a shepherd's pie.

'Just in time,' says Betty, swinging away from the oven. 'Do you want to wash first or scoff first.'

Taking her in my arms I give her a gentle snog.

'That was nice,' says she, pushing me away. 'More later, Detective Inspector. Let's eat while you tell me about your day. Take a seat.'

Betty has something she wishes to have a go at me for. What, I have no idea, but I sense it isn't too serious or we'd already be going at it like a pair of vultures over a manky carcase.

I wash my hands as she disappears, returning a moment later with a thick brown envelope in her outstretched hand.

After drying my hands, I take it from her and sit down.

'Delivered by hand, no less, Detective Inspector.'

'It's been opened,' admonishes I, noting the neat cut from a paper knife. 'This isn't on, Betty. Fancy opening a letter addressed to me without permission.'

'It wasn't addressed to you if you'd have bothered to look.'

'So it isn't,' says I, reading who it's addressed to. 'For Mrs Gough, no less.'

'There's a wad of pound notes in there,' says she, as I take them out.

'How much is here?' says I, knowing she would have counted them.

'Sixty pounds. I take it Mrs Gough is the poor widow of Constable Gough. So, I ask why would someone send her money via you, and, who is that someone?'

I give her the blank look. 'No idea my little amateur detective. Do you?'

'I can hazard a guess and will plum for William Boyle. Now then, Detective Inspector, either you tell me the truth, the entire truth and nothing but the truth or you won't get any shepherd's pie except that which is thrown in your face.'

'A good wife wouldn't dream of denying her husband a good meal, if he, chooses not to tell her anything he feels she'd be better off not knowing. Nor less throw a shepherd's pie in his face. It is police work and a secret. So please back off and leave it be.'

'I shall pop into the station tomorrow and ask Detective Chief Inspector Clump,' warns she.

'Very well. Have it your way. Dish up the dinner first, if you please, for I am famished having not had so much as a monkey nut since breakfast.'

'Really! Why ever not?'

'I lost my appetite. As you will appreciate once I tell you of my day.'

In between eating, Betty listened to my sorry tale without interrupting, apart from tuts, sighs of anguish and the occasional expletive. Once done I ask for her opinion and if there's any more pie left. She loads more of her delicious pie onto my plate before giving me her unbridled opinion.

'I wanted Bill and Bob to escape the gallows as you well

know. But no one would have sentenced them to any other punishment then death despite the fact their whole life has been a brutal tragedy that turned them into torturers and killers. Leaving you, I and others enraged at the injustice of it all. All those who sinned against the twins should have been punished, but of course they are the very people who do what they like confident in the knowledge that they will get away with it all. My problem is that Bill has become one of them in an odd kind of way. He believed it was acceptable to slaughter a policeman who was just doing his duty…'

'Don't forget how cruelly Gough goaded Bill.'

'I haven't forgotten, Detective Inspector. All I want to say is that, Constable Gough could just as easily have been Detectives Potter and Head, leaving me and Chloe widows.'

'Ah,' sighs I. 'So, you're saying I should have arrested Sally and forced her into revealing where Bill is hiding out. Assuming of course she knows.'

'Yes. The thing is, Detective Inspector, what if Bill lied to you and has no intention of ending his murder spree. How then will you feel if more policemen die at his hands.'

'Unhappy,' says I. 'Especially if Richard or I get it. The trouble is where do I go from here.'

'I don't know,' sighs she. 'Perhaps you should leave it all to fate.'

The sudden violent banging on the front door tells me fate has just arrived.

Having jumped out of her skin, Betty then angrily jumps to her feet.

'I'll go,' says I, holding her back.

Opening the door, I find a panic-stricken Nick standing before me.

'He's there, guv'!' gasps he. 'There right now, the bastard.'

'Who's there?'

'Joe Straw. Ya gotta come quick, *please*, he's in the house.'

'Hold tight while I get my stuff.'

'What's going on?' demands Betty.

'Joe Straws turned up at Sally's,' says I, slapping on my bowler, grabbing my jacket and holstering my revolver. 'I have to go.'

'Don't go alone,' says she. 'Pick Richard up. Straws too dangerous to tackle on your own.'

'No time, Betty.'

She digs her fingers into my arms. 'Make time, Gerald. Promise me.'

I swear I've never seen her look so terrified. 'I promise.'

Nick came in a hackney; we board and I give the driver Heads address along with demanding he pushes the horse to its limits.

We are at Heads within minutes. Jumping down I run up his path and bang on the door.

'This better be good,' growls Head as the door is flung open. 'Gerald!'

'Grab your things, Richard. No time to lose, I'll tell on the way.'

No arguments, he spins around and hurries away. Chloe then appears at the end of the hall with little Thomas in her arms.

'Whatever is wrong, Gerald?'

'Perhaps nothing, Chloe. Try not to worry…'

'I can't help but worry,' cries she.

Head appears, shoes in one hand and jacket in the other. 'Try not to worry, love,' says he, giving her and Thomas a quick kiss as the boy begins to cry.

Back in the hackney, with Nick squashed between me and

Head, Head says, 'What's up, Gerald?'

'Tell us what happened, Nick,' says I.

'We was watching the 'ouse from behind a bush across the road when Joe Straw turned up. He knocked on the door, we see the curtain twitch, then Sally opened it. She an' Straw spoke a bit an' then they went inside. Andy told me ta run an' get a cab over to yours. Cause I had ta pay the driver before he'd take me…'

'Don't fret, Nick,' says I. 'I will re-imburse you.'

'What's that mean?'

'I'll pay you back. Did you see if Straw was carrying anything? A bag or something?'

He shakes his head. 'He was in an orange-coloured tweed suit with a floppy hat. But he weren't carrying anything.'

Head is struggling to do up his shoe laces as he says, 'Straw's after finding out where Bill is. I reckon he had the same idea you had, Gerald that Sally might just know where Bill is hiding out.'

'It *was* Straw who Sally saw earlier walking down the passage at the rear of the houses. But why wait so long before confronting her. Straw must have known I was inside and probably saw me leave four hours or so ago…'

Head straightens up and sits back, 'Because he saw Bill leave and followed him.'

'Only Bill out smarted him and Straw lost sight of Bill,' says I.

'Sounds logical to me. Sorry, I need a fart.'

'Pooh!' gasps Nick. 'That smells like bad kippers.'

'Kippers for tea,' grins Head. 'But they weren't bad; they were bloody delicious, all four of them.'

I contemplate reaching over, opening Heads door and pushing him out, only I can't afford not to have him with me.

Traffic is light as we speed past the shops, houses and pedestrians to arrive at Sally's twenty minutes later, earlier than anticipated. I tell the driver to pull up a few houses back, I pay him, tell him to wait and we alight.

Andy is stood outside Sally's; he waves at us.

'What's been happening, Andy?' whispers I, as we step up.

'Nothin, boss. Straw went in about an' hour ago an' I crossed over ta listen out by her door. But I couldn't make nothing out until I heard her scream. Then it all went quiet. I ran back to me hiding place an' kept watch. Nothin'. Straw ain't come out an' I reckon he may have gone out the back way an' I missed him. After a bit I got brave and went an' knocked on the front an' then the back door. No one answered an' I tried peering through the curtains. I could just make out Sally sat in a rocky chair in the kitchen. I called out and banged on the window, her head moved but she didn't get up an' open the door…'

'We'll soon open the doors,' says Head, as he takes out his picks and goes for the front door. 'The key's still in the lock. Let's try the back door.'

We traipse around back, if the door won't open it will be window smashing to gain entry. Only the back door, we find, isn't even locked. I order Andy and Nick to wait outside as revolvers drawn, Head and I go in.

Sally is sat in the rocking chair, her head flopped to one side, her neck has been broken. I find myself so transfixed by the sight of her almost serene face, it takes away the horror of the sight of her dress having been ripped right down the front to expose her undergarments and what is left of her shredded drawers.

'You, poor little sod,' says Head. 'That bastard! Who the hell does he think he is going around raping and killing young women as if he has an absolute right to do whatever he wants?'

'It is time someone put a stop to Joe Straw's belief that he is untouchable, Richard. The trouble is where has he gone too. Sally may or may not have told him where Bill is hiding. She may even have given him a false lead and he's currently chasing rainbows…'

'Maybe several rainbows,' says Head, scanning around the room. 'No doubt Sally tried to mislead Straw to save Bill, but you don't fool the likes of Straw easily. Perhaps she gave him several options to try in the vain hope he wouldn't kill her. We'll never know unless we catch Straw and force it out of him.'

'No good arresting him, Richard when we finally do catch up with him. As ever the establishment will ensure he walks away from it untarnished. He knows too much about too many important people. Besides, Sally becomes just one more dead prostitute in their eyes. Hear today and forgotten about by tomorrow.'

I am still transfixed with Sally's face as I lay a tea towel over her lap. How can she appear so serene after the violent, disgusting way her life was taken?

'What's goin' on, boss?' calls Andy, sticking his head into the kitchen.

'Come in the both of you,' sighs I. 'But be warned, Sally has been murdered.'

They are tough lads, slum kids old before their time. Life and death go hand in hand in the world they live in.

'The poor cow,' says Nick, mouth and eyes wide open.

'I should have done somethin',' says Andy, as he stares at Sally. 'I could have distracted Straw. I could…'

'Have also got yourself killed,' says I. 'Do not blame yourself, Andy. Richard, you'll find a bottle of brandy in the larder. I think we all could do with a stiff drink while we consider where we go from here.'

Going into the parlour I open the front door and step up to the cab, handing the driver a half crown I ask him to find the first plod he sees and to bring him here, and then to carry on waiting.

Back in the kitchen, Head has already poured four generous brandies, which we take to the table and sit down. In silence we drink. Andy's watery eyes keep flicking over towards Sally, he is racked with guilt. What to do next? Straw may well have several places to go in the hope of catching up with Bill. Who knows, one may well bear fruit? We on the other hand have no idea where Bill might be. Unless, he has returned to Walnut House?

'Hopefully,' says I, addressing Andy, 'a plod or two will be here shortly. I think it best that you and Nick down your drinks and then go home. Tell no one about any of this. Your involvement must be kept a secret. I shall inform the plods and my superiors at the Yard that we had an anonymous tip off.' I hand the lads a pound between them.

'I don't deserve this,' says Andy.

'You do so,' says I, with finality. 'Right, clear off the pair of you, I'll try and catch up with you as soon as is possible.'

They go off with a final glance at Sally's body. I wash up their glasses and put them away. Head tops up our glasses and then goes to see if there's anything in the larder to eat. He comes back with a chunk of cheese, bread and pickle.

'Best get something into us, Gerald. It's going to be a long haul by the time forensics get here.'

'To tell us what, Richard? They've found loads of fingerprints. Bills, mine, Straws and Sally's. They'll tell us that Sally died of a broken neck and was probably raped just before she was murdered and that the post mortem may find a sample of the suspect rapist's semen, which, for all they now may have come from Bill. How much of that will stick to Straw in a court of law?'

'Probably none of it,' says Head, as he pushes a plate over. 'How much do you want, Gerald?'

'Cut me a small wedge of cheese and one doorstep of bread with a thick lump of butter on it.'

'Pickle?'

'I'll help myself. Thank you, Richard for being here.'

Head had consumed half a pound of cheese, half a loaf, most of the pickle and downed four brandies by the time two plods turned up. Which was about fifteen minutes after I'd sent the cab to find them.

I had pecked at a small piece of cheese and bread washed down with three double brandies. Did I feel tipsy? No, I may just as well have been drinking water.

After putting the plods straight that we'd acted on a tip off that Bill could be hiding out at Sally Pollards. Who we believed may have murdered her, where we think he might be heading and as to the reason why, we take our leave, and climb back into the hackney.

'Did you see the looks on their faces, Gerald when you spoke of Bill?'

'I did, Richard. Pure hatred in their eyes and I can't blame them. They couldn't give a damn about all those Bill killed before he done Gough in. What did the tubby plod say?'

'All cutthroats, near do wells and scum just falling out. There were no kind words for French, King or Shaver either. But Peter Gough was another matter. Well liked apparently, despite being a hot head and a prat at times…'

'But then he'd lost his own father back in seventy-nine.

Murdered by a thug while just going about his duty as a well-respected Police Sergeant.'

'All that aside, Gerald. As far as the plods are concerned the best outcome from all this would be Straw and Bill doing each other in.'

'I can agree with that, Richard. Bill will definitely go back to killing once he knows Sally is dead. And God help anyone who gets in his way because this time he will be utterly merciless.'

'And Straw will make it all far worse. It could go on for months.'

'Who is paying Straw now? We know Falconer paid him to hunt down the twins in order to cover up his son's affair with possibly his own mother…'

'What, Falconer's mother? She must be at least ninety.'

'You've had one too many, Richard. You know what I mean. Bill dropped his blackmail threats; the photographs were returned and no harm was done. So, I can't see why Falconer would continue paying Straw to hunt down Bill unless he is pretty sure Bill may well be paying him a visit one day? Anyway, we'll be there shortly, what is our plan of action?'

'The same plan we always go for when we don't have a plan.'

'Go in revolvers drawn and pray we come out alive.'

'It's going to be very dark in Walnut House, Gerald so we best keep close to each other or we could end up shooting each other.'

'Agreed. I doubt very much that Bill will be there anyway. It's too obvious.'

'Agreed. But trust me, Sally, the poor cow, would have told Straw about Walnut House and he'll no doubt turn up there at some time if he has had no joy finding Bill at wherever else Sally said he might be.'

'He may have already checked it out and is long gone. We shall check it out anyway. One thing's for certain, if Bill and Straw don't kill each other we *must* arrest or kill the both of them.'

'No more sympathy for Bill and no mercy for either of them,' sighs Head, giving me the cold look. 'Are you certain you won't back down if you come face to face with Bill?'

'I am. And I would rather kill him then arrest him. He would prefer that.'

We arrive at Marylebone High Street at eight thirty. The street is quiet, not much traffic and only a few people about. On spotting another cab pulling up outside Walnut House I order the driver to pull up.

'What's up?' says Head.

'I want to see who alights that cab up ahead before we go any further.'

A large shadowy figure jumps out of the cab.

'That could be Straw,' farts Head.

'Cor… Whose been eating rotten fish?' groans the driver, swinging his head around and glaring at me.

I point at Head.

'Sorry,' says Head. 'Too many kippers for tea. I often let rip when I'm nervous.'

'I often let rip when I'm angry,' says the driver. 'Especially if the wife's spent money on trivialities.'

While he and Head ramble on about all sorts of rubbish I am watching Straw as his cab pulls away, leaving him standing alone and facing Walnut house. He goes down the path only to return a few minutes later before heading towards us, then he turns onto the bridleway. Obviously, he knows where he is going. Even from here, Jack Straw appears very sinister. The sound of a dog furiously barking carries over to us and sounds as if it is coming from the rear of the houses. It stops barking as fast as it began.

'Listen in, driver,' says I. 'I want you to wait for us right here. We are going into Walnut House via a rear entrance in the wall down the bridleway. Now, should you hear the sound of gunfire I want you to make haste to the nearest Police Station and raise the alarm and demand they send armed assistance immediately. Is that clear to you?'

'It is, gov', but what about a retainer in case you get killed and I can't get the rest of me money.'

I hand him ten shillings and ask for a receipt for a pound.

'Typical,' scoffs he. 'You bloody coppers are a law unto yourselves. Anything to make a few bob on the side.'

'You will be forgoing your tip if you don't shut up,' snaps I. 'Just do as I ask, our lives may depend on it. Right, Sergeant, let's go.'

We make our way down the bridleway, weapons drawn should Straw suddenly appear before us should he be making his way back having not found a way in. Although I am certain that Sally told him about the hole in the wall. Head keeps farting while I am feeling very uneasy. There isn't much of a moon out, it's very dark and creepy and all made far worse by the eerie sounds of foxes barking and wailing in the distance.

On reaching the hole we find the cover hasn't been put back properly, Straw has gone in. By the hole we find Fabio's little body, his head has been caved in.

As silent as slugs, we make our way through the hole into the garden and follow the path, pausing and bobbing down, keeping close to the brambles but just out of reach of their thorns. Eyes now fully accustomed to the dark we can make out Straws shadowy figure standing and facing the kitchen. He is barely thirty feet away from us.

Sticking my mouth close to Head's ear I whisper, 'We'll

let him enter and then wait. Should Bill be inside and they cross swords let's hope they kill each other. If not, whoever comes out we will shoot them…'

'Even if it's Bill?' whispers Head.

I nod.

'What if no one comes out, Gerald?'

'Then we'll have to go in and hope we find them both dead or seriously injured enough not to shoot at us.'

'What if neither of them is injured?'

'Don't keep complicating matters, Richard.'

'I'm not. I'm just…'

'Shush. You're raising your voice. He may hear us.'

Straw suddenly turns and points a revolver straight at us. A glint of light from the moon shines on the barrel. Has he seen us? But then he turns away, and, after peering through the kitchen window he moves to the door and takes hold of the knob. Opening the door inwards just a crack he sidesteps away. After a minute or so he pushes the door open enough to go inside, silently closing the door behind him. Straw will wait until his eyes have adjusted to the extra darkness before he ventures beyond the kitchen.

'What now?' says Head.

'We wait a few minutes before going up to the back door where we will wait until we feel it is safe to enter.'

After a few minutes we stand and creep silently over to the door. There we stand stock still and listen. The sudden screech from an owl has us both jumping out of our skins. I can hear my heart thumping away in my chest. I am aware that the hand holding my revolver is trembling and my stomach is doing somersaults. Worse than that Head is practically standing on my shoes. He's that close to me his kipper breath assaults my senses like a bad omen.

Minutes pass, five, ten, fifteen, who knows? It is difficult to tell. Is Straw still in the kitchen watching and waiting for us to enter, having spotted us earlier, so he can kill us? Has he ventured further into the house? We can only surmise what is going on inside the gloom of Walnut House.

Head pokes my arm and gestures that we should go in. I don't want to change the plan, but I nod anyway. Opening that door could be the death of us if Straw is indeed waiting for us.

With my heart pounding even harder I gently push Head away out of the firing line. Should I get shot on opening the door at least Head will have a chance to drop Straw and maybe survive in the attempt. I open the door a crack, pause and listen. Nothing. It's now or never. Slowly I push the door open and step inside. Head follows, silently closing the door behind him.

We stand dead still and listen. Nothing, not even the creak of a floorboard, the scampering from a mouse or the squeak from a rat. It is as silent as death.

Head tugs at my jacket sleeve and nods towards the table. We step over to have the table in front of us and bob down, thus presenting a smaller target. Only the whites of our eyes peering over the table top would be a target for an assassin.

Forever seems to go by, I am becoming cramped in the legs and restless for something to happen. Then, at last, it has to be Straw who speaks.

'I know you are in here, William Boyle even if I can't see you. I reason you are hiding behind the corner of that huge book cabinet. Come out and face me. Let us see who is the better shot in this poor light, shall we? You ain't afraid now, are you? Of course, you aren't. Come on. Make a show.'

Straw sounds close by the drawing room entrance. Close enough to see inside while displaying a small target to fire at.

'Time is running out, Boyle. I'm giving you a chance of a

fair fight. Come out or I will kill you right through the cabinet.'

Not a word comes back to him. Either Bill isn't there or he is staying tight lipped.

Minutes drag by. Nothing. My heart has slowed and I've stopped trembling. Even Head has stopped farting. What's Straws next move? Search the house? Decide Bill isn't here and give it up? The second Straw's frame appears in the doorway; Head and I will shoot him to shreds.

Straws next course of action becomes very clear as mockingly he sounds off.

'That Sally was a good girl, Boyle. She gave me three places where you could be hiding out and how to access them. Two of them proved to be dead-ends. So, third time lucky, hey? Of course, I promised her I'd leave her be if she opened her mouth. Promised I wouldn't violate her and then break her pretty little neck. She held out for a little while. But, a little bit of strangulation while feeling her up nice and rough soon loosened her tongue and she sung like a robin. Sweet, sweet girl. Nice firm body as well. Raped her anyway and then snapped her neck like a twig. Or was it the other way around?'

No response from Bill. I am now convinced that he is not in the house and Sally told Straw a pack of lies to protect Bill.

More time goes by in absolute silence. By now I've even got the cramps in my anus.

Then there comes the sound of a match being lit. Light flashes along the hallway. Then two weapons are fired simultaneously. Rapid, fierce and deafening. I count maybe twelve shots from small arms, probably revolvers. Gun smoke drifts down the hall and swamps into the kitchen, the smell is sickening.

Head and I cock our weapons ready for whoever appears in the doorway.

'Knew you were there,' sounds Straw, his voice somewhat strangled. He's been hit.

'Speak up, Bill!' roars Straw. 'I know I hit you. Haven't you anything to say?'

No response. Bill is either dead, dying or just keeping quiet.

The sound of bullets being loaded carries into the kitchen. But it sounds laboured, metal hitting metal, whoever it is, they are struggling to feed the bullets into their weapon.

Head gestures for us to go in, then he drags a finger across his throat. Go in and finish it. I shake my head. Bill and Straw must play it out.

'I'm ready for another go,' says Straw. 'You up for it, Boyle? Or have you had enough? Or are you as dead as little Sally?'

Straw laughs, load and cynical. 'You ain't dead, Boyle, I know it. Call it intuition mixed with sheer experience. I just know you're still breathing…'

'Fuck you!' roars Bill as I picture him leaping out from his hiding place and blasting away to be answered by Straw's weapon.

I count eight shots before it falls silent. Them damn if I don't hear the sound of heavy metal hitting the floor. Either Bill or Straw have dropped their weapon. A sure sign that they are done for.

Someone is groaning in agony. The sound is coming nearer. I slip a finger around the trigger of my revolver. The groaning stops to be replaced by someone gasping for breath. Then, Straw speaks, 'You've done me in, Boyle. Damn you to hell!'

Then Straw appears, his bulk fills the doorway. One bloody hand is clamped to his stomach. The other, shattered beyond repair hangs by his side. Blood runs from it as if it is a grotesque stream. One side of his face has been ripped open. Rocking from side to side he staggers into the kitchen and stops. Rocking now, backwards and forwards the man is near dead on his feet.

Head can't resist it. 'How are you feeling, Joseph? *Fancy* letting a mere lad get the better of you. Never mind, you'll be knocking on the doors of hell in a very short while. You can then rest up for all eternity.'

Reaching out with the hand that was holding in his messed-up guts, Straw takes a step closer to us. 'Help me,' cries he, before crashing face down onto the flag stoned floor.

'That's the end of him,' says I. 'And good riddance.'

Head picks up an oil lamp from the table, strikes a match and at last we have more light.

Stepping over Straw's body we make our way towards the drawing room, the light bouncing along the walls.

'Who's there?' calls Bill.

'It is I, Bill along with Sergeant Head. Is it safe to come in?'

Bill clears his throat before answering, 'It is. I give ya me word.'

We go in. Head holds the lamp up high and it lights up the room, but we still can't see Bill.

'Bring the light over,' says Bill.

We do so to find Bill slumped on the floor with his legs splayed out and his back to the wall. Both arms are by his side, one bloodied hand still gripping a revolver. He has been shot to pieces with wounds in both shoulders, another close to his heart and one in his stomach. His face is untouched.

Bobbing down I gaze into his eyes, which are surprisingly bright, the kind of brightness I've seen a few times before, just before they fade and die.

'We'll get you to hospital,' says Head, holding the lamp to light up Bills face.

Bill smiles and says, 'I'll never make it, Mr Head. You know it and I know it.'

'Straw lied about Sally,' lies Head, bobbing down. 'She's alright. A bit battered and bruised but she'll recover in no time.'

'Oh… She's gone alright,' sighs Bill. 'Gone to heaven has Sally. Listen, I ain't got long. In my bag beside the book cabinet there's a small sketch book, Mr Potter. Take it and keep it, but don't let anyone else know you have it. Promise me?'

'I promise, Bill.'

'Good. Take what else ya want. There's money in there, keep it an' do something' good for the poor with some of it.'

Fetching the bag, I open it before him and take out the sketch book which goes into my inside jacket pocket. In an envelope there's a stash of cash, I take about two thirds and pocket it. Best to leave some as no one will believe Bill was without money to fund his crusade.

Bill gazes up at the ceiling where the lamp light has created a ring of bright yellow light like a halo.

'I see Sally, holding Bob's hand,' says he, as a trickle of blood seeps from the corner of his mouth. 'Ma's holding Bob's other hand. I see them so clear; they are all smiling, all waiting for me in Heaven. Ma's let go of Bob's hand, she's holding up the jumper that Mrs Potter gave me all those years ago. Ma just patted her tummy twice.'

He meets my eyes as his tears fall and his eyes sparkle. 'Ya gonna be a father, Mr Potter. A father to twins… How good is that?'

His head slumps forwards, a long sigh exudes from deep inside him. He has gone.

Reaching over, Head gently closes Bills eyes and then stands up.

'If nothing else, Gerald,' says he, his voice trembling. 'Bill was one hell of a brave lad.'

'A lad, but more man than most,' says I, standing up.

The poignancy of the moment is lost when we hear: *'Armed police. Come out with your hands up.'*

Walking on legs of lead we make our way to the back door where I call out, 'Detectives Potter and Head coming out. Lower your weapons.'

Half a dozen lanterns are raised high as we step outside to see a force of at least twenty armed plods.

'Anyone inside, sir?' asks Sergeant Bright.

'Two dead. One Joseph Strawbridge and one William Boyle.'

They erupt in cheers, whoops of joy and lots of giving thanks profanities.

Then everyone wants to shake our hands. We are heroes, even though we never fired a shot. One plod suggests that we all have a party while burning Bill's body. Other plods come up with even more grotesque ways to do away with the body. However, they all know that normal procedures and protocol *will* be followed. No one is interested much in the part Joe Straw played in the events and he is put aside as just being a common thug on the make who came unstuck.

Head went through Straws pockets only to come up with little of interest except for the expensive gold fob watch he was carrying and a wallet stuffed with notes. All of which was noted in Heads note book and Sergeant Bright's. No chance there then of anyone helping themselves.

Two hours later, once the bodies have been examined by forensics and photographed where they lay, they are loaded up ready for the morgue. Time to head back to the Yard.

Epilogue

Over the next few days Head and I find ourselves attending several slaps on the back meetings with our superiors, right up to the chief constable. We are up for bravery awards and all sorts. Rival newspapers came to physical blows in their efforts to gain exclusive rights to our story on how we took down the notorious killer, William Boyle, with all payments to go to the Police Benevolence Fund, thus leaving Head and I with no chance of making a few pounds on the side.

Bill's body ended up being handed over to medical science despite Reverend Shields protestations. No part of him was to be allowed to be buried with his brother. Bill would mostly be pickled. Preserved forever to be gawped at, with a death mask to boot, in the force's black museum.

Poor Sally ended up being buried with Pollard, as was seen to be fitting. She died intestate and with no known kin, so, no doubt the crown will steal her home if no one comes forward to legitimately claim it.

Joe Straw's body also ended up on the slab to advance the course of medical science. But not before the newspapers, looking for a scoop, ran a campaign to try and trace any friends or family he may have had. No one came forward. However, an anonymous person sent a note to the papers informing them where Joe Straw had been residing and that the man was a contract killer and bounty hunter, and not some vigilantly hero as the papers had supposed.

Once we had Straw's address, a posh apartment near Belgravia, Head and I, along with Clump as chaperone to ensure we didn't pinch anything, were given the task of searching the place. To say Straw was loaded would be an understatement, he had stacks of cash, jewels, art work, high quality furnishings, priceless artifacts, you name it and he had it. But our most important find was sets of ledger books spanning back thirty years. There was also detailed accounts for everything he had ever done for money, including those he killed, maimed, tortured, brutely warned off, or merely roughed up to gain information.

What the ledgers didn't tell us was who employed Straw to carry out his often-heinous crimes. Obviously, several different persons over the years who were, on average, undoubtably well healed and wealthy. Probably a mix of clients as far apart in social circles as a naughty Bishop or an up herself madam, such as Sadie Place. Straw had murdered six prostitutes over the years, including of course Mable Calver. But he had also done away with a young nun from a convent not too far from Westminster Abbey.

We could easily have found out who paid Straw to carry out several of his 'contracts,' there being enough information in his own records to investigate individual crimes and put two and two together faster than you would in a case where you start with nothing more than a body. Straw not only named his victims, he also stated why they were targeted.

According to Straw, all his victims deserved what they got because they had committed crimes against their 'betters'. Such as, amongst others, blackmail, theft, libel, slander and spreading rumours, to not knowing their place and being stupid. Such as the young house maid who went to the press to sell her story of having been seduced and made pregnant, before being thrown out of house and work to 'rot' in the gutter. The poor girl obviously had no idea that the editor of the newspaper wouldn't dare publish her story for fear of retribution from whomsoever had seduced the girl, and would instead have gone to warn the seducer. Thus, gaining favour, saving himself from a libel case that probably would have destroyed him and receiving a 'reward.' The maid, who was with child, died of a broken neck just two days after going to the papers.

Clump wasn't interested and assured us that the cases would never be investigated any further than they already had been. Maintain the status quo, and all that, so the rich and powerful can continue to escape retribution.

***

Three weeks went by before I opened the little sketch pad that Bill had given me. I had been very reluctant to look at it as I assumed it contained more depressing, gory pictures of he and Bob's pursuit for justice. I was to be amazed. The book contained drawings, often in colour, of all their few, but far in-between, fondest memories along with their dreams and aspirations for a future that would be gilded, serene, peaceful and productive.

Page after page of tiny pictures in accomplished infinite detail, such as: Bill and Bob picnicking with their mother in Hyde Park, with red squirrels and robins coming up to them for scraps from a luxury hamper set down on a blue chequered table cloth. In the background other families were playing cricket and other ball games. The sun beamed down with heavenly golden rays of pure fantasy. There was not a shred of dark thoughts hiding anywhere within any picture. Another was of Bill and Sally's wedding with the Reverend Shields conducting the ceremony while frowning at the obvious swelling of Sally's belly. This was Bill fantasizing at his best to push away the hell of his past along with his evil side. The last picture he drew was of myself holding hands with a small boy, who held hands with another identical boy, who was also holding Betty's hand as we crossed over a bridge towards a sun kissed meadow festooned with buttercups, butterflies and daisies.

Bill's dream was that Betty and I would one day have children, twin boys in fact. I carefully removed the page and slipped the drawing between my note book. I wanted to keep it, but wouldn't show it to Betty. Perhaps one day we will be blessed with children, but for now I didn't want to risk Bill's picture upsetting Betty.

I took the sketch pad to the Reverend Shields, as I did not think it appropriate that I should keep it. Certainly, I did not want to hand it over to end up in the black museum. The good reverend was over joyed with it, but amazed me when he said he wouldn't be keeping it. Instead, he intended to have the twin's mother's coffin exhumed and then reburied beside Bob's grave. In-between the two graves there would be buried a small waterproof copper casket which would house Bill's little sketch book forever. However, to keep those morbidly fascinated by the graves of violent killers and such from digging up Bill's casket, the reverend would not be putting up any kind of memorial for Bill.

I also handed over *all* the money that Bill gave me in the knowledge that the Reverend Shields would ensure the money was used wisely for the poor in the parish.

***

'At last!' whined Betty, several weeks later as I staggered into the kitchen barely an hour before midnight. 'Where the hell have you been! You said you'd be home by six at the latest. Your sirloin steak dinner is ruined. But if you still want it, it's in the bin. The champagne has lost its bubbles and I'm so fed up I think I'll piss off to bed.'

The kitchen table I note hasn't been set. Therefore, I'm assuming that dinner was to have been eaten in the dining room. Meaning that it was to have been a special occasion, what with steak and champagne. Furiously I rack my brains. Have I forgotten something important? It' isn't Betty's birthday or our anniversary. So, what the hell is it?

I plumb for dumb. 'Sorry my little angry hornet. An unexpected last-minute emergency came up. Some madman ran amok in the high street swinging an axe at passers-by just as me and Head were making our way home. By the time we disarmed him, arrested him and dragged him off to the nearest station, filled in our report and accepted a quick drink from the duty inspector in his office, three hours or so had gone by… I'm afraid, my darling, as a consequence I have forgotten what exactly we were celebrating tonight.'

She clamps her hands onto her hips and gives me the daggered look. 'That's because it was meant to be a surprise.'

'Oh! Lovely. So, what is the surprise?'

'It's ruined now. I was so happy. In fact, I've been bouncing off the walls with happiness all *bloody day* waiting for you to come home.'

With that she bursts into tears and buries her face in her hands. Going over to her I pull her into me while expecting to catch the strong smell of sherry on her breath. Nothing. She's as sobber as a sausage. She wraps her arms around me and crushes me to her while continuing to sob like a *child*. Call me a brilliant detective if you wish, but even a slow one couldn't fail to reason what this is about.

Gently I push her away and gaze into her tear-filled eyes, 'Are you having our baby?'

She nods.

'Are you sure?' says I, aware that my hands are trembling.

She nods. 'According to the midwife who I asked to call round I'm over two months pregnant. She then did the silver cross on a chain over my belly. Guess what.'

'She said you are going to have twin boys.'

'How on earth did you know that?' says she, wiping the tears from my eyes.

'I have something incredible to show you, Betty. It's in-between the pages of my note book.'

About the Author

David Burrows was born and raised in Suffolk, England. He lives there today with his wife Jenny. They have two daughters and three grandchildren.

Having had a few short stories published over the years, David still looked on his writing as a relaxing fun hobby. Now that he is retired, he has had more time to devote to his writing, resulting in the unique Fish Bone Alley series. This is the fourth book in the collection. The first was published in 2019.

To find out more about David and his work, visit his website at: **www.dfburrows.co.uk**